FORTRESS OF SHADOW

STARSIDE SAGA BOOK SEVEN

ERIC KENT EDSTROM

1

____

FOR HER MEDALLION

Garden Island was awash with the rain and wind of a fellstorm. The third of the season. The verdant jungle leaned hard to the north, the underside of leaves flashing a silvery gray as the ceaseless winds strove to rip them, root and branch, from the soil.

The ruins of Ori's Home soaked in it, unwitnessed, the few remaining novitiates and Sensuals having long ago fled to the center of the island. To Garden Tower.

Far to the north, the stilt huts of Pol's Vale lay empty as well. Those who chose to reside there had sheltered, once again, in a nearby cave to wait out the storm.

Kil's Keep stood near a precipitous drop at the edge of an ash-barrens. The oceanside cliff had once been fringed with vines. All now was ash, turned to a gray, sticky mud by the rain. No light burned in the high window of that tower. But a score of ragged outcasts now haunted the dank lower halls. They awaited with dazzle-eyed fervor the return of the Highest of Kil.

Inland, the Garden Tower stood atop the highest point of

the island. But from Docktown it was invisible, shrouded by the sheeting rain. Low, charcoal-colored clouds scudded over the top parapets, unloading a wash of moisture upon the thousand-year-old blocks of stone. Two figures stood there, exposed to the fellstorm's fury, dressed in oilcloaks. Pellets of rain snicked against the fabric, beaded and rolled away, keeping the wearers dry.

One was tall and lean, with manly fists jutting from her sleeves. Coin Inlina, leader of the Way of Pol.

The other was short, stocky, each hand fitted into the opposite sleeve and pressed close to her belly. Voluptuary Minn, head of the Way of Ori.

Two of the most powerful women in the world had come here for privacy. Highest Quiv's spies were everywhere, they suspected. And who knew what tricks the Sigh girl was up to? She could dymense after all.

It was those tricks that concerned Coin Inlina.

"We still don't know if Highest Quiv betrayed us or if he merely attached himself to Kila Sigh to keep an eye on her," the Coin said. She felt like she was repeating herself. She *was* repeating herself. Not a habit she wanted to start. But Voluptuary Minn had become obsessed with small problems, and the Coin needed the woman to turn her considerable intellect toward larger ones.

"He knew what was needed," Voluptuary Minn said in a pinched voice. "A promise -binding upon the Sigh girl. Nothing less. He even agreed to it, right to my face. You heard him."

The Coin sighed and reached for her medallion which hung upon a thick gold chain around her neck. But her oilcloak covered it. She settled for tracing the circumference of it with a long, pale finger. "He didn't agree. He merely said he saw the advantages of a promise-binding."

Voluptuary Minn huffed in disgust. The storm sent a sweep of wind to blast them, water pellets stinging Inlina's face. She turned her back to it. They stood on the Tower roof, walls to either side marking off the portion of the structure allocated to the Way of Pol. The roof was paved with slate and sloped just enough to shunt rainwater to wide scuppers that couldn't quite keep up with the torrent. Coin Inlina's feet were getting wet through her doe-hide boots. "Forget Quiv," she said. "Forget Kila Sigh for a moment."

That got the woman's attention. Piercing blue eyes, set in a wide, handsome face, peered from within the hood of the oilcloak. She was not accustomed to such address. "Forget the Highest of Kil? A child who infuses every mercus feat with emotion? You'd be rather more concerned about her if she had murdered one of yours, I'd wager." A bit of Voluptuary Minn's coastal curl-tongue accent crept in whenever she became angry. "Wager" had come out "weejah." She'd come from a small town south of Starside. Charton, Inlina thought it was called.

"Sensual Sliy was weak," Coin Inlina said. "You said so yourself." Kila had used a mercus feat to magnify her words, infusing it with a bolt of fear. The poor, meek Sensual had collapsed and died. The Coin's own emissary, Spin Moirina, had reported the assault to be only mildly disturbing.

"You encouraged Kila to study with that demayne," Voluptuary Minn said, shaking a finger. "Don't you tell me not to concern myself with her."

"Perhaps Flaumishtak would not have found her such a willing pupil if you'd prevented her torture at the hands of your Voluptuary Sennikt and Sensual Thine." That shut Minn up. The Way of Ori had been corrupted from the inside, and Minn had not interceded when Kila was shriven and had a *vaz'on* screwed into her skull. The Coin shivered to think of the thing, a be-gemmed crown that put the wearer into the control of any merculyn who knew how to use it. What Sennikt and Thine had done was unthinkable.

The Coin suspected she could have heard Minn's teeth grinding had the wind not been so sharp. "You relayed my message to Starside?" Minn asked.

"I told you I had." Just to humor the woman. The message had been coded of course, so Inlina had little idea what was in it. Her coin-code Spinster had relayed it to Starside a month ago. It was likely something to do with the Sigh girl. With Minn, *everything* was about the Sigh girl.

Coin Inlina let the woman stew a bit, then tried to change the subject. "What progress at Kil's Keep?" She had no desire to make the Voluptuary her enemy. In fact, friends were few in these times. It was essential that the Ways of Ori and Pol stay united to face what was coming.

"The last of the debris will be cleared out tonight. But I do not expect to find Kila or her companions. My Sensuals felt her and Henley's mercus potential vanish in an instant."

"We must look, though it's probable they dymensed to Starside." She could hardly credit that she was speaking such aloud. But the girl had dymensed right in front of her. A feat the Coin had thought reserved for demayne alone. The power had been appreciable, but more impressive had been the flurry of senses and emotions the girl had used.

"I have interviewed the few Donse Masters willing to speak with me," the Coin said. "They are firm in their allegiance to Highest Quiv. Most are still dazed by the collapse of their Fifth of the Tower. Many head injuries, not that you'd notice the difference, some of them."

The door leading into the tower swung open. A devotee of Pol ran out, white gown instantly soaked through and sticking to her lithe figure.

"Why are you out in this without an oilcloak?" the Coin demanded.

"It's Spin Ritten! Coin code coming."

Ritten would not have sent a devotee running unless the code was coming from one particular place. Starside.

"We must return inside," the Coin said to Voluptuary Minn. "Supper tonight?"

The woman didn't answer. No matter. She'd be there. She had only a handful of Sensuals and novitiates in her control here and no quick way to communicate with the Voluptuaries scattered across the realms of the world. In a word, Voluptuary Minn relied on Coin Inlina totally.

The Coin stepped across the threshold into a dimly lit stairwell leading to her quarters. Shedding her dripping cloak, she hurried to Spinster Ritten's rooms.

2

THE GOD-POWER

"Thrust!"

Kila lunged, driving Cayne forward.

Her teacher, a sour shadline called Jil Pokkti, gripped Kila's blade wrist and pulled, sending Kila stumbling and flailing to keep her balance.

"You put your weight too far forward, Sigh. Again."

And so it went. Onlookers were scattered around the otherwise empty courtyard in the shade of the Citadel's spire. A light snow had started just at the beginning of the training session, and the watchers were bundled in wool cloaks with fur-lined hoods. The cats were nowhere in sight, having wisely chosen to curl close to a hearth inside.

But Henley was there, a dusting of snow stark against his fiery locks. He grimaced at Jil's tone and gave Kila a cautionary lift of one eyebrow.

Kila bit down several choice remarks as she turned to face her teacher.

Her teacher. Bah! The woman hated her merely for being a merculyn.

Jil Pokkti was from Trine, well groomed, with short cropped hair and fine quality clothes. Like Kila, she had shed her cloak long ago. She wore a lace-up tunic over loose trousers tucked into fine leather boots. Her movements reminded Kila of Gian Delp's, fluid, dancerly, fast. The only tell of exertion was the steam rising from her skin in the chill.

Before Kila had caught her breath, the woman circled to Kila's off-hand side, forcing her to turn and retreat. Unlike Gian, Jil insisted they train with their shadline blades, not wooden ones. This struck Kila as ridiculously dangerous, especially since she had Cayne, a dagger, and Jil had Qinsh, a sword of unknown power. Unknown to Kila anyway. She just hoped it wasn't like Cloak Einlin's blade, which burned victims with magic flames.

"Thrust!" Jil commanded.

Kila took more care this time, but it made her lunge tentative. Jil took advantage and slapped the side of Kila's forward shin with the flat of her blade. The loud smack reverberated around the courtyard. Kila yelped and danced back, a mercus bolt forming at the same time.

Jil jumped as Kila's invisible mercus feat returned the favor on her backside. Her face became a mask of fury and she tilted her head to one side. "Repeat that, merculyn, and we'll see if Her Enlightened can put the pieces of you back together."

"You were toying with me," Kila shot back. "Now you know how it feels."

Henley rushed forward, clearing his throat. "It's time to stop now, anyway, ladies. Kila has her lesson with Flaumishtak next."

Jil blew out her cheeks and stalked off, murmuring about brats with magic and shadline pretenders. Kila was tempted to singe her hair, but Henley put himself in front of her and she couldn't see past him.

"She provoked me," she said. "She wants me to fail so she can stop these stupid lessons."

"You can stop these lessons any time you want."

That was true. Kila could do anything she wanted. Who was going to stop her? She was the Girl Who Could Fly and the Terror of Dunne Medow Plaza.

Three ten-days had passed since her battle with the Hargothe. Instead of feeling more rested, she was exhausted. And the city had not made much of a recovery either. Most of the debris had been cleared from the plaza, and Highest Quiv had already begun work to patch the giant hole she'd blown in the Cathedral of Til. But those who had witnessed the battle—and who had felt the byblow of her feats of fear and adoration—were not well at all. Many were dead. More injured. Some were calling for her execution.

And others . . . others had joined the Way of Kila. Not the Way of Kil. Just as Highest Quiv had predicted. Damn him.

That last group was especially problematic since there was no Way of Kil or Kila in Starside. Not officially. Not with her permission. But did Marlow listen to her objections? No. Did Her Enlightened listen? Ha! And now there was a camp forming in the ruins of the Blasted Quarter, full of lunatics who swore oaths to serve Kila Sigh and the Way of Kila.

These folks were not popular with the average citizen, who thought Kila ought to be trussed to a pole in Dunne Medow Plaza and receive the City's Justice.

Recently, late night raids by the infuriated citizenry had resulted in pitched battles in the Blasted Quarter, stopped only when Kila and the monarch had descended from the sky, engulfed in mercus light, voices booming for everyone to lay down their arms.

And then the ranks of her followers had swelled again as a third of those opposed to Kila switched allegiance due to "her fierce and radiant loveliness," as one man put it.

"Why are you training with Jil if you hate it?" Henley asked cautiously. "You can ash your enemies with ease. Stabbing isn't really necessary."

"I don't want to ash anyone. Ell says blade training is good for discipline and that the Dirth may wish to see my abilities at the Armory." She slid Cayne into its thigh sheath and swung her cloak over her shoulders. Black wool, very fine. The sleeves of her jacket bore black embroidered ravens that gleamed dully in the flat gray of winter. Ell had commissioned a wardrobe full of such clothing. "Let's go inside. Maybe I can eat something before—"

Nax darted toward her, voice filling her head with enthusiastic glee. *He's coming!*

"Kil's eyes, I missed my chance." Turning, Kila waited expectantly for the demayne to dymense into the courtyard. It wasn't long. A roll of green mist appeared first, followed by the hulking beast himself. Two and a half times Kila's height and swathed in black velvet robes, Flaumishtak might have been the image of Kil himself. Oly, cream-colored and fluffy, rested on the demayne's shoulder.

Nax leapt into Flaumishtak's open arms and received a good chin scratching courtesy of the demayne's cruel black claws. "Nax tells me you've been neglecting your health."

That's not true, ya little traitor! she sent to the small gray.

You didn't sleep last night and today you've only eaten an apple. Nax added a cringe to the sending, her opinion of apples being quite low. *You need meat!*

"Let's proceed, Flaumishtak. I have things to do."

Huff appeared and repeated Nax's leap so that the demayne's arms were full of cats. It might have been funny if Kila wasn't still fuming about Jil's treatment of her.

Flaumishtak gave each cat a bit of stinky something from a pocket, then urged them to disembark from his body. Finally turning his attention back to Kila, he said, "I recall we were exploring the interesting trick you call 'joining.'"

Kila threw up her hands. "I don't know how that works. And neither does Henley. You are supposed to be training us, not the other way around." In truth, he was supposed to train only her, but she refused to attend unless Henley could too. Flaumishtak seemed thrilled, but his insatiable interest in joining had begun to chafe.

"But I must understand the nature of joining, Highest Sigh." Mocking tones on her title. Always with the mocking tones. "You see, if you two have discovered a phasic bonding, then what is possible with the mercusine is greater than I ever knew. And you will require every advantage in the coming culmination."

Of course he had to bring up the stupid culmination. As if Dem-Kisk was something she might forget. She felt Henley's hand on her arm. Shaking her head to clear away the rising frustration, she blew out a breath and leveled a calm (well, calmer) stare at the demayne. For one burdened with the title of "Highest" she didn't seem to be much in charge of her hours.

"Henley explains joining better than I can." She nudged him.

The fiery-haired boy sighed and absently scratched the tip of his nose with his pinky. Kila knew that meant he was truly considering how to explain the inexplicable. He had far more patience than she did, which was one of the things she loved about him. She didn't know what she'd do if he . . . no! She cut off the thought.

Henley was already into his roundabout explanation to Flaumishtak. Kila barely listened, the fear of her thought rising against her resistance. The image of Henley lying at the Hargothe's feet, the seer's staff thrust through his body and pinning him. The boy had suffered so much at the old man's hands. The wounds had healed, but there remained a hollowness in his eyes. Even now she saw the boldness of his cheeks, the tightness of his eyes, the sharp hand gestures that strove to outline concepts he could barely grasp. It all spoke to her in a subtle language, revealing what Henley sought to hide. Pain.

"And then Huff rescued me from the lashes by bringing me into his mind. I did it with Kila later. Then she with me when facing the Hargothe."

"But what mercusine bolts were used?" Flaumishtak said, stamping a cloven hoof.

"None."

"But Miss Sigh said the Hargothe used the bond to penetrate her will and—"

"No, that was different," Kila said. "He used the force bond I had placed on Henley. I stopped the Hargothe by joining Henley to me."

The demayne growled deep in his throat. "That explains nothing! Surely there were bolts involved."

"Are you saying Huff is a merculyn?" Henley asked. He looked at the cat, who had taken up position on top of

Henley's feet to keep his body off the deepening snow in the courtyard. "Because he invited me to the joining. *He* did whatever it is."

The demayne tilted his head up and considered this. His mane of hair wavered in the wind, the loose ends ever-dissolving into tendrils of smoke. "Hmm."

A detail from Kila's first experience with joining glimmered in her memory. "Henley asked me to surrender. And when I did, he . . . embraced me."

"Yes, there is a pull," Henley said, "an invitation."

"Phasic mercusine. It must be!" Flaumishtak folded his arms and began to pace, leaving steaming hoof prints in the snow. "The felnithel are wise beyond my ken." He bowed to Huff, then offered the same to Nax and Oly who had jumped to a low wall in order to better survey their domain. "A dangerous feat, make no mistake. But think of what it says about the nature of the mind!"

Kila clicked her tongue. "When Yiothiziffra is dead, I'll be sure to sit back with a pint of trezz and give it a good cogitation. But right now I'm getting cold. Do you have anything to teach or shall I go in and find a nice fire to sit by?"

"Yiothizandra would torch you to ash if she heard you call her by that silly name. I like it!" He flourished his claws and shrugged his shoulder as if to loosen up. "Now. For your lesson today I thought we would work on dealing with the weather. You humans are so fragile when it comes to cold and heat. It's rather silly."

"Weather?" Kila perked up. "Can we make it stop snowing?"

"Ha! I would not say anything is impossible for you, my delicious sweetling, but such a feat is likely beyond even your long reach. What I propose is to show you how to shelter-cloak yourself. Once you master that, I can show you how to armor-cloak."

"Aha! That's what Marlow does. Not even Cayne can cut into his flesh. Not very deep, anyway."

"Marlow? That summer ninny? I doubt he has learned armor-cloak. He must have some other prank in his poke, perhaps a heller of some sort. He's a sneaky one."

Marlow did not use any artifact to stone his flesh, of that Kila was sure. It seemed there were feats that Flaumishtak did not know. That gave her some comfort since she didn't trust him one whit.

"Attend, pupils," he said, becoming mockingly solemn. "Form the bolts thusly." His mercus arose quick and powerful, a buzzing haze that Kila could see and feel and smell. As always it gave off the faint scent of burning hair.

She saw immediately that he formed a simple negation of the surrounding cold, then held the negation in place by the concept of rigidity. "You can't move about, then," she said. "Not much use."

"I'm not finished." He proceeded to dazzle Kila with slender threads of subtle emotion that she could not identify by name. But she realized she didn't need to.

"What're you doing?" Henley said to her.

She hadn't noticed her own hand reaching out to trace along the bolts the demayne had formed around himself. "Feel it, Hen."

He tentatively reached out. "Feel what?"

"The mercus. Can't you feel it? The texture. The warmth."

He flapped his hand around, passing his fingers right through the haze of Flaumishtak's shelter-cloak.

The wind had ceased to disturb the demayne's hair, and the snow that had accumulated on his shoulders had melted. Now the flakes hissed out of existence as they came near to him.

The weather-cloak was soft and yielding to Kila's touch. The mercus bolts had woven together more finely than a master tailor's work.

"Much of what we do with the mercus cannot be understood in detail," Flaumishtak said softly. The flames in his eyes had banked to orange embers as he watched Kila make her discovery. How long had he waited for her to come to this epiphany?

"Do you think I manifest my power as a human cook throws carrots and salt and chicken into a stock pot? No. The subtle realm of the mercusine is of the senses and emotion. The more you attempt to divide and divide again its nature, the less you will understand it. The less you will have control of it. That is your gift, Kila. You transmute pure intention into mercus action. This is the god-power in your blood."

Kila formed the bolts and was instantly warm. "That is so easy," she said.

Henley's face had fallen. "I don't understand a single thing he said, and yet you're already doing it. How does the rigidity in the bolt get leavened with flexibility?"

"Desire it," Flaumishtak said softly. "It is that simple. And that difficult."

A far door swung open. Her Enlightened Majesty, Ell LiMinluit, stepped out, dressed in a fine black fur. Beneath flashed a cream tunic and tight waistcoat above riding trousers. Boots rose to mid-calf and turned down at the top. Her usual tumble of black hair was pulled away from her face. She possessed the regal bearing of her station, purposeful but unrushed. But her usually equanimous face was brewing dark clouds.

Kila wondered what trouble she was about to get in. She ambled to meet the monarch and offered a polite nod. Neither Marlow nor Henley had convinced her she must bow to the woman. That Her Enlightened Majesty was not truly human at all did not disturb Kila nearly as much as the woman's assumption that Kila would simply do whatever she commanded. Still, she thought the monarch rather more trustworthy than Flaumishtak. That Harnzyne—a dragon of Day—showed the monarch respect and love also spoke well of her.

"Good morning, Ell," Kila said, wincing even as she finished the greeting. Wen had always said her tongue would get her into more trouble than her thief's fingers ever would. The monarch acknowledged Kila with a dark-eyed stare.

Jil and Dunne Marlow followed the woman into the snowy courtyard, though they kept more distance between them than such advisors might usually do. Also in attendance were two Radiants. The taller was Radiant Gilok, a middle-years dandy in pantaloons and so red of nose that Kila wondered if he'd breakfasted on a bottle of fine Tordanaise wine. Next to him strode Radiant Junisa Peline, Quinn's mother. Short, lovely, and fierce. She glowered at Kila and offered a nod. "Highest." She blamed Kila for Quinn's entry into the shadline order, even though Quinn had come into her blade before meeting Kila.

Gilok looked expectantly at Kila's left hand. The ring. The Kil-damned ring. A bloody garnet set on a thick gold band. She offered her hand. Gilok took it up with a delicate flourish and bent to press his lips to the stone. "Highest of Kil, how fare you this chill morning?"

"Is it cold? I hadn't noticed."

This provoked a squint of calculation from the man. But that wasn't new. He was always weighing and wondering and scheming.

Marlow and Jil stopped behind the monarch. Neither said a word of greeting to Kila, though Marlow offered a lopsided smile. He carried a rolled parchment three feet long.

"I fear the mercus lesson must end for the day, Flaumishtak," the monarch announced. "You may leave." She turned her back on the beast. Oly leapt from the wall and went to the demayne's arms. For once, Flaumishtak didn't offer a parting remark before dymensing in a flash of mercus green.

Nax came to Kila. It didn't take much effort to admit the cat into her shelter-cloak without dropping it.

Why haven't you done this all along?

I didn't know how.

You must spend more time with Flaumishtak.

Kila knew the monarch had bad news, else she would have waited for Kila to come at the usual time. Kila had been on the receiving end of a series of the dullest lectures imaginable. About governance, supplies, armies, realms, trade, treaties and every manner of court intrigue across every far-flung realm in the world. In truth, Kila rather liked hearing about the intrigue.

It was Gilok who did most of the talking in these sessions, punctuated infrequently by Radiant Peline, whose countryside upbringing gave her a different perspective.

Kila felt surrounded. They all wanted her to do something.

Exactly what that was remained elusive. They couldn't decide among themselves.

"It's time," the monarch said softly. "Henley, you must remain here. The Armory is for shadlines only."

Jil moved forward, hand on the hilt of her sword. "We must go at once."

"How do you know?" Kila asked. Even after all these ten-days of waiting, the moment seemed sudden to her. She didn't want to leave Henley.

"I listen and obey," Jil said stiffly. "As do all of our order."

"Why haven't I heard anything?"

Jil smirked. "I ask myself that every day."

"Enough, you two," Her Enlightened said. There was no bite in her tone, just a quiet assertion of authority. "You will learn to heed the shadline call, Kila. For now, trust in me."

Before Kila could make things worse, Marlow stepped quickly to the monarch's other side and extended his rolled parchment to Kila. "Study this in your spare time. It is quite valuable, so please try to keep it intact."

Taking it, she said, "What is it?"

"A gift. From Dunne Yples. A map."

Kila took it, but didn't unroll it. A servant rushed out, carrying a bundle. It was Kila's backpack. He offered it to her, half bowing and muttering, "Highest Sigh." Kila took it, frowning. "You have Cayne. You are ready," the monarch said. "Take my hand."

Instead of obeying, Kila turned to Henley. His green eyes locked with hers. She read the concern there easily enough, and the love. He put a hand on her cheek, and she could do nothing but press into its warmth. "I can dymense back easi-ly," she said. "I won't be away long."

I will always be with you, he said through their bond. His lips sought hers, and despite the presence of so many onlookers, she happily accepted the kiss.

If only there was a shelter-cloak to shield herself from tears. Trickles coursed down her cheeks. An ache in her throat strangled her words as she bade Henley goodbye.

"Take my hand, girl," the monarch said. "I will dymense us."

Kila hugged Nax close and did as she was told.

3
___

DIP THE SKULL

The bodies had been dragged away and returned to the nosg lands for burial—or ingestion—or whatever the old race of nosg-kin did with corpses. Most were charred to flaky blackness, unrecognizable as nosg at all.

Yiothizandra surveyed the great hall of Ceronhel, scrubbed and swept, and occupied now by a dozen nosg arch-shamans. They did not sit in the crude stools she'd had Noy fetch. Yioth would not permit it. The stools were there to be noticed, so the shamans would know they'd been denied even that most modest relief from their weariness.

The shamans had been summoned from across the Haelshock range, forced to come in haste for an audience with the new mistress of Ceronhel. The Hargothe was dead. No longer would nosg be sacrificed to feed his staff with power. Now there reigned a queen—a dragnithan, no less—who sought not to oppress the once-noble race of nosg but instead lead them to glory.

Aggalmas–alamas. The mire-tongue words for the nosg conquest of a world they thought had been stolen from them.

Yioth stood before the shamans, draped in luxuriant sable robes, wings unmanifested, in woman-form. Her armor and sword rested on a stand to the right, a reminder that hers was a martial empire and that the road ahead led to war. Total war.

No fire burned in the huge hearth behind her. Yioth was always too hot in this world, heated as she was by the dragon-fire within. The windows remained uncurtained and the outer doors braced wide, admitting swirls of chill mountain air. The shamans' breath plumed from wide nostrils, giving the impression of a herd of patient horses. They wore thick furs of goat and ox. Empty-eyed wolf and bear heads made for fearsome headpieces. The nosg were squat creatures, and hardy, of thick legs and striated hairy arms. Claw-fists adorned with crude rings gripped the skull-topped staves of their station. Those skulls did not have empty eye sockets. Instead, rough cut gems filled the voids. They could focus their shamanic swarmlight into rays of heat, ice, or other feats of magic. These twelve were the highest of their clans, lords of vast domains and innumerable nosg-kin underlings.

"Wic-Ok, Foy-Pan, Razk-Ka. One of you three shall be prime," she announced, refusing to use the honorific of Wurgu as she addressed them. This was the first declaration she'd uttered since their assembly here two hours prior. Her pronunciation of the mire-tongue was perhaps too precise, too agile, but the fact that she knew their names conferred more honor on them than omitting their rank had dishonored them.

A chorus of surprised grunts answered her. The individuals she'd named stepped forward. They glared at each other and showed their large pointed teeth. Wic-Ok and Foy-Pan were heads of rival clans; a feud had endured between them for a thousand years. The third—Razk-Ka—was noted for his wisdom, and his passivity. But Yioth knew what the others did not. Razk-Ka was a schemer who preferred a knife in his enemy's gut to a pitched battle in the passes. His alliances, trade arrangements, and enormous bevy of concubines gave him leverage, wealth, and ranks upon ranks of loyal sons to do his bidding.

Yioth mistrusted him. She needed him to be loyal or be dead. Dead was simpler.

"Bring me Razk-Ka's heart," she said to Wic-Ok and Foy-Pan. Before the reverberations of her command had faded, all three shamans set their skull orbs aglow with swarmlight.

The first to loose his power was Razk-Ka. The blue gems in his skull staff scintillated. He thrust the staff overhead and uttered a raspy command. Azure light oozed out, forming a dome of transparent blue around him. Half a heartbeat later, two rays shot from Wic-Ok's staff, amber like the first beams of morning light breaking free of a far horizon. They flashed against Razk-Ka's protective dome, sparking flares of fire all around it. But Razk-Ka's power was greater. Wic-Ok's effort failed and his attack sputtered out. Feverishly, he dug into a pouch at his belt, seeking a claw-full of the mimak mushrooms that gave him access to the mercus.

Foy-Pan's swarmlight had gathered more slowly. He now struck, the rays of his skull gems sizzling the air, nearly a matching blue to Razk-Ka's dome. The beleaguered shaman raised his staff higher, lips pulling back in a triumphant grin. Yiothizandra marveled at his wily defense. For the dome was not merely a shield. It absorbed Foy-Pan's power, such that Razk-Ka required little effort to keep the dome in force and at full strength. In fact, he had the spare concentration to reach into his own mushroom pouch, dip in and lift a bulbous red-cap to his mouth. He chewed with his mouth open, a clear taunt to his enemies. The noxious fungus turned his teeth black.

The onlookers roared, and just as Yiothizandra had hoped, the reaction revealed each shaman's allegiance. None wanted Wic-Ok to prevail. He was known to be weak and vain and cowardly. But the support for Razk-Ka was split. And those who urged on Foy-Pan were the louder. Perhaps those backing him were under Razk-Ka's fist in other ways.

Wic-Ok blasted another feat of amber fire at Razk-Ka. This time it rebounded and he had to dance back or be singed by his own flame. Cursing in a high-pitched shriek, the nosg cut off his magic and ran at Razk-Ka, staff clenched in both fists and raised to deliver a physical blow.

Razk-Ka payed him no mind, for his attention was entirely on Foy-Pan. The latter had ceased feeding his blue power into Razk-Ka's dome, and now retreated as Razk-Ka approached.

"Let us join to kill Wic-Ok, young Foy," Razk-Ka said. The onlookers screamed in delighted outrage at the insult. "You will dip the skull to me and I shall allow you to live, if our mighty mistress allows it."

Wic-Ok's staff came down, jounced from Razk-Ka's protective shield and lurched back to strike his own forehead. The skull upon the staff cracked and the jawbone fell off, teeth scattering across the stone floor. Wic's legs went loose and he staggered like a drunk sailor for a moment before falling onto his face.

Seeing Wic felled in such a ridiculous way, the onlookers cheered and pumped their own staves in the air. Foy-Pan summoned another gathering of swarmlight into his eye-gems and lashed out. The rays had no color, but merely distorted the air with heat.

Razk-Ka's bear-head skull began to smoke. Crying out in indignant rage, Razk collapsed his protective dome back into his eye-gems, preserving the power and allowing him to send forth a new feat without straining to gather the swarmlight anew.

He pushed the feat out, an inverted bowl shape of azure that turned back Foy-Pan's heat assault. Razk plucked a dried black deer-berry from a dangle of sinew that adorned his staff. This he popped into his mouth, then spat it Foy-Pan's feet.

The ball of dung exploded in fire and the great hall reverberated with the report. The floor beneath Yioth's feet trembled and the air filled with acrid black smoke.

Annoyed, Yioth manifested her wings and flapped away the smoke. Soon the air cleared, revealing the fallen Foy-Pan, feet seared off, stumps cauterized and black as coal. The nosg screamed in anguish, then lapsed into the breathless panting of a vanquished dog. Razk-Ka quenched his own power and strode forward, staff clonking on the stone floors. The great hall had fallen otherwise silent.

"Dip the skull," Razk-Ka commanded.

Foy-Pan had dropped his staff. He reached for it, but it lay half a span from his straining claw hand.

"I said dip the skull. I shall not repeat myself again." Swarmlight formed instantaneously in Razk's eye-gems. No matter they were sapphires; this light was a deep purple, sinister and full of dark resonances that made even Yioth's skin quiver. An answering vibration came from her belly. The Kil-notion quickening within her felt the pull of whatever forces Razk-Ka called upon.

Sensing worse agony about to strike, Foy-Pan scrabbled on hands and knees to reach his staff. Plucking it up he rolled onto his back and raised it. No swarmlight appeared in the gems. With a deep-throated growl, he slowly lowered the skull toward Razk-Ka until the forehead touched the floor. The slightest dry tap echoed from the walls.

Razk-Ka touched his own skull to the back of Foy-Pan's. He muttered something low, unintelligible. A scintillation arose and surrounded both skulls then faded.

Razk-Ka turned to Wic-Ok, who was just now coming out of his brain-addled sleep. He offered Yioth a side-eyed questioning look.

She nodded.

Razk-Ka smacked Wic-Ok upside the head with the butt of his staff. The nosg folded to the floor like an empty sack. There was no dipping of the skull this time. Razk-Ka stomped the staff skull under his heavy boot, smashing it into a dozen pieces.

He announced: "Wic-Ok is wurgu of G'galas Hael no more. There is no G'galas Hael, for it has been eaten by G'galas Woond."

The assembled shamans groused and stamped, but none chose to challenge his declaration.

Razk-Ka faced Yioth now. He bowed low, in the manner of the elnisian. A mocking gesture, she realized. She was tempted to flame him from existence for such insolence, but then she'd be forced to choose a Prime from the remaining unimpressive shamans.

"I bring you my own heart, mistress Yiothizandra," Razk-Ka said. "I am Prime."

She was not displeased with this result. The nosg were not

a sophisticated race, not comprised of great craftsmen and philosophers. As far as she knew there were no nosg books, no written form of their language at all. But that did not mean they were stupid.

"Razk-Ka, step forward and be branded mine."

A momentary hesitation, understandable given her words. But Razk-Ka knew when to be bold, and this was such a moment. He stepped forward and knelt before her, staff held upright so that the skull looked nearly into Yioth's eyes. She ignored it.

She was not like her little cousin, the so-called Enlightened Majesty of Starside. She did not play with the mercusine in such ways, for she had chosen other manifestations of her power. Her ability to summon wings and spit fire were the most obvious. But there were aspects of dragonfire that she could bring to bear in subtler ways. And now she did so, bending to press her lips to his forehead. The kiss seared him, marking him as hers. The Prime of all nosg-kin was subject to her now, and she would sense his whereabouts no matter how far he traveled from her sight. If required she could reignite this heat to remind him of her power, to punish him for transgressions, or to burn him to ash should he prove unworthy.

She explained none of this, but she thought he understood. Enough, anyway, to keeping him hewing close to her orders. The first of which came to her now.

"Whatever the Hargothe promised, I shall grant to you. But only in victory."

"Without victory, there will be no nosg remaining," he said in Ennish. His pronunciation was burdened by a thick tongue and mouth overfull of teeth, but she understood him well enough.

"The twelve g'galasi have been preparing to march," she said. "You've had more than enough time. Assemble the horde in the valleys and passes. Attend to the supplies carefully."

"Every drikk of nosgdom will happily starve to support our armies, Queen Yiothizandra. Even so we will be required to scavenge what we can from the vanquished men to the south."

"There will be plunder, I assure you. When this is over, you will possess all the lands of the world and the only men who live will be those you have taken for slaves."

A strange expression passed over Razk-Ka's face, a fluttering of his wide nostrils, a spreading of his thin lips. But it was the gleam in his eyes, like his own inner swarmlight, that told he battled a great passion of feeling. And now he did bow low, no note of mockery present. "It is truly *aggalamas-alamas?*"

"Oh, it is, Prime Razk-Ka. The elnisians called it Dem-Kisk. The return of Roon-Jek to this world."

The nosg worshipped the same gods as the other races did, but they had different names. Roon-Jek was the god men called Kil. But Yioth knew dozens of names that had been used for the god-notion that grew within her now.

"We do not seek Roon-Jek," he said flatly, some of the emotion draining from his face.

She placed a tender hand on his face. "I know. It is Shish-Jek who abandoned you." The goddess men called Pol. Nosg believed their misfortunes were the result of the goddess of luck turning her back on them. She was the one they always sought to appease and to attract.

"Shish-Jek is another face of Roon-Jek. You cannot have one without the other." Yioth thought their aggalamas-alamas prophecy pure idiocy, but she would happily use it to motivate the nosg to fight her war. "Trust in Yiothizandra. Aggalamas-alamas has come."

She again brought forth her wings and flapped to loft herself above them. The capes of their furs fluttered in her downdraft. "Aggalamas-alamas!" she shouted.

The shamans echoed her cry, and as one, knelt and dipped the skull.

4

SUCH NICETIES

In the center of Garden Tower was a round room accessible only by the heads of the Ways. Each entered through a hidden door in their quarters, latch activated by a lodestone emblazoned with the symbol of their Way.

Coin Inlina and Voluptuary Minn sat at an ancient round table within the room, each having brought their own supper. The Coin noted with sour distaste that Minn had once again brought the sweet squash soup she favored and a long stick of tough bread which she would rip apart and dip into the soup until it was all gone.

Inlina preferred to dine with utensils, and her kitchens had prepared for her a lovely filet of pikefish, potatoes, and some steamed greens. That she had no appetite at all was something she would never reveal to the Voluptuary.

They ate in silence, each daring the other to speak first. The Coin decided that time pressed too hard to delay further. "My coin-talker has received word from Starside. The Coin there has died, apparently at the hands of Kila Sigh, during a mercus tantrum that wreaked havoc in Starside. Even my aunt, Voluptuary Sinlop, was seen being carried away on a litter. The Hargothe is reported dead, also at Kila's hand. Ell LiMinluit was killed and resurrected by Kila Sigh. The Cathedral of Til has been partly demolished. Much of the Blasted Quarter has collapsed, and just as we feared, followers have flocked to Sigh, calling themselves the Way of Kila."

Voluptuary Minn listened as she stuffed soggy bread into her mouth, nodding for the Coin to continue as soon as the silence had returned.

"That's all there is," the Coin said. She took up her fork but couldn't bring herself to cut into her fish.

"That only affirms what we knew. Kila Sigh is Kil's creature and chaos is her aim. We must promise-bind her or kill her. Unfortunate that we no longer possess the *vaz'on*."

"It's been put to good use upon Dunne Yples brow."

"Aye." The Voluptuary nodded solemnly, but not without a skeptical tilt to her head. "But it would be better had he died. I do not like one of such power available for others to tap. He is with Kila and Quiv now."

It struck the Coin that her ally had a smug air about her. She sensed that she'd fallen into a bit of a trap. "What have you discovered? I can see it on your face."

Voluptuary Minn allowed a smile to curl one side of her mouth. She swallowed another chunk of soupy bread and delayed answering so that she might sip her wine. That finished, she said, "The last of the debris beneath Kil's Keep has been cleared. Beyond it lay a vast, empty chamber. All black. In fact, the first exploration revealed it to be too large for the space it occupied."

The Voluptuary waited for the Coin to add up the figures.

And then she got it. "A Derslin Wheel! Did they venture to the center?"

"All the way. Sensual Wighton instantly knew it for what it was. There was no sign of Kila and her party, not any leavings or tracks. No indication that they used any of the columns or if she simply dymensed them away."

Setting her fork onto the table, fish untouched, the Coin leaned back from her plate. The pain in her stomach had plagued her for a year now, and recent events had only made it worse. "Did Sensual Wighton activate a column?"

"No. He's too wise to attempt something so brash. I doubt he could do it alone in any event. He suffered a terrific backlash when he was abruptly severed from Yples's *vaz'on*. Besides, the columns are marked with symbols that have not been deciphered yet. My scholars are tearing through our library. Do you have any records of use in yours?"

Each Way maintained its own archives deep below ground level. What each contained was known only to those of that Way. "I will put the question to my archivists."

The Voluptuary swallowed the last of her bread and shoved her platter aside. Her handsome face had gone grim, but there was an eagerness in her eyes. "We will crack it and it will take us to Starside. But we do not yet have the strength to subdue Sigh should we find her."

That was indeed a problem. But not an unsolvable one. Kila could be brought down the same way Yples had been. With overwhelming force. But they did not have enough merculyns at their disposal here on Garden Island. They would have to fetch Sensuals and Spinsters from Towers and Baths across the world. The Derslin Wheel would make that possible. But the Coin did not plan to go after Kila just yet. "We are not going to Starside, dear friend. Not just yet."

"Where then?"

"My own city, Tordain. My aunt, the Autarch, will listen to our concerns with a sympathetic ear. And hers will be the first army to join our cause."

The Voluptuary was truly perplexed. She had set her mind on subduing Kila and had not looked beyond that. That was why the Coin was needed. For she had spun her medallion thousands of times upon the question. She explained: "Kila's rise to power presages Dem-Kisk, and she will be needed for the culmination. This I have seen in my spins. But war comes to the mainland. A great and horrible war. We know the shad-line cult has called an Armory. My coin-talker in Lockt speaks of nosg hordes gathering in the passes."

"Surely those were the Hargothe's pawns. They will battle each other now that he's dead."

"Some other warlord commands them now. I've instructed the Coin in Lockt to send parties north to discover who. Mark me, the coming culmination will pull the nosg south as surely as it pulls you and me to the mainland."

"And you intend to lead the forces of men to battle?" The Voluptuary scoffed and swirled her wine before tossing it back. "You are a strong woman, and I've no doubt Pol speaks more plainly through your medallion that she does through anyone else's. But battles are best left to military minds."

"Battles, yes. Wars, no. And the forces of humankind are too scattered, each bunched under the command of city-state leaders who hate their neighbors. They must be united, and only the call of the gods can inspire them to set aside their mundane and petty quarrels."

"But if this war comes, then it is imperative we control Sigh. The *vaz'on* looks a better crown for her with each passing moment, does it not?"

Coin Inlina could not argue against that. It would be better if Kila was under their total control. "Perhaps we divide our efforts. I to gather the forces of men under a single command. You to assemble our merculyns and make them ready to face Kila Sigh. But if we are to capture Sigh, we must approach her subtly. And I say this with all the respect due your station and your Way, but the followers of Ori are not of the right temperament for the task. If Sigh feels a circle of source-taps approaching, she will be on guard."

"Do you have someone else in mind to approach her?"

"I do. Raginalt Keel."

The Voluptuary soured at the mention of the lad's name. "He dotes upon your girl, Tia. I doubt you'll convince him to leave her bedside."

Tia had been the Coin's spy within Til's Fifth of the tower. She had posed as a Favored, serving the now-dead Highest Mancin Fley. At the Coin's command, she had released Dunne Yples from his prison beneath the Tower. Yples had brought the tower down with his rage. The collapse had stove in Tia's skull, but it hadn't killed her. She now lay in an unwaking sleep, attended by Raginalt, who had been with her at the time. And who had miraculously avoided so much as bruise.

"Raginalt was Sigh's close friend," the Coin said. "She would trust him."

"If you can convince him to leave Tia."

The Coin pursed her lips, as if considering the problem. In truth, she knew an easy solution to it. "I will speak with him.

Sending him to Starside to find Kila will not be difficult. Convincing him to betray her may be more challenging."

The unspoken answer to that filled the round chamber like a noxious fog. There were ways to make Raginalt comply, though all of them went against the ethics of the Ways of Pol and Ori. But given the exigencies of the moment, was it not required of them to violate such niceties in the service of the greater good? It was the sort of question devotees of Pol debated late into the night, faces flushed with wine and enthusiasm for the puzzle. How easy it had been to say that violating such rules would undercut the legitimacy of the entire Way. Coin Inlina had argued such in her younger days. But now, here, in the face of real disaster, it was just as easy to set such objections aside. She would do what was necessary. And so, too, would the Voluptuary.

They did not speak of what they knew they must do. By and by, the Voluptuary pushed back from the table and stood. "After Tia's funeral, we shall speak to Raginalt."

The Coin nodded and watched her colleague depart. Plucking her medallion from her necklace, she posed a question in her mind and flipped the coin high into the air. It jounced onto the table, bouncing and ringing. When it settled, Pol's face shined in the mercus light. A smile.

Such a grim thing, that smile. And how strong was the temptation to spin again, and again, to pester Pol like a child for a different answer.

But Pol held no sway over such things. Reborn or not, it was Kil who severed the cord of each mortal life, and Lumne pulled all into her never-waking embrace. But did death have to come so soon?

She plucked up her medallion and affixed it to her chain.

Enough of this inward reflection. Duty compelled her to look toward the living future no matter how little she would see of it. Perhaps she had a year remaining. Perhaps less.

Drawing upon reserves of will she had not often tapped, she took up her fork and resumed her dinner, small bite after small bite, pausing to clamp her palm over her lips and wait for her rebellious craw to accept the food. The coming days would demand much of her, and she would need all the sustenance she could consume.

5
______

WHEN YOU ARE READY

The Kovi-Mest river smelled worse than Cheapsgate. Kila and Her Enlightened Majesty, who much to Kila's relief insisted on being called Ell during their time away from Starside, walked on the bordering mule track toward Tearling.

"Why didn't you dymense us to wherever this confab of black cloaks is going to happen?" Kila complained. She didn't mind walking, but she just wanted to get the meeting over with and return to Henley. Everything Jil had told her about the Armory so far had left her feeling like a minnow about to be baited to a hook. Not that she'd allow that, but since her confrontation with the Hargothe, she was loath to use her mercus powers against anyone. Too many bystanders got hurt, or killed. They were the ones she was supposed to be protecting.

"I don't know exactly where the Armory will be held," Ell said. "My instincts bade me dymense outside of the city. We may hear and feel more as we approach."

As usual, Jil piped in with an unsolicited opinion. "There is a purpose to it, mark me."

I'll mark you, all right, Kila thought. Her hand brushed against Cayne, which was sheathed on her right thigh. She snatched it away. I'm almost as bad as Quinn. She wondered if the force of destiny had brought Jil into her life just to test her patience.

The thought of seeing Quinn helped soothed her anger. She moved her dagger hand to her shoulder and patted Nax's head. The animal had learned to drape herself around the back of Kila's neck and sleep while Kila did all the walking.

Kila considered how the shelter-cloak trick could be changed to keep out the stink. If she could use her mercus at all. Ell said she should remain masked on this journey.

The foul-smelling river, laden with debris and excrement from the city ahead, flowed swiftly behind them toward the Sorgeal Sea, a faint glimmer to the east. Ahead, the square towers of Tearling rose in the blue haze, backed by even hazier hills.

A mule team approached from behind them pulling a barge up the river. There was rarely a breath of wind here, which was why the stink was so terrible. The trio of women moved aside to allow the mules and their handler to pass by.

"We should jump on that barge," Kila said. Even after all this time wearing shoes, her feet had not become accustomed to being squeezed inside them. This lengthy trek was causing blisters.

"We must not," said Jil.

And so they did not.

The sun had long since peaked by the time they wound through the farmland on the outskirts of the city and came to an encampment alongside the river. Crude tents of sticks and hide leaned here and there, and young folk huddled around campfires, smoking pipes and singing. A banner, hand-painted on a bed linen, hung from a tree.

"Not here," Kila said. "This can't be." On the banner was drawn in a crude hand a familiar shape, an oval with spears jutting up from it. The crown of the Highest of Kil was depicted on an accursed handbill now in wide circulation. Below it, in even more crude shapes, a cat.

Nax, get in my backpack at once. She sent enough urgency to compel instant obedience and the cat burrowed in.

A long-haired, unwashed man trudged from the camp to greet them as they passed. A few other stragglers came with him. "D'ya have any spare coin, friends?"

Jil moved to keep him away from Ell, as if the dragnithan couldn't defend herself. But Ell smoothly stepped around the shadline to meet the man. She already had a gold skillet in hand but didn't offer it. "What is that on your banner?"

He chuckled. "The Way of Kil, but we call it the Way of Kila. She was born with nothing, just like us. She will build a Way for us. I have seen it."

His companions nodded solemnly to affirm that he had indeed seen this incredible future. Kila noted they were young women. Two had the dark skin of Iops. None were armed that she could see.

"You know Kila Sigh well, do you?" Kila asked, keeping her face down. The likeness on the handbill wasn't that close, and her hair had grown out enough that she didn't look bald as an atlen egg anymore. But she did not want to be recognized by these fools.

"Naw. Haven't seen her yet. But I heard she can fly and that she can raise the dead. She killed a demon in Starside."

Ell passed him the coin, which he took with a bit of awe. Kila doubted he'd held many like it in his lifetime. "Perhaps wait until Kila Sigh calls for followers," Ell said. "Tearling will not allow you to stay here long before they ask Tordain or Wantin to remove you."

"I hear your words, Lady. But we feel it's right to be here because seekers keep coming to join."

"Seekers?"

"Seekers of the Way. A man hears about Highest Sigh and he feels something. He leaves wherever he is, following that feeling. Doesn't know what it is or what it means. He just *knows.* That's how I got here. I thought you three might be seekers too, but I thought wrong. Thanks for the coin. We're hungry." He gave a weird sort of nodding bow and ambled back to camp, flipping the coin as he went.

Kila watched him go, fuming and clamping her tongue in her teeth to keep from yelling. A woman gasped. "It's her!"

The others scrutinized Kila, and one by one their mouths opened in awe. And then they were on their knees. The man who had taken the coin looked over his shoulder, saw the women kneeling and turned back.

He came up short when he finally saw Kila. "It's you. It truly is. I know your face, for I have seen it in visions." With slow, worshipful movements, he too went to his knees and then his belly. Others began streaming from the camp, first walking and murmuring to their neighbors, and then running.

Kila backed away, shaking her head. "No. You've mistaken me for—for her. I saw the handbill. She has no hair. She has—"

The man came back up to his knees, brows creased with earnest devotion. "Please don't deny us, Highest! We are yours to command. We are *yours!*"

First a dozen lay prostrate before her, then thirty. When the last came to greet her, the verge of the road was crowded, a hundred hands reaching toward her. The supplicants chanted in low, moaning urgency: "Kila. Kila. Kila."

A hand took hers. Ell's. She leaned close and whispered, "You must say something to them. They have no purpose. Give them one."

Heads started to raise as the congregation came up onto their knees. Some held their arms out in supplication, others hugged them close, as if being so near to Kila would make them explode with feeling.

She dropped her mask, looking for mercus potential in the flock. She felt faint buzzings here and there, from folk who had not awakened to their latent power. No threats.

An idea had formed. *Nax, come out.*

The cat squeezed from Kila's backpack and clawed onto her shoulder. Awe transformed into delight. A few people crooned at Nax, others folded their hands together and wept beatific tears.

Do you trust any of these people? Kila sent.

Nax surveyed the faces. *Yes. But they are very hollow.*

What? What does that mean?

Instead of explaining, Nax sent a strange feeling through the bond. Part hunger, part weariness. Lack.

What do I do with them? she asked.

The question seemed to confuse the cat, so Kila rephrased it. *Ell says I need to give them a purpose.*

Waggling her nose, Nax looked away from the crowd.

Perhaps instruct them to groom themselves.

"Kila," Ell urged. "They will follow us if you do not give them orders."

Orders. Kila could do that. And Nax had a point. "Do you seek to disgrace me?" she said to the man who appeared to be their leader, doing her best to sound as imperious as Quinn. "Is that what you wish?"

Horror twisted his face. "No, Highest! We only wish to follow your Way. To be what you wish us to be."

It wasn't her Way, but she hardly wanted them devoting themselves to Kil. So be it. If they wanted to play at being her devotees, they should Kil-damn well show a better face to the world.

"You live in squalor next to a filthy river. That is no place for you. Build homes. Clear farmland. Do none of you possess skill in craft that you may barter for food? And the banner on yon tree. Burn it, lest it become a sign to the world that only layabouts are to be found beneath it. Look to yourselves. Wash your bodies of common stink. Desist in pestering folk for coin. If you beg for coin, then I beg."

At first her followers were taken aback, stricken. But as she spoke, their spines straightened. Father had always gotten more from Kila and Wen when he demanded more.

"I have things to attend to. So do you." She marched away, motioning Ell and Jil to come with her.

"When will you come back to us?" the man called after her.

"When you are ready!" Which would be never.

Picking up her pace, she hastened down the road, mimicking Ell's bearing as closely as possible. "Are they following?" she whispered to Ell.

"No. I think you stunned them. It was well done, but now you have a following, whether you like it or not."

"When has liking it had anything to do with my life?"

The three of them said nothing as they continued. Jil tossed unreadable glances at Kila for a while, but Kila tried to ignore them. Ell was placid as ever, but when Kila began to slow, she pressed the pace.

Wishing to drop the topic of the Way of Kila, she took stock of the city ahead. There was no ring wall around it, which Kila found odd. Seemed like an invitation to Tordain or Wantin to come take everything in sight.

When she offered that observation, Her Enlightened said that Tearling was protected by long-standing treaties. "Starside, Jallisea, and Sorgan all agree to come to Tearling's defense should she be attacked."

The farms gave way to stone houses with large gardens. The deeper into the town they walked, the smaller the gardens became until the homes stood shoulder to shoulder and the road bumped up from rutted dirt, to gravel, to paving stones.

The homes here were of creamy brick, squared off and tidy. The main thoroughfare didn't wind in switchbacks as the Street of Sorrows did in Starside. It lay flat and straight, and the very end was interrupted by a squat palace with square towers at each corner.

Small atlens pulled open-air carriages along the streets in orderly procession. No one crossed the street but at designated corners. Kila counted no less than thirty sweep-teams, workmen in uniform, marching with martial precision, brooms on their shoulders in place of whipaxes.

The streets were severely clean. Ahead an atlen relieved itself as it pulled a wagonload of melons. Before Kila and her companions had reached the spot, a squadron of sweepers descended upon the offending stain with shovel, bucket, and broom. Within a minute nothing remained but a quickly-drying wet spot.

"They dump it all in the river, don't they?" she said.

"And it washes to the sea," Ell LiMinluit said. "Tearling is an orderly place, full of orderly people. They afford sweep teams because they do not pay for armies. The city was once surrounded by a great wall, extending down from the Hackwatch. The stones have all been carried away, used to build farm houses, bridges, and libraries."

The workmen marched away, steps lively and prideful. Citizens who passed the formation, doffed their hats and offered sideways nods, the women retracted their ubiquitous parasols and did likewise. Children stopped and knuckled their foreheads in grave solutes.

Seeing this, Kila laughed. "I wonder what these teams would do if they saw Cheapsgate?"

"They would be horrified," the monarch said. Her face was stony, but her voice belied her shame. And yet, she'd told Kila that she had allowed Cheapsgate to exist because her shadline instincts told her to. She'd never told Kila why. The woman was curious in that regard, rarely explaining anything except to say she relied on her instincts. But now she paled and was pointedly looking away from Kila.

But Jil wasn't. She wore the glare of a Terriside house-mother who had discovered her child with half a pie in her lap and engerberry smeared on her cheeks. Kila didn't see how it was her fault the monarch was offended. Kila had grown up in Cheapsgate, not Ell LiMinluit.

They seemed to be headed for the palace, which struck

Kila as odd. "Our little council of rogues can't be meeting there. Unless the king or queen are shadlines."

"They are not," Ell said. "And you are correct. I feel that we are not meeting there. Though you may be interested to know that Tearling has no monarch. They are governed by a council of elders. Some are merchants, some farmers, some scholars. Oh, and I advise you never to refer to shadlines as rogues in their hearing."

"It was a compliment, but I'll try to keep my tongue straight for your humorless friends."

They turned onto a wide boulevard running north and south. The street was lined with cream-brick inns and apartments. There were more people out here, men dressed in coats and trousers. The women wore muted burgundies and umber and black. All were primped like a Tilsday crowd.

They continued until the buildings began to thin again and the road, well paved, became empty again. A misty rain had started and Kila wished she could establish her shelter-cloak. A high fog pressed over the rolling fields, and the damp chill made Kila shiver.

They stopped where a narrower road split off to wind in switchbacks to a fortification barely visible in the mist atop a tall green hill.

"The Armory will be up there?" Kila asked.

"I feel that it is so," Ell said. "Jil?"

"I feel it, too."

Kila felt nothing but the chill and a deeper sense of dread, for there had been a note of concern in their voices. And Ell's brows were furrowed in a most uncharacteristic look of worry.

6

GIFTED AS SEEKERS

One could become lost in the Citadel of Starside quite easily. The bright corridors went on for miles, opening into countless halls and galleries, offices, and gathering areas. The entire governance of Starside and its surroundings was located here, and never in Henley's imagining had he envisioned so many scribes.

He'd been in his father's ledger rooms many times as a boy, had seen the serious and earnest bookkeepers bent over their rows of inventories and figures. It had seemed a dull life. Now he envied these people and their ink-stained fingers.

You don't seem to be going anywhere, Huff sent. The cat was perched on Henley's shoulder, long orange tail drooping over the other.

How to respond to the cat's comment? Fair to say it was an insightful observation in more ways than one. With Kila away, Henley had fallen into a low mood. Walking and exploring seemed to be the only answer to his sudden loneliness. After spending every waking moment with her, her absence left a lack in him he could only compare with the brief time he'd lost his bond with Huff. No. Not quite that painful. But close.

Here he was, with nothing specific to do. And yet the busy scribes wrote missives and did figures and issued payments and took taxes. The war was coming, and Marlow controlled everything now. He lent an urgency to the operation that Radiant Grilok, who had previously held these responsibilities, had never shown.

The greatest concern was food. Armsmen from Her Enlightened's forces were now guarding warehouses in lower Terriside, and flour was issued to bakers along with strict quotas for bread and hardtack. A flat rate of two copper plugs per loaf. The same for Baker Tel Ninon in Gristenside as it was for Axehead Shyne in Cheapsgate. Henley knew both bakers' goods and would never voluntarily eat Axehead's.

His meandering circuit took him to Marlow's office, which occupied a small room off a circular hall at the base of the main spire. Many, many stairs up were Her Enlightened's office and apartments. Henley was grateful he didn't have to climb them today.

Dunne Marlow was ostensibly still a Donse Master, but he'd recently shed the honorific in favor of Administrator Marlow. As Henley entered the office, full of ledgers, piles of parchments, stacks of books, and an enormous wooden desk close to buckling under the weight of documents it supported, the man looked markedly older than when Henley had first met him.

The Donse Master robes were gone in favor of more lordly attire, loose trousers, waistcoat, and ruffles. A salt and pepper beard gave his face a distinguished frame despite carrying a bit more fat than needed.

"Ah, Henley Mast, I was hoping you'd show." He nodded at Huff. "Hello, Huff. I'm afraid I don't have any bits of meat for you today."

Huff hopped down and went to snoop under Marlow's desk for the inevitable stray bits of the man's lunch that had landed there.

Marlow smiled and beckoned Henley to come in. In any other case, it would have delighted Henley to have someone happy to see him. But Marlow always had some agenda or other. If it hadn't been for the man's fatherly affection for Kila, Henley wouldn't have even come here.

"What is it?" Henley asked.

Marlow's answer was interrupted by the arrival of another man. This was Highest Quiv, the leader of the Way of Til. Scholarly and thin, and looking younger than his age, he was a handsome man despite his lank hair. In Henley's father's verbiage, he looked like "a scholar who woke up to find himself general."

He carried a familiar book in his arms. His face startled Henley. Exhaustion and worry had grayed his flesh. The man needed sleep. And sun.

"Where is Highest Sigh?" Quiv asked without preamble. "And Her Enlightened should hear this too."

"Both have gone to the shadline Armory in Tearling," Marlow said. "Please, sit."

"No. Come here." Quiv dropped the volume onto the corner of Marlow's desk, sending sheaves of parchment curling to the floor in all directions. Neither he nor Marlow seemed to care. Henley fought the urge to gather up the clutter. His father had captained ships and insisted everything be kept orderly.

Quiv opened the book, mumbling to himself. "Here. Look!"

Henley and Marlow scanned the text, written in the First Race tongue. The elnisians had a poetic way of writing Henley thought quite beautiful. It was also rather inscrutable at times. This was no exception.

Ixil savoia ees ixil decin.

"Seven wardens of seven houses," Henley said, interpreting the text as well as he could. The Ennish term "warden" only gave part of the meaning implied by *savoia*. He continued, looking for context. "On bended knee, bowed before Illizshian. Six heads sundered, six stones given. These her scepter received, begemmed and answering with swarmlight." He looked up. "What's swarmlight? What stones?"

Quiv nodded in vigorous agreement with Henley's questions. "What indeed? What indeed? But the begemmed scepter recalled to me another history, this of the nosg. You know of the fabled archer Sephie?"

"Who doesn't?"

"Just so," Quiv said, nodding. "In the 'Tale of Sephie of On'lin Keep', there's this bit:

> "Loosed her arrows, did Sephie
> At girnt and tsugu foes;
> And nosg-kin fell as wheat
> Into bloody windrows.
> With chants and vengeful fear,
> Shamans sought their might;
> With gem-eyed skulls on rods
> Called forth their magic light."

Quiv looked from Henley to Marlow. "You see it, don't you?"

Realizing that his audience perhaps could not read his thoughts, Quiv expounded. "The skulls on rods. Those are nosg shaman scepters, no? There are other sources that report of nosg mercus powers, derived through demented rites, where they sit alone in pitch black caves and eat poisonous mushrooms."

"Illizshian ate poisonous mushrooms?" Marlow asked.

"No! No. No. No. You miss the point entirely. The skulls have gems in the eye sockets. And here Illizshian is putting gems onto a scepter that 'answers with swarmlight.' Doesn't that sound like mercus power?"

Marlow threw up his hands. "I assume there is some conclusion you wish us to reach, Highest Quiv. Perhaps you state it now and save us a quarter of an hour guessing at your hints."

"I thought the conclusion obvious," Quiv said without a bit of irritation. "The elnisian queen and the nosg used the same power!"

"Ah." It was all Henley could say. He'd thought there'd be some revelation of import, but it had turned out to be a curiosity of interest only to a historian.

Highest Quiv deflated and thumped his book closed. "I thought it important."

Marlow returned to his chair, shaking his head. "Highest Quiv, we are facing a war. Unless this has some bearing on that, I really cannot give it more attention."

"It has everything to do with the war! Why else do you think I made the arduous trip here to the Citadel? These gems are important. Where do they come from? What gives them their power? What is the swarmlight? I've had every Reader in our library researching this. But we've uncovered nothing, even in the books declared Wrong. I wished for Highest Sigh and Her Enlightened to intercede with the Spinsters and Sensuals to open their libraries."

"Have you asked them?" Marlow asked.

Frowning the thin man said, "The new Coin here in Starside is a peculiar woman. She would hardly speak to me and refused to allow my Donse Masters into her tower. The Sensuals at the Baths ignore my requests entirely. I fear they have not even communicated them to the Voluptuary, if she still lives."

"Well, as you can see, neither Highest Sigh or Her Enlightened are present." Marlow bent to his work, offering a clear signal that he was finished with the topic.

Straightening and collecting his tome, Quiv stalked out of the office. He gave Henley a meaningful look and a jerk of his head. Henley followed after, Huff climbing again to perch on his shoulder.

Henley said, "I know the Voluptuary's sister, Finta Sahng. I think she's tending to the Voluptuary personally since . . . since what happened to her." Kila was what had happened to her. She'd ripped the Hargothe's strange bond right out of the woman's mind, nearly killing her in the process. "I'll go to the baths and see what I can discover."

"I'd be grateful." Highest Quiv paused and looked over his shoulder at Marlow's office. "But there's something else. I did not mention this to him, because I don't entirely trust him. But you knew Dunne Yples."

"Has something happened to him?" Dunne Yples had gone mad and had developed enormous mercusine powers.

He'd done all he could to kill Kila. He now wore a *vaz'on*, which kept his power from him.

"He's gone," Quiv said simply.

"Where?"

"I wish I knew. I came into his office this morning. You know how obsessed he'd become with maps and the Derslin Wheels. All his work was still there, inkpot uncovered, as if he'd just stepped out to visit a needs closet. The last person to see him was one of our acolytes, who stands watch in the nave of the cathedral. Since the destruction, all manner of folk come in at all hours. Just yesterday a group of thinnies was seen in one of the side chapels."

"I thought he wasn't allowed out by himself." Alarm was building now. Yples was an enormous well of power to any merculyn who knew how to access one of the *vaz'on*'s tap gems.

"The Donse Master assigned his watch is missing as well."

"The wards are still in place on the *vaz'on*?"

The man made an uncertain face, which made Henley's stomach boil. "I think they are. I don't see how anyone could undo them."

Kila had placed the wards upon the *vaz'on* herself, an intricate knot of mercus that would sting any mind that attempted to access the gems. But such wards were not absolute. "Where have you looked?"

"I have acolytes and Donse Masters out. From Gristenside to Cheapsgate. But you know how futile that is."

"His mercus potential should be quite obvious if a merculyn gets within ten paces or so."

"To you, young Henley. Not all of us are so gifted as Seekers. And you might recall our best Seeker is dead, praise be to Til."

That would be the Hargothe. Henley shuddered. "I think finding Yples is more important that getting into the library at the Baths."

"It is why I brought it up. I was hoping you might join the search." They came out of the Citadel into the broad court-yard. Two men of the Fell Guard stood like statues, flanking the entrance. A smart carriage with two gray atlens in harness awaited Highest Quiv. "You'd have my little conveyance at your disposal, of course."

It didn't take any more arguments from Highest Quiv. Yples absolutely had to be found, and Henley had no duties to occupy him anyway.

Let's go find Dunne Yples, he sent to Huff.

The cat meowed indifferently. Quiv eyed the animal with a mix of awe and suspicion. "What did it say?"

"That was a meow. I have no idea what it meant. If Huff wants to say something, he doesn't do so through is mouth."

Boarding the carriage, Henley relaxed into the mercusine and began to feel for the mercus potential around him. Quiv's showed up immediately, a moderate haze, indicative of the man's power.

"Let us take a tour of the Street of Sorrows," Quiv said to the driver. "And slowly, if you please."

The carriage soon began the long journey, downslope to Starside.

7

THE GIRL WHO FLIES

"The Hackwatch," Ell said, stopping a moment on their climb toward the hulking fortress atop the hill. "I have not been here for an age. For centuries the Kings of Kovi-Mest ruled over this land. Hard, unforgiving men. Their appetite for conquest outsized their capacity to govern. The Hackwatch was their stronghold, and woe to those who came here unwilling."

"Dungeons?" Kila said, perking up. She always liked stories about dungeon escapes.

"You could call them that. I suspect the depths below are hollow and abandoned now. The Iron Scholars live in the fortress now, studying the stars and reading portents in them. Though they pretend to be a martial order, playing with old swords and spears." Ell's gaze never left the looming fasthold, and a chill had come into her voice.

"The Scholars are aligned with the shadline order?"

"In one way of thinking. I doubt they give much credit to the creed of listen and obey. But perhaps they will have insights to offer. A few of them are wise."

"A few?"

Ell lifted a delicate brow. "There is at least one fool in every group."

"True even of our threesome," Jil said, eyeing Kila meaningfully.

Kila let it go. *I think I've fallen in with a band of daft ducks, Nax.*

I have never seen a duck. I think I could eat one. Beak to tail.

They have bills, not beaks.

Nonetheless, I am hungry enough to eat one entire.

I have an apple.

Nax sent the sensation of gagging up a hairball.

You can eat when we get to the Hackwatch.

How long?

I don't know. Several more grueling hours, by the looks of it.

Fly us up!

The temptation was strong. And Kila might have tried it, the monarch's consternation be damned, except she had found flying to be a rather unreliable feat of late. That was Highest Quiv's fault, for asking her in detail how the feat was done. The more she'd thought about it, the less she was able to do. Which, she supposed sourly, meant that Flaumishtak was right.

The day was dimming now, and the rain snapped hard against Kila's face, forcing her head down. The road narrowed as it climbed, and they soon overtook a man leading a large donkey. A figure was slumped atop the animal, wrapped in blankets. The beast was laden with panniers and a huge warhammer bound to one flank. The unmistakable shape of a tarred sailor's queue hung down the man's massive back. His ham-shoulders and oak-trunk torso were as familiar to Kila as Nax's face.

"Critt Sanglo!" she called cheerfully. "Yer no faster than a one-legged atlen."

The man turned, red-faced and ready to bellow an angry response, but his jaw flopped open at the sight of Kila. She ran to him, grinning. "Well met, old friend."

His arms engulfed her and lifted her from her feet. "Lass, yer cheery face fills me flaggin' mainsail. A long journey it's been and rough seas th' whole course from Starside to this Kil-damned game trail." A strange tic passed across his face, like a fleeting rag of cloud passing over the sun. He let her go and looked her up and down. "Yer hair! Did yer locks get caught in a windlass or are ya tryin' to look like young Jil o'er there?"

Jil coughed and Kila leveled an irritated glare at both of them. Critt's hands suddenly clenched so tightly the skin over his knuckles looked ready to crack. "D'ya got yer riggin' in knots, Critt?" Kila asked. She'd seen him angry plenty of times. It came with running a tavern full of trezz-fiends and thirsty sailors.

"No, lass. Ne'er better. And yer—and yer—" He coughed and a bit of spittle drooped from his lower lip. His face went pale. "And yerself, lassie? I hear—I hear—I hear strange things."

Kila straightened, seeing a wrongness in her friend. Skin prickling with alarm, she looked to the donkey. "Is that Quinn?"

"That be—That be—" He swallowed hard and spat on the ground. "And none too well is she." He heaved in a shaky breath. The cords at the side of his neck stood out, like a man straining under a great weight.

Kila uncovered the figure's head. Quinn's hair was wrapped in a kerchief to keep it from her face. She looked white as death, mouth open and drooling. "What happened to her?" Alarmed, she dropped her mask and brought mercus bolts to life within her.

"Hold, Kila!" Ell called before she could dive into Quinn's inner workings to find the source of her illness.

"Why? She's sick. I can—"

"I said hold!"

Critt's face went red. He gurgled and choked. "No. Not her!" The words tore from his throat as his lips pulled back into a guard-hound snarl. Lunging for the donkey, he pulled the great maul from its straps. He raised it in trembling hands. "Run, girl!" He shook so hard his heels juttered on the road.

His eyes changed to hatred. With a great cry, he brought the head of the battle hammer toward Kila's skull.

Shocked, she stood planted like a stump.

A clang rang out as Jil's sword intercepted Critt's blow. But such was Critt's strength, Jil's efforts merely diverted the strike. The maul grazed Kila's hair and carried on its way, twisting Critt with its momentum.

Jil blurred, arms swinging in a snakelike counter, taking the huge sailor in the back of the leg. The blade sank in deep. Critt howled, phlegm flying.

With a vicious yank, Jil sliced her blade free and lashed the tip up to bite into Critt's forearm. "You're out of practice, shadline," she said.

This wasn't right. Not at all. Kila staggered back, over-whelmed with the horrific strangeness of Critt's rage. Critt would never attack her. He had just hugged her.

"Move back," Ell said, coming to her. "Jil, do not kill him if it can be avoided. Kila, put your mercus mask in place."

Critt was kneeling now, sweating profusely and trying to wield his maul one-handed. Three more deep wounds wept blood onto the dirt track. The donkey skittered sideways, craze-eyed with fear. Ell darted to scoop up the beast's lead. With an eerie, crooning bolt of mercus the woman soothed the animal.

Critt continued to flail his weapon. Jil dodged easily, parrying with her sword the way one might play at swords with a child.

"Take the donkey," Ell said, thrusting the lead into Kila's hands. Ell formed more bolts as she waited for Critt's next feeble blow to swing his torso around. His strength was draining quickly even though some inner force compelled him to fight.

Ell smoothly stepped inside his reach and gripped his head in her hands, thumbs at the corners of his eyes. She overcame him, and with will or mercus, bade him return her stare.

Critt's eyes were wrong. They had always been dark, but now they looked infected with tiny white maggots that squirmed in the irises.

"Flecked with tresh," Ell said. "He's drunk a mooncrafter's brew. I'll wager the same is true for the Peline girl."

"What's a mooncrafter?" Kila demanded. "What's tresh?"

Jil answered as Ell prepared inconceivably intricate bolts. "You've heard of ferneaters?" She plucked a pristine white cloth from her pack and commenced wiping Critt's blood from her face.

"Of course. Vergent magic from chewing weeds."

"You truly are ignorant, aren't you? Don't answer. You're

too ignorant to even know how stupid you are. Have you heard of willshift?"

"I've been on both sides of it." A willshift was a mercus feat that took control of another person's body. Kila was sorely tempted to lay a heavy willshift on Jil and make the woman slap her own behind with the flat of her sword. Instead she asked, "That's what tresh is? A ferneater willshift?"

"Similar. Had you barged your powers into Quinn Peline's mind you likely would have succumbed to her state. Her Enlightened knows the byways of such spells. Allow her to attend to them and you to the donkey. Can you manage that much without causing a pitched battle?"

I could ash her, Naxie. I could leave her a smoldering pile of dust right there where she stands.

So do it.

Leave it to Nax to challenge her bluff.

Nax went on, *Why do you chase Jil's yarn balls? She makes a kitten of you.*

The admonishment made Kila feel silly. The donkey nosed her and she rubbed its snout. Jil reached up to pat Quinn's face to wake her. But it looked to Kila as if Quinn was halfway into Lumne's last embrace.

The donkey stamped and pulled at its lead, trying to go down the trail the wrong way. Kila fished her last apple from her cloak pocket. This got the beast's attention.

Critt slumped in Ell's grasp. She let him fall. "Move his weapon onto the donkey, Jil. Do not touch it. You may have to use Critt's hand to lift it so that you can secure a rope to the haft. You can lift it by the rope, but let no part of it touch you. Shatter is not friendly."

Ell wiped her hands on her cloak. "I closed his wounds. I

could not remove the tresh. A strong brew. Certainly slipped to him unawares. Whoever did this wished for him to kill you, Kila."

Suddenly chilled, Kila scanned their surroundings, certain that someone was watching. Skin thrilling, she twirled, searching the mist surrounding the pines lining the road. Nax's claws jabbed into her skin to better secure herself against Kila's gyrations. "I can feel them."

Ell faced up the path, eyes closed. Listening. "Someone comes."

"More than one," Jil said. She raised Qinsh, ready for battle.

The crunch of horse hooves and smash of trampled underbrush resounded in the air. Some came from uphill. More arose from below. Still more pressed from the flanks.

And then the horses emerged, bearing riders in leathers or chainmail, bearing swords, flails, hammers, and every other conceivable weapon.

Kila dropped her mask.

"No, Kila!" Ell shouted.

Kila ignored the command. She summoned her powers, furious that such a sinister trap had been laid for her. More insulting, they had turned one of her dearest friends against her, endangering his life as much as hers. Blue spheres of mercusine formed over her hands. Their glistening surfaces roiled with the oily black of her rage.

The men and women pressed their beasts forward, weapons raised. They circled, hemming the trio in.

Kila pulled her arms back, ready to hurl her feat into her enemies.

"KILA SIGH! DESIST!" Ell LiMinluit stood in front of her, blocking Kila's throw. Her face was pure fury. She held out a hand, and Kila thought she was preparing her own attack. But Ell did not hold the mercus at all. "These are allies. These are shadline."

The horses slowed and finally stopped. Kila realized the men and beasts were mostly facing away. They were guarding her and her companions. Kila released her mercus, and the spheres sizzled into nothingness.

One man dismounted and clanked forward, pulling a winged helm from his head. Tucking it under his arms, he fingered off his gloves. He wore a longsword on his hip.

Ell LiMinluit went up on tiptoe to kiss his cheek. "I had hoped to come quietly, Shad Lykea."

"Alas. The force of destiny announced you loudly." He eyed the donkey and Critt Sanglo, "And warned of great danger to you and your companions. I see we were not needed."

Shad Lykea was tall, fair haired, and closer to forty than thirty. His beard was braided on one side, well kept. His gray eyes swept over their surroundings. "We covered the terrain. I doubt a vole could have escaped our notice. We all heard the call at once. More than a hint. More than instinct. It was a hard shout. We obeyed."

"The danger must be grave," said an elderly man on a rather bony mount. His stooped shoulders looked utterly defeated by his mail coat. With soft presses of his heels he urged his horse into the circle.

"Shad Ault," Ell said, not so warmly. No effort to kiss a cheek, either. Ault had small eyes, but keen. He was looking at Kila.

"So this is the Girl Who Flies, eh? I dare say *she* is the grave danger we felt."

"I assure you, Shad Ault, Kila Sigh is our ally. Without her I would be dead. But more I will not discuss here. Let us proceed to the observatory, and to the Armory."

To this the old man leaned back and sneered. "We are not your subjects, Ell LiMinluit. Do not presume to order us about."

Shad Lykea waved his hands in frustration, glaring at the old man. Ault returned the stare by leaning forward and tilting his head to one side, a clear challenge. It struck Kila as foolish, for Lykea was stronger than the old man. But Lykea did not say more and did not put Ault in his place.

Before Kila could speak in her own defense, she felt a hand on her arm. It was Jil's. The woman didn't glare so much as shake her head at Kila.

Grudgingly, Kila let it go. She caught a glimpse of a man with an arrow nocked. Not drawn. But it would take mere heartbeats to put an arrow through her neck from where he sat his horse. She wished Flaumishtak had showed her the armor-cloak trick, though she thought she could manage something similar if pressed.

She waved at the man and smiled. He was older than Lykea, round-faced, and weather-beaten as a sailor. "Could ya stow the pinflicker, Sir Shadline? I get itchy when folk try ta stick me from afar."

He considered a moment, then snorted a wry laugh and stuffed his arrow in a saddle quiver. With smooth, practiced motions, he unstrung the bow and sheathed it in a supple leather bag.

Kila nodded a thank you. *See?* she sent to Nax. *I can be*

downright civil. All that it required was a man to return the favor.

She sent it with as much humor as she could muster, but Nax didn't reply. The cat was tense on Kila's shoulder. And for good reason. The feeling of being watched had not faded. Maybe it was because there were so many eyes on her at that moment. And they were not all men. One in four was a woman. Two were elderly, perhaps older than Ault. The youngest was fourteen, Kila guessed. A curiously cold-eyed lass with untamed curls cut short like Jil's. Despite her look of wildness, she had the face of a girl who should be back in her village pining for some boy she wished to dance with at Winternight festival. She did not blink as Kila regarded her, but merely raised a sword in a salute. Or was it challenge?

"Is that Critt Sanglo?" A middle-aged woman from the circle asked. "It is! I would know him anywhere. What have you done to him?" She dismounted and rushed to the fallen man. Her skin was dark and smooth, jaw wide and striking.

"He has drunk tresh," Ell said. "More I cannot say. Please, let's proceed to the Hackwatch. We are road weary and in need of rest and refreshment."

"I say the girl who flies should be restrained, to protect us from her power." Shad Ault was addressing the remainder of the Shadlines. Seeking allies. Several nodded, others seem to pass their unease to their mounts, which stamped and snorted.

Jil said, "And what relic do you have that will block her from the mercusine and prevent her from ashing you where you sit?"

This did draw a humorless laugh from Shad Ault. "I'm surprised at you, daughter. Do you think I would suggest such a thing if I did not have the answer?" He jerked his hand. A young man immediately urged his horse forward and extended a velvet satchel. Ault withdrew an object, the sight of which pulled a curse from Kila's lips.

It was a crown with seven gems around the band.

It was a *vaz'on*.

8

FATE BREAKER

"If ya think I'm gonna let you screw that into my skull, yer a slag-brained—"

Kila yelped as Jil elbowed her side. "He's one of the seven Shadline Knights. A simple 'no' will suffice. And stop it with the Cheaps-talk before you embarrass yourself further."

Kila lifted her chin. With egregiously fine enunciation she said, "No, Shad Ault. I will not don that trinket. And I suppose it is not necessary for me to attend your shadline congregation. I never swore the oath."

Ell's jaw ground has if she were chewing gravel to dust. "Impudent child."

"Didn't speak the oath?" Shad Ault crowed. "I see we have found a point of agreement between the so-called Highest of Kil and me. If she is no shadline, then she has no business here. Go away, girl. The adults shall discuss what to do with you."

"Peace. All of you." Shad Lykea stepped between Ault's

horse and Kila. The two had moved closer and closer as the spat had escalated.

"Does she bear a shadline weapon?" Lykea asked.

Kila drew her blade and held it up for inspection. "It's called Cayne. I've been told it's a shadline blade, but it's never done anything special but drink the blood of my enemies." As an afterthought she blurted, "Highest Annisforl called it Fate Breaker."

Shad Ault paled. His victorious smirk fell into a lip bite of consternation. "We must not let that blade leave the Armory without a clear decision. I withdraw my demands that Kila Sigh be bound with the *vaz'on*. It'll make little difference at the Hackwatch anyway. But mark me, girl. If you use your power to harm a single shadline in the future, I will see you crowned with this relic, and then decrowned with my very own blade, Lordmight." He tapped the pommel of an enormous sword, the scabbard affixed to the horse. The cross guard alone spanned two feet.

"Shadlines, please," Ell said. "Two of our own are grievously ill. Let us proceed to the Hackwatch and save the bickering for the Armory."

Shad Lykea rushed into the brief silence that followed her plea. "Yes, Ell LiMinluit is correct." He shouted orders for the shadlines to turn about. He secured the donkey's lead to his saddle, then offered Kila his horse. But Kila would not leave Quinn's side. And more than that, as weary as she was, she was also wary. She would not become indebted to anyone, not even for a small favor. She sensed that the same intrigues that pervaded Gristenside Radiancies were to be found among the shadline as well. A disappointment, but no surprise. And also a lesson. Quinn had told her that there was no escaping politics. That as soon as one accumulated a small amount of power, others would seek to attach themselves to it, use it, or simply steal it. To protect oneself and those one loved required constant vigilance. In short, nothing had changed since Kila had come to Starside with her father.

Scheming for power wasn't her strength. If she had a strength, it was her will to protect those she loved.

She huffed a weary sigh. Fat lot of good her will had done her. Everyone she loved had come to pain because of her. Wen, Henley, Quinn, Pennie, Ragin. Even Nax. None injured by her hand, but merely by being trapped within the fellstorm that swirled around her.

She kept her hand on the donkey's shoulder as they walked up the switchbacks. She made a show of ignoring Shad Ault, who rode behind them with the obvious intent of intimidating her. But she'd known bigger bullies than him.

I'd feel safer walking into Dox Viller's territory in Cheapsgate, she sent to Nax.

Then turn around.

Kila considered it. None could stop her. And yet . . . Dem-Kisk was upon them, and Yiothizandra would soon be driving her forces south to conquer a realm for Kil.

Strange, she sent to Naxie. *I have never met my enemy. I don't even know what she looks like. I don't know what she's capable of. All I know of her I've heard from others.*

Quinn's warnings rang anew in her mind. She resolved to hold her tongue during the Armory. She'd learn what she could from these people, and hopefully see Quinn and Critt nursed back to health. And she had a further hope. *Do you feel Lop?*

Yes. She waits ahead. She is hungry. I am hungry. Kila closed her eyes and sighed with relief. If Lop was there, so was Fallo.

Tell Lop to tell Fallo that Quinn is ill. He would want to be there when she arrived. Before the two had been separated, a little something had developed between them. As unlikely a match as Kila could imagine, with Quinn's exquisite beauty drawing every eye and Fallo's strange and off-putting visage making children cry. Also, he was a scoundrel. She suspected that was what attracted Quinn the most.

Kila had grown up surrounded by scoundrels. She didn't see the appeal at all. Which, she supposed, was why she'd found herself in Henley's arms.

Lop says she's not telling Fallo anything until Fallo gives her more of his chicken.

Kila couldn't help but laugh. But it was a sad laugh. Lop's typically selfish interference reminded her of the humorous insults the boys so casually flung at each other, the true language of fraternal love. Kila missed those days in the den— the boys, the cats, and a caper in the offing. So simple. So free. Now, every step she took forward she felt like she was leaving something precious behind—some hope, some dream, some life that had almost been within her grasp. She missed her band of thieves. Her family.

Ell was walking alongside Kila now. Her face had returned to its usual serene set, but there was a stiffness in her shoulders. And in one hand she toyed with a jade fish figurine. A worry stone. Maybe a mercus relic of some sort.

"Why didn't you tell me Annisforl had called your dagger Fate Breaker?" the woman asked.

"I'd forgotten it. It wasn't until Lykea asked about my blade that it occurred to me."

"You listen and obey without recognizing what is happening, Kila," Ell said softly. "It is a pattern for you. That moment just now was a fate-hand, such a subtle one. It might have eluded us and you might have returned to Tearling and missed an essential moment ahead. You must listen. Let the force of destiny whisper its hints to you and all will be well."

Kila had been harangued by Jil about listen and obey so much she could recite it like passages from the Theb. But she didn't hear anything with her shadline instincts. In fact, her instincts had led her into trouble as often as they got her out of it.

Ell seemed done with chastising Kila. "Fate Breaker was not among the hoard of shadline weapons used to found this order. But it was known at the time."

Jil had told Kila all about the founding of the order, how after the Synod of the New Pantheon, the Triumvirate's army had come to a monastery outside of Jallisea to rein in a rogue sect of Donse Masters who rejected the proclamations of the Synod. Only seven escaped, but they took with them a hoard of mercusine weaponry. For years they followed the doctrine of listen and obey, making many harrowing escapes, and slowly dispersing the weapons to those their instincts had led them to. In some cases, the weapons themselves had named their intended bearers. Legends like Linas, Reino, and Erig were well-known to the tavern crowds of Starside.

Ell continued: "Your blade was removed from the collection long before the original Seven left their monastery. It was stolen, actually. A Donse Master of good reputation had been assigned its study, to unlock its mysteries and discover its powers."

"So this Donse Master who stole it," Kila said. "Did you

ever think he meant to sell it? I could understand why a Donse Master would grow bored with his life and decide to exchange his robes and vigils for fine cloaks and carriages."

Jil snorted with exasperation from behind them. Kila turned her head, surprised to find the woman trailing so closely.

"No doubt that possibility was considered," Ell said. "And obviously, we don't know what he discovered about it. Except," she raised a finger to emphasize the point to come, "the name 'Fate Breaker' became attached to the missing blade. Perhaps he left some notes behind that were later lost. Perhaps he revealed something of the blade's nature to one of his friends. No record remains. Its legend has been a curiosity—usually dismissed as fanciful myth—until today. What fate can your blade break? The name alone is chilling to those who revere the force of destiny."

When Kila offered no insights, the woman pressed a shoulder to Kila's and spoke directly into her mind. *But it occurs to me that the man who absconded with your blade was a scholar of shadline weapons. Perhaps he listened and obeyed. Perhaps all that has happened to it, age to age, was to guide it to your hands.*

How do you do this? Kila sought the mercus bolts Ell must surely be using to speak into her mind, but she found nothing. Like sendings she received through her bonds with Nax and Henley, there was no mercus in the sending itself to detect. In Ell's case there was no new bond, either.

Some powers are reserved to demayne. Do not be distracted by it. Focus instead upon your blade and its power. Listen for guidance.

Kila still held the blade, she turned it in her fingers,

admiring the dark steel, the slender length, the memories it provoked of Wen and Father.

I suppose we'll know its purpose when the moment comes. But I have it now. I certainly won't be handing it over to Shad Ault.

Do not underestimate that man. He showed you the vaz'on. *Doesn't that strike you as strange? Now you know he has it. Now you are on guard. No, he would not show it to you unless he believed he could fit it to your skull if he so desired. Be alert, Sigh. Be wary. We felt a threat in those who approached. I feel it still. There is a snake in the nest.*

9

———

HIDEOUS VISAGE

A small dining hall had lain unused for generations. It was interior to the fortress and therefore less prone to leaks in the roof. Yioth bade it be cleaned and invited Rask-Ka to join her for a private evening repast.

The hearth behind her was cold, though she allowed nosg tallow candles to be lit and placed in wall sconces. They gave off a terrible smell but illuminated the space sufficiently.

Nosg hips being what they were, Rask-Ka would have sat awkwardly in a human-crafted chair, so she allowed him a stool. She lounged on a rather sturdy throne-like structure, presented to her just an hour ago by the Hargothe's favored nosg servant, a servile creature call Noi-Ick-Noi. The chair was even cushioned with rabbit pelt pillows.

"Razk-Ka, you will tell me if any of the other wurgus need killing, won't you?"

"Yes, Queen Yiothizandra," he said around a mouthful of stew. Even empty of mouth, he would have pronounced it "Yoshithanta." He didn't chew food so much as mash it a couple times before gulping it down.

"Speak your own tongue, Prime Rask-Ka."

The nosg made a crude bowing motion. "You honor me. And our conversations will be quicker if I do not have to gnash my tongue on Ennish."

He swallowed another slurp and continued. "Perhaps Tyl-Da and Um-Lot. But not yet. Um has many powerful girnts, heroic and hungry. Um is a god among them. Better to keep him living, for now. Tyl-Da of G'galas Chezk controls the southern passes in the west. Chezk are not accustomed to the cold as we of G'galas Woond are. Not much use for the siege of Lockt."

Yioth stirred a crude wooden spoon in her bowl. She forced a bite down, though her belly rebelled. The babe must be nourished. "I do not want you to lay siege to Lockt."

The nosg froze, bowl half raised to his mouth. "The only passable route to the south is through the city. Unless . . ." He set the bowl down and reached for his skull staff which leaned against the table to his right. Drawing it to him, he gripped the shaft and squeezed. The eye-gems did not begin to glow with swarmlight. This was a nervous habit, Yioth supposed. "You know of another way, Queen? It is winter, the high passes will be buried with snow."

"I'm surprised how little your people know of Ceronhel. Have you not explored its depths?"

"Yes. None returned."

"Finish your supper. I shall take you deep below this hall. And there I will show you a wonder. The elnisians called it *irl en hu*. Men call it a Derslin Wheel."

Noy shuffled into the room, bowing and murmuring apologies. "The caravanner the Hargothe summoned has arrived."

Standing, she fixed Razk-Ka with a glare. "Do not leave. I will show you the Wheel when I'm done with this."

Razk-Ka leapt up, accidentally knocking his stool over. He bowed. "Yes, Queen."

"Noy, have my chair brought into the great hall."

THE MAN STANDING before Yiothizandra breathed through his mouth. Every inhalation lifted his chest and raised his elbows towards his ears. When he let go, his whole body shuddered. It wasn't just the cold, though steam billowed from his mouth in the wintry hall. And it wasn't fear—at least not completely—that made him tremble so. It was exhaustion.

"The Hargothe told me of you. You are late." Yioth sat upon her throne-like chair, legs crossed, toes of one foot carving an agitated circle in the air. She regarded the man on the floor below the dais.

His thick fur cloak had likely started his journey as a very fine garment, as had the woolens, scarf, and beaver skin cap. The man himself had diminished, carrying the distinct sag of cheek and jowl of a man once plump, now gone gaunt. He pleaded now, which she rather liked. "I assure you that nothing could be done about the delays. There were storms, great snows, and not all nosg knew to allow us safe passage. I lost half my caravan to raids."

Yioth turned her head fractionally to aim her gaze upon Noy. "Discover who these nosg were, I want drikk and clan. And summon their wurgu to me immediately."

She returned her attention to the caravanner. He called

himself Tarek PiTorro, and claimed to be the greatest such merchant in Starside.

"How many men did you bring with you?" She asked. "I need blacksmiths, stonemasons, cooks."

"There are seventeen of us men who have survived the trip. I started with one hundred and fifty."

"Am I to infer by your poor result that you could not plan for the contingencies that any man might expect traveling here by wagon train?"

The man gibbered for a moment before falling silent. He made no defense, for he had none. He likely expected to die once he faced the Hargothe. And the Hargothe would have obliged. But Yioth would not be so wasteful. The man was here. There was no reason to extinguish his life when she could make good use of him. "You shall return to Starside."

"Now? May I not rest for a week?"

"Rest? What good to me is a man who rests? But fear not, I will not make you walk back to Starside. Time is precious." She placed a loving hand on her belly. "What contacts do you have among the Radiancies?"

"Many! I know them all. I have good relationships with most." He clamped his mouth shut, a wise instinct. "But how am I to get to Starside if not by walking? Even on horse—"

Yiothizandra rose from her seat and descended the dais to stand before the man. "I shall summon someone who can dymense you there."

The man's lips moved in an echo of the word he did not understand.

A summoning circle was now permanently etched in the great hall floor. Courtesy of Yiothizandra's sword and her dragonfire powers. It was a scorched channel thirteen paces across. "Yoznithan Flaumishtak, come."

He appeared in a fog of mercus green, again holding the creamy felnithel that had adopted him. As was meet, Yioth dipped her head to the Beloved One. The animal appeared to be asleep, but its tail flicked in response.

"Here I am," Flaumishtak said. "Did you call me merely to look upon my pulchritudinous face?"

Yioth ignored Flaumishtak's taunts. He sought to provoke her into some sort of attack, something that would break in the circle. He thought her a fool if he thought there was any chance of such a slip. Besides, if it came to battle, she would win.

"Encompass us in silence."

Yioth could feel the mercus come to life around the beast. She had no sense of what specific bolts he employed. Nor did she care. But she would be a fool if she did not test the bubble of silence the demayne had supposedly created.

"Tarek PiTorro, on your knees."

The man did not obey. She found him cowering as far away from her as he could get yet still be in her presence. He was more terrified of Flaumishtak than he was of her. But who could blame him, given the hideous visage on the creature. But she was satisfied he had not heard her command, so she proceeded with her questioning of the demayne.

"You were to provide me spies in all the elnisian cities where men still live. And yet I have none. Explain."

The beast lifted its shoulders. "These things take time. Recruiting a—"

"Recruiting takes no time at all. Point to the man, willshift him, weave slave-will shadows into his mind, do what you must, but give me my spies." Her wings manifested behind her, and she flapped them irritably before folding them back. "You do recall our bargain, do you not?"

Flaumishtak waved a claw in a placating manner. "Of course I remember. And it is true I can give you such spies easily enough, but I assumed you wanted ones well-placed. And it takes time, because you do not want them behaving in such a manner that people become suspicious. If you want useful spies, presumably ones who will endure, then give me time."

"What about this one." She motioned to PiTorro. "He claims to be well-placed, has relationships with the Radiancies."

Flaumishtak eyes flared with fire, which slowly receded until they became orange embers in the black. "Not a bad notion. He has possibilities. But his is not a common face in the Citadel. I assume that's where you wanted your spy."

"I think he has quite enough reason to be in the Citadel. After all, he's been here. Why can he not go to my little cousin and present what he knows about Ceronhel. As a concerned citizen. A loyal subject. He can get in her good graces, advise her on preparing her own forces for war. And then he can report all to me as their plans develop."

Rather than argue, Flaumishtak merely nodded in submission. "Do you require anything else of me?"

"Yes. Dymense this man home. Do what you must to make him compliant, and provide a means for me to communicate with him at my pleasure."

Flaumishtak's lips pursed out as he considered this last request. "Communication will require me to attach a little mercusine bow to your roiling brain. Will you allow such an intrusion?"

Yioth did not like it. She did not like it at all. She would no sooner allow Flaumishtak entry into her mind than she would him into her bed. Noi-Ick-Noi returned. He was followed by one of the wurgus. She couldn't recall its name. "He will do," she said, pointing at Noy.

"As you wish." Flaumishtak curled a claw and made a slight twirling motion with one finger. Across the hall, Tarek PiTorro stiffened for a moment before slumping forward, as if the last grain of strength had tumbled out of a hole in his pocket. And the same happened to Noy.

PiTorro gasped and screamed and tore at his hair. Noy growled in his throat and gnashed his teeth, flinging his head side to side as if he could shake the man's presence from his mind.

"Desist!" Yiothizandra commanded. Human and nosg fought to control their own reactions. She repeated her command three times. Finally PiTorro submitted. It took a minute longer for Noy to give in to the inevitable. "You two are now dym-bonded. You can speak to each other across great distance. Is that not true Flaumishtak?"

"It is."

"PiTorro, you will return to Starside. You will ingratiate yourself at court. You will make yourself indispensable to Her Enlightend Majesty and you will prod the Radiancies to rebellion. You will report all you discover to Noy. Do you understand?"

"I do," the man said, now weeping openly.

But his word would not be enough to satisfy Yiothizandra. She stalked toward the man, already bringing heat to her lips.

As she had marked her prime Razk-Ka, she burned a mark onto PiTorro's forehead. His scream was shrill, and his consciousness flooded away as the pain overwhelmed him. She did not bother to catch him as he fell. The mark would fade, and his lank mop of black hair would cover what little remained of it. But now, should he fail her, she could reinforce her control over him, delivering such exquisite pain that he would beg for death.

"Noy, carry this man into the circle and give him to Flaumishtak."

The nosg did as told. Flaumishtak took PiTorro by the collar of his fur coat and held him out the way a man might hold a dead fish. He did not wait to be dismissed.

Yiothizandra turned her attention to the wurgu that Noy had fetched. "You attacked that man's caravan and confiscated half of the goods that were intended for Ceronhel."

"I gave no such order."

"And yet it was your g'galas that this man passed through coming from Lockt. So among your clan were drikks who robbed from me."

The nosg shaman had no reply for this. Perhaps he had issued the order to allow the caravan to pass, but some drikks had simply seized upon the opportunity out of pure greed.

"What is your name, Wurgu?"

"Bizt-Ma, my Queen." He showed no fear. Yet he knew his life hung upon a partially severed rope. "I apologize for the behavior of my g'galas. I will search out those who attacked the caravan, and I will deliver you their hearts."

"There is no time for such things. One day I will call upon you to make amends to me. To demonstrate your loyalty. You will remember my mercy."

The shaman knelt and dipped the skull.

"Leave me."

The shaman hustled away, leaving her alone with Noy. "When PiTorro speaks to you, you will search me out immediately. You will relay what he says, word for word."

"Yes, Mistress." He hesitated then rushed on. "There is rumor from the clans to the north. Of dragons."

"Why were you so hesitant to inform me of this? I have called the dragons of Night to me."

"These dragons . . . they are dead."

10

A SUBTLE WEB OF POWER

The carriage's wheel lurched into a particularly large hole, making Henley's head smack into the side. Highest Quiv wasn't there to hear his curse.

He rubbed his head. There would be a lump. Just another ache to add to the general throb in his skull. He'd been riding up and down the Street of Sorrows for hours now, adrift in the mercusine, feeling for Dunne Yples.

He'd felt other Donse Masters, a few Spinsters, and a Sensual. All these were obvious as soon as he looked at them, busy on one errand or another in Terriside.

Gristenside had shown him a few hazy glows, the signatures of House Donse Masters in the greathouses there. But he knew what Yples's potential felt like. For one, it was immense. Nearly as strong as Kila's. For another, Henley had spent days confined in a cell next to Yples's and he was sure he'd recognize the man's power. It had a chaotic buzz to it, very much at odds to the muted haze that hung about everyone else.

Henley thumped a fist onto the roof, signaling the driver to watch where he was going. He got a thump and a garbled response in return. Couldn't blame the man. It had to be mind numbing work, and the atlens were likely irritable, unaccustomed to hauling a carriage so slowly for so long.

Either he's masked somehow or he's not near this street, he sent to Huff. Starside was very large, and many areas were distant from the main thoroughfare.

Let's run the roofway!

That wasn't a bad idea. Henley knocked on the roof again. The driver stopped. Climbing down and stretching, Henley gave the man a silver skillet. "Return to the abbey. I'm going to walk."

The driver knuckled his forehead and gave the birds a sharp "yah." Henley found himself not twenty paces from the Cheaps. The driver had not wanted to go through the Cheaps. The only accessible area that way was the docks. Henley decided a quick run would show up Yples if he was there. Not many merculyns in Cheapsgate. Not on purpose, anyway.

Though Highest Quiv had lifted the bounty on cats, the Watch guards at the gate gave Huff a greedy eyeing over. Rather than assert his own importance as Highest Sigh's friend, he brought forth a few copper plugs and had no further challenge.

The stink hit him right off, and he had to pause in wonder that he'd lived in Cheapsgate for a while. In truth, the slums had saved him when Hackworth Keel had burned down his father's house, killing his entire family.

He climbed onto the roofs with Huff and began to run, not fast, just quick enough to cover the area between the gate and the Warren. Seeing the dilapidated old warehouse, Henley felt a pang of loss. Some of his happiest days had been spent in the cramped little den there.

The feeling came over him so strongly he couldn't help but climb to the jagged roof and find his way to the secret entrance, carefully pushing aside the loose plank to peer in.

Either Parlo Odok hadn't found anyone to rent it, or the current tenant wasn't home. Henley went in. Everything was as they'd left it. The little fish oil lamp, unlit. Four pallets of rags on the floor. With barely a thought, he added heat to the lamp until the wick ignited. The stale, yellow glow spilled over roughhewn planks, and a curl of acrid smoke lifted from the lantern's blackened chimney.

Huff nosed around. *Startle was here for a while.*

The fifth cat. A black and white fuzzball, nearly a twin to Lop. Kila had named it Startle because it always had a surprised look on its face. *Is he back?*

No. Startle is gone.

And not just gone from Starside, according to Huff. Gone from the world. Not dead. Just gone. Taken by Flaumishtak . . . elsewhere.

A strange ache took hold of Henley's throat and he sat on Kila's pallet, lost in the past. *Ah me, Huff. I do miss Kila.*

The cat came into his lap and began to purr. *It is strange how gone feels,* Huff sent after a while. *Gone, but still here.*

Yes.

The last of the fish oil burned up and the lantern smoked out. They sat in darkness a while longer before the urgency to find Yples returned. But where to look next? He was too tired. The temptation to sleep right where he was came over him so strongly he slid down onto Kila's pallet of rags. Huff, always indifferent to where he slept, snuggled in.

The mercus arose to Henley's awareness as it so often did these days. A subtle web of power that pervaded his entire awareness. And as he sank deeper, he felt his awareness begin to expand, first filling the den, then the Warren. Soon it had stretched to the ring wall surrounding the city.

The image in his mind continued to gather in homes and streets, creeping west, pulling in Dunne Medow Plaza, the abbey, the mercus potential of the Donse Masters there appearing like hazy smudges.

Henley realized this is what true Seekers did. Had he not been so exhausted, he doubted he'd have accessed this power. It required the opposite of effort. Surrender.

Marlow stood out to him, as did Dunne Quiv and the Voluptuary. Those in Pol's Tower did not shine so brightly, but there were many merculyns there. By the time the entirety of the city came to him, he knew Yples was not anywhere in Starside.

And then he slept, and the subtle realm filled his dreams.

11

YOUR ONE TRUE LOVE

The funeral rites of Pol were austere, quick, and ended with the deceased upon a pyre atop the Garden Tower. Few attended, save the Coin and a few of the decedent's friends.

And so it was that the heap of ash blew away in the trailing winds of a fellstorm, carrying Tia On'Liette into memory. Coin Inlina cared little for such rituals. When the heart and breath stopped, the soul was already in Lumne's embrace. The body was a useless husk, and burial or burning merely a practical task to get the meat out of sight before it rotted.

Raginalt Keel did not seem to share that opinion, for he wept openly. The Coin felt compassion for him, but there was no time to allow him grief. "Ragin, the Voluptuary and I would like to discuss something with you. Would the rest of you wait near the door?"

Voluptuary Minn's mouth was pinched, for the task ahead would be bitter indeed.

Spinsters Moirina, Rippa, and Heleen filed away, faces solemn. Ragin probably thought them overcome by the loss of their friend. The Coin knew better. The task ahead weighed heavily upon them.

The young man was seventeen, tow-headed, with such pale skin he might be thought ill if not for the healthy flush that colored his cheeks and throat. Wiping his eyes, he came to her. Always respectful, always serious. He had joined the Way of Til just prior to the collapse of the tower. He'd forsaken that vow, but still wore one of the acolyte robes, though cut off to tunic length. Trousers from Docktown stopped mid-shin, a fine belt cinched around his slender waist to make him look as respectable as such garments could.

He waited for her to speak.

The Voluptuary spoke instead. "Allow me to soothe you, my son. No, I will not strip away your sacred grief. But I see that you have not slept these past few days."

"Tia was recovering, Voluptuary. She spoke just yesterday."

"I know. But that is not uncommon. Life is full of reversals, as you well know. Here, allow me." She took his face in her hands and smiled serenely. "A little mercus is all. Hold still."

Ragin had little mercus power. The Coin doubted he would've ascended to Donse Master had he stayed in the Way of Til. But he surely noticed that she flared to life upon the mercusine, as did those waiting by the door.

He had no chance to react. The circle formed and the Coin herself offered the combined power to the Voluptuary. The flow was immensely pleasurable while it lasted. Minn's efforts were practiced, swift, and effective, if not nearly so elegant as what that Sigh girl could accomplish.

First, she marked him. The mercus bolts were simple combinations of scent and light, with which she etched her name into his skull, beneath his skin. It did not hurt him, he felt nothing more than a strange weight settling upon him. Not too heavy. The mark would allow her to track him wherever he went.

Next she formed bolts leavened with love and urgent need. The Voluptuary's face went red as she felt the emotion she would implant into Raginalt. Perspiration beaded on her forehead. Forming such bolts outside of certain rare marriage rituals was forbidden. Even then, Sensuals usually prepared for weeks to bear the feelings they had to endure in order to create the mercus bolts.

Ragin's wan face changed. From drawn and haggard to eager and energetic. He smiled and began to bounce on his toes a little. The Voluptuary crooned. "You are done with Tia. She had your heart for a while, but now you must return to your one true love. Do you know who that is?"

The eagerness vanished. He shook his head, trying to fight the press of emotion the Voluptuary was provoking in him. "I —no. Not her."

Taking more power from the circle, the Voluptuary probed deeper into Ragin's mind. She was not particularly skilled, for such things were not well understood to the Ways.

"Your one true love, son. You know who she is. Say her name and let your devotion be sealed."

He fought it. The Coin was rather impressed by how long he fought it. But by degrees, his face relaxed until he beamed with holy devotion.

"Who is she? Who is your one true love?"

"Kila Sigh," he confessed. "It has always been Kila Sigh."

"And so it shall always be." The Voluptuary released the

feat of mercus and stepped back from the boy. "You've been parted from her too long, haven't you?"

"Oh yes. Kil's eyes, yes. I must go to her. Please let me go."

"You may go, but do not race to Docktown for a ship. I know a different path. A swifter path."

His enthusiasm was so great all he could do was nod and bounce on his toes.

"Come then, Raginalt."

THE ATLEN-DRAWN wagon had been waiting, the travel packs each woman would bring already on board. The drive through the ash-barrens to Kil's Keep took three hours due to the mud. Ragin rocked back and forth the whole time trying to lend the birds speed. The Coin assured him several times that this was indeed faster than a ship. He must trust.

Along with the Voluptuary and the Coin were Spinster Moirina and Sensual Roon. They knew the mission. They were committed.

"Kila is the Highest of Kil!" Raginalt crowed as they entered Kil's Keep. They were met by a rag-tag band of hopeless folk. They had come here to find the Highest, to enter the Way of Kil. They had found an empty keep, no food, and no leader. They watched with blank stares as the Coin led her party through the keep and to the descending stair.

Half an hour later, the party came to the center of the Derslin Wheel. Sensual Wighton greeted them somberly. He had a little camp set up here. Tables, chairs, baskets of fruit and links of smoked sausage to sustain him.

"I have deciphered another symbol," he said, showing her a list. "It leads to Ittiti in the Shudderlins."

"Well done, Sensual," the Voluptuary said. "Now, please open this one," she said pointing.

"You're sure she's there?" Raginalt asked, brow creased with anxious worry. "I need to see her. I need her *now*."

"I received notice in coin-code from Starside this morning. She has gone to Tearling for the shadline gathering. Be swift, Raginalt. The shadline are not to be trusted. Kila is pressed from all sides by those who seek to use her."

"Ah me!"

Sensual Wighton approached one of the strange columns, then began to walk in a circle, waving for Raginalt to follow. "The columns are never in the same place," Wighton said. "Let's see. We're looking for a great block with two slits and a maw."

They continued to walk around the circle until Wighton abruptly stopped. Immediately he brought forth mercus bolts of need. The man was moderately powerful in his own right, and he'd made a quick study of the forbidden senses and feelings since the Voluptuary had charged him with opening portals here.

A shimmer appeared in front of the column then shined in a vertical line so bright the Coin had to look away. When it faded, she discovered a fiery opening in the air where the column had been. Remarkable!

On the other side was a Derslin Cavern. Raginalt did not hesitate before stepping through. Wighton released his feat and the portal squeezed out of existence.

"And you?" he asked the Voluptuary.

"Wantin."

"Of course, Voluptuary. You recall the bolts for the portal so you can return?"

"Yes."

The process repeated and the Voluptuary—accompanied by Spinster Moirina—disappeared through Wighton's next portal. He wiped his brow and took a swig of wine before nodding politely to the Coin.

She'd known her destination at the instant her plan had formed. Pol had smiled upon them in this regard, allowing Wighton to discover her desired destination early in his research.

"Tordain. But you must allow me to open the portal. I wish to practice, for we'll be moving on from there."

"Of course. He handed her a copy of his list, a directory of all the known symbols. Ten had destinations next to them. She found the one for Tordain and made the circuit of columns until she found the two circles connected by a horizontal line.

The bolts formed reluctantly and she fumbled with them for a few minutes. But soon the tear in the air formed. She stepped through, her companion Sensual Roon following close behind.

She stepped into another Derslin Wheel. The air was cool, dry, scentless. The scholarly part of her mind, the one so taken with books and ideas when she was younger, wished desperately to bask in the miracle of traveling so far so quickly.

But there was no time for that. No time for anything.

The young Sensual Roon, barely eighteen, but apparently unshakable, merely glanced around. "Shall we?"

"Yes. Would you provide the light? Voluptuary Minn suggested I have you practice your feats whenever possible."

The Coin and the Voluptuary had decided each to travel

with an underling from their opposite Way. This would smooth negotiations in places where one had a stronger presence than the other, and each had different skills.

Sens Roon produced mercus light, rather feebly at first, and floated it ahead of them as they walked into darkness.

12

THE REVULSION

"Can't this beast move any faster?" Kila said. The donkey looked strong, but it plodded slower than she could walk. "Maybe I should fly Quinn up."

"Can you do so reliably?" Ell asked softly.

The monarch knew of Kila's near disasters in that regard. During battle, flying had been effortless, the bolts coming to her as easily as the desire. Kila *thought* she could do it now, desperate as she was to get Quinn off the donkey and into a bed, but if she failed . . . Hard to explain to herself or anyone else that she had dropped her dearest friend to her death.

Her mood was not improved by the worsening weather. The higher they ascended toward the Hackwatch, the denser became the mist. Tiny ice particles needled her face now. Her cloak cut the chill somewhat, but it had grown heavy with the damp.

A wall loomed ahead. "Are we there?"

Jil said, "No. This is the outer battlement. I told you the Hackwatch was once a fortress." The donkey's hooves echoed as they passed into an arched tunnel. The wall was so thick,

Kila wondered if it could possibly be solid stone all the way through. Overhead, light shone down from murder holes, through which armsmen of old loosed arrows or flaming pitch.

Midway through, when the light of the openings was dimmest, two huge braziers smoked and spattered, casting angry light to cut the murk. The brief warmth was welcome, but not long lasting. Shivering, Kila again eyed the ceiling, ribbed with supporting stone arches. It was the work of men, reminding her of the Cathedral of Til. It lacked the elegance and effortlessness of the First Race builders.

The weight of the wall made everyone's shoulders hunch over. Except for Ell, whose face was serious but placid. Shadlines pulled their cloaks more tightly about themselves and a few tapped their ears three times. Kila hardly resisted the superstitious ritual herself, and she never gave such things any mind. Most times.

A cold wind met their faces near the exit and then they were out into a whitewash of day. The trees were cleared away here, leaving a rough stretch of rock-strewn grass left and right. Beyond it, and still further upslope, hunched the Hackwatch.

If not for Quinn's need, Kila was sure she would have turned back. For the fortress stood against the sky, black as shadow, walls and towers thick and low, tops crenellated and overhung with rotting wooden hoardings. Though surely not by design, this vantage gave the Hackwatch a face, for it had only two windows visible. Left and right, each on a squat tower.

A vast gate, standing open, yawned at them like a mouth.

"You say scholars live here?" she said. "I can't imagine

anyone wanting to. It's—" Lost for words, she looked to Ell. "Can't you feel it?"

"I feel it. I daresay all the shadline do a little bit. Discomfort. Unease. You'll feel as if your collar is too tight, the air unsustaining of breath, the damp colder and the shadows deeper than natural. This is the Hackwatch. It will be worse for you inside, I'm afraid."

"Why hold the Armory here?"

Behind her Jil laughed, a cold, harsh, biting laugh of contempt. "If you knew what it was to be shadline, you would not ask such a stupid question. We listen and obey."

"Jil, enough," Ell said. It was the first rebuke Kila had ever heard the woman give to the sullen shadline. "Kila must be free to decide whether to speak the oath or not. Her ignorance is not her fault."

"Forgive me, Ell. My apologies to you too, Highest of Kil." There was no attempt to hide the sarcastic twist in her voice.

Kila didn't think much of Ell defending her. Not if she was going to say Kila was ignorant.

Ell pointed to the left tower. "That was the first structure to be built here by men. An outpost overlooking the town that eventually grew into Tearling. But the elnisians were here first. You'll find yourself going to the Stardome without meaning to. The atmosphere is lighter there." She sighed. "That tower is where executions once took place, at the very top. The very name of the fortress derives from that favorite pastime of the elder kings. King Mannustir bade his enemies be decapitated by means of a small hatchet. At the time, a wooden platform jutted out at the top. The condemned were bound there, head on a sloped block. The executioner hacked at the neck, fifteen or thirty blows, until the head came free and fell to the ground below. If it landed in the basket, the executioner received a gift from the king."

"Hack. Watch. This Mannustir fellow reminds me of Dox Viller back in Cheapsgate."

"A very similar taste for cruel violence," Ell said. Her mouth clenched in and her eyes gleamed. But she swallowed the emotion.

"That doesn't answer why the shadline would hold the Armory here."

"The ill ease you feel . . . it makes you want to leave. To avoid this place. To a shadline that is a clear sign that one must approach and enter. The way is discomfort, Kila. Of all people, surely you know the truth of that." But Ell did not sound entirely convinced.

The upward trudge continued, straight toward the leering face of the Hackwatch and the gaping maw of its gate. Kila now discovered the donkey's steps a bit too spritely for her taste, her own feet dragging.

A hard rain beat onto their heads as they finally reached the gate. Two scholars in brown robes stood just inside, faces pale as maggots. The men had no hair on their spotty scalps, and only slightly more teeth when their thin lips spread in smiles. They made welcoming motions with their hands, but Kila's skin went gooseflesh. She'd known men in Cheapsgate who lured girls and boys into dark corners using the same smiles and motions.

One man fixed a stare on Kila and would not release it. The look of a hungry man, and not for food. "Are there women here?" she asked, ashamed to hear her voice break.

"Among the shadline," Ell said. "Do not worry about these men. They know shadline are dangerous. They also have no strong urges of the kind you fear. They drink a brew each morning to quench such fires so that they might focus entirely on their studies."

They passed through the gate and into the courtyard, and Kila still felt the man's eyes on her. Did he know who she was? He did. She was suddenly certain of it. Those Lumne-touched followers of hers by the river had known her too. That damnable handbill! She felt her gorge rise. Something was very wrong here.

"Kila!" came a voice, resounding from the black stone walls surrounding her. The courtyard was cramped and muddy. A man skittered down a set of stairs, calling to her. "Quinn is in trouble!" he called. "We have to find her."

It was Fallo. The same hideous face, the flop of black hair atop his head, the single bushy eyebrow over his eyes.

"She's right here." Kila handed the donkey's lead to a boy in the same robes as the scholars. "Here, Fallo. Help me get her down."

The young man brushed past her and scooped Quinn off the animal. His journeys with the Cloak had thickened him, made him stronger than the alley boy Kila had first met. Quinn looked small in his arms. Fragile as a fevered child. "What happened to her?" he demanded.

"She was given a ferneater potion. Some sort of willshift." Kila put a hand on his shoulder, tried to soothe him. "Carry her inside. I will tell you all I know. But we must get her help."

"Zirhine!" he cried as he dashed away.

Nax, stay close. I don't like this place. It feels . . . wrong.

It is thick. I smell rats.

Kila trailed after Fallo, ignoring Ell's calls not to disrupt the quietude of the fortress. But climbing the steps took enormous effort. Her legs resisted, weighed down by some unseeable weight. A deep pressure seized her chest, like a fist gripping her heart.

Gasping and straining, she bent double, unable to go farther, unable to take the last step that would carry her through the threshold of the door. Fallo's hollow cries carried to her, "Zirhine! Zirhine!"

He had taken Quinn. Kila had to follow. Had to make sure Quinn lived. Muscles failing, she did what she always did. She reached for the mercus.

It wasn't there.

Absence. The weight upon her was caused by the total absence of the mercus. She had not recognized it until now. Panicking, she strained for it, as one clawing toward the surface of a lake, desperate for breath. It was not there. Instead, an oily foulness sloshed in her awareness.

"You feel it now," Ell said, bending next to Kila and rubbing her back. "The sludge that separates us from the mercusine here. That is called the Revulsion. It congeals in certain places. The Hackwatch is the one of the worst I've felt."

Retching and coughing, Kila tried to crawl the last step. Nothing would keep her from Quinn's bedside. Nothing.

"Easy, Kila. Allow yourself to adjust."

"Why—aren't you—down here—with me?"

"I've been here before. It is easier the second time, I assure you. But I am also a dragnithan. I cannot be totally separated from the mercusine, for I am *of* the mercusine. The mercus will be there for you when you leave this place. You see why Shad Ault so readily relented about the *vaz'on*."

Kila fought down gags, then failed. Lips wet with spittle, she gasped in air. "Discomfort is the way, you said."

"Aye. For you more than most."

Nax butted her head into Kila's shin. *Stand up.*

Naxie, this place is vile. The mercus is buried.

Stand up! It's just a place.

Doesn't it bother you? The Revulsion?

Nax sent a flurry of sensations, of creeping silently, stalking prey. Of the exhilaration of exploring dark, scary places. And oddly, of a sort of respect for the Revulsion. Not love for it, nor even attraction to it. But of an acknowledgement that it is there. *It is always there. Thicker here than elsewhere. Haven't you felt it before?*

No. Kila felt for Nax's soft head, drew strength from the little gray's indomitable spirit. *You feel it always?*

Always. Stand up.

Slowly, Kila obeyed. The weight of absence still pushed her down, but Nax fortified her spirit. Heaving out a great moan, she lunged through the door. Ell caught her and held her upright until she recovered her breath.

The weight did not entirely release, but was much less now. A quick search for the mercus revealed nothing but the horrid sludge of the Revulsion. "Are you sure the mercus is beyond that?" she asked Ell.

"I am."

"Nax says the Revulsion is always there, but just more so here."

Ell bowed her head to Nax, eyes gleaming. "Honored Felnithel, thou art wise and courageous and holy. I am not as sensitive to it as Nax. And for that I'm grateful."

Nax took this as her due and slunk ahead. *Fallo went this way.*

The nausea had passed and Kila felt more herself now. She followed after her cat, only dimly aware of the shadlines who followed.

It is dangerous here, Nax sent. *Be wary.*

You just said it's just a place! Now you tell me to be wary?

Just so. It is nice when you listen.

A chirp of outrage escaped Kila as she stormed deeper into the fortress. And after three turns, became completely lost. The ways were narrow, dank, and swarming with shadow. There were no windows, and the oil lamps were wicked low to conserve fuel. The effect was suffocating.

Only Nax's clear presence in her mind guided her true. Turning a corner, she nearly smashed into Fallo's back. He stood, holding Quinn before a shadline woman in a drab shirt. Her face was sun-wrinkled and handsome, with eyes as piercing as a hawk's.

The Cloak stood behind her, Tosuin in hand. A lick of flame coursed down his blade, casting lurid shadows of all present against the damp walls. "She's had ferneater poison," Fallo said. "You have to undo it. You must."

Zirhine palmed Quinn's cheeks, pressed her nose close to the girl's lips and held there for a moment. "Tagleseed and whiskey. And something else . . ."

"It's tresh," Ell said. Fallo gaped to discover Her Enlightend Majesty standing next to him.

"Bring her," Zirhine said, and then led the way into the keep. Fallo's breaths seemed to scrape in the air of the narrow corridor as he twisted to keep Quinn's head and feet from brushing the strange, sweating stone.

A bitter taste hung in the cramped space, of lantern smoke and unwashed skin. A scholar motioned them to an empty room, but he kept pressing a finger to his lips, urging them to stay quiet. Fallo set Quinn onto a cot but refused to leave the girl's side when Zirhine urged him to make room.

"I will stay here until she wakes," he said. "I must. I hear it. I hear it and I will obey."

Zirhine nodded. "Someone fetch my pack from my room. Touch nothing in it."

Footsteps trampled away as one of the shadline ran for her pack. Zirhine knelt next to Quinn and again placed her nose close to the girl's lips. She felt along Quinn's arms, pressed fingers under her wrists. "The other man on the donkey. Tresh also?"

"Without a doubt," Ell said. "It is Critt Sanglo."

"Ah, Critt is strong. This is very subtle. The work of an absolute master."

"What is tresh?" Fallo demanded. "Poison?"

"It can be. But the purpose is to control a person's will. Once consumed, the mind becomes susceptible to deeply placed commands. Such commands can lay dormant for days, even years. But I have never seen tresh make someone fall into deep sleep like this."

The runner returned with Zirhine's pack, and she tore into it. "I can bring her to wakefulness. But I cannot discover what commands she may have been given. Waking her will not remove the deeply laid command. Whatever it is, she must act upon it to be relieved of it. Bring hot water and a cup."

The runner darted away again.

Zirhine laid a white cloth onto the floor. Then she opened pouch after pouch, vial after vial, pulling out bits of weed, twigs, stone, powders, and even legs and wings of insects. These she arrayed on the white cloth then placed a finger near each one as if counting. When she was satisfied she pinched the four corners of the cloth and drew it up into a small pouch. She shook it to mix the ingredients together.

Kila knelt next to Fallo and circled an arm about him. He didn't seem to notice.

The runner returned with a steaming cup. Zirhine dunked the pouch into it. "It must steep a moment. I pray we are in time."

Fallo's murmuring stopped. He looked at Kila, then the others. "Our gathering in this room is a fatehand."

Zirhine, Ell, and Jil bowed slightly to him, acknowledging his statement with remarkable solemnity. Cloak Einlin, who had ghosted into the room without her noticing, merely nodded grimly. Kila hadn't the slightest idea what a fatehand was.

"Close the door," Fallo said. Jil obeyed immediately, roughly urging two leering scholars from the opening in order to secure the door.

"What else are you hearing?" Zirhine asked Fallo.

He closed his eyes, and doing so revealed enormous pain. And then resignation. "This gathering, in this room, is a fate-hand. I've said all I know."

13
———

TO THE FATEHAND

"**A**ssembled in this room are the only people we can truly trust," Ell LiMinluit said. "Fallo PiTorro, the forsaken son, and bearer of Telt and Skeye. Zirhine, mooncrafter of Trine, and bearer of Reft. Cloak Einlin, shadline blademaster, bearer of Tosuin. Jil Pokkti, shadline merculyn hunter, bearer of Qinsh. Quinn Peline, bearer of Black. Kila Sigh, Highest of Kil, bearer of Fate Breaker. This is a fatehand, as Fallo has said. The order of the shadline has been corrupted."

The room was too small for the number of people in it. Kila didn't like being so close to Zirhine, who she suspected of poisoning her friends. Fallo was tugging at his collar laces, strange face flushed. Seeing Kila looking at him, he edged away. Did he believe she'd start throwing mercus spheres at Zirhine?

He was the first to fill the tense silence. "I don't want to be one of the only people we can trust. I just want to return to Starside, forget about adventures, get married, have a passel of children, dogs, and friends . . ." He trailed off sadly. It didn't take any shadline instinct for Kila to know that none of that was to be. At least not now. Fallo obviously knew it too.

Kila found Zirhine staring at her. She stiffened and returned the stare.

"You can trust Zirhine," Fallo said.

Without breaking eye-contact Kila said, "If it was ferneater potions that poisoned my friends, then one must look to the nearest ferneater."

Zirhine did not take offense at Kila's use of the derogatory term. Instead, she clasped her hands together and regarded Kila with a look of great patience. "I understand your mistrust. But you are far from Starside. Perhaps you do not know that there are many who derive power from plants. I know your suspicion is rooted in ignorance. Allow me to ease your fears. I did not know of Quinn Peline prior to coming here. I have no reason to harm her or Critt Sanglo."

Kila pointed at Fallo. "How can you know him and you don't know of Quinn Peline? I can't imagine he's gone more than a minute without talking about how he kissed her. Surely he's talked about little else."

"Quinn is who you were talking about?" Zirhine said turning on Fallo. "You said your girl was hideous."

"Would you have believed me if I told you the truth?"

Kila blew out a sad laugh. "Maybe she poisoned Quinn so she could be the one to save her. That'd make her a real hero, wouldn't it? Maybe your love for her is blinding you."

"Stop," Ell said. "I'm telling you that those in this room can be trusted. I feel it as an absolute, stronger than I have felt any whisper of the force of destiny. Put aside your suspicions."

Everyone looked at Kila. She sagged under their gazes, and tossed her hands out to the side in surrender. She turned to Quinn and brushed the girl's hair back from her forehead.

"I never told you I loved her," Fallo said softly.

"But you do."

Ell began to pace, and everyone made room for her to walk back and forth. "It couldn't have been Zirhine. Whoever did this got to Quinn and Critt in Tearling or before."

"What about Shad Ault?" Kila asked. "He hates me."

"He is protective of the order," Cloak Einlin said. "But poisons and such are not the shadline way."

Jil confirmed this with a quiet, "Aye. True words, Cloak. And you know I am no friend to Shad Ault."

"It could have been anyone," Zirhine said. "If Critt carried a flask of drink, I would like to inspect it. If tresh-tainted, a small daily sip would renew the power of the tresh without him realizing it. He was the kind who would share it out, too. That would explain Quinn's state."

"So they might have fallen under its sway far from here," Fallo said.

Kila thought this even more chilling. It would mean someone knew Kila would be here and knew of her friendship with Critt and Quinn. "Kil's eyes, they would have to have known that Critt was a shadline! I hate to say it, Cloak Einlin, but that suggests the poisoner is a shadline. Who else is a ferneater here? Seems like they should be questioned first."

"Questioned?" Fallo said. "Hello there, sir Shadline. I heard that you're a filthy ferneater. Would you have by chance be the one who poisoned Quinn and Critt?"

"I was thinking of something more subtle than that."

Zirhine looked troubled. "We must consider this from a higher vantage and look down upon our order in its entirety. Let's not single out those gifted with the mooncraft. It could be that someone seeks to direct our suspicions upon those of the craft, so that we do not look elsewhere."

That seemed awfully convoluted to Kila. Whoever these other ferneaters were, she intended to give them a head-to-toe looking over. Nobody poisoned Quinn and—

She stumbled over the word. Poison. "Why was Quinn in Lumne's dream and on the donkey? Why wasn't she as hale and feisty as Critt?"

Zirhine was quiet for a while, chewing her lower lip as she considered the question. "I wondered that myself. I understand that Critt attempted to fight the impulse of the tresh for a few moments. It looks to me that Kila cares deeply for Quinn. Perhaps that feeling was returned?"

"Of course it was," Fallo said, now looking at Kila with a softness she'd never seen in him before. "They were as sisters."

"I see. If strong-willed, one can overcome the demands of tresh. If the tresh be particularly powerful, the inner war can wreak havoc upon the mind. Perhaps we see the consequence of a stalemate. I believe Quinn has nearly died for refusing to betray Kila."

Kila let out a soft moan and dropped to her knees next to the cot. She hugged Quinn's head and placed her cheek on her forehead. Quinn's eyes popped open, and she drew in a ragged breath. Kila jerked back in surprise. Rising on the cot, Quinn's hand searched out Black. Drawing it, she sprang up.

Fallo reached for her, but she thrust the stump of her right arm into his chest. With unexpected strength she pushed him down. Zirhine scooped up her steeping brew and scampered backward.

Quinn pointed Black at Kila, her arm straight out and head tilted at an angle. Her mouth moved, but Black's power silenced her words. No one trained in blade fighting would hold a weapon in such a stiff overhand grip. It was the pose of a Lumne-touched madwoman bent on murder.

The blade arm came back, readying for a strike. The shock of seeing her friend so strangely possessed froze Kila. Fallo scrabbled to catch Quinn's elbow. The Cloak and Jil reacted a moment later, wrapping the girl up and slamming her back onto the cot. Quinn struggled and jabbed with her blade, and Fallo heaved back on her to keep Black from stabbing Jil in the neck. Ell leaped into the fray, adding her strength to hold the young woman down.

"We have her," Ell said. "Zirhine, prepare your brew!"

Kila reached for Quinn, wanting to soothe her. And in truth, wanting to wrest Black from her hand so she could hear what her friend was saying.

The Cloak had thrown himself across Quinn's knees, clamping her legs in his strong arms. Jil and Ell held Quinn's arms, twisting them back to a position of weakness. Fallo grasped her head, pressed his chin to her forehead, and held tightly. Her mouth moved in screams and curses silenced by Black.

Zirhine collected her steeping ferneater brew. Jil twisted Quinn's wrist until her fingers loosened. The blade clattered on the floor. Quinn screams rose, high-pitched and full of wrath. "Kila Sigh! Why won't you—"

A huge, shuddering inhalation interrupted her words.

"Why won't you—Ah, please, no!" She was fighting it.

Kila's vision blurred to see her friend's agonies. The final words came out in a defeated rasp. "Why won't you die?"

With swift, sure movements, Zirhine dipped a pinky into the brew. With her other hand she pried open Quinn's left eye and shook two drops from her finger.

Quinn screamed in fiery agony. It was all the shadlines could do to hold on as the girl writhed and bucked. "Hold her still! One more!" Zirhine urged.

Again she dipped her finger, and this time went for the right eye. But Quinn had squeezed it shut in her pain. Zirhine did not relent, her own knuckles going white as she strained to pry Quinn's eyelid up. And when she had, she let drop two more splashes.

The effect was instant. The girl's eyes opened wide. The pupils narrowed to pinpoints, and the irises—so brown they were nearly black—paled to an icy silver.

The fight went out of Quinn, and a hot hiss escaped her lips. The smell of it made Kila crinkle her nose and recoil. It wasn't the halitosis of the sick, but a dark sweet stench, like a body decaying in a Cheapsgate alley.

And then the odor was gone, dissipating into nothing.

"I must administer more," Zirhine said. It required no effort now to turn Quinn's head to one side and then the other, each ear getting two drops. "You two men, step outside," Zirhine said.

The Cloak and Fallo went out, and Kila followed, unwilling to see whatever the ferneater planned to do next. Her belly clenched so tightly she was sure she'd lose her last meal. "She tried to kill me."

"You know that wasn't Quinn's will," Fallo said, stooping to scoop up Lop. "I don't know if I'll ever be able to forget that look in her eyes. I've never seen her filled with such hate."

"You trust this Zirhine woman? Truly?" Kila said.

"With my life. With Quinn's. Without question. You saw what she just did."

Kila saw such sincerity in his face, such unguarded feeling, she realized she was seeing him for the first time. The dry wit, the selfish talk. It had long hidden the young man's soft heart. And such a heart it was.

And then, to her own astonishment, Kila hugged him fiercely. It was not just an embrace of greeting. There was something desperate in it, and she trembled like a rain-drenched puppy in his arms. He patted her back and kissed the top of her head. "Who cut your hair?" he asked. "The blind Barber of Regent Row?"

Kila disengaged herself and punched his arm. "You could use a haircut yourself," she said. "Or is that a bear pelt on your head?"

He smiled broadly, then roughly pulled her back into his embrace. Ah, it was good to see his ugly face. With Wen gone and Henley so far away, Fallo was her only true friend here. He would never seek to use her power or steer her like an atlen under harness.

He eased back, still holding her arms in unexpectedly strong hands. "So they say you can fly."

"That's true. Would you like me to make you fly?" She offered her most ingenuous smile.

"I'll let Lop go first."

"How long has Jil Pokkti been with you?" Cloak Einlin asked her, barging into their reunion.

"A month," Kila said. "She was in Starside with Her

Enlightened—I mean, with Ell. She's been 'training' me in the use of my blade. She's insufferable and she cheats!"

"She never tried to kill you?"

"No. But I think she would like to."

The Cloak nodded but said nothing more. His lips mashed into a firm line. He was thinking his usual cryptic thoughts, and likely listening to the subtle call of the force of destiny. But whatever it told him he kept to himself, praise be to all gods in all times.

"Is she really Ault's daughter?" Kila asked.

The Cloak nodded. "So she claims. Ault does not dispute it, though he did not know of her until she found him. By then she had come to possess Qinsh. Father and daughter share one thing in common. A hatred of merculyns."

"Then why is she so close to Ell?" Kila asked.

The Cloak pursed his lips and considered it. "She listens and obeys. And Ell LiMinluit is a shadline. The oath means much to us, and Jil is no different. Perhaps you could learn from that. Perhaps you should quieten the chatter of your own mind and listen and obey."

"Kil's guts in my stew!" Kila threw her hands up, disturbing Nax who had climbed to perch on her shoulder. "I'm so tired of that phrase."

"Perhaps if you listened to it, it would not be uttered so frequently in your hearing."

Fallo offered Kila a sympathetic look. She could tell he'd resigned himself to the shadline way already and agreed with the Cloak.

The door swung open, and they were admitted into Quinn's room. She was asleep, clothes neatly folded and set onto a chair across the room. Blankets covered her, feet to chin. Her raven hair was pulled into a loose bun atop her head. Her pale grayish face sagged under the exhaustion brought on by her inner battle.

"She will sleep now," Zirhine said. "I think she will be well. I must go see to Critt Sanglo. I will recruit others to hold him down. We will need seven or eight I think." The woman collected her ingredients, her pack, and the cup of her mooncraft brew, and departed.

The Cloak nodded respectfully to Zirhine then took stock of those present. "I fear we have little time to give to our worries for Quinn. She is hale and I have little doubt she will recover. We must return our attention to the fatehand. Such encounters should not end without a decision."

"Yes," Kila said, "I've decided to find the rot in the shadline and burn it out."

No one seconded her statement. She looked to Fallo, but his chin was tucked as he stared at his feet. One hand stroked Lop, who slept snuggly in his arms. "I don't know if Quinn was poisoned by a shadline or someone working for a shadline. I cannot feel it. But say it is so. How could a shadline traitor be listening and obeying and do such a thing?"

Jil swore softly. The Cloak said nothing.

Ell said. "The force of destiny moves us all toward necessary events. Even Yiothizandra is not excused from it. But Kil's growing presence in this world might bend the force of destiny toward new ends. The course of a boulder from cliff top to the ground below is invariable if the drop be sheer and unimpeded. But put trees and other boulders in the way and who is to say how it will bounce, split, and shatter? The Cloak is correct. We must come to a decision. And the decision is not about finding who poisoned Quinn, is it Fallo?"

"No. It's about Kila."

The door pushed open. It was Shad Ault.

"Sanglo is dead," he said. Without another word he walked out, leaving the door open behind him.

And then Kila was in Fallo's arms again, weeping like a child.

14

DEM-DISK, MY DEAR

Two dragons lay atop each other, lodged in the crook of an outcropping thrust from a jagged mountain peak. Yiothizandra saw immediately what it happened. They had battled high in the clouds and become twined in a deathlock, claw digging under scale, teeth clamped into serpentine neck. Their wings had become tangled, making it impossible to fly.

The resulting plummet had been a test of will. Who would relinquish the grasp first to make the desperate glide to remain airborne? But neither had relented, and so they had impacted here, throwing up a ring of ice, stone, and dirt, and setting off an avalanche that collapsed half a mountainside.

Yiothizandra flew over the bodies. The impact had mangled them, but she recognized these dragnithors. The white one was a dragon of Day, Haptenar. Only two thousand human years old. Inexperienced, foolish.

The other was black, but the scales shone under the gray winter light enough to make the body glimmer a silvery gray.

Oksyosh, who had flown by Night long before Yiothizandra herself had come into existence.

She alighted next to her fallen friend, placed her hands upon the scales of its twisted neck. "You shall be avenged. All of us shall be avenged."

She took again to the air, circled once more, and headed south to Ceronhel.

UPON HER RETURN to the now-humming halls of her northern holdfast, she observed with satisfaction the men who had come with Tarek PiTorro unloading wagons, setting up their smithies, and detailing nosg work crews to move slabs of stone and fresh timbers to the worksites.

Bizt-Ma had sent his drikk-folk with the stolen goods. Much would still be in transit as there was a long distance to cover, and much of it would be through the subterranean ways due to the snow in the passes.

The Hargothe had intended Ceronhel to be the first fortress of his new empire, and he had planned to restore it to its former glory. But he had not intended to live here long. His aim had always been in Starside.

Foolish man. He had been too much consumed by greed and hatred for her little cousin. Yes, Starside was extremely defensible. But the same qualities that made it so—backed by impenetrable mountains and secure in a narrow bay—made it difficult to use as a base from which to project power through the world. Starside was rich and strong, but her little cousin did not rule over subjects beyond a few days sail north or south. The Hargothe would have squandered most of the nosg forces taking Starside, leaving him little strength to turn west-ward and begin the conquest of more realms.

Yiothizandra would not make that mistake.

On her flight home she had overflown growing encampments of the nosg armies, which had gathered in the passes and valleys. The endless constellations of cookfires and shelters had impressed even her, who had seen a hundred wars. The uncountable masses roared as they saw her soaring overhead. And she spoke to the babe growing within her. "Behold, Kil, the time of your return is come. The forces of Night gather to gift you a world."

But Yiothizandra was not content. She still needed to move this ravenous horde out of the mountains. And there was only one Derslin Wheel in the north. It would take months to file these creatures into Ceronhel and down the twisty passages and stairs into the Derslin cavern. The nosg were not noted for their patience nor their orderliness.

So she bade Razk-Ka send only a fraction of her forces to disperse through the Derslin Wheel. The main body would traverse the western passes, first to take Stallid. But the way west through the Haelshok range was blocked by heaps of snow.

Delays. Delays. Always delays. But she knew of a method to clear those passes quickly: Dragonfire.

She retired to her private room, a solitary chamber high on one tower with a northerly view to admit the iciest mountain air. Here she bedded down upon a nosg-crafted pallet, closed her eyes, and settled her mind. As a dragnithan, the mercusine was her essence, and if she listened closely, if she silenced her thoughts long enough, she could call to her kind.

Dragon-kin of Night, I have summoned you and yet you do

not come. Hurry to me. Hurry to Ceronhel. I offer you freedom from this hateful world.

She was not long waiting before a reply came. And the voice was one she expected. Bazron. The oldest of the dragnithor. *Patience, child. We come. Are the eyries above Ceronhel clear of Day or will this be the long-foretold battle?*

The eyries have been clear since the elnisian left this place. They have been clear for an age. The battle you seek lies ahead. We must prepare.

We come. And then we shall counsel.

Yioth sat up, irritation warring with satisfaction. She did not intend to counsel with anyone. They would do as she commanded, for she was the mother of Kil. But she would address that when the dragnithor were present.

She settled once again, sinking deep into the mercusine. It was not a comfortable state for her. She disliked the thoughtlessness of it. She preferred to plan, to act. But the coming war would be vast, and even Kil required allies.

Dragnithan come to me. Hear me, Eckso. Hear me, Klayne. They were the two dragnithan of Night who had been imprisoned with her here since that hateful day. She wished there were more, for each could answer for thousands of mortal men. But she did not intend to send them into battle just yet. There were other tasks for them, ones requiring more subtlety, more stealth. More patience.

She had called them once before, before the Hargothe's death. But they had been stubborn, as usual. Now her words carried the resonance of Kil's power. They would not be able to ignore the power of her summons.

As Yioth had devoted her essence to flight and fire, the other two had devoted theirs to the mercus. And so it was that

Eckso and Klayne dymensed into her chamber, thankfully eschewing the excess of mercus green that Flaumishtak loved so much.

Yioth sat up and greeted her guests with an imperious lift of her chin.

Klayne had his arms crossed and a skeptical look on his face. He was man-formed, and though he could manifest wings, she had never seen him do it. He wore a loose white tunic over baggy trousers. His feet were wrapped in the curious sandals common to men in Losstra, far to the west. Around his neck and wrists were gold chains. Gold hoops pierced his earlobes, and his wavy brown hair was swept back and oiled such that it stayed perfectly in place as he moved. "Well met, Yioth," he said in his silky baritone. He looked like a man of thirty, though he was nearly Yiothizandra's age. "I believe you were lying in bed when I last saw you. Well satisfied I might add."

Eckso snorted and threw her hands up. "You two are depraved."

"And you, dear sister, are a prude," Yiothizandra said, not deigning to rise. "What name do you go by this time around?"

"Lady Winnea, niece of His Majesty, Worran Pozzti. I'm quite content with my station. It leaves me to my pleasures. But I suppose Trine is much warmer than Ceronhel. Too warm for one of your disposition."

Yioth's younger sibling had huge floofs of blond hair, painted eyelids, and rouged lips. She wore an elegant gown, something appropriate for a ball. She'd always enjoyed the frivolous frocks of the posh classes. With her mercusine powers she could be a queen like Ell, but instead chose to be a lesser noblewoman, biding her time, aging and appearing to die, then being reborn and coming into some new society to begin her slow social climb. She never wearied of it. But unlike Yiothizandra, Eckso had flown at twilight. She had never been fully committed to escaping this wretched world of mortal flesh. Never fully committed to Night, for that matter.

"Is it true you have finally gotten with child?" Eckso said. "Why now?"

Yioth stretched languorously before stalking toward her sister, relishing this moment of revelation. "Dem-Kisk, my dear." She placed a hand on her belly. "Surely you feel him upon the mercusine. I bear Kil within me. And so it is time for you to choose. Support Night, and live. Support Day, and be destroyed utterly." Yioth raised a finger and cut off her sister's retort. "Don't think you can return to obscurity and hope Pol smiles upon you when Dem-Kisk comes. Unless you support me with your full will and power, you are my enemy. When Kil comes into this world, he will reward those who helped establish his realm here. Refuse me and he will feed upon you. I think you know what that means."

Eckso blanched, hand going to the sapphire and diamond necklace at her throat. She toyed with it, likely not realizing she had acquired such a foolish human tic.

Klayne still had his arms crossed, but he nodded and pursed his lips. "And you have spoken to the Hel Lords?"

"What need I of their counsel? Do they bear Kil within them? No. They shall grovel at my feet when I leave this world." Smiling, she placed her hands on his chest and pressed her lips to his. When he returned the kiss with eager appetite, she pulled away.

"Is that what you want of us? Groveling?" Klayne asked. His tone of amusement was betrayed by a twitch beneath his right eye. An age-old tell of his inner rage. His ambition had never been matched by his discipline. He thought he should be emperor of all domains, but the truth was he was lazy. "Who bestowed this honor upon you?"

"A qiznithan, indirectly. Can you believe it? It started with a young merculyn called Tenn. So hungry for power was he, that he entered a blood ritual in Ittiti, where a qiznithan was summoned. In return for a large sacrifice, it granted the young, ambitious man oracular powers, heightened his mercusine such that he had to pluck out his own eyes and retire to solitude. He proclaimed himself Hargothe and schemed to remake the world under Til's law." She laughed merrily. "What a fierce and unforgiving god he supposed Til to be. If he'd only known . . . He'd served Kil from the first moment."

Yioth enjoyed seeing Klayne and Eckso pretend disinterest. She knew they burned with curiosity. She continued, "You see, the qiznithan's true blessing was passing into the Hargothe the seed of the Kil-notion. The gods have long forgotten who they are, barely existing as minds. But each is drawn to its nature, and this world is so delightfully full of darkness, isn't it? Perhaps that is what caused the Kil-notion to stir, to wake enough to whisper to the qiznithan its wishes, guiding it as one guides an atlen with tugs on the reins."

Klayne scoffed. "But why you?"

"Ah, see, this is where it becomes more delightful. The qiznithan did not intend for Kil to come through me. He was meant for another." She laughed with delight. "I stole him."

"Who was the intended mother?" Eckso asked, biting her lip and already sagging with defeat.

"I believe it was a thief girl from Starside. Kila Sigh. She has enormous mercus power, according to the Hargothe. He was obsessed with her, though he thought it only because of her power. It was the only aspect of her he *would* find attractive, for a pretty face or figure was of little interest to him even before he removed his eyes."

Klayne released his arms from their tight clench across his chest, now showing more sign of agitation. "Kila Sigh? The girl who flies?" He dug into a trouser pocket and pulled forth a folded slip of paper. He handed it to Yiothizandra.

The sketch was worn, torn at the edges, and stained with rings where sloppy cups had been set. Yioth had not seen Kila Sigh before. In the likeness she appeared small, shaven of head, wearing the crown of Kil upon her brow. A felnithel, poorly drawn, peeked from behind the long cape of her station as Highest of Kil.

"This is Kila Sigh?" Yioth began to pace, studying the picture, emblazoning the girl's features into her memory. The Hargothe had been obsessed with her. And she understood why the qiznithan had planted such a compulsion into his mind. This explained the old man's unresolved need for her, his soul-void that could only be filled by her. He claimed to want her power, but Yioth had always known his hunger was seated lower in his body. This girl was the true desire of his loins. Had he captured her, and possessed her, he would've gotten a child upon her. And that would have been Kil. The qiznathan's scheme had been turned. It had not anticipated him bedding a dragnithan instead. Yiothizandra smiled and handed the sketch back to Klayne. "She flies? I find her most curious. What gives her such power?"

Klayne relaxed and smiled. He had the air of someone who knew a tasty secret.

"Tell me, Klayne. How does a human girl become so powerful? To be known to a qiznathan?"

"She is god-blooded."

"Impossible. Til barely exists in this world. Pol and Ori haven't borne offspring so recently or all demaynia would have rung with the power of it. Besides, they hardly exist now as ideas, much less as thinking entities."

Klayne said nothing, but merely smiled, enjoying her frustration.

Yioth lunged, gripping him by his throat. In three strides she carried him to her window and thrust him out. He dangled there, a five hundred span drop beneath his feet.

Yioth's skin thrilled as mercusine bolts formed around him. She didn't care. "Try to harm my babe and your death will be a mercy." She squeezed, feeling the soft, human flesh of his throat compress under her fingers. "You've grown weak, Klayne. Did you know the yoznithan can come and go from this world? Perhaps I should summon Flaumishtak and have him dymense you home."

Without breaking free of this prison, such a return would doom Klayne to untold tortures at the hands of the Hel Lords. Yioth had realized the destruction of this world was their high aim and the reason she and her brethren had been exiled here. They would not be free until they freed themselves.

"No! No!" Klayne's words came out choked and desperate. "Let me go. I'll tell you what I know."

Yioth complied, releasing him. His scream echoed from the far peaks as he plummeted. She turned and found him on the floor, panting, encircled by mercus green.

"I'm pleased to see you retained some of your old skill," she said. "It will be needed."

Eckso wrung her hands and stared at Klayne. "You dymensed while falling. That's—that's—"

"Impressive," Yioth said. "Klayne is very skilled. He even taught our little cousin a few tricks before she betrayed us to walk beneath the sun. Now, Klayne, tell me what you know of Kila Sigh."

Red fury shone in his eyes. More mercusine hummed around him as he got to his feet. He staggered—a feint! With a yell he threw his hands out, sending forth arcs of violet light. They flashed toward Yioth, searing her vision purple.

She felt nothing.

"Impossible!" Klayne said, panting.

Yioth's vision cleared and she found him four paces away, shoulders and arms flexed in rage. Sparks of power scattered along his form. "Eckso, lend me power."

"No, Klayne," Eckso said. "Yioth should be convulsing on the floor from that bolt, but you saw how it arced around her and dissipated. She must have a relic of some sort protecting her."

"No relic," Yioth said. "Merely Kil inside me. Your attempt to kill him is noted, Klayne. As of now you are doomed to his caprice once he's old enough to understand your betrayal. But perhaps you can earn mercy yet. Now answer my question. Whose child is Kila Sigh?"

He looked up at her, angrily, rubbing his throat. "She is of Kil's blood. Through Semūin."

Yioth's wings manifested and unfurled behind her, brushing the ceiling of her bedchamber. "Semūin? That wanton nymph? I thought she was one of Til's whelps." She pulled her wings in and wrapped them around herself like a black cloak. A new realization stoked the dragonfire in her.

"But she isn't . . . is she? How marvelous." Yioth laughed with delight at the ancient scandal, just discovered. "I wonder if Til ever knew Lumne bedded his brother. I wonder if Semūin even knows her true father's name."

Klayne smirked. "I doubt it or she'd have thrown it in Til's face. She's petulant and capricious like that."

Eckso shrugged one shoulder and tilted her head toward it. Such a weak show of nervousness. She had grown insecure by habit and needed a strong reawakening to her dragnithan power. Yioth wondered if she had even used her mercusine in recent memory. Eckso said, "Semūin is a rebellious child. Til forbids her mortal love, so what does she do? Lures mortals to her vale and ravishes them, body and soul. And now the Sigh girl is half mortal, half something else. The perfect vessel to receive the qiznathan's Kil-seed through the Hargothe. But it's so . . . incestuous."

Yioth dismissed Eckso's human moralizing. "Where is she?"

"Where do you think? Semūin's Vale, of course," Klayne said, once again smiling broadly at Yioth's frustration. "Just fly there."

Just fly there. But Semūin didn't allow anyone into her hidden grotto who she did not want there. It would be nearly as difficult for Yioth to find that place as it would be for any unwelcome mortal. Yioth abandoned the project before starting it. "She's more vergent than goddess, being Lumne's child. I'd waste too much time and gain nothing of use. Kil will decide her fate, either to bestow upon her his love or his wrath. But this Kila Sigh might be a problem. Kil may favor her. And she was powerful enough to kill the Hargothe." That made her intriguing and dangerous. Yioth couldn't help but muse about how she might turn the girl to her own use. "The Hargothe was foolish to face her in the flesh."

"All I know is what is on this handbill," Klayne said, pointing to the sketch of Kila. "The rest is wild rumor, having traveled thousands of leagues, such that one can hardly credit any of it."

"But this says she's the Highest of Kil," Eckso said, peering at the sketch. "Doesn't that make her our ally? For when the babe comes, she can lead his Way, draw followers to his glory—"

"There will be but one Highest of Kil," Yioth said. "Me. When he comes of age, Kil will destroy this world and release us so we can return to the demaynic realms. Have you not been listening? There is no need for a Way of Kil or human followers." She moved to stand close to her sister, who had always resented being a hand shorter. Now Yioth emphasized the difference, wrapping her wings around Eckso and drawing her even closer.

Eckso threw up panicky hands and swallowed hard. A strange buzzing came from her and Yiothizandra knew she was forming mercusine bolts of her own. She was about to dymense.

"Klayne, stop my sister from leaving until I dismiss her."

Klayne raised a hand and more resonances passed through Yiothizandra. She didn't know what either of them had done, but Eckso's building feat fell silent. Her face transformed, going from frightened noblewoman to imperious and outraged dragnithan. This was Yiothizandra's sister in her true form. Yioth released her.

Eckso spun on Klayne. "If you dare to bleed my feat again, you'll find Loveheart in your chest." She pulled a slender blade from her sleeve. The hilt was ivory, the steel a five-inch piercing design, a round spike tapered to a point. A rondel dagger, perfect for dark-alley kidney stabs and bedchamber heart-thrusts.

Klayne raised an eyebrow and clucked his tongue. "A shadline are you? You disappoint me."

Eckso sheathed the blade as quickly as she had drawn it, but the look of warning did not leave her face.

Yiothizandra took a subtle step backward. She was wary of shadline weapons. Her own sword had come with her from the demaynic realms. It had its own powers and its own needs, but these elnisian blades were tricky. "Possessing such a weapon does not make one a shadline," Yioth said softly. "Not unless you've spoken the oath. Have you?"

Eckso lifted her chin and attempted to look down her nose at Yiothizandra. It made her look like a petulant child. "I do not have to tell you anything. But if I had spoken the oath, what of it? Such vows aren't binding on our kind. If anyone should know that, it would be you, sister."

Yioth had spoken many vows during her imprisonment in this world. She said whatever was expedient. But such vows were water in a river to her. They had no form, and no power to bind her. Night protected her from men's silly notions of honor. Night allowed only for one loyalty, to itself. She wasn't so sure about Eckso. Yioth would have to take measures to ensure her sister's loyalty.

"This is quite convenient," Klayne said to Eckso.

"What is?"

"That you are a shadline. Surely you mean to attend the Armory, no?"

Yiothizandra's wings unfurled. "What is this about an Armory? The Dirth convenes?"

Klayne relaxed and crossed his arms across his chest again. He had shaken off his anger and fear and again looked quite pleased with himself. "They convene at the Hackwatch above Tearling. I have two shadline friends who are attending."

"Are they loyal to Night?" Yioth asked.

"They are loyal to me." He chuckled softly. "Though I find their oath to the order quite diverting. I've gone on some of their adventures, just to see them suffer through their wanderings. Mack'Ti is from Slirya. His sword is a hungry one, but he's mastered it. For now. He's a gallant man unless he drinks. And then he's ravenous for certain pleasures that the Way of Til frowns upon. The other young man, Cinnon, came into his weapon when he was only three years old. A great wooden club called Bash. He's thin as a rail, eats like a starving dog, but can't seem to put on enough flesh to sustain himself. It's the club. It gives him immense strength despite his puny stature. But if it's not strapped to his person, he's as weak as a baby dove."

"What rewards did you promise?"

"What all such men want. Wine. Wealth. Women. These two will remain on the periphery of the Armory, hardly noticed. That's what the order does when weapons settle for unimpressive wielders. But in Stallid they live like princes, and the force of destiny be damned."

"Oathbreakers cannot be trusted," Yioth said.

"But they can be used."

Yioth turned her eyes to her sister. "You will attend this Armory. I want to know all that is said. I want to know who was there. Klayne, you will turn your shadlines over to Eckso's command."

Eckso threw her hands up. "I was already planning to go when you summoned me. We could have saved a lot of bother if you would've left me alone. But I'll never trust those under his sway."

"Nevertheless. You will use them, perhaps to get close to our little cousin, who will certainly be there. She never could keep her nose out of everyone else's affairs."

"We never shared the same animosity that you and she did. I could ask her directly what she plans."

"She knows you are closer to Night than to Day. She will not trust you. She will poison the others against you. No. You must go disguised."

"That is the first sensible thing you've said," Eckso grumbled. "I had intended to wear a hooded cloak. None in Trine know I'm a shadline, and I would keep it that way. It isn't seemly for a lady."

"A hooded cloak?" Klayne said, choking. "That wouldn't look suspicious at all, you ridiculous twit! But allow me to help. Would you like to be a woman or a man?"

Eckso stomped her foot, face going red. "I don't trust you. You're just as likely to turn me into a mule, or a hound."

Klayne put a hand on his chest and mocked a wounded tone, "Me? I can't believe you'd even suggest such a thing."

Yioth gave her wings a flap and called heat to her eyes. Klayne might be able to resist her dragonfire, for a little while. But Eckso was not so powerful, and she well knew the pain of such flame. Seeing this, her sister relented. "Leave me as I am, but for my face. But keep me beautiful."

The mercus resonance grew again in Klayne, and he flourished a hand across Eckso's face. She transformed totally, her nose elongating, her mouth narrowing. Her eyes went dark, and her hair reddened. Not beautiful at all, which Yioth thought rather more fitting.

"Ell will feel this mercus glamour," Eckso said, a note of victory in her voice.

"She will not," Klayne said. "You can sense it because you are inside of it. But no one on the outside will notice it, unless they try to heal you. And of course you must remain quelled until you get into the Hackwatch. I assume you have an artifact or two that can achieve that?"

Eckso's anger flared again. "How dare you! I've been able to mask since I was—"

"Enough!" Yioth said, stamping her foot and cuffing her sister upside the head with the tip of her wing. "Go to the Armory. Learn the shadlines' plans. And when I summon you next time, be swift."

Eckso growled, but said nothing else. Yioth was happy to have awakened the dragnithan rage within her sister. Eckso needed that reminder. She had lived too long as a human woman, had adopted too much of their lazy weakness. "Go."

Eckso dymensed, leaving behind a thick cloud of mercus green out of spite.

Klayne waved his hand in front of his face and coughed. "So rude. Why do you tolerate it?"

"Does the carpenter throw away his saw because it is dull? No. He sharpens it. And then he uses it. And if it should buck occasionally, that is its nature. And now I will deploy you. First, bring me Eckso's children."

Klayne clucked again, lips going pale. "I see. Regrettable. But I see."

"After that you will go to Tordain. The Autarch has found the Motherlight. You will take it from her."

He smiled, genuinely now. "This might be truly interesting. And in truth I do itch to leave this world."

He made an unnecessary flourish with his arms and dymensed, leaving behind just the slightest wisp of dymension smoke.

15
___

STRIKING YOUR FACE

The scholars did not pay Kila much attention as she and Nax explored the narrow halls of the Hackwatch. Most of the space was given to tidy combination offices and bedrooms, where men of scholarly bent studied and thought deep thoughts. There was a vacant look in their faces as she encountered them in the corridors, as if they were not truly aware of their surroundings. That did not stop the hunger from coming over their eyes when she passed. None spoke, for they had vowed themselves into silence.

She puzzled over the relationship between the Iron Scholars and the shadline. It seemed both groups sought to know the future in one way or another. One by studying the heavens and reading the portents there, the other by listening to their instincts and the subtle pull and push of their own desires and aversions.

It all seemed silly to her. The mere fact that these people came to the Hackwatch on purpose—and *lived* here—spoke to their idiocy. Ell had told her the scholars chose it because it had been abandoned and that it offered clear views of the night sky. Their weapons training was a bit of an afterthought, a tradition more than a practice.

Had it not been for the Revulsion, the Hackwatch would have been rather impressive. For it was a small town unto itself, though most of the structures within the walls lay empty. What drew Kila now was an enormous dome occupying the central area of the stronghold. The ceiling was painted to match the stars that supposedly stood directly overhead. She had stood beneath it earlier, marveling to see the fresco slowly moving. Stars rising in the east and setting in the west.

The Revulsion didn't retreat as Kila passed into the dome, but the weight of it lessened a bit. A quick reach for the mercus met with black sludge. Shivering and rubbing her arms, she crossed the mosaic floor. Scenes of elnisian life covered the expanse, including a central red dragon, nostrils smoking. But the beast did not scorch the First Race warrior standing before it. Instead, it seemed to bow to a central figure, a woman with scarlet hair . . . and a cat on her shoulder.

D'ya see that, Naxie? Who is it?

Nax climbed onto Kila's shoulder to get a better vantage. She looked at the mosaic cat, nose twitching and tail flicking. A sense of unease came through the bond. *I don't know. It looks like a cat.*

It does. Flaumishtak and Ell call you a felnithel.

Felnithel . . . that has a feeling. Nax didn't know the word for the feeling so she sent a barrage of sensation to Kila. Caught off guard, Kila swayed where she stood. It was as disconcerting as the catsight, except this came as sound mostly, as hundreds of simultaneous echoes. Voices in strange tongues, some guttural, some songlike, some distinctly meows. There also came a rising drone, like a deep note on a nickleharpa struck again and again. Nax sent all this, louder and louder into Kila's mind. "Nax! Enough!"

Her cry resounded in the dome, and a scholar passing through glared at her. She ducked her head and waited for him to leave. Nax had stopped sending the resonances, but they continued to ring in her ears.

That hurt, she sent to Nax.

I didn't mean for it to hurt you. I forget sometimes.

Forget what?

That you feel only a small part of the world.

Critt Sanglo lay in state under the dome. He was surrounded by braziers, a thread of gold blanket covering him, a thin veil over his face. His shadline maul lay atop him. He had never mentioned owning it in all the years she'd known him.

Kila had fetched two copper plugs from her backpack to place over his eyes. Cheapsgate tradition. In Gristenside they used skillets. The payoff to the undertaker. It was fitting to give him a good Cheapsgate send off. He would have laughed to see it, barrel chest pumping as he bellowed out mirthful barks.

"The maul is called Shatter. It is legendary."

The voice brought her around. The fourteen-year-old girl she'd seen in Shad Ault's gang earlier walked toward her. The mop of red hair had not seen a comb in an age. Her eyes were dead-cold. She wore a short sword on her hip, though she had dispensed with the armor.

The girl continued, "You've heard of Erig, I'm sure."

"Jil never shuts up about him." Erig had been one of the original Seven Shadline Knights.

The girl didn't laugh. She held Kila's gaze, almost challenging. That wasn't how one survived long in Cheapsgate. And yet Kila felt certain this girl could hold her own against most she'd encounter in the stinky slums.

"You knew Critt Sanglo?" the girl asked.

"I did. He was very kind to me."

"I wonder why."

Kila wasn't sure if it was meant as an insult or not. The girl had a queer manner about her. It reminded her of Dox Viller's long-dead son, Pons. That boy had never been able to read people. He always stood too close, or asked impolite questions. It had gotten him killed.

"May I touch the cat?"

Nax was still perched on Kila's shoulder. She complained the floors here were too cold to walk on. But Kila felt the tension in the cat. Nax did not like it here, even though nobody seemed to harbor animosity toward her kind.

"It's up to Nax. I'll ask."

That got the girl's eyes to widen a bit.

Nax, can this girl touch you?

Nax inspected the girl with squinty lack of interest. *Are her hands clean?*

They appeared so to Kila, maybe a bit of black under the fingernails. That was a good sign as far as Kila was concerned.

I will allow it, Nax declared.

Kila encouraged the girl to pet Nax. "Gently, now. She's not a hound you can roughhouse with."

"I like hounds. They understand me. People do not understand me." She stroked Nax's fur, down to the tail. So gently. "This animal is soft."

Again, Kila could not tell if that last bit was meant to be a compliment or a criticism. Her tone was so flat.

"What is your name?" Kila asked.

"Aggy. That's all I know." She continued to pet Nax, who decided she rather liked the attention. "Jil says you are not very skilled with your blade."

"Do you think Jil a good judge of such things?"

"One of the best. She will be a Cloak one day. So will I. She said I was good. Can I see Fate Breaker?"

Kila pulled her weapon and held it for the girl to inspect. "I don't hand it to people, so don't ask."

The girl blinked, but did not appear to be offended. "I'm disappointed, but I understand you. Many get angry with me because I do not let them hold Swife." She drew her own blade and held it so Kila could see it.

"That's—that's a beautiful sword. How did you get her?"

Aggy froze for a moment. "How do you know Swife is a she?"

"Just a guess."

"She has never spoken to me. Has Fate Breaker said anything to you?"

"No. He's quiet as Kil's Cathedral on Tilsday."

Aggy laughed, a sudden, sharp chirp. "I think quiet blades are the best kind. Some shadlines have to argue with their weapons. Jil does. It wants to kill merculyns. All of them."

That explained a lot. "My friend Quinn has that problem. Her dagger wants to fight all the time."

"I do too, but I don't anymore. I'm a shadline. I don't give in to such nonsense." She sounded like she was repeating something that had been pounded into her head. A dangerous girl indeed. Kila decided she liked Aggy.

"Jil cheats in training," Kila said. "She uses her longsword while I have this."

"Your enemies will cheat, too."

Such a simple statement. And true enough. A sudden thought came to Kila. "Would you like to practice with me? I feel like a caged animal in this place."

"I will train you. You should put that cat aside. I do not want to hurt her."

Nax moved to a bench at the edge of the dome's open space. She had perked up now that violence was in the offing.

With Critt's body as backdrop, the pair faced off. But to Kila's surprise, Aggy removed her belt and scabbard and set her weapon aside. "First learn to use your hands and feet. These are the first principles of combat. All else is derived from this mastery."

In truth, Kila was happy not to have a shadline facing her with a sword. She unbuckled her thigh sheath and set her weapon on Critt. He wouldn't mind.

The girl fell into a ready stance and Kila saw instantly something she recognized. "You're Alnassi, aren't you?"

For answer, the girl came at her in a flurry of hands and feet. Her blows struck Kila's stomach, thighs, shoulders. Hard enough to jostle Kila, but not so hard as to bruise.

"You have met an Alnassi lay-esh before?"

"Yes. But her Ennish was a bit hard to understand." Kila struck, trying to trip Aggy with a surprise swing of her foot. She met air and was rewarded with a slap upside the head as the girl skirted by her. Two blows in the kidneys finished the counter and then the girl was well out of range.

"You are very unskilled," Aggy said. "I was to be a lay-esh, but then Swife came to me. I'm surprised you survived your previous encounter with a lay-esh."

"To be fair, Yiqa was not trying to kill me. Just injure me a little."

Aggy straightened and cocked her head to one side. "You fought Yiqa?" A true look of awe filled her face, the strongest expression the girl had shown yet.

"You know her?" Kila asked.

"Every Alnassi knows of her. Now, prevent me from striking your face." The girl launched herself at Kila, hands driving in blurry jabs and swings.

Kila deflected the first three, stumbling backwards under the speed of the assault. Aggy was smaller, lighter, but her blows carried tremendous force. The fourth, fifth, and sixth blows struck home: cheek, jaw, temple, hard enough to jar Kila's vision.

Kila did not fear pain, but her pride stoked hot under the younger girl's assault. Backpedaling, Kila gathered her focus and began to circle, hands out as Yiqa had taught her long ago. The first and only lesson she'd received had been atop the Warren. Yiqa had left Kila bruised and exhausted. It hadn't been enough training to make the skills stick.

Instead of waiting for the next attack, Kila lunged. She attempted a strike, which Aggy turned aside—with her foot, no less—before swatting Kila upside the head again. "You are as unskilled as a babe. You are fortunate that nobody but the cat is here to witness this."

Dropping her mask and spanking the girl with mercus was out of the question. Nevertheless, had the Revulsion not been lurking, Kila might have figured a way to offer some slight retribution. Instead, she straightened and bowed. "I'm impressed. I want you to continue to teach me."

"Stand as I stand," the girl commanded. Kila obeyed, one foot back, hands up. "Strike my hand." Aggy held up her hand, palm out.

Kila punched at it, but did not connect. "Too slow. You are so slow a turtle would yawn before having to move out of the way. Collect power from the floor, rotate your hips. No swinging of the arm and elbow. Thrust out. A snake striking!" she demonstrated. Kila mimicked.

A half hour passed, marked by deep, lethargic bells somewhere outside in the dome. Another half hour passed. Kila's clothes were drenched, her raven-sleeved jacket long since flopped over Critt's legs. Nax curled up and went to sleep. Lop wandered in and joined her.

Over the course of two hours the stars on the ceiling moved overhead, a moon had risen, and a few scholars and shadlines had come in to watch Kila's lesson.

It was hunger that finally defeated Kila, and she collapsed, cross legged on the floor. Aggy joined her, brow glistening and wild curls darkened by sweat. "You are a good pupil," she said. "We shall train again in the morning?"

"Yes. Unless the Armory starts."

The girl stood, offered a curt bow, then departed, sword in hand. Nax wandered over and sniffed at Kila's face.

One of the shadlines who had been watching was Shad Lykea. He had shed his armor and was dressed in a cream-colored tunic, unlaced collar filled with wiry chest hair. "Aggy likes you. That is a remarkable achievement."

Kila rubbed her jaw. "Are the bruises bad?"

He eyed her face. "Not yet. May I ask you a question?"

"Yes. I can fly."

He smiled. It was a lopsided smile. Charming and open. He had one prominent tooth on that side. It didn't look too bad. She might have developed a heart-fix on such a man in the past. But now that she was at least sixteen years old, she wasn't so susceptible to such things. Besides, this man was over thirty, middle years for most men. Still, he had a nice face. "I wasn't going to ask you that. I want to ask about your father."

"Wenton Sigh. He was a locksmith, hunter, and an exceptional thief. He died when I was twelve or so."

"And Cayne was his?"

"Yes."

"Where did he come by it?"

Kila knew the answer now. She hadn't known for most of her life. But then Annisforl had unlocked her memory. Her mother was the capricious water spirit Semūin, who had given her father Cayne for some purpose Kila didn't know. She told Lykea none of this. "I suppose he stole it, or bought it, or maybe he won it at dice." That last was unlikely. Father never gambled.

Lykea's gaze turned up to Critt. But he wasn't looking at the man, but at the blade she'd put atop him. Kila said, "I won't let you hold it."

"May I see it?"

Grunting, she got up and collected the blade. She drew it and held it for the shadline to inspect. Two other shadlines hurried over to see. An odd-looking woman with a sharp nose and pointed chin. She wore a gown, out of place among all these warriors. The other was Cloak Einlin.

She was not happy to see him. They'd left the silly fate-hand meeting without a satisfactory decision, which he never seemed to stop talking about. But after Critt had died, she hadn't been willing to have them all in Quinn's room, filling it with their tense silence. And what sort of decision could there be if the question was so vague? It's about Kila, Fallo had said. She would decide about herself, and Kil take 'em all if they thought they could control her.

Lykea introduced the two shadlines. "Highest Sigh, you know Cloak Einlin. And this is Shadline Winnea Frost from Trine. She swore her oaths only recently. To Cloak Wright, correct?"

Winnea curtsied. "Yes. May Lumne hold him close for all eternity." Her gown was very fine, cinched under her ample bosom.

Lykea and the Cloak both nodded solemnly. "A powerful man, he was," the Cloak said. His eyes were nearly golden in the brazier light, which gave him a particularly wolfish look. "I shall miss him."

"That blade is as black as midnight," the woman observed. "May I?"

Lykea caught her reaching hand. "One does not grab at another shadline's weapon. It is a pity Cloak Wright died before you could learn these things."

"Oh, I'm sorry!" She pressed her hand to her throat, as if clutching a necklace that wasn't there. "I feel a twit now. Forgive me, Highest." She ducked her head and made a curtsy that would have been expected in Gristenside.

Shad Lykea's voice was a full baritone, resonant in the

echoey dome. "I have seen a hardblade of similar make once before, but it wasn't so fine. Was the bonding ecstatic?"

"Ecstatic?" Kila didn't recall her father ever using that word, and knew a lot of odd ones. "I don't think so."

"Oh, you'd know," he said, teeth flashing. "When it bonded to you, did you fall into convulsions, see visions, raise from the ground? Was it delightful? Painful? Does it demand you not allow others to touch it?"

"No. My brother handed it to me. It's a knife. I don't let others touch it anymore, but that's my decision, not Cayne's."

Three reactions, all different. Lykea laughed. Winnea snorted. The Cloak frowned.

"Fate Breaker," Lykea said in wonder. "I never thought I'd see it. Cloak Einlin, do you remember our arguments about this blade? I swore to you that it was pure fantasy. That no such weapon existed."

"And I held a different view. I do not know if I am pleased to have my belief vindicated. I am ashamed I did not recognize it when I first saw it." He regarded Kila with appraising eyes, but they did not betray what his assessment was. "And yet even Critt Sanglo did not recognized it, and he knew both the girl and the blade much longer than I did."

"Don't blame Critt," Kila said, rising to her old friend's defense. "He was just a tavernkeep."

"Just a tavernkeep?" Lykea said. "Ha! Critt could have been a Shadline Knight. But he said the force of destiny told him to abide Starside. He never budged. That maul there—" He pointed to Critt's weapon. "It does not choose unworthy wielders."

"I don't doubt it," Kila said. "Critt was a fine man, one of the few I could trust."

"And poisoned like a rat!" the woman said. "A travesty. And that girl was your friend too. I hope Lumne doesn't pull her all the way under." For the first time since being introduced, Kila noted that there was no weapon on the woman. Strange. She had never seen a shadline without one.

Kila sheathed her blade and buckled the scabbard to her thigh. Both men observed this with different degrees of incredulity. The Cloak shook his head. "That is not a wise position to secure your weapon. Speak to Crafter Exalin about a proper belt. And requisition new leathers for that hilt. There is an art to wrapping it properly, so ask for instruction."

She would wear her weapon how she liked. "Who's this Exalin?"

"She's the commander of smithies and accoutrements for the order. She will provide you whatever you need, from mundane weapons and armor, to clothing and horses. You will need her instruction if you are to have access to resupply stores in your travels."

She didn't know what travels lay ahead, but having a source for supplies sounded mighty intriguing. There was a time not too long ago when she would have taken everything in sight and tried to sell it. "Where is she?"

"I'll take you to her," Winnea chirped. "I was just there. Come."

Kila nodded a parting to the two men. Shad Lykea offered a slight bow. Cloak Einlin said, "Listen and obey."

She started to follow Winnea out of the dome, but turned to call to Lykea. "Do you know when the Armory will begin?"

"An hour, a day, a month. It will be called when it must be called. In the meantime, continue your training with Aggy. Something tells me you will need it."

Exiting the dome, she said to Winnea, "What I need is food."

"I don't have any of that."

"Can I get something on the way?"

"The dining hall is not on the way. Come. We'll dine after we visit Exalin."

16

A RONDEL DAGGER

Winnea didn't say much as she guided Kila through the Hackwatch's winding corridors. Kila was content with the quiet. She was exhausted from her training and so hungry she could eat a chickenbug, legs still wriggling.

They came out into a courtyard. The clank of a smithy resounded from the walls and so did the grunts of two men practicing with wooden swords. More shadline watched from the periphery. Winnea skirted around them, eyeing one of the bare-chested swordsmen with prudish distaste before waving to a man so thin his collarbones protruded. He leaned on a crude wooden club and munched on a strip of jerky.

Upon seeing her, he straightened and made an awkward half bow. The man next to him did the same. The second man was shorter and stouter, his long loose shirt draped to his knees. His black beard was oiled so thickly that it gleamed like lacquered ceramic. Winnea introduced them. "Shadlines, this is Highest of Kil, Kila Sigh. Highest, these are my friends, Mack'Ti and Cinnon."

"A pleasure," said Mack'Ti, bowing with extraordinary grace. Skinny Cinnon swallowed his bite of jerky and offered another awkward bow.

"I'm taking her to see Crafter Exalin. After, we are going to the dining hall."

Cinnon perked up at hearing this. "I'll join ya."

Mack'Ti shrugged. "If it is not too much of an imposition, I too would take great pleasure in joining you in your repast."

They left the men and continued to what had been a horse stables, but was now a fully operational smithy. Several men labored there, working a forge and hammering upon anvils. Kila had never seen a woman blacksmith before. Crafter Exalin smiled patiently as Kila got control of her surprise. The woman was short, thickly built, and wore a leather apron. When they arrived she had been measuring out strips of leather and cutting them with heavy shears. She said nothing except to bow slightly.

The Crafter's eyes went to Cayne. She made a motion to the table. Kila put the blade on the table, but kept her hand on the hilt. Exalin took no offense. She stepped away and found a similarly sized blade and began to show Kila how to remove the leather from the hilt, then how to wrap it. Still saying nothing, she placed out an array of choices, indicating that Kila should press the leather into her palm to see if she liked its feel. All of this was done without words, and it finally occurred to Kila that the woman could neither hear nor speak.

Winnea wandered during this, frowning at a blacksmith who had shed his sweaty shirt and dumped a bucket of water over his head and torso. When Kila had selected the leather she liked—a deep brown doe hide stained an oxblood red— Exalin shooed them from the smithy.

"I like that woman," Kila said to Winnea as they headed toward the dining hall. "She didn't bow and scrape at me, didn't lecture me, and didn't call me Highest. Not that she could."

"What? Do you not like your title?" Winnea thought this most shocking, if her collar clutching was any indication. "Kil is powerful, god of death and war and fire. To be chosen by him . . . Do you mind my asking, how *were* you chosen? I thought the Triumvirate wished Kil banished from the minds of man."

"The Triumvirate had nothing to do with it." Kila left it at that. She didn't know this woman, and given her high class dress, couldn't completely trust her.

The dining hall was sparsely populated when they arrived. Winnea took her to the kitchens where one of the junior scholars showed her a slip of paper with what was warm and what was cooking. Kila asked for a platter, but Winnea let slip that she was Highest of Kila and the young man nervously forked and spooned an enormous pile of everything onto the platter for her.

Finally seated before a sorry array of charred ham, charred potato, and something that had once been green, but was now a grayish brown, Kila bent to her meal with a will. It was very overcooked, but a life of eating refuse and stolen bread had gifted her with a very tolerant palate.

The dining hall here at the Hackwatch reminded her of the same at the Baths of Ori in Starside. A wide space, high-ceilinged, with trestle tables enough to seat a hundred. Fires burned in three hearths, but the flames were banked low, barely softening the damp chill.

Shivering, she nibbled on a gristly mouthful. Under the

ham she discovered some beans. They left a weird greasy smear on her platter and smelled of charcoal. She didn't get much down before her belly began to rebel. She wondered if the Revulsion had infiltrated the kitchens.

No surprise if it had. The huge, rambling castle and surrounding compound smelled old, musty, vaguely rotten. Everything was damp. Even now, the walls glistened here and there where moisture seeped through. "Bleeding walls," the shadline called it. At least the air moved in the dining hall. The corridors were little rat burrows, dark for long stretches. Stuffy and silent.

That heavy, expectant silence filled every corner of the Hackwatch.

Except for at this table. Winnea chattered about gossipy things, speculating on which Shad was married and which was available. Soon Cinnon arrived, bearing a platter so overloaded with meat and potatoes that stray bits hung over the edges. Bean grease dripped down his arm. His club, called Bash according to Winnea, was now strapped to his back in a fashion that looked very inconvenient, uncomfortable, and impractical.

"Can't be parted from her," Cinnon explained about the club, "or I'll fall over. Gives me strength, but I can't eat enough to keep up with her."

He tucked in, eschewing fork and knife and instead grabbing up handfuls and shoving them into his mouth. His face was so emaciated that his jawbones protruded. Kila couldn't help but marvel as he chewed the enormous wads he'd shoved in. Not that he did much chewing before shooting his head forward and swallowing like a sea bird slipping down a large fish.

Mack'Ti brought only a mug of beer. Upon seeing this, Cinnon swore around his next mouthful. Jerking his head forward, he swallowed. "Keep yer blades handy tonight," he said. "Mack'Ti's drinkin' again."

"Now, now, dear friend. This mug is my first of the day. And last. If you think I'll risk reprisals among this crowd you're a bigger fool than I. Too many sharp blades about."

Seeing Kila's perplexed look, Cinnon explained. "Ol' Mack is a gennleman, most times. But in his beers he's a right raving hound. Can't control hisself, and his throbbin' needs take him over."

"If he comes to my cot," Kila said, "he's going to become a drift of ash in the corner." Only after she'd said it did she realize the emptiness of the threat. Without the mercus, she would be left to rely on Cayne. That had never been a fear when robbing marks in Starside, but if a trained shadline attacked her . . .

She pushed her platter away. Cinnon eyed it questioningly, so she shoved it to him.

Mack'Ti had stopped mid-swig, eyes wide. He put the beer down and pushed it aside. Cinnon snortled, loosing flecks of food across the table. Winnea's eyes shot daggers at him. "That's no way to conduct yourself in front of the Highest!"

"Or anyone else, for that matter," Kila said. "I'll be going now."

Winnea jumped up to walk with her. "I apologize for those buffoons. They don't have any manners. Mind if I ask you a question?"

Kila didn't tell her not to, so Winnea asked, "Who commands the Way of Kila? What I mean is, have you named Highests of Kila in all the cities? Or do they draw lots, cast ballots, or simply fight it out? And how does it rank compared to the Way of Kil? I confess, with all those followers of yours, I don't know what to think!"

That brought Kila to a dead stop. "Where have you seen those Way of Kila fools?"

Winnea blinked several times, as if the question violated several assumptions she had not questioned until that very moment. "Fools? You mean your followers?"

Followers. That was the last thing Kila needed. She'd thought the ones she'd seen near Tearling were a fringe band of trezz-fiends, a silly offshoot of the squatters in the Blasted Quarter. "Are there any in Trine?"

"Trine, Jallisea, Tordain, Sorgan, Wantin. I suspect all the way to Slirya by now. So you don't control them?"

"They wouldn't exist if I controlled them. Kil's guts in a bucket, I could throttle the anvil-brained fool who printed up those handbills."

The Way of Kila, she groused to herself, cheeks flushing. If Father had heard of such a thing—or Wen—they'd never let her hear the end of it.

"Huh. I thought perhaps Ell LiMinluit had counseled you to form a new Way, to separate yourself from the Despised God." She indicated Kila's garnet ring and whispered. "I'll confess I never understood why everyone says Kil is so bad. Death is part of life, no?

"And hatred and pestilence, too, but those aren't good things. Why would I want to head a Way devoted to evil? I may be a thief, but I tried never to steal anything a mark couldn't spare."

Winnea put a hand on Kila's shoulder and urged her to continue walking. Kila had been heading to Quinn's room, but she wasn't about to bring this stranger there. She turned to go outside where the air was fresher. There she'd make an excuse and leave Winnea behind.

"I'd never heard of Fate Breaker until today," Winnea said as they passed into misty gray daylight. She could change subjects as quick as Quinn could change clothes. "What does it do? Oh! I'm not supposed ask that. Etiquette has never been my strength. My mouth gets ahead of my brain sometimes. I'm sorry. Here's my shadline weapon." With a swift jerk, she pulled a slender dagger from her sleeve. The steel was rounded, a spike with a hilt. "Loveheart is a rondel dagger. The only shadline of its type." She made a stabby motion with it, twisting up her lips in disgust. "I can't imagine poking some-body with it. La! I don't know what Loveheart sees in me. But she was quite insistent I be the one to bear her."

As they walked along a quiet path, Kila sought some excuse to shed the woman. She was friendly enough, but there was something strange about her. Kila didn't know if it was just her obvious posh upbringing, so poorly masked by her bubbly baseness, or something else. She wished Nax was near. Cats had a good sense of people.

Pol smiled then, for Cinnon appeared and took Winnea away. Apparently, Mack'Ti's beer hadn't been his last of the day. There was talk of mops, angry scholars, and Shad Ault threatening to make a public example of him.

Finally alone, Kila headed back toward Quinn's room. She couldn't do anything about the Way of Kila right now. Hope-fully those woolheads would just get bored and go home. Otherwise she would have to start paying them visits, and they would not like Kila at all after such an encounter. She would make sure of it.

17

RAGGED CHASM SPLIT

enley Mast stepped from the carriage outside the Baths of Ori, boots squelching into the winter slush. A fresh snowfall had descended overnight and covered the dome and tower like sweetbake frosting.

He groaned and put his hands on his lower back to help him straighten. Sleeping in the Warren hadn't been the smartest idea.

"Never seen so much snow, sir," the driver said. "Be long?"

"I don't know. Best return them to the barn." He paid the driver, then proceeded up the steps to the Dome of the Gentle Goddess. It was indeed warm inside, thanks in part to the many braziers surrounding the three pools. But also due to the pools themselves, which lifted tendrils of steam into the air.

A Sensual with very dark skin waited at a desk just inside. The Way of Ori received citizens here at all hours, especially the elderly seeking succor for their aches and pains in the pools. It was more unusual for a young man like Henley, who had just recently turned sixteen. "Ori's Blessings," the woman said. "I'm Sens Taht."

"I'm Henley Mast. I need to see Finta Sahng. She knows me."

"Finta is not of the Way."

"I know that. I also know that she's the Voluptuary's sister and that she has not likely left her bedside since events in Dunne Medow Plaza. I have important things to discuss with Finta. Urgent for the realm."

This did not impress the Sensual in the slightest. She narrowed her gaze, scrutinizing him down to the bone.

Huff, please find Finta, he sent.

The cat had slunk into the dome behind him and kept to the shadows. Henley had worried this would happen, that he'd be stalled at the door. He'd been a guest here once before, under the protection of the Voluptuary. That meant all the Sensuals knew of his friendship with Kila. And she was not well thought of among the Way these days.

Huff sent back a frison of irritation, since he was already sneaking off. He knew where the Voluptuary's rooms were, having explored the Baths from kitchens to belfry.

"That's as may be," Sens Taht said icily. "It is not our practice to admit shady interlopers into the Voluptuary's presence." Henley had met many folk from the island nation of Iops. They had been uniformly friendly, even jolly. Of course, most he'd met had been sailors on his short stint aboard one of his father's merchant ships. But he'd never encountered one so irritable as this woman.

"I stayed here for days and days. I've met you before."

"And?" She arched an eyebrow.

He sighed and shook his head in mock defeat. "I won't trouble you further, Sensual Taht. May I enjoy the warmth of the Dome for a while before I leave?"

She couldn't refuse him that. Nobody was refused admission to the Dome unless they were causing a disturbance to the quietude of the place. Even Cheapsgaters were welcome here. Unfortunately for them, they were not allowed in Gristenside, which made accessing the Baths rather a challenge.

He ambled around the periphery of the dome, mostly to irritate the watchful Sensual. He used the opportunity to consider his meeting with Quiv earlier in the morning. The man had been perplexed, vexed, and anxious to learn that Yples was no longer in Starside. "You might check the Derslin Wheel," Henley had said as a parting thought. "It's the only place I think would escape my notice." He didn't think Yples had gone there. Even if his Donse Master chaperone had been willing to go, the man would certainly not have the skill to open a portal there. Henley tended to agree with Highest Quiv. Yples had either been abducted, or he'd schemed with someone who could get him out of Starside quickly.

The door is closed, Huff sent, his presence deep in the complex of wards and halls.

Show me.

The catsight came instantly. Henley was ready for the disorientation of having his vision filled with what Huff was seeing, and from Huff's perspective close to the floor. It no longer made him want to sick up his last meal, but he did have to reach for a column to steady himself.

Look the other way, he sent.

Huff's vision spun to look down the hall leading to the Voluptuary's quarters. Wide, lushly carpeted, with side tables laden with bronze statuary—mostly of the goddess Ori in her various poses of allure, anger, haughtiness, adoration, and so on. Close by he spotted something that would serve his needs.

A service cart stood on the other side of the hall. A few goblets and plates were on it. Food brought for the Voluptuary, Finta, and whoever was on nursing duty.

Food! Huff sent.

You can eat what you find, but first knock those goblets off the cart. That'll bring someone, then you can slip through the door when they—

Huff jumped and Henley reeled in response. Huff tiptoed over empty platters and a silver bowl containing a heel of bread. Disappointment flowed through the bond. *They ate it all! Your kind is worse than hounds.*

Just knock the goblet off.

Huff swatted one and it tumbled off the cart. The catsight conveyed all the sounds Huff heard, as well as the smells. That bread would be very good, though Huff felt nothing but disdain for it.

Another! Henley sent.

Huff complied. *I'm good at this! I don't see why you get mad when I do this in other circumstances.*

The door to the Voluptuary's quarters opened. Huff darted from the cart and slipped between skirted legs. A surprised "eek" arose, then cut off.

"Huff, you lovely darling!" came a quavery voice. "It's you! Oh, come here you sweet little baby, let Finta scritch your wee little chin-chin."

Henley's vision blurred as Finta picked Huff up by the scruff and smothered him with squeezes and kisses. The distinct spicy smell of Finta Sahng came keenly through the bond.

Huff squirmed free and went back to the door. With tail

high he uttered a demanding meow. Finta cackled and followed.

Sens Taht glowered at Henley when Finta Sahng swept into the dome. The Iopsi woman clearly did not like either of them.

Finta took hold of Henley's shoulders and pecked his cheek. "My, my. You're looking right fine. And I hear you've become quite the merculyn."

Henley liked the ancient woman, but there was something stormy behind the cheery greeting. She was all in black. According to Kila the woman had worn mourning dress since her husband had died long ago. Her face was a mass of wrinkles, all bunched up around smiling eyes and lips. She was known to be a great healer, a master of weed and seed, concocting all manner of brews and tinctures to soothe whatever ailed those in her lower Terriside neighborhood.

But she was also Voluptuary Sinlop's sister.

"Is Kila well?" Finta asked, guiding Henley to a bench.

"Last I saw her. But she is not happy. I wonder if she'll ever get a chance to be so."

The smile firmed into something less cheery. "Her father was the same."

Henley called to Huff through the bond, a strange sense coming over him that they may need to leave in a hurry. Odd. There didn't seem to be any threat here except for the habitually displeased Sens Taht.

"Kila may have nearly killed my sister." Finta's voice was tight. "I know she did not mean to, but . . ."

"What is must not be denied," Henley finished. "That is why Sens Taht treats me like I'd just escaped the Westbunk."

Finta huffed. "That one would be better suited for Donse Master robes, if they took women into their order. What a sour apple. But yes. My sister was well respected here. But now the Sensuals smell a vacancy at the top, and they can't but yearn to take my sister's place." She leaned closer to Henley. "Word has come from the Garden. All followers of Ori are ordered to find and capture Kila. Have you noticed there are five Sensuals in the Dome with us now?"

Henley hadn't paid the others here much attention. But now he noticed the visitors had all dried off and departed, leaving only Sensuals and a few older novitiates. They were busy cleaning up towels or mopping splashes.

"They intend to trap me here, don't they?"

She nodded. "Fools. They think they can use you to lure Kila."

"Kila has gone to Tearling for a shadline Armory. They may have to wait a while. But since I'm staying, is there a place more comfortable for us to talk? I have some questions."

She leaned back, surprised. "You mean to let them capture you?"

"I doubt they could combine their powers enough to keep me from leaving if I desired to do so. But I'm happy to let them believe their plan is working if I can continue to speak with you."

Cackling, the woman led him deeper into the Bath's of Ori, finally coming to the Voluptuary's quarters. The cart and fallen goblet had been removed. "Would you like to see her?"

The Voluptuary's bedchamber was bright and quiet. Incense smoldered on the bedside table, sending blue snakes of smoke to the ceiling. The smell was thick and cloying. The woman Henley owed his life to lay on the bed, a thin sheet over her. A mask of mud covered her face and two strange flower blossoms rested on her eyelids. It reminded Henley of his mother's wake. He shivered.

"Is she quelled?" he asked. Merculyns were easy to recognize by the haze of their potential power, unless quelled or actively masked.

"No. Sens Renna tells me her power has fled. I'm no merculyn. Come. Let's have tea in the other room."

The tea was minty, which Henley did not like. He sipped at it anyway. Huff sat on Finta's lap and luxuriated in her gentle attention.

"How did word to capture Kila come from the Garden? Has a ship come?"

"Now that is curious," Finta said. "A Spinster arrived yesterday. She met with a few Sensuals, then left."

"Coin code," Henley said, nodding absently. "I'm not surprised that Coin Inlina and Voluptuary Minn are working together to catch Kila. They tried to promise-bind her before we left there."

Finta set her cup down. "But they failed."

"They failed. Voluptuary Minn wanted Kila to vow to use her power only for healing."

"By the Lightshades! That would be the ruin of us all. Kila must choose from within her own heart what course she will take. The force of destiny already herds her toward the culmination. How could those women be so stupid?"

"You didn't see what Kila did. What she nearly became when she faced Dunne Yples. I understand why they want her promise-bound. I disagree with them, but I understand it."

Finta sighed in relief then offered him a flat smile. "You are honest in your thinking, young man. But do not make the mistake of believing those who oppose you will be so fair minded. And if they used coin talkers to spread this message, then Kila must be wary wherever she goes. The Ways of Pol and Ori will not be her allies."

"Strange that you mention that. Highest Quiv helped us escape. I never thought I'd see the day when I trust a Donse Master more than I do a Sensual. Strange times."

"Strange. And fraught."

"I had hoped the Voluptuary was awake. I promised Highest Quiv I'd ask her a favor on his behalf. He would send a Reader to the library here to research elnisian magic."

"Elnisian? I would think his own libraries would have the most resources on that topic. Which they declared Wrong not that long ago."

A figure stepped from a corner. Henley spilled his tea as he leapt up, already dropping his mercusine mask.

"Hold, Henley," Finta said. "It is only Yiqa."

He had seen the Alnassi woman once before, in a dark alley when she had been beating Kila into submission. Hooded and veiled, she was a tense bundle of killing power. Her gray eyes stabbed at him, confronted him. She did not have the bearing of a friend. Huff sent cautious alertness through the bond, which help to slow his rapid heartbeat.

"Henley Masst. You vill commme vittt meee." She turned and strode from the room, heading back to the Voluptuary's bedchamber. "Heal herrr."

"I—I don't have Kila's skill."

"Heal herrr."

He looked to Finta for guidance. The ancient woman merely blinked.

Henley moved to the bedside and gathered his mercus. He was skilled with mind bolts, having learned them first hand from the Hargothe's intrusions. Taking Finta's silence for permission, he plunged into the Voluptuary's mind.

There was nothing there. A void. At the periphery, the energy of the body hummed. It kept the heart beating, the chest rising and falling. The absence of anything else chilled him. He wanted nothing more than to retreat. Kila had done this, not intending to. She had merely ripped the Hargothe's bond from the woman's mind. It should not have drained everything away. He had enough sensitivity to see the flow of blood through the body, saw how it permeated the brain. It still lived. But could it be restored to wakefulness?

The mind usually appeared to Henley as a landscape, as if he were a bird flying above a person's thoughts. There were clouds, seas, firm land. But here, darkness. He knew it was not the actual mind he saw, but a representation. His own imagination making sense of the incomprehensible.

Light. It was a thought in his mind, and then it was a lantern-beam in the darkness of the Voluptuary's. And there lay the terrain, clear, still, barren. But not without contour. The surface was not where the true mind existed. The Hargothe had always plunged deep, boring inward to find the fears and secrets he so desired. And deeper still lay the connection a merculyn had to the subtle world of the mercusine. That was where the Hargothe latched and suckled upon the flows meant for another.

Henley dove, more gently than his teacher. All was blackness, but not as still as the surface. Here the disconnected thoughts of a mind deeply asleep rose and fell on susurrating waves. She was alive. Perhaps deep in a dream she barely noticed.

He went deeper.

In the center of the Voluptuary's mind, a ragged chasm split what should have been whole. In the pit was a blackness so complete it made the surrounding lightlessness appear gray. The void-within-the-void pulled at Henley, bringing terror into his own mind. He knew with absolute certainty that to be sucked into that blackness would be to surrender himself to an eternity of hollow suffering. And that was where the Voluptuary was.

Her only hope for release was the death of her body. And even that would not guarantee escape. He recoiled from the horror and opened his eyes. "She is beyond my reach." Shivering he stepped away from the bed.

"There isss nnnoo hope?" Yiqa asked. The steeliness in her eyes did not soften with the words.

"I would never say that. But—"

"You withhold something," Finta said. "Speak it."

"I know of only one being who might have insights I do not."

Flaumishtak! Huff sent, hopping onto the Voluptuary's bed. *Yes! Yes! Yes!*

"There is no man in Starside more capable than me," Finta said. "And with Kila away, no woman."

"I do not speak of a man. Or woman."

Flaumishtak! Huff nosed Henley's hand to encourage a chin scratch. He complied.

Yiqa stepped over the unconscious Sensual. "Summonnn heemmm."

Though he was loath to do it, Henley obeyed. "Flaumish-tak! I know you're listening, you Kil-damned goat. Come here."

The beast appeared in his usual cloud of mercus green. Oly hissed at Yiqa and then leapt down to bat Huff's ear. Huff ignored this and meowed at his favorite yoznithan demayne. Flaumishtak bowed slightly to Huff and offered him a disgusting bit of meat from his pocket. Huff ran off with it, Oly chasing after.

"See?" Flaumishtak said, spreading his arms. "No circle needed to make me behave. All I require is respect."

Henley thought what kept him in line was the cats. He respected them, so likely spared their bonded humans out of kindness. Finta and Yiqa were in more danger, but since Huff liked both of them, Henley thought they were safe, too.

"The Voluptuary's mind is . . ."

"I've looked in there," the beast said, leaning over the woman. "Even awake I was never impressed with her. Did you know she once tried to use a light-searer on me?"

"A what?"

He put his huge paws close together. "A bright gem, about this big. Very dangerous. I believe you call it a bane eye. Very rude to wield one of those when a demayne is simply trying to fulfill a bargain."

"Can you bring her back or not?"

The beast's hair-smoke wafted up in wavy billows as the massive head tilted side to side. "Hmmm. Very dangerous. If you slip into that void, you become . . . elongated. Not pleasant. If I did draw her back, she would not be the same woman. Not at all. Madness would be the least of her ailments. But I can attempt it. For a price."

"And what is your price?" Finta asked, voice firm, head up. She did not appear even slightly afraid of the beast. "Mind you, I will grant you no kills."

Flaumishtak huffed and snorted. "I've had my fill of killing. This city bores me with its mundane villainy. And the most delicious ones are too important."

In his bargain with the Hargothe, Flaumishtak had gotten permission to commit many murders. Henley knew that the demayne had been seeking out the worst of the criminals in the city and slaying them, what he called "villainy." Not out of any sense of justice, but from a perverse sense of humor. Henley knew the creature's true reason for stopping its spree. The bargain had been struck with the Hargothe. That man was now dead, severing the permission from Flaumishtak.

The demayne made a transparent shrug of false disinterest. "I suppose there is one thing young Henley could assist me with. Tarek PiTorro has recently returned from a caravan expedition to the north. He claims to have news of Yiothizandra's plans, which he would like to share with Her Enlightened Majesty. Out of patriotism, you see."

"How do you know of Tarek PiTorro and his comings and goings?" Henley demanded, more suspicious than ever. Fallo had told him how his father, Tarek, had tried to have him killed, so that his younger brother Deni would be next in line.

"How does anyone know anything?" Flaumishtak asked, shrugging his huge shoulders. "One roams about and hears things here and there. And what harm is there in making the introduction? You can tell Her Enlightened exactly who recommended Tarek to her. That ought to put her guard up sufficiently to protect against any duplicity on my part."

"I'll take him to Marlow. He'll decide who gets an audience with Her Enlightened. I don't have that authority." And he didn't want it.

"I accept." The mercus rose around the beast in intricate whirls as he dove into what little remained of the Voluptuary's mind. His claws lowered and extended toward the woman's face, fingers waggling in a totally unnecessary display of mysterious magic. The Voluptuary responded to his movements with an arching back and a great, noisy inhalation. Her eyes popped wide and her head shook side to side.

Flaumishtak withdrew his hands and let the mercus go. Hair tendrils swirled up toward the ceiling and his flaming eyes were banked to near darkness. He opened his mouth then shut it again, leaning close to regard the woman's pale face. Finally, he straightened. "She's back, mostly. I caution you all. I sense a wrongness in her. I'm not sure what it is, for her mind thrust me out as soon as she returned to this world. But mark me on this, she will not be the same woman you knew. And her connection to the mercusine has been irreparably severed." He sounded as though he truly regretted that last bit. "Tarek is waiting for you outside the Baths, Henley."

Oly blurred into his arms and he dymensed away. Henley couldn't shake the impression that Flaumishtak was fleeing the place.

Finta and Yiqa had moved to examine the Voluptuary, who seemed to be struggling to wakefulness. Henley backed away, stomach souring. If Tarek had been waiting this whole time . . . But how could Flaumishtak have known a bargain was in the offing?

The Voluptuary sat up and screamed, frantically pushing at her coverings and flailing at Yiqa's attempts to calm her. A crack resounded in the room, Yiqa's hand connecting with the woman's face. She went still, blinking hard. "Yiqa? Finta?"

Henley started to back out of the room, but Finta held a finger up. "Stay, young man."

It took ten minutes and some special tea to calm the Voluptuary, but she eventually accepted that she was surrounded by friends. "The last thing I remember was standing on the execution platform in Dunne Medow Plaza. The prisoner had escaped. He had . . ."

"You were in the Hargothe's thrall, sister," Finta said softly. "Kila removed his evil bond from you, but your mind was lost. Just for a while."

"How long?"

"A month."

"A month? And yet I live. And that means the Hargothe did not prevail."

"He is dead, Voluptuary Sinlop," Henley said. "Killed by Kila Sigh."

The woman had no response to this. From the haggard look on her face she found little relief in the news. "And where is the girl now?"

"At a shadline gathering. In Tearling."

"The Dirth has called an Armory, eh? I'm surprised it took them this long. Well, that is good. Perhaps they can come out from behind their secretive curtain and help in the battle to come."

"What battle?" Henley asked, eyes narrowing. If the Voluptuary had been unconscious this whole time, then she could not know of the threat Yiothizandra posed.

The woman returned his look, eyes very clear. "I learned much where I was. The demaynic realms are in turmoil, alliances shatter and new ones form. The call of Night has gone out, and many seek passage into this world. It must be Kila who brings Kil forth, lest his essence be molded by Night."

Yiqa bent to the woman's ear. Henley's heightened senses did not pick up what was said due to the woman's accent.

"Truly?" the Voluptuary asked.

Yiqa did not nod or speak, allowing instead for her stillness to confirm her statement.

Henley remembered that the Alnassi woman and been on a mission for the Voluptuary. She'd apparently just related whatever it was she'd learned. He did not want to know what it was. In fact, he felt a tingling urge to be gone. Similar to what he'd felt in the dome earlier. A sense of being hemmed in. Probably a memory of his time in the cell beneath the Cathedral of Til, but still . . .

"I have to go back to the Citadel. Thank you for your wisdom, Finta. Voluptuary." He turned to go.

"Hold!" the Voluptuary commanded.

By the tone of her voice he knew he was cooked and Kil-damned. He did not look back, but merely faced the direction he hoped to go and waited.

"Have you learned to dymense yet?"

"I know the principles."

"You'll have to do better than that. You're going to Tordain."

"With respect, I am not a Sensual for you to command."

"And I would not send one. You'll take Yiqa with you. She will show you what needs done."

He did turn now. "Which is?"

"A return to your thievish ways."

"You want me to steal something? Why can't Yiqa do it? She's stealthier than I am."

"Only a merculyn—a very powerful one—can do this."

Every word she said made the task sound worse. But he asked the inevitable question. "What are you asking me to steal?"

"The source of the Autarch's recent increase in power. A mercus stone. The most powerful mercus artifact ever known. The Motherlight."

Finta's shocked reaction told Henley more than the Voluptuary's words had. He had never heard of the Motherlight. But he knew of the Autarch, a woman of enormous mystery, having never been seen outside her palace for the past twenty years. She was reported to be richer than Her Enlightened and greedy for empire. Her armies had marched all over the southern peninsula a ten-year ago, only to be beaten back by the combined forces of the city states of Wantin, Jallisea, Sorgan, and Starside.

"You are sure she possesses the Motherlight?" Finta asked. "It must be a recent acquisition or the whole southern peninsula and the Kovi-Mest would be hers by now."

The Voluptuary's face looked soft as dripping candle wax. She made three false starts, then said, "And so we must remove it from her grasp. Henley?"

"The Autarch is a merculyn?" he asked. The idea startled him. While everyone knew that Starside's monarch had incredible powers, the rest of the world had formed laws to prohibit such people from rising to power.

"She is a—She is a—" The Voluptuary's lips drew back, a grimace of agony. Her body began to shudder and her eyes rolled up into her skull.

Henley recoiled as the woman's skin flashed over with scales. But just for a moment, before her crepey skin returned. The cabbagy stink of a kitchen middens pushed Henley further back, gagging. Huff charged from the room.

A voice that was not the Voluptuary's erupted from her mouth. "I have her now!" She began to rise, posture hunched, fingers curled into claws. Her lips had gone white, but they pulled up again. White teeth gleamed, not human. Fangs!

"She's o'erwhelmed by a demayne!" Finta cried. She produced a small pouch from a pocket and fumbled to loosen the ties. Yiqa put her body between the elderly healer and the possessed Voluptuary.

Henley knew little demaynic lore. He'd only recently learned that they were classified with names like yoznithan and dragnithan. This thing did not look like either of those.

The Voluptuary threw herself at Yiqa, arms rigid with strength beyond the limits of her flesh. Flaumishtak had warned she would not be the same woman. Henley had never imagined he meant it literally.

Henley drew the mercus to him, forming azure spheres over his palms, the glassy surfaces aswirl with black fear.

Yiqa fended off the Voluptuary's unskilled swipes and lunges with sharp blocks and kicks. Clearly she did not wish to harm the woman to whom she had shown so much loyalty. "She is no longer the one you served!" Henley cried. "Strike her down!"

Too late. Henley barely registered the bolts forming within the possessed woman before they released. Yiqa slumped as if all the strength had drained from her. Henley smelled the bolts of willshift, but these were laden with despair. So much so, he blinked away tears as the byblow of the feat washed over him.

The Voluptuary was on Yiqa in an instant, hungry fangs flashing, seeking the Alnassi woman's throat.

Finta shrieked and thrust her hand at her sister's face. With a hard puff from her lips, she blew a billow of dust into the Voluptuary's eyes and mouth.

The effect was instant and horrific. The Voluptuary's eyes squeezed shut. Crimson tears traced down white cheeks. The mouth clamped shut, just short of biting Yiqa, and the Voluptuary began to choke and retch. The mercus failed in her and Yiqa stumbled to regain her footing.

Seeing his opening, Henley released both spheres. They took the Voluptuary in the chest. She flew back into the wall and crumpled onto the bed.

Finta staggered to her sister's body, thumbed back an eyelid, felt at her throat. Crystal tears streaming down her wrinkled face, she bent an ear to the Voluptuary's chest. "Oh, my dear sweetlight. She's gone. Ah me." Covering her face, Finta wept.

Yiqa refastened her head covering and veil. What she felt, apart from cold rage, did not show in her gray eyes. Eyes which were turned on Henley.

"I had to strike," he said.

"You deed vell. A sweeft detth." She strode toward him with such menace in her steps he again gathered his mercus power to defend himself. But she swept past him. "Vee leef een onnne hour."

"Where should I meet you?"

"I vill ffffind you." She left.

Finta bade Henley help her straighten the Voluptuary's body and cover it. She sniffed and coughed throughout these ministrations. When there was nothing left to do to set the

Voluptuary's bedchamber into order, she took him into the sitting room. Huff huddled under a chair.

"She must have struggled to retain control the entire time we spoke," Finta said after a long silence. "I do not know what class of demayne possessed her, but surely nothing lower than a baalnithan. You saw how ravenous it was for life. Pol smiled that we banished it so swiftly. Had it consumed any of Yiqa's blood . . ." She trailed off and swallowed hard. "But it did not."

"I'm surprised Flaumishtak allowed such a creature into this world. He's been helping us."

"Helping? Flaumishtak's aid serves his aims. If what you seek aligns with his schemes, he will surely assist you. But do not fool yourself that he has a beneficent bone in his body. He is a trickster and chaos is his great amusement." She poured lukewarm tea into a cup and sipped.

"And yet he possesses knowledge we need. He taught me the power I just used against that thing in there. He taught me the principles of dymensing. He was the one who warned us about Yiothizandra. The cats love him."

"I did not say he wouldn't benefit you. I merely mean to point out he has no loyalty to you. When he brought my sister back, mind infected with a baalnithan, perhaps he saw the main chance. A way to shortcut to his true aim. For such a demayne, this world is a ready feast."

"If he wanted this world destroyed, then why hasn't he thrown in with Yiothizandra?"

"Perhaps he has." She set down her cup and smoothed her black skirt over her knees. "I'll point out that his teaching Kila to be more destructive has not served this city well."

Henley had no counter to that. He respected Finta, and

her words wormed into his mind. "Can we trust your sister's demands that I steal the Motherlight? Or were those the baal-nithan's words?"

"A baalnithan wouldn't have broken through to attack if its true aim was the Motherlight. It would have remained hidden until you brought it the relic. And I know the Autarch well. If she possesses such an artifact, it must be removed from her grasp."

"And how do you know her?" He wasn't sure he wanted to hear the answer.

"She's our sister, Saralina. The youngest of us, and a brat." Finta stood. "I suggest you prepare for your travels. Yiqa is not a patient woman."

Henley kissed her cheek. "It is a great blessing that you have been Kila's friend," he said warmly. "I know she is grateful to you, for all you did for Wen. Thank you for your counsel. I wish I could have done more for your sister."

Her eyes welled and gleamed. Pressing a hand to his chest, she smiled. "You have a kind heart, son. Before all is through, Kila will have need of it. Go. Complete this task, then find your girl."

TAREK PITORRO STOOD on the Street of the Diadem just outside of the Baths of Ori. Same flop of lank black hair as Fallo, but a handsomer face. He looked like he'd failed to eat for the past month. His chin was unshaven and he had the haggard droopy flesh around his eyes of an ancient woman.

"I am to take you to the Citadel," Henley said to the man, bypassing greetings. Tarek was detestable for one simple fact.

He had tried to have his own son murdered, sacrificing guards and drivers to make it look like a raid upon one of his caravans. "Hold onto me." Henley offered an elbow.

Seeing Huff on Henley's shoulder, the man recoiled.

"Do it!"

Whatever the man had endured, it had made him skittish. He jumped at Henley's sharp words and quickly obeyed.

Henley formed the bolts, mostly out of irritation. If he was to leave Starside in an hour, he had no time to ride a carriage to the Citadel. Even so, trepidation filled his guts. He'd seen what a slight error in dymension could do. Quinn had lost a hand because of it.

He released the feat and felt an icy wash over his flesh as he and Tarek PiTorro passed into dymension. They appeared a moment later in Marlow's private office. The man jerked back in his chair, loosing a sheaf of papers he'd been reading.

"Til's tears, boy. I nearly soiled myself."

"Apologies, Marlow. Here's Tarek PiTorro. He was recently with Yiothizandra, according to Flaumishtak. He can report what he saw at Ceronhel."

Henley didn't wait to hear Marlow's objections. He went into the corridor and dymensed again, leaving a maid's screams behind. Now in his room, he began to shove his belongings into his satchel. There wasn't much to collect except a change of clothing and spare socks. The satchel held the crimson dragon scales he'd scavenged from the ash barrens, a pouch of coin, and a knife given to him by Coin Inlina.

He dymensed to the kitchens and searched out Kinnon Swile, mistress of kitchens, in her office. She looked up at him sharply. "Are you the cause of the screams in my kitchens?"

"I apologize for that. I dymensed pretty close to old Mam. I need provisions for travel. Quickly."

Kinnon Swile was the calmest person he'd ever met. Young for her position, she had the level eye of someone invulnerable to nonsense or scandal. Henley supposed she'd seen or heard everything in her role here. She called for a kitchen boy and scribbled a list of items. "Gather this in a bag."

"None of it will spoil for a ten-day," she said after the boy had scurried off. "After that, you're going to have to hunt or buy your food. Is there anything else?"

"No. Thank you."

Loaded down with his provisions and his satchel, Henley moved to the courtyard. Yiqa was there. How she knew to be there at that moment was a question for the gods.

"Cann you dymmennz usss?"

"I can dymense to Jallisea. That's as close to Tordain as I've ever been. It will be dangerous."

"Hide your cattt. Jalliseeannns vill eet heem." She took hold of his arm. Huff squeezed into Henley's satchel, sending irritated fur-ruffle feelings through the bond.

Henley formed the image in his head, hoping the docks had not changed location in the past three years. The mercus bolts formed and he and Yiqa slipped into dymension.

18

THE DRAGON TOOTH BLADES

Kila held up a hand, stopping Fallo in mid-sentence. She cocked her head and listened to her bond with Henley. He had moved, suddenly.

Huff moved, Nax sent.

Yes. I felt Henley shift too.

He had dymensed far enough for Kila to sense it. Confirmed by Nax. He had never dymensed before, which meant he'd worked on it in her absence. Or there had been great need.

"Kila?" Fallo asked. He was leaning against Quinn's cot, feet straight out and Lop on his lap. The cat had turned onto her back to make stroking her belly convenient.

"Henley just dymensed. I think well south of Starside." She wanted nothing more than to dymense into Marlow's office and see if he'd dispatched Henley on a mission of some sort. But she couldn't unless she left the Hackwatch. And even if Marlow knew, Kila could do nothing to help Henley.

Frustrated, she settled back against the wall and forced her attention back to the conversation at hand. "You were saying something about Cigil-Tine?" She wouldn't have believed Fallo's story at all if Cloak Einlin hadn't corroborated it earlier. Not that he'd said much other than, "It's true."

"And there were ghost nosgs," he said. Then he told a ridiculous story about fighting nosg in the streets of Cigil-Tine and of finding a frozen elnisian queen. "Quite lovely. She would have been a nice cuddle except for when she turned into a dried-up corpse."

Kila told Fallo of her adventures on Garden Island, of Kil's Keep, Annisforl, and her ridiculous ascension to Highest of Kil. Fallo eyed her garnet ring with skepticism. He resorted to having Lop ask Nax for confirmation, which cost him a chicken wing.

"And then I destroyed a big portion of the Cathedral of Til and the Blasted Quarter," she said, wrapping up her summary of failures. "But at least I killed the Hargothe." She didn't mention the details of how she'd squeezed the old man's heart with mercus touch, nor how—inexplicably—she'd discovered herself holding a handful of ash in the aftermath.

"I don't remember the first time I met Critt Sanglo," Kila said, changing the subject as the silence in the room grew too intense. Fallo had changed. His face wasn't handsome, but no longer was it as hideous as she remembered it. There was a new strength in him. His shoulders broader, his eyes . . . silvered.

"I remember," Fallo said softly. "I had just returned to Starside from Misen-Tine. I came up through the thinnie tunnels. My father thought I was dead and I thought it best to keep him thinking that while I figured out what to do. I spent a lot of time in Cheapsgate after that, mostly keeping my head down and doing odd jobs to supplement my atlen egg supply."

Kila smiled at the memory of the old atlen barn where she'd found Fallo and Henley. "And Critt helped you, didn't he?"

Fallo snorted and waggled his single, black eyebrow. "He's the one who told me and Henley that some sailors had cats. Kind of put the idea into our heads that we might swipe the one Ragin was taking for the bounty. He didn't give us any free trezz or ale though."

"No. Critt counted his coins. I wonder what'll happen to his tavern." The thought that it would be taken over by someone less worthy made Kila immensely sad. "Funny how things don't last."

"Some things do." He put on a haughty face. "The Radiancies and the monarchy does."

Kila wasn't so sure. "What do you know about Semūin?" she asked after another silence.

He licked his lips and recited:

> "Hunter do not wander
> Toward those lovely calls;
> 'Tis the voice of death,
> Lovely 'neath the falls.
> Semūin! 'Tis Semūin!
> Luring you deeper down;
> To take away your final breath
> Where in her arms you'll drown."

He grinned, a flash of the old Fallo. "Or would you like to hear the good one?" He flashed his brow again, an assurance that this other tale wouldn't leave out the bawdy parts.

"She's my mother," Kila said.

Before he could laugh, she bade Nax relate the truth of it to Lop. For once Lop didn't demand payment for relating information to Fallo. Perhaps because Nax asked nicely. Or, more likely, she threatened some catty retribution that Lop truly feared.

Fallo's strange features passed through shock and horror and disbelief before finally settling into an amused nod of appreciation. "So you're saying my dearest friend is a goddess of some sort?"

"I can't speak for your friend, but *I* certainly have some of mama's blood in my veins. Didn't stop me from nearly being killed by Shinane."

Instead of chuckling at Kila's wry humor, he sat up. "The third dragon tooth blade? You've seen it?"

"Seen it? It's in my backpack over there. Why?"

Chuckling, Fallo drew his blade. "Ol' Rusty. He's Telt. Remember?"

Kila nodded. "Yes. So two of the three legendary blades have surfaced. You'll forgive me for being unimpressed. Weird and strange events are the habit of my daily life these days."

Fallo hiked up his trouser leg to reveal another blade tucked into his boot. Lop mewled angrily when these gyrations upset her comfortable snoozing. Fallo drew the blade. "I'd hand it to you, but it's got a nasty disposition. *This* is Skeye. Illizshian had it."

It was Kila's turn to sit up. "The elnisian queen you mentioned was Illizshian?" That name had come up frequently of late. Highest Quiv had shown Kila the queen's private journal, and Kila had found an illuminated history of her in the Way of Kil's library. Quiv had immediately appropriated the tome. "She was alive?"

"Briefly. She's not any more. Corpse, remember? Cloak Einlin's got her brain gem in his pocket." He looked down at Lop. "The cats have them too. I suppose that means Illizshian was a demayne. The gems are fate's-pieces now."

"Every Kil-lickin' thing in the world is a damned fate's-piece if you believe Ell and Jil." *Do you really have a gem in your head?* she sent to Nax

A what?

She waggled her ring in front of Nax's nose. *A colorful stone like this.*

Look in my ear and see.

Fallo looked at her backpack. "Can I see Shinane?"

Kila drew the backpack to her. She had never liked Shinane, probably because she'd been stabbed by it. She slid it across the floor to Fallo. He reached for it, then pulled his hand away before touching it.

Scooping Lop from his lap, he deposited the cat on Quinn's bunk. Tail flicking, the fuzzy black blob of a cat snuggled close to Quinn's flank, pointedly turning her face away from Fallo.

Fallo stood and licked his lips. "I hate this," he said to himself. "I don't want to pick it up."

"Then don't."

"Every shadline instinct in my body is telling me I must. And so I shall."

He bent and grasped the hilt. He relaxed as he straightened. "Ah. Nothing. Ha ha." There was perspiration on his forehead. Kila had never seen him this nervous before, even when he was about to pick a pocket.

He withdrew the blade from the scabbard. His visage changed from relief to jaw-clenching anger. He dropped the scabbard and slowly bent to raise his trouser leg. Retrieving Skeye, he straightened. An eerie flicker in his eyes was all the warning Kila had before he lunged with both blades.

She countered reflexively, kicking his gut the way Aggy had kicked hers. The impact jarred him enough that he shook his head. He shook it again. "Kil's eyes!" He bent forward, knuckles white on the hilts of the blades. A dangle of spittle came from his mouth and his face went red. Kila realized he was resisting the impulse to attack, surely coming from the blades.

Lop was standing atop Quinn's chest, fur sticking straight out as she hissed at Fallo. Nax joined her, spitting, tail high, fangs bared.

Kila reached for the mercus, felt the sludge of Revulsion sluice into her mind. Retching, she shoved it away.

Fallo was clearly fighting with the daggers now, blades raised before his eyes and defiance on his face.

Lop stopped hissing and abruptly curled up to snuggle against Quinn. Nax quieted and sat primly, watching Fallo with mere curiosity now.

"No," Fallo said to Shinane. "You be still. You too Skeye."

And then it was over. The strain went out of his posture and he was just a young man holding two daggers. "Sorry about that, Kila. Skeye sets a bad example, appeals to the darker side of Shinane's nature. I've got them wrangled. Skeye is acting all sullen now. Sneaky blade, this one is. It wants me to kill all my friends all of the time. I don't pay her any mind." He set the offending blade on the tiles, then put Shinane next to it. Finally, he unsheathed Telt and added it to the lineup.

"That doesn't look like the Telt I remember," Kila said, eyeing the pristine dagger. She knew the blade well, having confiscated it for a while after Henley had threatened to stab her with it. It had been the sorriest, rustiest, dullest dagger she'd ever seen. That had been long before anyone knew its true nature.

"Ol' Rusty got a bit of a burnish in Cigil-Tine when I killed an elnisian warden. Both blades went in." He made a thrusting motion with both hands. "It sort of drew the warden's blood into me, according to Zirhine. That's what happened to my eyes, in case you were wondering. I'm part elnisian now. Part vergent, too, though that's harder to explain."

Despite her earlier statement about her weird and strange life, it was rather breathtaking to see all three of the dragon tooth blades in front of her.

"Shinane just bonded to me," Fallo said. "That caught me a bit wrong footed and then Skeye tried to take over again."

"Shinane freezes its victims," Kila said. "The smallest cut will do it. The death is slow. Don't count on that power in battle."

Fallo sneered a bit as he considered this. "Now I have to carry three of them. Too bad I've only got two hands." He chuckled and began sheathing his blades, but the humor trailed off and he eyed Quinn. He leaned back again, motioning to Lop to resume her position on his lap. The cat ignored him.

Oly is that way now, Nax sent, pointing her nose east.

Close?

Far. Not as far as last time.

Kila had asked Nax to tell her anytime she sensed Oly move suddenly. That always meant Flaumishtak had moved too. Nax could never say exactly where Oly was, only offering a subjective notion of his proximity. Kila retrieved her rolled up map and spread it out. Placing a finger on Tearling, she dragged it east along the Kovi-Mest river to the Sorgeal sea. North and east was Tordain, due east of that was Jallisea. Beyond that was the Ansin Ocean and the islands of the Archipelago of Scin.

And last time?

Nax moved her head to face a bit more northerly. Starside.

What was Flaumishtak up to? She'd have to ask Henley. She could feel him out there, right in the direction Nax had looked. Was he with Flaumishtak? Perhaps she should walk out of the Hackwatch and dymense back to Starside, see if Marlow knew. Maybe sleep in her own bed. How nice that would be. But she wouldn't leave Quinn.

Soft snores arose. Fallo had passed out.

Henley? She sent, pushing with her mind in hopes of reaching him. No answer. She hadn't expected one, but she longed for it. Longed to feel his arms around her, and his lips on hers.

As tired as she was from her training with Aggy, she found herself brooding in weary wakefulness. She noticed her pack and retrieved the hilt leather Crafter Exalin had given her.

Well, Naxie. I suppose this room isn't much worse than the den in the Warren.

It's better in every respect.

Kila snorted softly and set about rewrapping Cayne's hilt. She wanted to argue with Nax, explain that the Warren den had been good because it had been familiar. It had been home. She'd been happy there.

Fallo snuffled in his sleep, right hand reaching for Telt. He didn't draw, but kept his hand on the hilt. Kila watched him a moment longer, then returned to tightly wrapping Cayne's hilt. Satisfied, she held it up, assessing the grip. A bit tackier, less prone to slipping.

Why do you use a knife when you have the power to turn foes to ash? Nax asked. The cat was still nestled next to Quinn, chin on dainty white paws. Her eyes were open just wide enough to show a sliver of amber.

When I practice with the dagger, I can't think about anything else. Like how I have the power to ash people.

If you don't want to think about it, don't think about it.

I can't seem to control my thoughts. I don't like being able to harm so many so easily.

So you practice with the knife to harm fewer people with more difficulty? You are strange. Nax's head shot up. *Oly is that way now.* She faced northwest. Kila didn't need to refer to the map to know that Jilin and Trist lay in that direction. The demayne was up to something, which was no surprise. She considered summoning him, but decided she wasn't particularly well liked here already. Summoning a demayne wouldn't improve her standing. And of course, he wouldn't be able to dymense here anyway.

The demayne seemed to be visiting major cities. She didn't like it. Since the Hargothe had died, he'd been able to move with more freedom than before. And yet he had not wreaked general destruction as Marlow had feared. For some reason that did not comfort Kila.

19

DO YOU FEEL IT?

The Katteshan Palace covered over twenty square miles of land in the northern quarter of Tordain. A city unto itself, it was surrounded by high walls topped with wrought iron spikes, and held the two largest domes ever built. Between these enormous structures were miles upon miles of covered galleries, apartments, small mansions and palaces, and a treasury so full of priceless wonders it required a staff of one thousand scribes and coin counters to inventory.

Coin Inlina regarded it all as waste.

She had been here an entire day and still her aunt had not deigned to grant her an audience. And to think, this woman had sat upon Inlina's knee and listened with rapt attention to stories about Pol. Yes, it had been strange to be older than her aunt, and the roles certainly had been switched. Inlina thought they'd had a good relationship, until her aunt's rather scandalous marriage to Tordain's heir had put Saralina upon the Katteshan Throne when her husband suddenly died. Eschewing the title of Queen, she declared herself Autarch, dissolved the nation's assembly of governors, and began a series of ill-considered wars to conquer Jallisea and Sorgan.

Fool girl! Coin Inlina was most disappointed in her, and she would hear about it. If she would ever allow an audience.

The apartment given to her by the Autarch's castellan was much too large and came burdened with a dozen servants, a kitchen, and five armsmen. Though those last may just as rightly be considered guards to keep her in.

Nothing was denied her but what she wanted. And so she plucked her medallion from its chain and gave it a vicious toss. The question she posed as it flipped in the air was, "Do I wait?"

It came up frowns, so she left her uneaten dinner and made her way toward the Katteshan Throne, young Sensual Roon at her heels. The armsmen flanked her, so she went quickly, forcing them to keep pace in their burnished armor and hefting their ridiculous halberds.

The so-called Katteshan Throne occupied the entirety of the eastern dome. The spire burst from its top, rising to dizzying heights. Coin Inlina had been there before, once. But that was prior to her aunt's ascension to power. At the time, the dome had been a tourney field, where displays of horsemanship, atlen racing, and gladiatorial battles had left hundreds bleeding before a delighted audience.

Now it was given over to one chair.

Because of its former purpose, many enormous arched doors let into the structure. These had all been bricked up, save one. More shiny armsmen stood guard there. The Coin suspected a hundred more men lined the path to the chair. She didn't know and she didn't care.

If needed she would melt their armor off their bodies and

turn their halberds into slag. Thanks to that idiot Mancin Fley, the former Highest of Til, she possessed some powerful mercus artifacts.

The heller on her finger was a simple band of gold called Roop's Wild. It doubled her power. Her favorite was a bracelet fashioned artfully into a crane, wings encircling her wrist. With it, she could summon great winds to blow foes from their feet. She had hardly tested its power. The final trinket was a necklace of three chains, gold, silver, and steel. Should one of her aunt's armsmen become exuberant with his halberd, he'd discover her flesh hard as marble.

So it was with great confidence that she approached the gate. The armsmen did bar her way. "I'm Saralina's niece. I'm also the Coin of Pol, First Spinster, and Medallion Bearer of Garden Island."

The captain said from behind his pointy visor: "Our orders are inviolable. No one enters without invitation."

Chafing under this unaccustomed treatment, Coin Inlina weighed her options. She chose not to blow the men from their feet, but simply plucked her medallion free. "Will these men live if they bar my entrance?" The coin flipped up and landed on the stones that separated her from them. Her guards leaned forward, plate armor screeching and rattling.

Pol's face frowned up at them.

The men at the gate shifted from foot to foot, visors turned this way and that. But they had been chosen for their loyalty and they all soon found their spines.

Sighing, the Coin plucked the medallion from the stones with her mercusine. It shot into her fingers. Such feats were rare. The men should have stumbled back in shock. But they didn't.

"The Autarch will see you when she chooses," the captain said. If anything the Coin's trick had firmed his stance a bit. Curious.

"Do you feel it?" Sens Roon asked softly. She had her eyes closed and one hand up, as if trailing her fingers through imperceptible air currents. Roon was very sensitive to the mercus, with much greater potential for it than Inlina. The Coin cocked her head and tried to sense whatever it was.

"The power in the dome is immense," Roon said again.

The Autarch had possessed a small measure of mercus as a child. But after a few years as a novitiate of Ori, she had left the practice. It did not seem likely the girl had grown in power since.

Now the Coin was more determined than ever to gain entrance. She squared her shoulders and ignored the ache in her belly. She took three bold steps forward.

The men closed ranks, forming an armor wall.

"Very well," she said. Calling on the power of the crane artifact was as easy as thinking it. The bracelet supplied all the mercus power. She flattened her hand on the captain's chest and let the fellstorm wind blow.

The men before her lifted from the ground and flew twenty paces back through the great arched gate. Cries sounded from her honor guard. Sens Roon had wisely flattened herself upon the ground.

The Coin walked forward, stepping over men who moaned and men who did not make a sound. The captain was the last she passed, legs and arms bent at impossible angles, helm caved in from where it had struck the stone arch.

Sens Roon caught up. "Was that truly necessary?"

"Time does not slow, it only hastens. War comes and I will have Tordain's forces on my side, else they are on Kil's."

Three more confrontations ended in similar ways. Her armsmen finally raced ahead to announce her arrival.

As she passed from the long entry tunnel into the dome, the air became light and fragrant. Gone was the huge dirt floor of an arena. Now a rambling garden spread out to encompass acres and acres. The greenery and blossoms climbed the tiers of bench seats where spectators had once cheered on their favorite warriors.

At the center of this was the foot of the spire, a massive column with a wraparound balcony. From there, the kings and queens of earlier ages had been able to keep an eye on the entirety of the battles and races below.

Now it held a chair. And upon that chair sat Aunt Saralina, the Autarch of Tordain.

20

WHAT IS EVIL

The eyries above Ceronhel lay north of the fasthold. Yioth stood on the ledge of the largest mountainside cavern. This was no natural formation, though to the casual eye it would appear so. The arched opening loomed overhead, high enough that a dragon could land safely in storm winds. There were more such caverns in the Haelshocks. She would leave it to Bazron to sort out which dragnithor would occupy which eyrie.

And the dragons were close now. She could smell them on the frigid wind. The blustery air swirled around her, cooling her wings. She relished the cold almost as much as she enjoyed the view. Ceronhel lay thousands of feet below her.

She turned to face the children Klayne had brought her. A boy of perhaps eight. A girl of twelve. "What are your names?"

In answer she got sobbing.

Such weakness offended her. She was tempted to throw Eckso's children from the eyrie. But that did not suit her aims. Besides, if she were to throw them to their deaths, it would surely be better to have Eckso there to witness it. They were dead regardless, for once Kil was done with this world, no mortal here would survive the destruction.

She knelt before them, smiling. "I asked you a question. It is impolite to ignore me." She cuffed the girl's head. "Speak!"

"Poli! I'm Poli. This is Trev."

For now they would serve a good purpose. Yioth had summoned her sister an hour ago, knowing she would have to leave the Hackwatch before dymensing. Still, she was wroth with her sister for the long delay in coming.

But Eckso finally showed, a billow of mercus green quickly carried away on the wind. Her back was to her children, so she did not see them. Hands together she pleaded, "I apologize for the delay, Yiothizandra. I was among the shadline and had to make excuses to leave the Hackwatch."

"Turn around. But remember your face."

Confused, Eckso did as told. When she beheld her children she took two steps toward them, arms reaching. But she caught herself. They did not recognize her, beglamoured as she was. Shoulders trembling, she turned back to Yioth, who offered such a soft, sympathetic smile that Eckso's face burned to be mocked so.

"No harm will come to them, sister. I thought it best to bring them here where they may be protected during the war to come. Don't you agree?"

"I—" But she couldn't get out anything else. Lips trembling, nostrils flaring, she became full of mercus. Yioth merely raised an eyebrow, daring Eckso to attack, daring her to then witness the consequences of such action.

The effort to pull back the feat was matched by the hard swallow that accompanied the surrender. Eckso was not stupid.

Yioth began a circuit around her sister, forcing the drag-nithan to turn. Stopping behind Poli and Trev, Yioth put her hands on their heads. Delicate things. Such soft hair. "Their mother is my sister," she said to Eckso. "Do you know her?"

Eckso nodded but said nothing.

"They'll be safe here. Do you think that is a good idea?"

"Of course. Such lovely, sweet children must be kept safe. At *all* costs."

Excellent. "Come with me to the ledge, dearie." Yioth took Trev by the hand and led him to the great arched opening. Having no fear of heights, she moved to put herself right at the edge. The boy resisted, planting his feet and pulling back. But his little boots lost grip and he slid to her, then out over the drop, held only by her grip.

Eckso and Poli cried out. The boy shrieked pathetically. Yioth laughed.

She let him dangle a while before returning him to firm footing. "Be careful, dear. Now, be brave and peer down. See how far it is?"

The boy cried and refused and again struggled to pull away. Yioth let go of his hand and allowed him to race back to his sister. Beyond the girl, Eckso stood wringing her hands, desperate to comfort her children but unable to do so without confusing them.

"Come to me," Yioth said, waving to her sister.

Now out of the children's hearing, Yioth put an arm around Eckso's shoulders and bade her look at the drop. "I have no compunction about throwing your children over. You do understand that, don't you?"

"I do." Eckso shook violently. Such fear was embarrassing,

really. The children were half human, which meant they should be beneath notice.

"Now tell me what you've learned at the Hackwatch."

The narrative did not go on long. And when Eckso finished, she leaned away, as if expecting to be struck. Not a bad instinct either. "You were with Kila Sigh and you did not bring her to me? Surely without the mercus she is but a twig of a girl, easily overmastered."

"I have to get her out of the Hackwatch to dymense her to you. This cannot be done with scholars and shadline looking on. Have patience."

"What of our cousin? What has she been doing all this time?"

"Ell does not walk about alone. There is always a shadline woman with her, Jil Pokkti. She is Shad Ault's girl, I understand. Besides, Ell is rarely out of her room or that of a sick girl from Starside. Kila Sigh's friend, Quinn Peline."

Peline? Yioth knew of the girl's mother. The Radiant Peline. Which made Quinn the Hargothe's niece. "Is the Peline girl a merculyn?"

"I don't think so. I haven't gotten into her room to see her yet."

"What of the Sigh girl's felnithel companion?"

"There are two there. I don't know which is hers. And I dared not approach them too closely. Masks do not fool them easily."

That was true and wise. "We must not harm the felnithel."

"I have spoken to Kila. She does not love Kil as he is thought of in this world. Death, war, pestilence, hate, and all the powerful feelings of Night repel her. I do not think she will be loyal to Night no matter what you say to her."

Yioth chuckled. "Pestilence? Such naive children these humans are. Do they not pause in their moralizing for even a moment to consider that what they call evil is merely a perspective? What is truly evil is our imprisonment here. What *is* evil is Day's banishment of Night. What *is* evil is Til's subjugation of his brother, and Pol's hubris to dare speak for the force of destiny, and Ori's celebration of weakness. Kil fought them alone, on all fronts. By banishing him, they thought they'd won. Fools. Behind the daylight sky is the evernight. And someday the final light will fade, and the evernight will reign eternal. *That* is good, for it is the total truth of all realms. In the end, darkness."

Her voice had risen, and her last word resounded in the cavernous eyrie. She lowered it. "Bring the Sigh girl to me."

"And Ell?"

"Kill her."

"That will not be easy. Loveheart will drain her blood, but the mercusine will sustain her unless it can be freed or drained."

"Free it, or drain it. Take as many shadlines from the board as you can. You will have nosg to aid you in that. But above all, bring me the Sigh girl. Alive."

"Yes, Yiothizandra. I suppose I should mention that someone else has tried to kill her. Two of her friends were placed under the sway of tresh and commanded to attack Kila on sight. The man Critt Sanglo has died of his wounds. The girl, Quinn Peline, seems to have fought off the compulsion."

Yioth did not like it. Not at all. "Someone among the shadline?"

"I doubt it. Someone from Starside. There are many there

who detest Sigh for the destruction and terror she rained upon the city recently."

"Yes. I see that. But the attempt failed, so I shall not concern myself about it for now. You have your orders. You have two days before young Trev must once again face his fear of this drop. He will not find me so patient the next time. Now begone!"

Eckso's eyes glimmered with tears of frustrated hate. But she said nothing before she vanished.

Yioth turned to face the children, wings spread wide. She knew she was cast in silhouette and reveled in the terror in their eyes as her wings shadowed their wan faces. "Did your mother ever tell you what you are? That you are abominations?" She stalked toward them, reveling in their fear as they cowered and shrieked. "But what lovely abominations you are. Now, what shall we do with you?"

Leave them with me! came a dragnithor's voice into Yioth's mind.

The whole chamber fell into shadow, and the children erupted in piercing cries. Yioth smiled in satisfaction, turning to greet the great black dragon Bazron with a polite nod. She waited for the beast to lower its carriage-sized skull in a bow of respect. But it did not offer it.

The vast leathery wings folded in and the beast slunk forward, quiet despite its immeasurable weight. A thick carrion stench blew in with it.

Bazron's eyes were mere slits that glowed with green fire. Yioth suppressed a gasp. This was the legendary dragnithor who had flown at demaynic midnight. His dark nature had deepened in the past thousand years and that had blackened his scales, and had likely hardened them just as much.

Hold still, girl, Bazron commanded, pushing his immense snout toward Yioth and snuffling such that her hair flew back. *I smell him. Kil! Dem-Kisk comes at last. The elnisian scryers spake truly.*

"Bow, Bazron," Yioth said. "Demonstrate your fealty to our Lord."

The dragon grunted and sulfur stinking smoke billowed from its nostrils. Yioth did not have the weak stomach of humans, but neither did she relish such foulness.

I will bow before the babe when it cries in open air before me. And to no one else.

This would never do. The rest of the dragnithor of Night must be brought under her absolute control. That meant Bazron had to submit.

She drew her sword, a lordblade of Sc'avin. It was nameless in this world, but in the demaynic realms it was known as Flayshui. No Shadline blade, this. For it was not of steel, but forged of invur, an element only found in the demaynic realms. The sword was heavy and expectant of its due in blood. Red flame coursed along the flat of the single-edged sword. "I will have your obeisance, Bazron. Dip your head to me or I shall force it to the floor—upon your neck or apart from it."

Bazron did not rear up or gather an attack, but instead snaked his tail in a long arc. Yioth heard the wind of its approach, but could not see more than a faint gray line blurring toward her. She leapt, wings catching the air, blade slashing as she glided toward the beast. The tip of the invur lordblade struck a scale, focusing her rage, her fire, and her will into a tiny area.

The beast writhed and spat, ridged skull bucking back to strike. Yioth lost the air beneath her wings. Tucking, she struck the floor and rolled to her feet, slashing wildly to counter a bash from Bazron's sail of a wing. Her blade bit deep into the weaker scales of the underside. Inky ichor splurted down upon her, scalding her skin. She released all of her human form, allowing her dragnithan nature to arise fully, allowing her skin to give way to scales. Hers were not as strong as a dragnithor's, but they communicated less pain to her.

"You dare attack the mother of Kil?" she screamed. "Are you so proud that you no longer seek escape from your imprisonment here?" She breathed fire at the beast. Bazron endured it as if it were merely the wind. His maw spread wide and emitted his answer, engulfing Yioth in the impossible heat of a starheart. To her it was nothing, for she, too, was of fire.

Other dragons had alighted upon the ledge of the eyrie to watch. Good. They needed to witness Bazron's defeat or they would forever question her command.

"I tire of your insolence," she said. "Dip the head to me!"

You are but a brood mare, a flesh sack for Kil to shed and consume. I owe you nothing.

Yioth had hoped it wouldn't come to this. She would have preferred to keep the depth of her power hidden, to be used later when the need arose and surprise offered more advantage. Alas, it was time to reveal the extent of her superiority.

Taking flight again, she held her blade before her and opened herself to its hunger. "Lordblade Flayshui, vanquish this beast!" The lordblade's voracious need took hold of her, mind and body. Even her quick brain could not follow what the blade made her body do. She became a blur of shadow, darting in and out in thirteen snake-strikes, too fast for Bazron or any creature to see. Each blow brought the full force of the blade to the same point until the scale finally exploded, sending shards in all directions. And upon a final blow, the lordblade bit into the dense flesh of the dragon's neck and lodged there to feed.

Yioth screamed with unbearable pleasure as the dragnithor's life flowed into the blade and into her as well. But she did not wish to kill Bazron. She needed him. Now it became a battle of wills as she gathered hold of herself and imposed her command upon the lordblade. *Desist!* she commanded. With a cry she yanked it free of Bazron's flesh and glided to the floor.

Bazron's eyes were squeezed shut and short puffs of smoke came from his nostrils. He was wounded, but not grievously so. The lordblade had left its own sort of poison in him, and the wound would fester if not tended.

She smacked his snout with the flat of her blade. "Look at me, Bazron!"

One lower eyelid drooped. The vertical pupil fixed on her.

"You cannot kill me for I bear Kil within me. But I can kill you, and I will if I must. Dip the head to me and command the dragnithors in my service. Kil will reward those who aid in securing this realm for him. He will punish those who stand in my way. Death is no bar to him, remember. You can suffer eternal misery even should I slay you here."

How came you by this accursed blade?

She owed him no answers. "Dip the head, Bazron."

A pool of steaming black ichor fingered across the floor from where it spilled from the dragon's wounds. The thick liquid would cool into a flaky stone in the next few days. Yioth noted it, for it was a valuable resource, ideal for arrow and spear tips.

She knew the dragon could have killed her in those first moments had she not been large with Kil. And so did he. His head lowered to the floor, followed by his body, wings folding tight to his flanks.

"I shall assign the human children to tend your wounds and keep them clean. Do not eat them or ash them until I say. They are my sister's offspring and are here to assure her continued cooperation."

I understand.

"Fourteen dragnithor of Night come?"

No, mother of Kil. Oksyosh has gone silent. There remain but thirteen. The rest await your orders.

Good. Bazron was speaking the truth. "I saw our brother Oksyosh in deathlock with Haptenar in the mountains to the north."

A great loss. May the Hel Lords feast mightily upon his soul, and may the Lightshades choke upon Haptenar's.

Now that they had come to their understanding, Yioth was willing to nod in respect to Bazron's fine words. "Much needs doing, Bazron. Send firebreathers west to melt the western passes so my nosg army can reach Stallid. The rest of your flight shall feed and strengthen for battle. Do not eat the nosg. Do you feel the presence of the dragons of Day?"

They hide themselves well. They cannot number more than five with Haptenar's death.

She called to the children, who had fled to an interior passageway. "Come out Poli. Come out Trev."

They straggled out, heads down.

"Poli, Trev, you have important work to attend to. Your mother is away, serving Night, and so shall you serve Night. You will be provided with rags and herbs and firewood and food. You shall abide here with the dragnithor and tend to Bazron's wounds. In the battles to come, more may return for such care. It will be your duty to tend to them. Show them the respect they are due and you will live. If not, you may not get to choose between being eaten or dropping from yon ledge. Do you understand?"

They nodded without looking at her. The girl said, "What are you?"

"I am Yiothizandra, child. Didn't your mother mention me? I'm your auntie. I am also the mother of Kil. The glorious day comes and you might be witnesses to it if you obey and see to your duties with diligence."

They would die within a ten-day, she guessed.

21

____

THE NEW WOMAN

Sweat poured into Kila's eyes, despite the damp chill in the air. She and Aggy had come to a high garden overlook to train. All but the Hackwatch's towers lay below them. Here they sparred amidst the choked thorny trees and the jagged stones that thrust up like tilted grave markers.

Aggy spun in, leg lashing out. Kila jumped. Not fast enough. Aggy hooked her foot behind Kila's ankle.

The earth slammed into Kila's back, pushing all the air from her lungs. Rolling onto her side and gawping for air, she came eye-level with a broken off stone. It _was_ a grave marker.

The lock in her chest broke and she heaved in a breath. Aggy stood over her, hand extended. She helped Kila up then bounded away, ready for another bout.

But Kila knelt to look at the stone. The carving on the fragment was so weather worn she couldn't read it. But tracing a few lines with a finger showed her it was indeed elnisian writing. "Strange that the First Race would build anything in such an awful place."

"They are dead. We live. Now fight."

Groaning, Kila got into position. She'd shed her shoes long ago. Though her feet had lost their toughness, she reveled in their filthy state. The cold, damp soil felt good on her soles.

Kila knew she would never best Aggy with speed alone. She needed to draw her in, get her into a tangle of arms and legs and use her greater weight to drive the girl to the ground.

Lunging at her didn't work. Kila had the bruises on her ribs to prove that. Feinting didn't fool the girl at all. So it was back to dancing in and out, staying far enough from Aggy that her blows fell short, but hoping to lure her into extending too much. In short, she needed Aggy to make a mistake.

So far, that strategy had left Kila worn out, bruised, and scraped. Aggy's clothes weren't even dirty.

Abruptly Aggy straightened and pointed down to the main courtyard. From here it was just a tiny square, half obscured by a nearer rooftop. A lone figure staggered in wearing a gown more appropriate for a ball than a shadline gathering.

"That's the new woman," Aggy said.

"Winnea. She's posh or I'm a sailor's beard. Nice enough, but nosy."

They stood close enough together that Kila thought she could tackle Aggy. The thought hadn't gotten entirely into her own awareness before the girl struck, lifting Kila from her feet and driving her back to the ground.

"Enough! I say we're done for the day. That was a Cheapsgate cheat if ever I saw one."

"You were about to attack me," Aggy said. No judgment, just fact.

"How could you tell?"

"You shifted your weight and bent your knees."

"I did no such—"

A bell clanged. It wasn't from the bell tower. It was a tiny, high pitched chime. It rang every five seconds.

"The Armory?" Aggy asked.

"What else could it be?"

Aggy tilted her head and nodded. "I feel it is time. Yes. It is time."

"So where do we go?"

"Can you truly not feel it? The Stardome."

Kila began shoving her feet into her shoes. Aggy did not wait, nor did she bid Kila farewell. She simply collected her sword and began to jog downhill.

So it was about to begin. After all this waiting. And Kila still didn't know exactly what the Armory was. In truth, she didn't much care. She had come here to recruit the shadline, to focus them on the war Ell said was coming. And so she would, for what it was worth.

Buckling Cayne to her thigh, she went after Aggy, knees and back aching the whole way.

22

LITTLE NIECE

"You had no right blasting my men," the Autarch said to Coin Inlina.

The imperious woman sat on her chair, which was the size of an atlen-drawn carriage. It was so massive she had to bend forward to look down at them past her own knees. The effect—from Coin Inlina's perspective at the base of the monstrosity—was to make the woman look like a child.

"They refused to allow me to see you," Inlina said. "My own aunt."

"I appreciate the familial bond, dear niece. But I am the supreme ruler of this realm. There are protocols that must be followed." She emphasized this by rapping her scepter on the arm of the chair.

"It's not her," Sens Roon mumbled to the Coin. "The power is below her."

That was good to know. The Coin did detect a fuzziness in the air around her. It made her skin prickly. So the Autarch had a mercus relic, did she?

"There is little time for protocol, auntie," Inlina said. "Dem-Kisk comes. War."

"You refer to the child Kila Sigh. I do not fear her."

"I have witnessed the carnage she leaves in her wake. Her power is unimaginable. The handbill you've surely seen claims she can fly. She can."

"I do not fear her. My power is uncontestable now, niece. Do you not feel it?"

"Sensual Roon says the power in this place does not emanate from you."

"And yet I wield it." The Autarch's face pulled back, her feet pulled up and she came to stand on the seat of her throne. Arms out to the sides, she called forth an enormous feat of light. It seared away the world, until there was nothing but brilliance.

And when it was gone the woman was too.

"She's descending behind the throne," Roon whispered. "There must be stairs back there."

The Sensual's eyes followed the route the Autarch took, so that Coin Inlina knew where to look when the woman finally appeared. A concealed door in the base of the throne swung in. More white light. When it was gone, the Autarch stood there, gown strap over one shoulder, the other bare. All in white, gold belt and ring of golden leaves upon her head.

"You killed my armsmen," the Autarch said, hands on hips. "Are you the one who brings war to Tordain?" Handsome and plump, she carried herself with a sensuality Inlina considered wanton. But such things were essential to a person, she supposed. And no amount of correction would rid the woman of her allure. Inlina had surely tried with her, to no avail.

"Your armsmen would not see reason. We have no time. Kila Sigh is surely a danger, but we will need her in the end. I come to requisition your troops. The realms of humankind must rally their forces. Nosg hordes prepare in the north."

The Autarch trilled a laugh. "Nosg! Oh, my dear niece. You always had such a fertile imagination. But come, I shall forgive you for killing my guards. Merely apologize and agree to my penance."

"I'll do no penance for doing what I must."

A fist of air gripped the Coin, squeezing her aching bones with suffocating power. The Autarch had both fists up. The Coin couldn't move her head, but she heard a muffled groan behind her. Apparently Sens Roon was bound up, too. The constriction did nothing to constrain Inlina's mercus. She tapped her heller ring and flicked a whip-crack of touch onto her aunt's bottom. The woman jumped and rubbed herself. Inlina let her have another and another, until the woman was hopping about, shrieking.

"I'll crush the life out of you!" the Autarch cried. Inlina continued to deliver strike after strike. The Autarch lost her concentration and the air slipped away and Inlina found herself able to breathe. She stalked to her aunt and took hold of her ear. "Pay attention, Saralina. I have no patience for another tantrum. Do that to me again and you'll learn the meaning of pain."

For all the young woman's power, she had little skill. Sens Roon came forward, panting and gray-faced. "There is an enormous reservoir of mercus in that throne."

Saralina's red face became fierce again.

Roon said, "Coin, if you please."

Inlina immediately offered her mercus as a source tap to

the Sensual. Though less skilled in most regards, Roon had been on the ash barrens when Fley had contended with the giant forms of Dunne Yples and Kila. She had learned the techniques of the mind.

Taking Inlina's power, she lashed into the Autarch's mind and easily quelled her mercus power, severing her from the artifact hidden in the throne. Once the quelling was in place, Roon released Inlina's power.

The Coin nodded her appreciation to the Sensual. "Now, let's see what little toy she's got socked away."

The Autarch opened her mouth to scream for her guards. The Coin slapped her face. "Ignorant prat! Be still and cooperate lest you lose this ridiculous throne altogether."

Leaving Saralina with Sens Roon, the Coin went through the throne door. The passage was narrow and smooth. Marble. She ascended a winding stair and came out through the seat of the throne. The Autarch's flash of light had been a silly trick to hide her slipping through a hatch in the seat.

The view was remarkable. And from this vantage, Coin Inlina saw the throne stood upon clever wheels set upon iron rings that circled the entire balcony. The throne was moveable, allowing the Autarch to survey any area of the garden she wished.

Such waste. Such shameful waste.

But the mercusine artifact was not up here. She went back down the stairs and quieted her mind. If Roon could feel it, then the Coin would wait until she felt it too. It did not take long, for the buzzing was quite noticeable here.

The little corridor inside the throne was smooth of floor and wall. She ran her hand across the wall, feeling for the buzzing. There had to be another hidden door. "How do you open this, Saralina?" she called.

The woman answered with a curse and a petulant, "You'll never figure it out and I won't show you. It is mine."

"What is yours?"

Coming back out to face her aunt, Coin Inlina put on her most severe expression. The one reserved for misbehaving devotees. Fingering her medallion, she came around to inspect the woman. Short, bright-eyed. Haughty.

"It's mine, niece," the Autarch said, chin up. "You cannot hold me here forever, and now you truly have committed an act of war. I shall sear the Way of Pol from my realm and put every Spinster to the torch."

"You'll do no such thing. Why do you even utter such nonsense? Sensual Roon, can you keep her quelled while inspecting that little corridor?"

"Of course, Coin Inlina." Sens Roon seemed quite eager to find the source of the Autarch's enhanced power. As soon as she entered the throne's secret hall, she let out an awed gasp.

"What would Aunt Marnie and Aunt Finta say if they saw you behaving like this?" Coin Inlina asked.

The Autarch looked away, cheeks reddening again.

A man's voice called from somewhere around the balcony. "Saralina? My dear girl, where have you gotten off to?"

"Here, Klayne! I'm here. Come quickly."

A handsome man rounded the curving walkway that hugged the massive central column. He had on a long shirt and sandals. Upon seeing the Autarch's distress he picked up his pace.

Inlina snorted. The last thing she needed was a useless man

interceding and having to be killed. "Sensual Roon? Have you found it?"

"No . . . I don't think there's a door here. It must be accessed from below."

"Is it?" Inlina asked her aunt.

The Autarch refused to answer.

"Who is your guest?" Klayne asked. He had a charming smile, a quality the Coin despised in men.

"This is my niece." To Inlina's amazement, the Autarch pouted. "She barged in and killed some of my guards. I wasn't ready for her."

Putting a proprietary arm around the woman, he drew her into a little hug. She leaned into him with the obvious familiarity of a lover. "The other quelled me!"

"Ah. That is rather impolite. I see you are a Coin of Pol. Surely you didn't do all the Autarch says."

"I did. And I will do more if she continues to behave like a brat. Who are you?"

"Klayne Itopolo. From Stallid. I have the pleasure of being the Autarch's chief counselor. Of course you must direct your assistant to release the Autarch immediately."

Sens Roon emerged from the hall, biting her lip and frowning. Upon seeing Klayne and his oiled hair and gold chains, she coughed and smoothed her skirts. She was in travel gear, so wore none of the flimsy gauzy skirts the followers of Ori favored. But the Coin thought the blue dress a bit too low cut. Klayne did not, for he eyed Roon up and down, an appreciative smile on his face.

He made a magnanimous gesture toward the way he'd come. "Please. Let us retire to the Autarch's small throne room and hear what happened. I'm sure some accommodation can be made in the name of familial harmony."

Inlina doubted her sullen aunt would agree to anything now. But that didn't matter. Inlina was going to have the young woman's armies and that hidden relic.

"I'll have you both executed," the Autarch spat as she led the way to another door behind the throne. "If you're lucky."

Klayne put an arm about the Coin's shoulder and the other around Roon. He hugged Roon rather a bit more vigorously. "She's hungry. It makes her puny-tempered. Let's eat and talk."

The Autarch's mood did improve after eating. She subsisted entirely upon various sweetbakes and cow's milk. Klayne preferred to eat the cow. Roon nibbled at fruit and vegetables, and the Coin forced herself to try a bit of everything. Her stomach rebelled at every bite, and only sour determination got anything down at all.

The small throne room was enormous of course, filling the base of the spire column. The garden itself wandered into this area through great archways. A central fountain spewed water high into the air. The Coin thought it as annoying for its noise as it was for its impracticality.

"Perhaps we got off to a bad start," Klayne said. His manner was so smooth and pleasing the Coin thought she'd be sickened by it if she wasn't already ill. "Let us begin anew. Coin, please explain what brought you here."

"I do not know you, nor do I trust you. But seeing that my aunt will not part with you, I shall speak as plainly as I can. I have it on good authority that nosg hordes assemble in the Haelshoks. It does not take a particularly sharp mind to see that Dem-Kisk comes. There will be war, and likely one with many sides. It is my aim to pull as many realms of humankind under a single banner as I can."

"An intriguing notion. May I ask who is providing this information about . . . nosg." He allowed the slightest laugh to color that last word. Just the tiniest indication of how silly he thought the notion of nosgs. Fool man.

"You may not ask me. But let us ask Pol for confirmation." Removing her medallion she tossed it high over the table. "Do the nosg gather in the north?"

The coin bounced and showed smiles. She collected it, tossed again. "Do the nosg gather in the north?"

Again, smiles.

This she repeated a dozen times until Klayne begged her to desist. "I believe you, Coin. Truly, I do. That is a remarkable run of smiles. No fool I. Now about the armsmen. It is quite impossible that the Autarch's forces would be deployed under any commander save one of the Autarch's own choosing."

"She has the military mind of a puppy," Inlina said.

The Autarch sat up straighter, eyes blazing. Roon had still not released her quelling. Saralina was a truly unimpressive merculyn. Without her secret mercus artifact, she would have no ability to fight at all.

"She does not have to command them directly," Klayne said. "But look at her. Such beauty must be *seen*. Her face will inspire her armsmen to great valor. I daresay any who come to her banner will bend the knee and pledge their lives to her service. She has that effect on people." He patted the woman's knee and returned her beaming smile.

The Coin knew the futility of arguing against Klayne. The Autarch was smitten with him and would do anything he said. Fine. She could live with that. Tordain had the largest standing army in the east. She would have it. "Agreed. But what commander have you to manage the influx of forces I shall recruit from Sorgan and Jallisea and Jilin? Who have you who can delegate leadership to armies as far flung as Slirya? It must be a person of uncommon skill and insight."

Klayne bowed in mock humility. "Why, I could serve in that role quite well."

"Yes!" the Autarch said. "Oh, do let it be Klayne. Imagine him ahorse, arrayed in armor and a blue cape with gold fringe. What a noble figure he'd strike. The nosg would run in terror just to behold him."

The nosg would likely run him down and eat out his throat. The Coin kept this to herself. Klayne could be disposed of later. The main thing was to get the forces moving. "The Sablefort will be our forward base. Patrols can range the Sackwood and up to Lockt. I will have Jilin and Traye send forces to Trist. That will put hundreds of thousands of horse and boots bracketing the Neer Plain."

Klayne arched a brow. "You've considered this well, Coin Inlina. You overlook many great logistical difficulties, however. It will take years to build roads for fast communication between the Sablefort and Trist. We'll need atlens. Many, many atlens."

"We will use Derslin Wheels. And we do not have years. We have but a few ten-days, I suspect."

For a split instant, Klayne appeared shocked. He recovered and said, "What is a Derslin Wheel? A new fast carriage?"

The question was a lie. He knew very well what a Derslin

Wheel was. And that was concerning. "You're from Stallid, Klayne Itopolo? That is not a tribe name with which I'm familiar."

He shifted with the Coin's change of subject as gracefully as a dancer. "Ah, well. It is not one of the Barrazh. But it is an old tribe. You'd be surprised how far back I can trace my lineage."

"And do you have standing with the Delp tribe? We could save much time if you journeyed there yourself, spoke to the Queen. Stallid must prepare."

The Autarch laughed. "Queen Delp is dead! Didn't you know, little niece?" She leaned into Klayne. "She's spent too much time on Garden Island. What a sad little outpost it is. Have you been, Klayne?"

"To Garden Island? No. I regret to say I have not."

She kissed his cheek and giggled. "You've missed nothing." Then she glared at Inlina. "Unless you fancy dour old women who poke into everybody's business."

Pushing her plate aside, the Coin leveled her stare at the woman. "The queen is dead, eh? Sad news indeed. And the Voluptuary on Garden Island just recently was host to her heir, Gian Delp. He fled the island because of Kila Sigh. I should think him quite amenable to our requests."

Klayne's smile did not manage to hold any semblance of genuine humor. But he showed it anyway, like a horse chomping its bit. He would never concede to going to Stallid, she knew. He thought this whole enterprise silly, despite her medallion spins. But she didn't need him to believe, she needed him to get men moving to the Sablefort. Arguing and prodding further would not produce the results she needed. It was time for her to withdraw and think through her options.

Standing, the Coin bowed respectfully to her aunt. "Autarch. It has been good to see you. I wish it were under peaceful circumstances. Now I wish to see this artifact you've kept concealed from me."

Klayne laughed now. "Oh, you'll need Pol's help with that. The Autarch will not show it even to me. Perhaps after Dem-Kisk she will reveal it."

"I suspect she will have need of it during Dem-Kisk. But may I ask you one last question?"

"Of course, Coin," Klayne said with immense magnanimity.

"Does the Autarch know you are a merculyn?"

The woman's reaction was more surprised than the Coin had hoped. It explained much about their relationship. He had no love for her. He did love her power. More than that, he wanted the artifact. No doubt it was why he was there. The Coin would not allow that to happen. "Sens Roon, release the Autarch. Klayne, please do me the courtesy of sending me a roster of armsmen you intend to send to the Sablefort. I will go ahead of them and prepare the garrison there to receive your forces."

Klayne nodded, though he looked at the Autarch sideways. She was studying him with a narrow gaze. The Coin doubted her revelation about him would drive much of a wedge between them. If he was as skilled as she suspected, he may have used mind-lulling feats upon her already. "It will be my honor, Coin Inlina. When will you be leaving Tordain?"

"I haven't decided, but time runs thin."

The Coin exited the small throne room, Roon in tow. Once they were out of the dome, Roon looked back. "I have felt Kila's power. I have felt Dunne Yples's. Whatever the

Autarch has hidden there, it is a match for either of them. What could it be?"

"It can only be one of two things."

"Oh?"

"Either it is Dunne Yples himself, which I doubt. Or it is the Motherlight. Klayne Itopolo wants it for himself. Something is stopping him from taking it and it is not my aunt. Her power is great, but her skill is laughable. There must be a protection upon it that a merculyn of Klayne's power cannot easily overcome."

"He is powerful, but not more than Henley Mast or even you with that heller ring."

That was quite powerful enough to do great harm. Stallid was not known for producing merculyns. They manifested power through their own strange religions that had nothing to do with Pol or Til or Ori. That made him a riddle to the Coin, and she did not like riddles. Not one bit.

"What next?" Roon asked as they returned to their apartment full of useless, fussy servants.

The Coin did not know. The meeting with the Autarch had not gone as expected. The forces of Tordain might never go the Sablefort. No. Merely thinking of failure was unacceptable. The Autarch must do as told.

"Klayne must go," was all the Coin said before retiring to her room. The statement played in her head for hours as she considered how she would rid herself of the man.

By the time she had settled on a course of action, the servants had given up on her and gone to bed. She fetched a loaf of bread from the pantry and pinched small bites into her mouth. It tasted of dust, but she swallowed.

23

UNRESOLVED MOMENT

One hundred and fifty shadlines assembled in the Stardome. They were of every nation, every conceivable shade of skin, every size. More men than women. Some wore fine tabards over their chain shirts, others wore the dress of their trade, still others the finery of wealth.

Among them were a handful dressed all in black. The Cloaks. Most serious of face, some scarred on cheek or brow, and all radiating the potential of extreme violence. Cloak Einlin stood near to Zirhine and Fallo, wolfish face showing true eagerness for the proceeding ahead.

The pointy nosed Winnea wormed through the throng, smiling broadly at Kila. Cinnon and Mack'Ti trailed after her like loyal hounds, Cinnon chewing on a hunk of bread.

Jil and Ell stood in the front ranks, facing a curved table where the seven Knights of the Dirth sat. At the center, Shad Ault leaned on the table, looking left and right to make sure all were present. A cloth in front of him covered a lumpy object.

Everyone wore their weapons. Swords and daggers were

the most common. But here and there a shadline leaned on a battle-axe or hammer. One woman held a pitchfork-like weapon Kila had never seen before. The short, dark bearded man next to her juggled two black spheres, roughly the size of apples. It looked habitual to Kila. But could those balls be weapons?

"The Armory will come to order," Shad Ault said. Though his shoulders slanted sharply down, his tone was imperious. The dome magnified his words so that all heard and went quiet.

She recognized Shad Lykea to Ault's right, with his beard and bright eyes. A truly handsome man. Kingly, even.

Sitting to Ault's left was a lumpy older woman in a sack dress. Maz Nool had served on the Dirth nearly as long as Ault. She had been a Cloak before being raised. Kila couldn't imagine the woman dancing, much less fighting.

One seat down was Shad Grickel, a short man with incredibly large arms and legs. A great golden beard poofed from his lower face and coursed down his mailed chest like a pelt off a northlands yak. Jil had mentioned he was the only shadline other than Fallo to possess two shadline weapons.

The others Kila didn't know. A dark-skinned Iopsi man with a striking bluish hue to his flesh. A woman Jil's age, so slight and delicate in frame it was a wonder she'd survived the wounds that had scarred her face. A very elderly woman sat at one end of the table, gaze vague, grin toothless.

"The final shadline has arrived, just this morning," Ault said, nodding to someone Kila couldn't see on the other side of the crowd. There were no chairs. Shadlines stood lumped together in small groups. "He is one of our two newest oath-takers. Please come forward, shadline."

A young man emerged and strode into the clear space between the assemblage and the Knights. He had dark hair, broad shoulders, and moved with a grace Kila would never forget. Neither would she forget the shape of his jaw, the intensity of his eyes, or the soft warmth of his lips.

It was Gian.

The memory of kissing him, of losing control of her mercus such that they floated above their sparring ground at Ori's Home, rose fresh in her mind.

But he had left after her battle with Dunne Yples. *"I can't be so outshined,"* he had told Henley. She'd thought him so powerful, so brave, so skilled. But he was a vain coward, afraid to tell her those words himself.

She had Henley now. She didn't want this young man, no matter how charming and beautiful he was. Yet the hurt was still there, reopened by his very presence.

"You wished to speak first," Shad Ault said. "Go on. Speak."

Gian moved to the end of the table and faced along it, so that the Knights and the common shadlines could see him. His eyes caught Kila's. Stiffening, he clenched his jaw. Kila hoped it was shame that made his cheeks flush so brightly.

"I swore my oath a ten-day ago when my mother died and her sword, Revenir, came to me. My coronation will follow this Armory. Losstra needs me back in Stallid. It is my hope we can conclude our business swiftly. But I will stay until it is finished, for I have seen the great danger that threatens this world. I have seen the malice and power of Kila Sigh first hand."

Heads turned to face her, but she was only dimly aware of those expectant looks. Her vision narrowed until nothing but

Gian's visage filled it. She noted his hand on the hilt of his sword, the tension in his shoulders. And those stiff arms. Could they be the same warm arms that had so easily wrapped her up over and over as they trained that night?

"I was with Sigh when the horrid Dunne Yples appeared amidst a fellstorm. He grew to enormous proportions and became like black smoke, a hellform of mercus evil. He laid waste to Ori's Home in his efforts to kill Kila and her companions. I had the misfortune of being among that number.

"Kila Sigh is susceptible to great rage, and Yples's attacks provoked within her an equal response. After removing us by means of a mercus feat known as dymensing, she became engorged with her own hateful mercus evil. She, too, grew to enormous size and contended with Yples. I saw and felt her hate as she turned on her friends.

"In the end she was brought down. Highest Fley was killed, unfortunately. Kila escaped and soon declared herself Highest of Kil." His voice cracked as emotion overwhelmed him. Steeling himself, he continued. "I think now she may have used her mercus to manipulate my heart in her favor. I was utterly smitten with her. Only her frank display of power and desire for dominion over all people broke through the glamour of her charm spells.

"I have not trained in the shadline ways, but I do know the principle of listen and obey. I urge the Dirth and the entire Armory to seize Kila Sigh while she is unable to use her magics. Keep her at the Hackwatch forever. Whatever you do, do not let her go. The race of man will not long survive should she once again embrace the fullness of her power."

With that he strode back to the crowd, pointedly not looking in Kila's direction.

His speech was so audacious, so completely wrong in both fact and assumption, that Kila did not know how to respond.

Shad Ault did. With a casual tug, he uncovered the object on the table before him. It was the *vaz'on.* "It can be no accident that this relic came into my possession. It is clearly a fate's-piece."

The shadlines murmured to each other, raising a tense rumble in the Stardome. Winnea leaned to whisper in Kila's ear. "You knew the Prince of Losstra! Why didn't you tell me? Did you truly transform into a giant devil?"

Kila couldn't exactly deny it, though her memories about the encounter were vague at best. Yples's hatred had reached into her and sparked a response she wasn't proud of.

Shad Ault pounded his fist on the table. "There will be silence."

And there was.

"I sense another wishes to speak. Step forward, shadline."

This was the woman with the pitchfork weapon. She wore the plain woolens of a lower Terriside housemother. "I was in Starside when the Girl Who Flies attacked. She threw great spheres of magic that destroyed the Cathedral of Til. Other spheres demolished people's homes, including mine. My son and daughter were crushed under heavy beams. Fire swept through before they could be freed. They were burned alive. And though I did not see it, I know that she smashed buildings in the Blasted Quarter to drive the poor from them. Many died as the fragile structures collapsed. The dust spread through the city, stinging our eyes and choking babies in their cribs. She used magics on our minds, shouting commands that we worship her. I was among hundreds in Dunne Medow Plaza to witness an execution. I was made to fall prone and raise my palms in supplication by the sheer brutality of her mercusine commands."

"Thank you, shadline," Ault said. "Next?"

A raggedly dressed man with filth covering his face hobbled into the clearing. His weapon was a short sword.

"M' name be Varl Akton. I live in Cheapsgate out the city walls. I knew of Kila Sigh and 'er brover Wen. They was thiefs of turrible repitation. So much gold they robbed in Terriside the Watch got rough on everyone dared to go into th' city. She was known t' tackle a man an' threaten bloody death on 'im. Such behavior gave us all bad names and shamed us. Now she's killin' everybody in sight and tearin' up the city with 'er power. Can't be good fer us or nobody."

Throughout this recitation, Ell's jaw muscles bulged more and more until Kila thought the woman's teeth would crack. If anyone could be as mad as Kila was at hearing this, it would be Ell. It was her city, and she knew what twists these last two tales were.

But when Shad Ault bade the next person to speak, Ell did not step forward to defend her. Kila's heart hammered even as her lower jaw thrust forward in outrage. For Jil Pokkti took the floor.

Oh, she must have been waiting for her chance to pillory Kila before the Armory. All this time, knowing the day would come, she must have planned and relished this moment.

"Kila Sigh is indeed powerful. My sword, Qinsh, has a singular power. It can smell merculyns, can trace the scent of their magic. Qinsh hates them. I cannot help but feel the same, though I am the master of my blade.

"The shadline instinct led me to Starside. I did not know why at first, but soon I uncovered a string of murders, all committed by a merculyn. Later I discovered a man of small power who had murdered a scribe and her grandbabes. It was not Kila Sigh, but a trapper who had been corrupted by the Hargothe of Til. A man of horrific evil."

Jil drew her sword and ticked the tip onto the mosaic floor. "Even now, Qinsh wishes nothing more than to lop Kila's head from her shoulders."

Now Kila's hand went to Cayne. She knew she didn't stand a chance against Jil's superior skills, and without her mercusine, the battle would be short.

"But to do so would not be just. I know facts these others have not related. Kila did indeed rain destruction upon innocents of Starside, but it was not her intention to do so. She fought a valiant and righteous battle against the Hargothe, a merculyn who had spread his corrupt mind-bond through the Ways of Starside. In the end, Kila was victorious. The Hargothe is dead, by her hand. This council owes her its gratitude, not condemnation." Finally turning to face Shad Ault. "And you, Father, know that."

Again the shadlines erupted in shocked discussion. But nobody present was as shocked as Kila. Jil had just spoken on her behalf. Judging by the looks on the Knights, her narrative carried a lot of weight.

The conversations continued even as Ell finally strode forward. She patted Jil on the arm as they passed, nodding in respectful gratitude.

When she spoke, her voice was soft, almost a whisper. But the dome enhanced her words and immediately the Armory returned to silence.

"I came here as a shadline, though I am also the monarch of Starside. I can add yet more detail to Kila's feats in Starside to support her goodness. Not only did she kill the Hargothe, she saved my life."

That final fact hung in the room, and Ell allowed it a moment to penetrate into the minds of all present. "I had been stabbed by my very own shadline weapon." She drew her dirk and held it up for all to see. "Merculyns possessed by the Hargothe's foul bond were overtaken by his deeply laid command. They struck and I bled, nearly to death. But Kila Sigh came to my aid, and through the immensity of her power and skill, plucked me from Lumne's fingertips. I cannot but be grateful for that.

"She could have just as easily left me to die. She could have crowned herself. Starside could be hers. Easily."

Kila nearly choked. The idea had never occurred to her. And now that Ell had planted it, the wiry and thorn-burdened notion sprouted in hideous tangles, showing her the horror that could have been had she harbored any ambition to be a queen.

But the idea had come to Ell naturally. And apparently to Jil, for she nodded along with Ell's words.

"Had Critt Sanglo lived, he would have told this audience of Kila's many disadvantages. Of her father's untimely death. Of her brother's lingering sickness. Of the tremendous responsibility she bore to provide for him by whatever means she could. Critt would have told you that he had sacrificed all thought of being a Shadline Knight because his instinct bade him abide in Cheapsgate and look after Kila. Not too closely, but simply to be there when she needed aid. And could Quinn Peline be here to speak on Kila's behalf, she would tell of a loyal friend, whip-smart and fierce.

"Yes. There are those who Kila has harmed, but the force

of destiny cannot always be kind when it moves one person among the uncountable peoples of the world toward a culmination. The battle to come will claim many lives, for it will be waged upon sky and land and sea, and the powers yet to be brought to bear will make events in Starside look like mummer's magic."

Shad Grickel coughed and said, "You speak of the war to come. I believe that is the subject of this Armory. Surely Kila Sigh will play her part, but she is not even a shadline. The *vaz'on* is indeed a fate's-piece, but given your testimony I do not think it meant for Sigh's brow. Let us set aside this discussion and turn our minds to this fatehand."

"I disagree," Shad Ault said. "While Ell LiMinluit and my daughter have offered powerful statements to Kila's credit, the fact of her actions remains. I am especially troubled by Gian Delp's story, for it makes clear that Kila Sigh cannot control her power."

A new voice filled the dome, this one full of hard anger. "And so should you control it?"

To Kila's astonishment, it was Fallo. He took Ell's spot on the floor now, eyebrow dipped with such fury his eyes peered through a thicket of black hairs. "Do you bind a racehorse's legs with chains? Do you place bags of sand upon its back? You do not. It must have its head. If I have learned anything as a shadline it is that the force of destiny can use only those who are free to serve its ends. 'Discomfort is the path.' Is that not central to the shadline way? Kila is a fellstorm, yes. She *is* discomfort. If we shackle her because we fear her, she will be unable to act when the culmination comes. If anyone needs restraining, it is the enemy who gathers nosg-kin hordes in the north. How is it that we did not begin by discussing this grave threat?" Catching his temper and taking a nostril-flaring breath, he smiled. "Besides, Kila has bonded to a cat. That alone speaks all one needs to know of her character."

Kila wanted to hug her friend. She would have covered his face with sisterly kisses. But showing such gratitude could only sap the power of his words before this audience. And so she stayed put.

Nax. Tell Lop to tell Fallo I said thank you. And promise Lop whatever food she requires as a toll. I'll pay it.

Lop says Fallo would do anything for you, and so would Lop.

Eyes misting, Kila looked away from her friend.

Shad Ault pounded the table until he got silence. "I respect the noble words of Kila Sigh's friends. It speaks well of them. But we cannot give the testimony of her allies the same weight as we do that of these other, more impartial complainants. Perhaps there were extenuating reasons for her dire and destructive acts. And young Fallo speaks wisely that shadlines must remain unhindered to answer the call of destiny. But Kila Sigh is not a shadline."

Shad Maz Nool waved her meaty hand, clearly out of patience with the proceedings. "Let her speak the oath, then, and let us move our discussion to the nosg."

"I fear it is too late for that," Shad Ault said, shaking his head with false regret. "With a sentence hanging over her head, such vows would have no meaning. No. I fear we must decide against her, for she is too dangerous to remain unrestrained. Shadlines, bring the girl forward."

Fallo and Jil moved first. Jil with Qinsh up in guard position, Fallo holding a dagger in each hand. Winnea came close to Kila's back, her little rondel dagger out of her sleeve.

"Stand down!" Shad Ault commanded Kila's defenders. "I said stand down!"

"This is wrong," Fallo said. "Can't you hear it? It is wrong, wrong, wrong."

Cloak Einlin stood between Fallo and the Knight's table. All of the Knights were standing. A few were gripping their own weapons in fury, but they were looking at Shad Ault.

Shad Maz Nool clicked her tongue and flapped her hand again. "Enough of this. Shad Ault is first among us. His command carries. Move aside, children. Allow your betters to escort Kila Sigh forward."

This speech made no impression on Jil or Fallo.

"Let's run," Winnea hissed to Kila. "If we get outside the Hackwatch they can do nothing to you."

But the door was blocked by a throng of shadlines. Kila stood no chance against even one of them.

It was Ell who interrupted the stand-off. "We must obey Shad Ault. I disagree with his judgment, but we must honor it. The debate can continue, but let us not have sister and brother shadline battle each other. Unity is the only way to victory in the days ahead."

"Well spoken, Ell LiMinluit," Shad Ault said. "Cloak Einlin. Zirhine. Bring the girl here."

Ell glared at Jil until the woman sheathed her sword. Winnea slid back into the crowd, cursing under her breath. Only Fallo remained at her side.

"Fallo PiTorro," Ell said. "Your defense of Kila does you honor. Do your instincts bid you to die here, or do they simply declare Kila's restraint wrong?"

His jaw worked left and right as indignant pride warred with Ell's cooler reasoning. Kila loved him all the more for this bold act, for she knew how he prized his reputation as one interested only in his own advantage.

"Listen to Ell," Kila said. Lifting her voice, she continued: "Shadlines of the Armory, I will not fight against being thrown into a cell. But if anyone tries to fit yon crown to my head, I will die from your swords and hammers before I will submit. I have worn one before, and it is a punishment beyond cruelty. And there is no need for it here. The Hackwatch itself guards against the mercus. Aggy and Jil will testify that my skills with Cayne are no threat to any of you."

Jil gave a sharp nod. Aggy spoke from the rear of the dome. "She is no threat to anyone here. I say she be allowed to keep her blade, for it must not be touched by another. I feel it is so."

"I second that," Cloak Einlin said. Kila glanced at the man, surprised to hear him advocate for Cayne. He had handled the blade before, so he knew there was no danger in doing so. "Fate Breaker came to her. Let it not be wrested from her until we ascertain her true ambitions, be they for mankind or against."

"I don't see the point of the *vaz'on*," Maz Nool said. "If she fears it so, then all the better not to use it yet. Let the mere threat of it rest upon her head, all the better to keep her in line."

"So be it," Shad Ault said. "For now the *vaz'on* will remain with me. The blade Fate Breaker will remain with Kila Sigh. Should she draw it and threaten anyone, it will be removed from her possession and her hand with it. Now, take her from the Stardome. I've asked Scholar Yips to prepare a comfortable cell for her."

Nax, they're locking me up. Stay hidden for now.

I want to come with you.

Better for both of us if you remain free. Shad Ault doesn't remember you exist. I'm not going to—

"And what of her cat?" asked the Cheapsgate man, Varl Akton. "Such creatures be thought possessed by demayne. Donse Master's club 'em every chance they get."

Ell snapped her fingers. "No harm will come to the Beloved One. Anyone who touches a hair on either of them will answer to me as monarch, not as shadline."

"You are no monarch here, LiMinluit," Ault said. "We'll find the girl's cat and put it in a box."

Hide, Nax. They're coming for you.

I'll care for her, Ell sent into her mind. *Though I suspect they will never find her. Be patient.*

Varl Akton shoved her, an act that would have got him a fistful of Kila's rage had it happened on the rooftops of her home quarter. Cloak Einlin made a noise in his throat and the man backed off. To Kila's horror she noticed a crude tattoo on his forearm. Of a curved blade called a "gutter" in Cheapsgate. It marked him as one of Dox Viller's thugs. How had such a man become a shadline?

Fallo stiffened, head twisting around. "Quinn?" He sprinted away, shouting her name.

Nax, what's happening to Quinn?

I'm not in the room with her. Lop says someone is attacking her.

She made a move to follow Fallo, but the Cheapsgate man yanked her around by the elbow. "It's Quinn," Kila cried to Ell. "Someone's attacking her."

The Cloak and Zirhine shared a glance, but neither moved

to go after Fallo. The Cloak said, "Fallo will handle it. I have no doubt. Come, Kila Sigh."

Feet dragging, Kila followed Zirhine out of the dome, Cloak and the Cheapsgate scoundrel following close behind. Scholar Yips met them at the door, hands clasped, maggoty-white face saggy as candlewax. He led them across a scraggly garden to a block building barely larger than a toolshed.

The door squealed open exposing stairs. The scholar fumbled to light a lantern with a flashtaper, then led down into blackness.

Nax?

Fallo tried to stab the man, but another shadline stopped him. The villain was a brown-robe. Quinn is unharmed. The man was trying to remove Quinn's clothes.

A scholar? A vile image came to Kila's mind of a man like Scholar Yips groping the unconscious girl. "I thought scholars deadened their desires each morning," she said.

Yips jerked around, scowling. He held a finger to his pale lips.

"Quinn is well," Kila said for the others' benefit. "A scholar tried to rape her."

Zirhine hissed. The Cloak's jaw bulged and he gripped Tosuin's hilt. Varl Akton made a sad sound. More disappointment than disapproval.

"You're one of Viller's men, I see."

Cackling, he said. "Ol' Dox don't like ya one bit. An' if he don't like ya, ya don't have much prospect fer a long life."

"Are you a shadline or a murderer?" Cloak Einlin demanded.

"What's the diff'rence? I spake me oath, an' I list'n an' obey. Maybe I hear diff'rnt whispers than some."

"We shall continue to argue for your release," Zirhine said to Kila. "But do not expect it to happen soon."

"Fatehands end in decisions," Cloak Einlin said. Kila understood he meant the previous fatehand, in Quinn's sick room. "Without a decision, the unresolved moment frays. A chance passes into history, never to be recovered. I fear Quinn's attack and yon cell could have been avoided had we given the fatehand its due."

"Yes, Dunne Cloak," Kila said icily. What was the point of this lecture? *She* was the one being locked up.

The stern man did not appreciate her humor, but the Cheapsgate man snickered. "I like that. Dunne Cloak."

The stairs opened into a dank hallway lined with iron bar doors to either side. The scholar led them to the last cell. A whale oil lantern hung on a hook inside. The floor had been swept and strewn with straw. A cot, chamber pot, and basin completed the appointments.

Kila's skin itched as she passed into the cell. Zirhine looked around, frowning. "There is no privacy here." True enough, the bars went floor to lintel. Anyone coming here would be able to look in on her.

The scholar shrugged and motioned for the shadlines to exit the cell. He swung the door closed and turned a big iron key in the lock.

Varl Akton leered and made a mocking bow. "Goodbye, Highest Sigh." Then he was hustling away, chuckling.

Kila rubbed her arms. Not because of the chill—thought the jail was cold and damp—but because the air held such malice. The prospect of being locked down here became a fully realized terror.

But she would not beg. Would not show any weakness before the disgusting scholar.

"Thank you for coming to my abode," Kila said to her friends. A tremble in her words betrayed her.

Zirhine reached into a pouch and pulled forth a hank of gray fur. "Wolftuft. Tear off a pinch and roll it in your fingers. Put it under your tongue until it absorbs. You will sleep. Now, put your face closer to the bars."

When she hesitated, the Cloak jerked his hand, commanding obedience.

Zirhine popped a handful of weeds into her mouth and chewed vigorously.

The scholar rattled his ring of keys, impatient to go. His gaze never left Kila's face.

Zirhine hooked her forefinger into her mouth and pulled out a black glob. "Hold still. This aided us in Cigil-Tine. It will remain above the Revulsion and offer some protection against it. If you have the heart for it, pray. You may find the gods attentive."

Zirhine drew a rune on Kila's forehead. It was cold and then it warmed, spreading slowly across her scalp and down her throat. A release came over Kila's shoulders and the darkness receded. "Thank you. And . . . I'm sorry for thinking you poisoned Quinn."

Zirhine nodded and departed. The Cloak's gaze lingered a moment, then he turned away. The scholar's lantern glow moved down the hall, shrinking and then fading as they ascended the stairs.

A moment later the door at the top of the steps slammed shut, followed by the rasp of a lock sliding into place.

24

TO CROWN A QUEEN

Yiothizandra was right, Eckso decided as she left the Stardome. She had become too enamored of her human life, had forgotten what it meant to be dragnithan. Her hand was clutching the throat of her gown. She snatched it away. Such rank weakness!

How had she come to this horrific pass? Weakness.

Ah, but her sweet babies . . .

Cinnon and Mack'Ti trailed after her. It was well the mercus was inaccessible to her. She felt her rage alone would have turned them to cinders. "Leave me. I must think."

Cinnon steered toward the dining hall. Mack'Ti went with him, after first offering a courtly bow. The other shadlines were dispersing throughout the Hackwatch, each seeking their bed. What an enormous waste of time the whole confab had been.

After Kila Sigh had been led away, the business had turned to the mind-numbing sharing of fate's-pieces. Even as a shadline herself, Eckso had never truly given such superstition much credit. All the random objects, the slips of paper, the snatches of graffiti committed to memory, sightings of ravens in Wantin, corpses of villains in Starside. It amounted to a mess of disconnected information that they so solemnly tried to puzzle together.

Eckso had claimed a freestanding building on the edge of the compound. It had been a servant house of some sort. The scholars had left it abandoned, so now all that occupied it were rats, spiders, and silence.

She'd had Cinnon bring in mismatched bits of furniture. Two lanterns gave just enough light to cut the heavy murk of the place. A tattered rug gave her feet a soft surface upon which to pace.

Kila Sigh was out of reach. Damn that girl and damn Shad Ault! Eckso had less than two days now to kill Ell and capture Kila. Not enough time. Not enough time at all.

Yioth was right about Eckso's softness. She was also crueler than a qiznathan, a creature fully devoted to Night. Eckso would never trust her to release her children. How could she?

"Klayne, you duplicitous blackguard!" she steamed to herself. He had snatched her children from their beds. For the first time in an age, Eckso missed her own dragnithan friends. They had been few, but they had been loyal. Alas, they were on the other side of the seal that kept her in this world.

Ell was not her friend. She would be of no assistance whatsoever. Not unless she volunteered to be decapitated.

Eckso went to the basin and splashed cold water on her face. Looking up at the glass, she composed her face, lifting her chin and lifting her brows into the well-practiced cool disdain required of her station in Trine. "You must save Poli and Trev. That's the sum of it. So how to proceed?"

Again she began to pace. She had no mercus here, but she

did have Loveheart. That wasn't nothing. And Cinnon and Mack'Ti had obeyed her thus far. Not inconsiderable tools, despite their dullness of mind.

First, Ell. The mercus above the Revulsion persisted here, else the shadline weapons themselves would become merely mundane. And Eckso's glamour would have dissipated the second she walked through the gate. If Eckso had a mercus stone or some other reservoir, she could kill them all with ease.

She did not have such. Killing Ell would require more than Loveheart. A dragnithan was infused with mercus, the source of life itself. Untappable power, but also difficult to drain.

Eckso stopped in the middle of the rug. She had it. She knew exactly how to kill Ell. Risky. But what choice did she have?

Pacing again, she considered the problem of Kila Sigh. The answer came to her just as abruptly. Oh, it was quite a lovely answer. It might even do to get her children away from Yioth.

There were too many uncertainties remaining to allow a smile onto her lips, but they did press in determination. There was a Derslin Wheel below the Hackwatch, full of Yioth's hideous nosg warriors. She'd hoped to leave them there to rot, but she needed them now.

The goddess Pol did not merit much respect, but Eckso offered a prayer to her now. Such beings barely knew they existed, and demayne did not like to grant them power through beseechment. But it seemed they were all due to awaken soon anyway. Dragnithan did not have many superstitious wards in their repertoire, but humans did. Eckso tapped her ear three times and said, "Die, Yioth, Die."

FINDING SHAD AULT's room was not difficult. As expected it was high in one of the towers, above and separate from the other Knights. The man's self-regard was the equal of any lord's. That would be to Eckso's advantage.

Smoothing her skirts, she tried to prepare herself for the filthy task ahead. Having lived a hundred lives upon this world, she had experienced a wide range of existences. She preferred the life of a noblewoman, but this called for something a bit more streetwise.

At her knock his voice barked, "Come!"

The chamber was well appointed, and she realized he had taken over a senior scholar's room. Rugs spread across the floor, tapestries to soften the walls, a crackling fire. He was enjoying a solitary repast at a thick round table, piled with delicious smelling food.

"Is all that from Tearling?" she asked after a curtsey.

"Winnea, is it? I hope you have something important to say."

The food was certainly not from the Hackwatch kitchens. The man lifted a cup and eyed her over the brim as he drank. "Loveheart came to you, did it? I knew shadline Egriss well. She never blooded the thing. Pity to waste such a fine weapon." He put the cup down. His eyes were watery and gray. His stooped shoulders had not gained an inch with the removal of his mail shirt.

Eckso saw his great two-handed sword on a stand near the bed. Lordmight was so legendary that even Eckso knew the songs by heart. She approached the table, slippered foot in front of slippered foot so that her hips would sway just so.

She'd loosened the laces of her bodice a little. No man would notice the technique, but he would notice the extra fraction of exposed bosom. "I came to discuss Kila Sigh. My instincts have been shouting to me about her."

He brightened at this, but he did not ask her to sit.

She moved close to the table, holding hands together and worrying them in the manner of someone nervous to be in the presence of a superior. Men liked that. Fear aroused them.

"I believe it was a mistake—I beg your pardon. I mean to say the question of the *vaz'on* bothers me greatly. I do not think Kila Sigh should be without it." She rushed out the words, as if getting a great burden off her mind.

She gave her lips a nervous swipe of her tongue, knowing how it made them glisten. Knowing how the pinkness of her tongue provoked certain thoughts in a man's brain. Had she her mercusine, she would be done with him by now.

"Sit," he said.

She chose a chair next to him.

"The *vaz'on* won't do ought while she's here," Ault said. "Not that I disagree with you. Had I my way, no merculyn in this world would be without one. In truth, if I truly had my way, I'd send Jil after them and unburden their heads from the necks. Every last one. Qinsh is wasted on her. Jil had killed but five merculyns the last time we spoke." He sighed and took up a leg of turkey and began to tear great mouthfuls from it, juice dribbling into his white beard.

"Where is the *vaz'on?*" she asked, smiling demurely. "I thought it quite beautiful."

"Oh, it is!" His eyes glazed across her throat and chest. Scooting back his chair he spryly went to a trunk at the foot of his bed and retrieved the *vaz'on*. He brought it forth in both hands, like a Donse Master about to crown a queen.

Shuddering, Eckso dipped her chin and allowed him to set it on her head. The points of the screws were dawn back, but they still pricked the skin.

"Do I look like a queen?" she said, laughing.

"You look like a princess, fare and smooth." His voice had changed so quickly, Eckso was caught surprised. She had thought this encounter would take hours.

Standing, she approached him. He was not tall. They stood eye to eye now. She took up a cloth from the table and wiped the juice from his face, gently. Tenderly as a mother. His nostrils flared. She had him.

"Keep it on," he said, hands reaching for her skirts.

Base desire. It had always been her least favorite weapon, the one she resorted to in the last extreme to get what she wanted.

She allowed him to do as he willed, waiting until he reached the peak of his angry lovemaking. Then she slid Loveheart into his breast, threading the ribs, and penetrating his aged heart. It poked through as easily as a needle into cloth, for it was a shadline weapon.

She rather enjoyed the reaction Loveheart provoked in its victims. As they died, they sought her gaze, hungered for it. Death was a sweet ecstasy for them under its power. And the dagger passed that feeling through her.

Shad Ault did not disappoint, gasping out his final words: "Ah, my dear. How I love thee."

She left his body on the bed, a growing stain of crimson spoiling the linens. She swallowed the last of his wine, removed the *vaz'on* from her head and put it in the canvas sack.

The *vaz'on* went into her little room, under the cot. Just a temporary hiding spot.

She undressed and cleaned herself with chill water from the basin. She feared Shad Ault's reek would remain with her forever. But she would do anything to save her children.

Now the truly difficult part began.

25

A MILLION HARD LEGS

Lop got hurt, Nax sent.

Kila popped up from the cot, mind fuzzy from wolftuft. The lantern was still lit, and eerie shadows danced across her cell. Beyond, the bars cast long shadow lines onto the filthy stone of the corridor.

Water dripped somewhere in the darkness. Tick. Tick. Tap.

Is she . . . ?

Lop will be fine. Zirhine did something with weeds to her.

I'm surprised Fallo didn't kill that scholar. Is Quinn well?

Quinn sleeps still. Unharmed. I am with her and Fallo. Ell is here.

Kila's vision abruptly shifted, the cell vanishing and Quinn's room appearing as seen from Nax's position on the floor.

Nax let out a chirp. Ell squatted low and peered into Kila's eyes. "Are you there? I must assume you are. Nax is such a blessing to us all. I cannot speak to your mind unless I can see you. Shad Ault is allowing no one into your cell except a scholar to bring food and water. This will serve. Quinn is well. The villain did not get very far in his advances. Lop was thrown across the room, but not before giving the man many terrible scratches and bites. He lost an eye to Lop's fury.

"The Cloak went to search the man's room, but the head scholar refuses to admit him. Alas, the man is dead now. He dosed himself with rat poison mixed in wine. His body was not . . . You are glad to not have seen it. We believe that someone sent him to kill Quinn, but he sought to enjoy her before killing her. What sickness! This place . . ." Ell shivered, face was as pale as alabaster. "Shad Ault refused to hear any entreaty on your behalf. The remainder of the Armory today was a presentation of fate's-pieces. Fallo, Zirhine, and Cloak Einlin withheld the pieces they carry. None of us trust the Dirth. There is a corruption in the order. Cloak Einlin told me of the Cheapsgate man who spoke against you and the things he said to you. I am aware of Viller's Killers. He should never have come into a shadline weapon. I don't know if it is the Revulsion or if Kil's growing presence in this world twists all things toward darkness. You see now why you are needed!"

Kila did not see it, but couldn't speak back through Nax.

A sound behind Ell drew her head around. "Quinn wakes."

Ell went to the cot. Fallo was there, too, bending over the girl. And then Quinn sat up, blinking and confused. Fallo hugged her. She resisted for a moment, then seemed to realize who he was. She embraced him so fiercely that Kila had to wipe tears away.

Nax, go to Quinn.

Kila's vision bounded and wobbled as the cat leapt onto the cot. Quinn's face came very close, very quickly. She smiled wanly at Nax and kissed the top of her head. Kila felt the kiss on her own head. She ached to wrap her arms around her friend.

A pounding on the door startled Nax. A loud voice boomed.

"Nax, hide!" Ell hissed.

The catsight vanished, and Kila was left sitting dizzily on her cot. Quinn had wakened, but someone had come. Someone unwelcome. Had they come for Nax? Or had they come for Quinn?

Frustration lifted Kila from her own cot. A burning rage tensed her arms, made curses fly from her lips. The lantern light jerked and danced, and shadows lunged and retreated. The wolftuft was wearing off. The smudge rune on her forehead smeared off on her palm.

She kicked the iron bar door. It rattled and the black corridor answered with jangly reverberations. Rats squeaked and scurried in a nearby cell.

The inky corridor chilled Kila. A presence hovered out there. Someone—some*thing*—lurked just out of range of her lantern light. The unseen eyes feathered over her mind, lingered upon her body. A scholar? She hadn't heard the stair door open.

"Hello?" she called. What a small voice she had. "Speak, man!" she said, more firmly.

Perhaps it was her imagination filling the darkness with nightmares. Yes. That had to be it. Of course nobody was there. If one of those maggoty-faced men were down here, his white skin would fairly glow in the lantern light.

The corridor held its breath. Had it grown darker? No.

How could blackness be blacker? The lantern was sputtering. The light was less. Surely.

Kila longed for her mercus senses. They would show her every contour of the stone down here, every whisker on every rat. And she could ash them all.

Just wishing for it drew her attention deeper, to where her power resided. The Revulsion met her with eager fingers. She recoiled and hugged herself, shivering.

She'd never noticed how the mercus had occupied her body before, but with its absence, a sucking void held the core of her. The Revulsion knew of it, hungered for it. It wanted to fill her up with its essence.

A scuff in the corridor, like a foot dragging over gritty stone.

No. It was just an answering echo to her own foot sliding upon the straw.

Another scuff, something heavy.

"Go away! I've got Cayne. You'll not find me pliant to yer gropes, scholar."

No answer. The lantern spat and hissed. The acrid smoke coiled from the glass chimney like an ethereal black serpent.

This was ridiculous. She was Highest of Kil, the Girl Who Flies. What could she possibly fear from darkness? Her god *was* darkness.

She went to the center of her cell and began to move through the fighting forms Aggy had taught her. Punch, lunge, block, kick. Over and over until her body warmed. But still her neck thrilled with the tingle of watchful presence in the black corridor.

She froze, sweat instantly chilling her. Was that sharp breath an echo of her own gasp, or the eager intake of someone just behind her? Her skin thrilled with the dread certainty that something was almost touching the nape of her neck. A taloned hand extended, reaching, about to stroke her skin, about to pull her into shadow.

She squeezed her eyes shut, covered them with her hands. She stomped her feet and let out a high-pitched squeal. Noise. Any noise of her own to mask the sound that was about to come. The guttural desire of a phlegmy mouth stretching wide.

What would it do if it grasped her? What would it do?

It didn't matter. The horror was if she saw it! What if she turned right now and saw the horrid pale, maggoty face?

She mustn't look. She mustn't turn.

What had Zirhine said? To pray?

In desperate whispers she blathered whatever came to mind. "Ah me, Kil. What do ya want of me? I didn't ask to be yer Highest. Don't let it touch me."

Touch me . . .

She shouted, "I didn't ask for power!"

Touch me . . .

Terror made the Revulsion surge, forcing her gorge to rise even as the black sludge flowed to fill the spaces left hollow by the absent mercusine. Retching and still covering her ears she fell to her knees, spine thrilling. Something brushed her neck.

Light flooded into her vision, glorious, sweet and warm. The Revulsion skittered away upon a million hard legs, driven to shadow. The entity behind her pulled back. Warmth spread from her heart to every pore.

The catsight took hold of her vision and suddenly Quinn was looking directly at her.

"What is it, Naxie?" Quinn asked, gently stroking the cat

from head to tail. Fallo sat beside her, holding Lop in his arms. He looked at Kila with grave concern.

"I've never seen Nax do that," Fallo said, sucking on a scratch on one hand. "Ah. Lop says she's showing us to Kila. Hello, Sigh. Is the food better down there than it is out here?"

Quinn elbowed him. "Shush." Brows knitting, she came very close and kissed Nax's nose. Tears traced down Kila's cheeks, but her vision did not blur. Nor did it move. Nax held her friend's gaze, held the light and warmth and presence of that room. Held it for Kila.

Thank you, Naxie. By Mayla's blood and all the small gods, thank you sweet friend.

The Revulsion wants you. I will not allow it.

Crawling and feeling her way, Kila moved to the cot. She was used to the catsight and it no longer made her head swim. But it was better if she stay still. The cell and the blackness outside of it was gone to her now. She was in the room with her friends.

How long can you do this? I know it tires you.

Until you no longer need it.

"I'm sorry I attacked you, Kila," Quinn said. "I don't remember it."

"I understand. You were treshed—"

"Zirhine said I was poisoned. It must have happened on the ship. Critt and I did not stop in Tearling." Quinn continued over Kila's response because she couldn't hear it. "I wish the man who did it could feel Black's bite. I grew quite fond of Critt. A good and wise man, he was."

Fallo said, "The man who did it knew that Quinn would name him when she woke. That has to be why he sent the scholar to kill her. I suspect you know who I'm talking about,

Kila. Who else traveled to the Armory with Critt and Quinn?"

Quinn picked it up, not giving Kila a chance to consider it. "Viller's Killer. His name is Varl Akton."

The Cheapsgate man. He'd found a corruptible scholar and probably made him many tempting promises. Probably enticed him with visions of a lovely, sleeping girl, unable to defend herself. Unprotected by any shadlines while the Armory was meeting. Vile, disgusting man!

"He kept out of sight for most of the voyage," Quinn said. "Cloak Einlin is meeting with the other Cloaks. He doesn't trust Shad Ault."

"For good reason," Fallo said. "The Cloak realized the connection when you brought up Dox Viller. He's the one who captured the villain. And lucky for Varl he did, or I would have ended him."

But why would Dox Viller want Kila dead? And why go to the trouble of treshing her friends? Kila had no doubt they had the right man, but he wasn't the only one. Someone had sent Varl on this mission, going so far as to secure a shadline weapon for him.

Fallo was already walking the same path of thoughts. "So who sent him, you're wondering. It wasn't Dox. Akton says it was a side job offered him by some Sensual named Taht. Iopsi, he says. She was acting on orders from the Voluptuary of Garden Island. Taht originally asked him to capture you. But when he said he didn't want to be ashed by Highest Sigh, she agreed that he should find a way to kill you."

Varl would join the scholar in Lumne's embrace. And it would not be a gentle one. Not for a man with such crimes upon his soul.

The topic moved away from the bad things. Quinn spoke of the sea voyage. She spoke very fondly of her donkey which she'd named Tolky. She'd been relieved to discover the beast was safe in the stables. Kila lay back and feasted upon the sight of her friends. Nax never wavered, only occasionally blinking.

And in this wonderful light, Kila eventually slept.

26

THE BLADE PUSHED

She'd enjoyed countless lifetimes upon this world, appearing to age, feigning death, then moving to a new city. Eckso had savored almost every minute of it. She loved the challenge of ascending the social strata, often giving herself the lowest starting point.

Woman of a pleasure house.

Orphan selling posies in the square.

Once she'd played at being blind and destitute and had risen to be a queen. How long ago had that been? Prior to the last war against the nosg.

In all those cases, she'd had plenty of time. Now she had none.

Nosg! How she hated the wretched beasts. But she needed them now. If only she could find the accursed Derslin Wheel. It had to be here somewhere.

At the moment she was wandering the sub-cellars beneath the main keep. Not even the hideous scholars ventured this deep. The Revulsion manifested itself more openly down here, making the rats larger, the shadows blacker, and the stone slicker.

One hand bracing against a greasy cold wall, she crept down a promising pathway, lantern held high. The giveaway was that this was an elnisian corridor. Very fine work compared to the roughhewn blocks of men.

The way sloped downward, twisting and turning and finally coming to a dead end. It appeared to be blocked over, but Eckso knew better.

She strode confidently at the wall and passed right through it. Even her dragnithan blood couldn't resist a slight shiver as she crossed into the elsewhere of the Derslin Wheel.

The nosg were there, nearby campfires spreading elongated shadows of the hunched figures bent over their meals. More flames blossomed and danced in the distance. But the endless space of the cavern took the smoke away and even kept the nosg-kin stench to a low riot in her nose.

Reaching for the mercus to amplify her voice, she said. "Shamans, come to me!" The return of her power gave enormous relief, like a lungful of sweet air after a long-held breath. The Revulsion might one day seep into these places, but since the Derslin Wheel was not truly at the Hackwatch, it was as good as being miles from the walls.

Surprised grunts and shouts arose in the nosg's lurkmire tongue. Silhouettes flittered across the campfires as the creatures dashed to pick up their spears and axes. Soon a throng of beasts emerged, the glowing eyes of their skull-topped staves tilting to and fro in cadence to their steps.

She produced a glowing sphere above her, shedding red light down. The creatures revered red, and her display of the mercus would keep them from acts of precipitous stupidity.

"I am Dragnithan Eckso. Queen Yiothizandra wishes for you to take the fortress above this place."

"What is the fortress?" asked the lead shaman, an older beast with a green-eyed skull. His necklace of fangs, ripped from snowcats and wolves, dangled in heavy loops.

A human cry came from far away, muffled, as if gagged.

Eckso ignored it. "It is the Hackwatch near Tearling. I will lead you into it. Slay all you encounter." Most of these creatures would die. A single shadline, if trained, could count for dozens of nosg warriors.

The cry came again, this time more frantic.

"The gr'hils are ready," the shaman said. He tapped his staff on the ground. Swarmlight intensified in his skull eyes. *"Aggalamas-alamas!"*

The nearby nosg responded in a roar. The long-awaited day had come. They believed they would reclaim the lands of man and elnisian. Eckso didn't care enough about it to pity them. Perhaps they would enjoy a brief dominion over men, but in the end Kil would destroy them all.

The human cry again pierced the nosg chants.

"Who is that?" Eckso demanded. "Did you venture out and abduct someone?"

"No. Boy came here through column circle. Maybe eat him later."

Through the Derslin Wheel? That was . . . alarming. Eckso bulled past the shamans and followed the continued cries of the human. She found him next to a campfire, bound hands to feet, greasy rag placed over his mouth.

She knelt next to him. His pale eyes filled with hope upon seeing her. His hair was nearly white, and his skin exceptionally fair. Yanking the gag down, she said, "Who are you?"

"Raginalt Keel, mum. Get me out of here. Please."

"How did you operate the Derslin Wheel? I feel the barest haze of mercus within you. I doubt you could light a candle with your power."

"It was opened for me. From Garden Island. Please. Get me away from these beasts."

Garden Island was where those fools who ran the Ways taught and trained merculyns. Kila Sigh had been there. That's where those ridiculous handbills had come from.

"You came seeking the Sigh girl, didn't you? Are you one of those Way of Kila fanatics?"

"No. I'm her friend. From Starside. Take me to her. She has to know about these nosg." The oddity of the nosg standing by and allowing Eckso to question him finally sank in. "Why don't they kill you or tie you up?"

Eckso frowned as she considered the boy. He likely knew some things that Yioth would like to know. But Yioth didn't know about him at all, so maybe Eckso could question him. Later.

She replaced his gag and patted his head. "Rest easy, young man. I'll return for you when I'm done upstairs."

The boy moaned and cried, which she did not like to hear. But there was nothing for it. She wasn't about to bring him into the coming chaos where she might lose track of him.

Eckso picked up her pace as she led the nosg from the cavern and into the cramped passageways beneath the Hackwatch. She needed to get ahead of them, for there was a chance—a very slim chance—that the nosg might kill Jil before Eckso could get to her. That would never do.

Though she had never made a practice of exercising her body, her dragnithan blood gave her strength and speed to spare. Emerging into the populated corridors of the keep well ahead of the invading nosg, she cried an alarm. "Arise! Arise! Nosg attack!"

She burst out of doors, shouting and screaming to rouse the shadline. Confusion and chaos were her allies now.

Answering cries arose, demanding to know who was playing such a trick. Scholars stumbled out of their quarters, iron swords and axes in their fists.

Screams came from deep in the keep, followed by clashes of steel upon steel. Rumbles and vibrations shook the floor as shamans unleashed their swarmlight magics.

Reflexively, Eckso reached for the mercus, intent on throwing up a protective ward for herself. The Revulsion sluiced around her mind, seeking entry with oozing fingers. Recoiling and cursing her own stupidity, she snatched her attention away from the implacable sludge that so eagerly sought to embrace her.

Ugh. What foul madness it was. Still running, Eckso wound around the main keep to the entry courtyard. She wanted the battle to be in full fury when she made her move.

Outside her own building, she shouted for Cinnon and Mack'Ti. They hurried out, armed ready for battle thanks to her forewarning. "Ignore the nosg," she said. "Come!"

The men fell in behind her without asking a question.

A few skirmishers had come out into the night. Nosgs alone and in groups of three contended against single shadlines. Their gr'hils had been broken with the loss of their commanding shamans. They would not last long.

But there were hundreds more still filing up from the Derslin Wheel. They were quick and eager. The Iron Scholars might have a martial name, but their rusty weapons and unfit limbs made them slow fighters. The pale men became chaff before the blades of the gr'hils swarming up from the lower levels.

Jil Pokkti's room was just up ahead.

And there she was, Qinsh flashing in the blue and violet glows of shaman swarmlight. Nosg lay in piles at her feet. With a dancer's fluidity, she ducked and sliced, stabbed, and hacked. Beams of light flared from eye-gems, but Qinsh rose to meet and turn aside these attacks.

"Take the shaman," she commanded Cinnon. The man cried out and raised his club overhead. Skinny limbs corded with effort, he brought the club onto the shaman's head, obliterating it. The skull staff fell.

"Get back!" Eckso cried.

Cinnon dove away just as the unspent swarmlight exploded, ripping apart the surrounding nosg. In the ear-numbing aftermath, Jil still danced. Eckso shook her head and yawned, trying to get her ears to stop ringing.

Slowly the cries and clangs of battle came back to her. Jil was a beautiful creature to behold as she clove the second shaman's neck. The skull staff fell and Jil tumbled backward, a handspring twisting in midair, landing in a huddled crouch as the blast of energy blew past her.

"Mack'Ti?" Eckso said.

The man stepped forward, sword flashing at the woman.

Jil deflected the blow, face twisting with fury at the betrayal. Mack'Ti fell back under her flurry of swings and thrusts.

Her shadline instincts were remarkable, and Eckso noticed the very instant they told her to look for Cinnon's club. But there was simply no time for her to do more than flinch.

Her body flew back from the blow, slammed into the wall. Her head cracked against the stone. Vacant eyes turned toward Eckso, not seeing anything. The woman slumped forward and collapsed onto her face. Qinsh came free from her hand and clanked onto the floor.

Mack'Ti approached, face grim. Sword hilt in both hands, he lifted and stabbed straight down, driving the blade through Jil's neck until the tip clicked into the stone.

Again. Then once more.

Eckso lifted her skirts and tiptoed through the blood and bits of nosg that littered the floor. Plucking up Qinsh, she braced herself.

Nothing happened. No ecstatic bonding, no violent refusal of her touch. Lifting the bloody blade, Eckso grinned. The delight faded as she continued to turn the blade tip toward her own throat. A compulsion tensed her muscles.

With a will, Eckso dropped the weapon. A quick search of Jil's room produced a cloak. She wrapped the blade in the wool, careful not to touch the hilt. "It truly does hate merculyns," she said. The thing had almost forced her to kill herself.

"Pity havin' ta kill this lady," Cinnon said, toeing Jil's body. "She was a fine lookin' woman. Wounta minded having a go with her."

Mack'Ti spat on the floor. "Had you touched her, I'd have killed you myself, sir. A fine and honorable woman like her had no need of a wrecked man like you."

"Silence yourselves!" Eckso said. "We are not nearly finished this night."

She turned from the scene of murder and fled down the corridor. A sharp turn at the intersection. Hall blocked by fighting. Cloak Einlin's flaming sword hewing and torching nosg. If Jil had danced through her moves, the Cloak flowed through his like a creature of smoke. One moment solid, the next dissipating only to reform suddenly at the moment of a strike.

She detoured, taking a long route through abandoned corridors where the nosg gr'hils made room for her to pass. She had discovered Ell's room earlier. Barging in, she found it empty.

She retraced her steps and ran, skirts pulled up in one hand. The stomps of Cinnon and Mack'Ti kept pace with her.

Rounding a corner, she skidded upon the soles of her blue satin slippers. A fierce battle filled the hall outside of Quinn Peline's room. The girl herself was in the fray, though outmatched in skill by her assailants and her companion, Fallo PiTorro. The young man moved in rapid jerks and charges, dodging nosg strikes he simply could not have seen coming.

No sign of Ell LiMinluit. "This way," she said to her followers.

Where had her cousin gotten to? It wasn't like her to avoid a battle. They came back outside between the main keep and a walkway leading to the Stardome. That had to be where she'd gone.

A minor battle spilled out in front of her. An entire gr'hil of thirteen nosg warriors backed by a shaman fought against a girl with wild red hair. Aggy. Eckso recognized the girl who had been training Kila Sigh. She considered sending Cinnon to kill her, but there was too little time to spare.

Eckso made a wide course around the battle, astonished at the girl's swiftness. She upended nosg three times her weight with trips and shoulder thrusts, all the while severing throat and hamstring with blurring swings of her sword. She wove through the gr'hil and severed the shaman's arm. The staff tilted and fell, dismembered hand still clutching it. The skull exploded before his own head struck the ground. Already retreating, Aggy was thrown high into the air. She balled herself up, flipped and landed on her feet.

Her head whipped around, eyes locking on Eckso. "Why don't you fight?"

"The Stardome!" Eckso cried. It wasn't an answer of any kind, but Aggy seemed to interpret it as one. The girl sprinted ahead and disappeared into the dome.

"You two, go up to the garden. I'll bring her."

They obeyed, Cinnon flush with battle joy, Mack'Ti serious and grim.

Eckso discovered chaos in the dome.

A dozen shadlines fought a hundred nosg. Scholars lay here and there, some inert, some mutilated, others crawling for safety. Critt Sanglo's bier lay on its side, the dead man in several pieces. As she watched, a nosg reached for Shatter, the great maul. When its claw closed over the shaft, a shudder of agony shook the beast. The maul rejected the creature, driving it up and arcing through the domed space and falling into the midst of a gr'hil fighting with a short woman in trousers and jacket. Black hair tumbled over her face as she danced under axe heads, leapt over sword blades, and stabbed down with her delicate dirk. It was Ell.

She did not fight like Jil, or Aggy, or Cloak Einlin. Her grace even struck Eckso as wondrously beautiful. She dealt merciful deaths, striking only instant kills in eyes, or hearts, or throats. A shaman fell, and she caught the staff before it struck stone. Instead of exploding, the swarmlight faded. Then she bashed the skull into the face of a warrior and his head vanished in a puff of smoke.

Eckso raced to her. "Your Majesty! Come quickly. They have Highest Sigh!" Eckso did not wait for her words to register before racing from the dome. With all her speed she ascended the path toward the garden overlook. Ell ran behind her, calling out frantic questions.

The bundled sword was clenched in Eckso's hand. She felt it throbbing with what she could only guess was lust. Lust for her blood, lust for Ell's.

At the entrance to the garden, Eckso called out: "Just there. By the stones." Feigning a stumble, she fell onto hands and knees. Ell flashed past, desperate to save Kila.

"You are a fool, cousin. And so predictable." Eckso jogged after her cousin and found her facing off against Cinnon and Mack'Ti. Both men held their weapons ready. Neither bothered answering Ell's demands to know where Kila had gone.

Eckso steeled herself and let the cloth fall from Jil's blade. Teeth grinding, she grasped the angry hilt in both hands. It wanted her to turn the blade toward her own throat. And its want slowly began to become hers.

But like a hound distracted by a new scent, the blade abruptly swung back down. Toward Ell LiMinluit.

Eckso said, "Men, attack."

They obeyed. Ell evaded their wild swings with ease. But her own thrust stopped short as Eckso drove Qinsh through her back. It required no strength at all. The blade *pushed* through Ell's flesh, found a path through her heart and out her chest.

And still Qinsh was not done, for it began to feed.

Ell shuddered and dropped to her knees.

Eckso released the blade and wiped her hands on her skirts. What a horrid weapon. The hate it bore for Ell, for her, left a stain upon her mind.

Ell fell onto her side, hands grasping the bloody tip of the blade that impaled her. "Why betray us?"

"Why indeed, cousin?" Eckso motioned for her men to follow.

"Eckso? Why didn't you come to me? We could have—" Pain severed her words and she curled in on herself, groaning.

"Yioth has my babies. Your death was the price for their lives."

Ell's gasps and moans followed her down the trail toward the keep. One task complete. Now for Sigh.

If anything, the battle had grown. More shadline were outside now, and concussions of power rattled the Stardome. Flares of red and yellow swarmlight streamed from doorways.

Eckso did not join the battle. She instead stopped before a little shed. The door was locked. "Cinnon?"

The man slammed his club into the latch, breaking it off.

27

DOUBLE-STAB

The nosg lay in heaps around Fallo and Quinn. A few moaned and twitched, but none were a threat now. Quinn's mouth was moving, but Black kept her words silent.

Fallo embraced her, relieved to see her whole. Where had she found the strength to fight as she had? A Radiant's daughter she may be, but not soft. Not his Quinn.

He held Telt in one hand. His other two blades were screaming at him, each demanding to be wielded. Each demanding blood.

"Kil be a merry maiden, where'd these nosg come from?"

Quinn's weight sagged against him.

More come, Lop sent.

"Get into your room," Fallo said to Quinn. "Bar the door."

All weariness vanished from Quinn's face. Her lips moved and he didn't need her voice to know what she said. "Kil's piss, mother of dogs! You'll not treat me like a little girl."

Fallo kissed her nose. "Get ready then."

The racket of an approaching gr'hil thundered from

behind him. Quinn's eyes widened a moment, then narrowed as she began shoving dead nosg aside with her feet.

Are you safe? Fallo sent to Lop.

I'm trapped in a fortress full of nosg, you idiot.

The ones in Cigil-Tine didn't harm you.

I was almost pierced by an arrow there!

They were shooting at me.

A sudden rush of genuine fear—and love—poured into Fallo through the bond. *You, me. Same.*

Blinking back tears, Fallo bent to retrieve Shinane from his boot. He already knew the consequence of double stabbing a foe with Telt and Skeye. His enemy's life essence would pour into him. Quite a bracing feeling, but it also left him shuddering and immobile for many seconds. Not ideal amidst a battle with dozens of nosg.

What would happen if he did the ol' double-stab with Skeye and Shinane? Maybe this wasn't the best time to experiment.

But then the nosg rounded the corner and were on him.

He counted seven warriors and one shaman. The shaman was the most important target. If they were to live, they had to get to him.

This one was behaving differently than the others he'd faced, for it sprinted at the front of the gr'hil, skull staff raised like a club. The eye-gems were glowing green. Fallo knew that instant death could blast from those eyes.

The light engulfed the skull. He didn't have time to consider it further for his shadline instincts pulled him to the right, daggers crossed into a vee to catch the descending staff.

A jolt went through his arms. The grinning skull stopped

an inch from his face. The green glow blurred his vision. It smelled earthy, like a mound of leaves left to rot.

Quinn danced by, thrusting with Black. The blade caught in the shaman's loops of necklaces but didn't penetrate skin. A jagged nosg sword swept down, nearly taking off Quinn's nose. She retreated.

Fallo shoved up, forcing the skull face away from his. The green glow began to expand. Dropping to the floor, Fallo scrambled on hands and knees between the shaman's legs, popped up and stabbed with both daggers.

The blades buttered into the nosg's back. Fallo absently wondered if the creatures had kidneys in that area. No jolt took him, no prolonged inrush of energy left him vulnerable. Only a wash of heat over his arms told of any effect beyond the stabbing itself.

The nosg warriors shrieked and swung their blades. Fallo dodged as the shaman fell. Releasing Shinane but holding onto Skeye, Fallo snatched the falling skull staff, knowing he must get it far away from him and Quinn.

Turning, he raised it for a throw.

The nosg warriors backpedaled, mouths gaping, upthrust fangs glimmering with green light.

They seemed suddenly terrified of him. He feinted forward. They turned and fled, screaming. Fallo threw the staff after them. It struck the floor and exploded in a flash of green, flattening the retreating nosg.

"That was easy," he said, turning to Quinn.

She was still in battle stance. Facing him.

Her eyes darted from him to the fallen shaman and back. "Are you injured?" he asked.

Her mouth moved. He read her lips. "Stay back."

He took a step toward her, she retreated making warning thrusts of her dagger.

"Quinn? What's—?" He choked a moment and looked at Skeye. Looked at his hand gripping the hilt. Not a human hand. A nosg claw. And his arm was clad in hide armor. His other hand was a claw, too. He pressed a long-nailed finger to the back of one hand. It was smooth, normal. His chest did not feel any different under his palm. No necklaces of teeth and claws, but looking down at himself, they were surely there. A quick survey of his head and face revealed the usual mop of hair and thick eyebrow.

He held up a hand and eased into Quinn's room. Lop hissed at him from under the cot. Still side-stepping to stay out of Quinn's reach he peered into the glass above the basin.

He was a nosg.

Not just any nosg. He looked like the shaman he'd just killed. But when he tried to touch one of the tooth necklaces, his hand passed right through it to press against his shirt.

"A glamour," he said. "Like in 'Whispy in the Swamp.'"

Quinn was still staring at him, licking her lips. "Fallo? How . . ."

"It's these damned knives. Telt and Skeye drew in the elnisian warden's blood or life somehow. That's what Zirhine thinks, anyway. But I used Skeye and Shinane this time and now I look like a Kil lovin' nosg!"

It's rather an improvement, Lop sent.

Ignoring his Beloved One, Fallo stomped into the hall and retrieved Shinane from the back of the dead shaman. The sound of battle carried down the hall.

"If I go out there, every shadline I see is going to come after me."

"Don't go out there, then," Quinn said. She slumped onto the cot. Her fierce energy had drained and she looked as haggard as a Cheapsgate pleasure girl at dawn. Not that he would speak of that image to her, even under pain of death.

"How long will that glamour last?" she asked, rubbing her eye and yawning.

"Not long," he said, certainty rising. Not long at all. Because he was going to end it. Bending, he pulled up his pant leg and pressed the tips of both blades to his shin. Gritting his teeth, he applied a bit of pressure, then a bit more. Both blades bit at once, stinging like hornets. They drank eagerly, urging him to sink them deeper into his own flesh. "Selfish blades, aren't ya?" he said. Sucking air through his teeth, he pulled the daggers away. The wounds burned, but did not seep a drop of blood.

"Til be praised!" Quinn said. "I wasn't sure I could kiss a nosg."

The basin revealed what Fallo already knew. The glamour had vanished. He waggled his brow at himself. "I must say, I do look rather smart by comparison, don't I?"

Quinn hefted herself up from the cot and wrapped her arms around him. "You do indeed." And then she fitted her lips to his and he forgot about pretty much everything, including the nosg battle raging throughout the fortress. But then Quinn spoiled it by stopping kissing him. "We must do our duty as shadlines. The fight continues."

"I'll go. You're much too—"

She arched an eyebrow.

"I was going to say much too beautiful. I just don't want the shadlines to be distracted from their fight."

She allowed his lie to stand, and even rewarded it with

another short kiss. "I recommend you not use Shinane and Skeye together. Unless it's against Shad Lykea." Her lips pursed for a moment as she mused upon the idea. "With his permission, of course."

"Wanton harlot!" he said affectionately. He put Skeye away.

That left one other combination. And he had no doubt that the consequences of a double-stab with Telt and Shinane would do something extremely uncomfortable. So as he drew the blade, he resolved to do only single stabs.

"Stay with me, Lady Peline," he said. "If ought happens to you, I shall swiftly embrace Lumne to follow you down."

Lop returned to her hiding place under the cot as Fallo and Quinn charged from the room and sought more nosg to slay.

28

SAVAGE ACCELERATION

Nax had released the catsight while Kila slept, but when she woke she was completely blind. Flailing about, it took a moment to remember where she was.

The lantern had gone out.

Total blackness.

But not silence. Rumbles carried through the floor, then a boom shook the whole cell, making the iron bar door rattle. Dust and bits of stone tumbled from the ceiling, pelting her head and choking the air. The Revulsion surged, again offering itself.

Shaking and moaning, Kila shouted at it. "Go away!"

The floor shook again.

Nax! What's that sound?

Nosg have invaded. I'm hiding.

Nosg? Here? How?

They appeared in the halls.

Light seared her eyes though it came from a long distance.

Far down the corridor, an orange lantern. The skinny shadline Cinnon carried it. Mack'Ti came with Winnea behind.

The Revulsion did not retreat, but the light gave Kila strength. She ran to the door. "Winnea! Get me out of here."

"Stand back, girlie," Cinnon said, passing the lantern to Mack'Ti. With only the slightest wind up, he smashed his club into the door. The crash made Kila jump back and cover her ears. He struck again and again, each time deforming one of the bars until it bulged inward.

"Yer a skinny lass," he said. "Squeeze through."

"Thank you! Ah me, thank you!"

"Quickly," Winnea said. "This way."

She was running back down the corridor. Kila chased after her, spurred on by the oily Revulsion that tried to push itself into her grasp. They came out into chaos.

The space between the prison shed, the Stardome, and the main keep was filled with nosg. Here and there a shadline stood alone, or back to back with a partner, killing with efficient ferocity.

The dead lay everywhere. Winnea stood on tiptoe to see over the fray. "Damn!" It seemed the way she wanted to go was blocked. "We need to get you out of the Hackwatch so you can use your mercus. Come. I know another way out."

The two men followed close behind as they left the pitched battle behind. They wound through abandoned buildings, then turned into a narrow courtyard. The booms of shaman magic resounded behind them.

Nosg. Kila could not accept that she was truly seeing such creatures. Fallo had told of fighting them in Cigil-Tine. She had no idea how fearsome they were. The squat limbs, the wicked blades. Wide mouths with upthrusting teeth. Beasts!

Eckso slowed. "Men, go scout the way ahead."

The men started to brush past. Alarm flared in Kila's mind. On instinct alone, she dropped to her knees. Her short hair ruffled in the wind of Cinnon's fist passing over her head. It hadn't been a killing blow, but a hard enough one it would have knocked her senseless.

Mack'Ti circled around her, arms out. His sword was sheathed. "Come here, Highest. We surely do not want to hurt you. Cooperation will spare many a bruise."

Behind them, Winnea watched with impatient focus. "Hurry."

Drawing Cayne, Kila fell into a fighting stance. Aggy's lessons had shaped her, had honed her natural dexterity and speed. "Why are you doing this?" she demanded. "I thought you were helping me."

"We are," Mack'Ti said. "You must trust us."

"Trust you? Cinnon tried to brain me!"

"Just a gennle tap ta get yer attention." Now he had his club in hand. He swung. Kila lunged under the blow and thrust with Cayne. Cinnon's scrawny body arched inward just enough that her blade sliced through the top layer of skin rather than disemboweling him. Roaring, he set about with vicious blows. Each missed but gouged huge divots in the earth. His final swing hit the corner of a stone building and sent fragments flying.

Kila scurried away, dove past Mack'Ti, and came up face to face with Winnea. "Get back," Kila said, making warning jabs with Cayne.

Winnea stepped back, arms out, blocking Kila's escape. She held her little rondel dagger in one hand.

Cinnon stormed at Kila, flailing at her with his club. His

skill was not a match for his strength and Kila evaded easily. More divots appeared in the ground.

"I need her alive, you fool!" Winnea cried. "Yioth will have your hide if you kill her."

Yioth? As in Yiothizandra? Kila carved the air with her blade, pressing Winnea back. Mack'Ti tried to wrap her up, so she rammed her elbow into his gut. He bent double and her knee drove into his face. Nose blooming blood, he crumpled.

Eckso stabbed, tip of her dagger catching in Kila's shirt sleeve. Falling back, Kila lost her balance. Cinnon swung. The blunt tip of the club swept across her flank, ripping cloth and abrading flesh. Had he been an inch closer, her ribs would be spread across the courtyard.

Stinging pain erupted, making her vision go red. Winnea closed, again stabbing at Kila's arm. Her blade arm. The woman was attempting to disable her.

Retreating and grasping her blood-seeping flank, Kila again sought a route for escape. The stone walls were old, the mortar long eroded away. She could climb easily. But for those first moments she would be exposed to their attacks.

Winnea rushed at her, again. Her movements were fluid, practiced. This was not the untrained noblewoman she had pretended to be. Cinnon kept his club moving.

No time. She had to face Winnea, dagger to dagger. The pain in her side hunched her over. The point of the rondel dagger became a white gleam.

Without thinking, Kila threw Cayne. The Revulsion flowed in as she instinctively sought to guide her blade upon the mercusine. The foul sludge threatened to choke her, to make her lose her gorge.

And yet . . .

A bolt coalesced from it. Kila felt Cayne's form in her mind, and with savage acceleration drove it at the woman. Cayne plunged into Winnea's shoulder, throwing her back, screaming.

Cinnon staggered and mouthed a curse. Kila stumbled forward to collect her blade. Her vision had turned a metallic red, the world glimmering as if seen through a sheen of blood. Inside of her, the Revulsion twisted and begged for more release. She discovered she held it at the ready, that it filled the entirety of the void left by the mercusine.

Another bolt formed, purely from intention and anger. This would annihilate Winnea in black flame. An ecstatic glee overrode Kila's nausea.

Cinnon swore and raised his club. Another sound came to Kila's Revulsion-heightened senses. A drag of metal.

A searing agony exploded on the top of her head. The red vision flashed white. Buildings tilted and fell sideways in her view. But it was Kila who impacted the ground.

The last blurry image was Mack'Ti, sword held upright. "A pommel to the head, my friend. A reliable ploy in such cases. Might you have the leather sack, dear Cinnon? Good. Cover her head. I'll see to Winnea, for we are in the flames ourselves should she perish."

Kila! Nax sent. *What did you do?*

Kila lost consciousness before she could answer.

29

AWFUL MEMORIES

Sweat poured down Fallo's face, mingled with blood and mud, and dripped from his chin. Another dead shaman lay at his feet. Quinn was kneeling, catching her breath and dabbing at a deep scratch on her cheek. She'd come so close to decapitation that Fallo felt enormous fear and rage simultaneously.

The shaman's face was turning blue as Shinane's slow freeze deepened. A terrible way to die. Kila had called Shinane Bone Chill. An apt name. A useful blade for a slow kill, Fallo supposed. But in battle, the power was not immediate enough. To satisfy Skye's insane bloodlust, he used the blade to put the shaman out of its misery by way of its left eyeball.

Fallo and Quinn were in the courtyard now. The dead lay everywhere, mostly nosg. But many shadlines had fallen. Fallo did not know them.

Quinn wiped her brow and struggled to her feet. For someone who had been unconscious for days on end, she had made a good showing in the fight.

"Enough, Quinn. You can barely keep to your feet. You've done your duty."

"Just—need—a moment."

Stubborn woman. The thought came with a rush of pride. While she was not yet skilled with her blade, she had exceptional instincts for tactics. Perhaps that was the shadline gift coming through. She knew she was overpowered in every encounter with the nosg, and so she had learned to keep to the shadows, circle, and strike from the rear. In battle her footsteps would not have been heard anyway, but Black seemed to confer a bit more stealth than mere silence. On a few occasions Fallo had lost all hope for her survival. But each time she had crouched, slipped aside, and held perfectly still as enemies passed her by. She'd hamstrung three before they realized she was there.

One of the huge doors to the inner hold blasted off its hinges and tumbled across the courtyard. It gave one final bounce then smashed into the iron bars of the portcullis.

A roar of rage resounded from within. A man shrieked, then flew through the doorway to join the shattered door.

"Fallo … That didn't sound like a nosg."

Another rumbling roar was followed by a rattle of chain. Three shadlines burst from the opening and skidded into the courtyard. Shad Lykea, Shad Grickel, and a man holding a weapon Fallo had never seen before. A spear with three tines, the middle one longest.

Their faces were covered with blood, lips clamped in the grim look of ones certain of their own imminent doom and ready to face it.

Another roar, another rattle of chain.

"Stay back," Fallo ordered Quinn. She pulled back her hair

and slunk across the courtyard to crouch in the shadows. Fallo wondered why he said such things. They seemed to produce the exact opposite behavior from what he wanted.

"Fallo PiTorro!" called Shad Lykea, "Gather all the shadlines you can—"

The source of the roars emerged from the hold, ducking under the doorway then straightening to its full height.

"Kil be a merry maiden …"

It stood twice the height of Lykea, more than twice as thick. It stood upon legs like oak trunks, armored in layers of crudely stitched hides. Its arms were bare save for bracers made from the staves of huge barrels, cinched tight with crude cordage of ten different fibers.

The head was nosg-like, with upthrust tusks. The wide smushed nose recalled the face of the cattle dogs Fallo had seen on caravan. It wielded a heavy chain in one fist, the loose end connected to an enormous double hook, like a ship's anchor. The other fist clutched an axe with a long, curved spike on the back end.

The creature bled from several deep wounds which seemed to enrage it more than hinder it. The shadlines spread out, seeking to flank it.

Fallo looked around for more shadlines to call, but it wasn't necessary. Five more ran toward the beast, weapons ready. The kid, Aggy, sprinted at the front, her sword twirling through flourishes.

Lop, you wouldn't believe what I'm seeing.

I don't care what you're seeing. Is it safe to come out?

No.

The giant nosg began to swing its chain over its head,

sending the anchor in a long circle of death. The iron hunk made the air hiss and the chain links whistled.

The shadlines backed further. With a grunt, the beast jerked its arm forward, sweeping the arcing iron at Lykea. There was no deflecting it with a sword. The man had no more ground to give, his back nearly pressed to the wall. The only recourse was to go forward. He dove, rolling flat onto his back. The chain passed over his head, the anchor slammed into the stone wall.

The shadlines struck all at once, racing in over the now slack chain, dodging swipes of the enormous axe. Shad Grickel wielded his battle axe now, neck corded and flushed crimson. The axe bit into the beast's calf.

Aggy blurred between the legs, slashing three strokes, hamstring, hamstring, groin. Fallo went next, careful not to use both blades at once, he jabbed Skeye into one of the wounds Aggy had opened.

The beast's muscles convulsed as a shock coursed from the blade. Pulling Skeye out, Fallo thrust in Telt.

And then the man with the three-pronged spear was there, stabbing upward into the groin. The moment it struck the spear came to life with a white glow. The man squinted and held on. The energy built and suddenly released, lifting the giant nosg from the ground.

Others leapt in as the beast fell, striking, stabbing, smashing. The nosg giant screamed and flailed about with its axe. The spike caught a swordsman in the neck and tore his head free of his shoulders.

Another figure appeared from the shadows, leapt onto the giant's head and stabbed down. It was Quinn. Black arced into the thick neck, then withdrew. Again, again, again. Blood poured from the wound.

The beast curled into a ball, then flung its arms wide, sending Aggy flying. Quinn stumbled back and fell.

With slow, agonized movements, the giant got to its feet. The chain began to swing. The nosg creature blinked furiously and swayed unsteadily. "Back off!" Fallo cried. "It's done."

The giant stumbled again and the chain continued its arc, this time wrapping around the enormous body. Tilting, catching its balance for a moment, then losing it, the giant fell sideways, nearly crushing Quinn under its weight. The great mouth drew in a few quick gasps and then death claimed it.

The shadlines relaxed and looked at each other, awed by the foe that had withstood so much before falling.

"Fallo!" Quinn cried.

He spun, hairs on the back of his neck warning him. Up came Telt, edge striking the incoming arrow shaft, diverting it from its course just enough that the fletching brushed through his hair. The arrow whumped into the giant a pace behind him.

The arrow had come from above. His eyes sought the offender, but found only shadow. Another arrow zinged in, aimed for him, but he leaned away easily. He never saw it. He no longer needed to be convinced of his shadline instincts; they clearly guided his every move during battle.

And now they guided him through a narrow alley and up a ladder to a fallback tower inside the compound. At the top he discovered several dead nosg and even more dead scholars. A single nosg remained, loosing arrows at men below. It had not heard him come up.

Pulling Telt and Shinane, he saw the opportunity for what

it was. No other threats around. Driving both blades in its back, he gritted his teeth and waited for whatever shocks and convulsions the combination of these two had in store for him.

The nosg didn't react. The arrow it had nocked fell. But the nosg simply froze, elbow back as if still preparing to loose.

Fallo felt nothing at all. Yanking hard, he pulled at the blades. They would not come free, and the nosg was dragged backward.

Fallo couldn't open his fingers to release the hilts. "Kil's eyes, what now?"

The nosg was making a sound now. A guttural whisper. Fallo leaned around, saw its lips moving. Lurkmire nonsense, probably. The small eyes were moving. Fallo leaned further until he was bent awkwardly over the nosg's shoulder, still holding both blades. He peered into the creature's eyes.

And then his breath failed as surely as if someone clamped a hand over his mouth and pinched his nostrils.

A flash of brilliant red seared his vision. He was in a cavern with no ceiling. A figure lay tied up near a great fire. Nosg sat around, eating, drinking. The figure called out. Fallo stood and bent over the figure. A man. Tow-headed. He slapped the man's face and shouted in lurkmire to be silent.

The face stared back, terror stricken.

Ragin?

The vision shifted. A woman approached. The shamans went forth to meet her. Winnea. The new shadline woman who had befriended Kila.

Then fighting. Killing. Blood in his mouth. Battle rage. Climbing to the tower. Throwing scholars to their deaths. Unlimbering the bow, nocking, loosing at a tiny figure below.

Pain in the back. Fierce agony.

Fallo sucked in a huge breath as the daggers slipped free. The nosg tilted forward and pitched from the tower. Someone cried out and cursed from below.

Panting in gulps of sweet air, Fallo regarded the two blades. They'd shown him the nosg's memories. Awful memories.

Ragin had been tied up. That had to have been recent. But the fire had not shown any thing around. No trees or stones, nothing identifiable at all to show where the nosg camp had been.

Sheathing his blades, Fallo surveyed the battle below. It was over except for a few small skirmishes. The remaining nosg were outnumbered now. The fighting would be over soon.

As he descended the ladder his limbs told him of extreme weariness. He could not afford to be weary. Forcing himself into a trot, he angled toward a gr'hil that had lost its shaman. It was surrounded by three shadlines. Aggy, Shad Lykea, and Shad Grickel. "Spare me one," Fallo said, pulling Telt and Skeye.

The battle was brief and ended as Telt and Skeye drove into the gut of a nosg warrior. Fallo was ready for the convulsions this time. The inflow of energy shook him and shocked him. But when the blades finally let go of their victim, Fallo felt strong, as if he'd slept a full night and had eaten hearty stew.

The shadlines were watching him with great interest. He shrugged. "The blades like to work in pairs." He didn't owe them any explanations. "I think I know how the nosg got in. Winnea is a traitor."

Quinn found him, circled an arm around his waist. She

felt wispy in his embrace. "You don't need rest," he said. "Don't argue. The battle is over, but your duty as shadline is now to deplete all your strength."

She simply nodded and yawned.

"Aggy, see that Quinn finds her cot," Shad Lykea said. "Go."

The young shadline did not like this order, but she obeyed. Quinn leaned on the girl as they went away.

Cloak Einlin and Zirhine found Fallo, both showing relief to discover him alive. The courtyard soon became the rally point for the survivors, shadline and scholar alike.

"The gates were closed, as I had requested," said Shad Nool. She was covered in blood, but despite her lumpy physique and advanced years, she did not seem in the slightest wearied by the battle. "The turf around the gates outside is not disturbed enough for that to have been their point of entry."

"They can't have dymensed in," Fallo said. "The mercus doesn't work here." He told of the nosg memories, of seeing Winnea come among them. "But there was nothing around the fire. Just a stone floor and endless blackness."

"That sounds like a Derslin Wheel," Zirhine mused. "This place was elnisian before men overbuilt it with this fortress."

"Whatever it was. Raginalt Keel was there, bound and gagged. So where is this Derslin Wheel?"

A chorus of questions arose, but Shad Nool cut them off with a sharp whistle through her teeth. "Scholars! Where is this Derslin Wheel?"

Only one had the courage to step forward. He was rotund, middle aged, and sported a beard so long it was tucked into his belt. "I'm not a scholar here. Merely a long-term guest. I do not know where the Derslin Wheel is, but if there is such here, one should probe deep into the cellars. They are oft hid by false walls, glamoured to appear impenetrable. Or so I've read. I would very much like to see one."

"I'll find the headmaster," Cloak Einlin said. "If he knows of it, he will tell me."

"Spread out," Maz Nool ordered. "Search the entire fortress for stray nosg. Has anyone seen Shad Ault? It is unlike him to avoid battle."

No one had. She sent a man to search his quarters.

Fallo didn't need to clean his blades. They drank the blood they drew. He was happy to return Skeye to its place and Telt to its. He supposed he was now part nosg, having sucked in one's life energy.

Lop, you can come out.

That took too long. I'm starving. Oh, and Nax says Kila is in trouble.

What else is new? What kind of trouble?

Nax doesn't know. Kila went to sleep a little while ago. And then she moved.

Moved where?

Nax isn't sure. The Revulsion is cloudy here.

The what?

Kila is in trouble. Lop put more urgency into the statement this time. All the cats loved Kila. All except Oly. Fallo sometimes thought Lop was more loyal to her than to him.

Swearing, Fallo ran for the prison shed to check on his troubled friend.

30

LOADS OF DEAD

"I never seen a wound like that," Cinnon said. He was somewhere to Kila's right. Cold, rocky ground poked against her stomach and breasts. The thick smell of wet leather threatened to suffocate her. There was a bag over her head.

She tried to roll, but jerked to a stop. The barest movement reawakened a lurking agony at the top of her head and sent white flares across her vision.

Mack'Ti would learn a hard lesson soon, she thought. How dare he clunk her head so hard?

The villain in question was speaking. "Yes, Cinnon. The wound *is* ever so mysterious. 'Tis strange, the workings of shadline blades. I saw the Highest's blade fly in a strange curve, as if borne upon wings. It struck our benefactress with tremendous force. It is a wonder she lives at all."

"But the wound should bleed! Why don't it?" Cinnon's voice was very trembly. Despite his strength, the man had the heart of a coward. Kila would soon free him of it such a useless organ.

Her palms gripped grass. Her first awareness upon waking had not told her the most important detail of her situation. But now she realized it.

She was outside. Out of the Hackwatch.

With anxious need she reached for her mercus. These men would—

She met with a barrier like a wall of glass. The lovely, sweet mercus was there, just out of reach. And the Revulsion had thinned here, just a skim of foulness like the aftertaste of sour milk.

The glass . . . She had experienced this before.

It required all her will to push onto her knees. The pain in her head disrupted her balance and she flopped onto her side. She lay there, panting, trying not to groan.

"Highest Sigh's blade came free easily enough," Mack'Ti was saying. "Perhaps its power is to partially heal the wound it creates. I've heard of such a blade. Quite cruel."

"Why don't she wake, then? If she's healed up as you say."

"Dear Cinnon. You recall just minutes ago that she *was* awake? Long enough to crown the Highest? But remember, she struck her head when she landed. If we had light I would show you the wound. Rest will remedy her ills. Mark me, lad."

"If she dies ol' Klayne will do that thing to us again!"

"Ah, quite so. Hmmm. But only if he finds us." Mack'Ti did not sound so certain now. "Perhaps wisdom guides us to make a quick end for both these women. We could race to Tearling, take a room, and keep our noses tucked in like wee mice."

"D'ya think the nosg killed everyone by now? They won't spare us if she's dead. Won't spare any in Tearling neither."

Nax, do you feel me?

Yes. Fallo is coming.

Have him hurry. These betrayers are talking about killing me.

She did not have Cayne. The mercus was beyond her reach.

The Revulsion was here, though. Perhaps . . .

Even thinking about using it again made her stomach rebel.

Her hands were free. A leather sack covered her head. Her fingers found a cord knotted at her chin. Trembling, she dug her fingernails in, searching for a loop to pull and loosen. The filthy thing came off, caught on something. She knew what it was.

Fresh air swept into her lungs. The air was cold and clean.

The world remained black. No moon. Clouds obscured the stars.

The men were a dozen paces away, arguing over whether they should kill Kila and Winnea. She couldn't make them out except by voice.

Tentatively she felt for the crown. The *vaz'on* was cold to the touch. No point trying to twist the gems, the bolts driven into her skull would not turn without aid of the mercusine. Whoever Winnea was, she was a merculyn. And she knew Yiothizandra.

Winnea put the vaz'on on me, Nax. Tell Fallo to bring Ell.

She can't come.

Why?

She's missing. Nax sent the sensation of curling into a ball and hiding. *Jil is dead.*

Is Quinn safe?

Yes. She comes with Fallo and Cloak Einlin. I come too. They go as I direct.

"Don't hear nothin' from the fortress now," Cinnon said. "Suppose the nosg won? Winnea sleepin' won't help us none. We'll be supper fer them."

"The nosg stand no chance against the shadline. Did you not see the carnage?"

"I saw. Loads of dead shadline too."

"But each shadline told for dozens of nosg. No. Harken to me, lad. The shadline will come forth, victorious. If we kill Winnea now, we can claim—"

Shouts came from the distance. Not far. Kila realized her captors had not bothered to carry her more than a hundred paces from the fortress.

"Come, Cinnon. Allow me to speak for us, for you will betray us with your stammering lies."

"The women?"

"Leave them. No time to end them without chancing witnesses."

More shouts. Kila thought she recognized Fallo's voice among them. With Nax along, she didn't need to cry out. In truth, she didn't dare lest she force the men to reconsider sparing her.

But now she heard Mack'Ti calling to the approaching group. "Over here, shadlines. We chased a gr'hil of nosg into the night. Alas, they got away. They carried two women with them."

A nearer sound drew Kila's attention. Someone crawling over grass and loose stone, groaning with the effort.

Nax, tell Lop that Cinnon and Mack'Ti captured me. The new shadline Winnea is a merculyn. She put a—

A strong hand gripped Kila's arm.

The mercus was out of Kila's reach, but she could feel bolts forming close by. A fast swirl of power and need.

Nax! She's going to—

The mercus green filled Kila's nose, and a slosh of ice passed over her flesh as Winnea took her into dymension. The world rushed back just as quickly as it had faded. The rocky grass beneath Kila became smooth stone. The blackness remained.

Winnea felt along Kila's body until she reached the *vaz'on*. Sighing with relief, she released Kila and scrambled away. A door swung shut and Kila was left in silence.

Beyond the pain in her head, Kila sensed the contours of the room. A small closet, barely deep enough for her to straighten her legs.

Nax?

But Nax was too far away now. Henley only somewhat closer, to the north.

Kila tried to get to her feet, but dizziness drove her face-first onto the grit of an unswept stone floor. The air was much drier here than at the Hackwatch. The Revulsion . . . the thinnest skim in her awareness. Had it always been there as Nax said? How could she have not noticed?

She knew she needed to stand. Needed to break down that door and run. Again she worked herself up, bracing with one hand on the stone wall. If only there was a light. Just the faintest glimmer to see by.

Working her way around the room, she found the door. Wood. Thick. Latched on the outside. It didn't even rattle when she shoved it. Nor when she kicked it. And when she screamed, her voice came back to her, surrounded her in the small space.

Pressing her back to the wall, she slid down and hugged her knees.

31

A SMATTERING OF BLOOD

"Jasyn! Get down here!"

Eckso lay on the bottom few steps of the cellar stair. It had taken all her energy to get that far. The piercing agony of her wound kept interrupting her determination to climb the steps.

"Jasyn!"

The door at the top swung open. Light spilled down the stairs. A man skittered quickly down and pulled Eckso to her feet. "Madam! You have been stabbed!"

"I'm quite aware. Carry me up and fetch Hazel."

Within minutes she was resting on a divan in her mansion's parlor, an elderly woman administering mooncrafter's healing onto the wound. Hazel had rheumy eyes and waggling jowls, but she possessed a deft hand with healing concoctions.

"What blade made this? Most unnatural."

"Shadline." Eckso had Kila's blade. She'd hidden it just outside the little cell she'd locked Kila Sigh into. Fate Breaker.

The name alone sent shivers through Eckso's body. What did it mean? And how had the girl controlled its flight without the mercus?

Hazel knew Eckso was dragnithan. It was why she had taken up residence in the mansion, for Eckso could acquire rare ingredients with ease. In return, the woman supplied her benefactress with all medicines and potions that might be handy in her intrigues. This allowed Eckso to remain masked and avoid the attention of suspicious merculyns. Especially Donse Masters, who had been a burr in her skirt for a thousand years.

"There is a girl in the old storage closet in the cellar, Jasyn. See that she receives water and food. Don't go in alone. She's unarmed, but feisty."

"Yes, madam."

Hazel's ministrations closed the gash and sapped the pain. It would have to do until Eckso could rest. Which would be soon, if her plans worked.

Dismissing her servants, she changed into travel clothes and dissolved Klayne's glamour from her features. She regretted the tear in her filthy gown where Kila's blade had gone in. It had been such a fine garment. How had Sigh thrown it so hard? It had to have been mercusine bolts. But that was impossible. The Revulsion had been too thick there.

She found an old shawl in her closet and settled it over her shoulders. A quick glance in the mirror showed her a weary woman. She hoped it would serve.

Eckso pulled the mercus to her and formed the bolts to dymense. The night outside the Hackwatch was still black, but the ramparts of the fortress were lit with watchfires. A few Iron

Scholars patrolled it with flickbows in their hands. Nearer by were squads of torch-bearing shadlines, searching the open spaces for stray nosg.

Putting the shawl over her head, she moved to the fortress. The gate was open. Two Iron Scholars stood guard. She told them she was a weary traveler, seeking shelter for the night. Her unglamoured face was not known here and they swallowed her story like a honeyed biscuit. Their eyes lingered on her as she slipped through, ostensibly to follow their directions toward the kitchens.

As expected, the nosg had lost. Nobody looked at her when she came through, dagger tucked away in her sleeve.

Shad Lykea was conferring with the short and stout Shad Grickel near a towering bonfire. The bodies of dead nosg were piled high within. Many exhausted and bloody faces were lit by the angry light. Shadlines and Iron Scholars huddled in bunches, many with bandaged limbs.

Eckso skirted along the fringe of the firelight, pausing to listen into Lykea's conversation with Grickel. "Fifty of our order dead. A dozen missing. They took Kila Sigh. I should never have allowed her to be imprisoned."

"You think she charmed Winnea into leading the nosg in?"

"I don't see how she could have done. No mercus here. And PiTorro claims Winnea kidnapped Kila. Kila surely didn't murder Shad Ault. And Cloak Einlin believes Jil was murdered, not slain by nosg."

"What about the men we took?"

"Cinnon's not woke up yet. Mack'Ti said he was listening and obeying. Says the shadline order will one day recognize his deed for what it is."

"Did he admit to killing Jil? Did he explain why Jil's sword was found in the high garden?"

"He claims to not know anything about it. Says maybe nosg took it up there."

"Hmm. But no nosg bodies were found there. Just a smattering of blood."

Eckso frowned. Just blood? What about Ell? Surely she had died there.

The men turned to look in her direction, forcing her to continue her circuit. She had to dodge into a narrow niche between the library and the keep when a familiar group came out of the keep. It was Cloak Einlin, with Zirhine, Fallo PiTorro, and Quinn Peline. The last two held Beloved Ones in their arms.

The Cloak held a large parchment in his hands. "If she was dymensed south and east, she could be in Sorgan or Trine. Best to go by ship. The Kovi-Mest coast is difficult by land."

"Did you know Winnea?" Fallo asked.

"No. She's new to the order. The Cloak who heard her oaths died suddenly. I think we now know why."

Eckso stifled a curse. They knew where Sigh was. Her Beloved One could sense her, of course. Eckso should have remembered the bond. And the girl must have told the felnithel that Winnea had abducted her. She watched the group pass as they headed toward the fire. Their shadline instincts did not alert them to her presence. A grim reminder that the force of destiny sought its own ends, which could be good or ill for Night or Day.

Eckso ducked through the door and swiftly wound her way down through the abandoned passages to the Derslin

Wheel. The nosg fires had burned out, but her mercus was available. Sending a brilliant sphere of white light high overhead, she quickly found the tow-headed Raginalt Keel lying where she'd left him. He blinked furiously in the glare.

She dymensed with him back to her cellar.

32

THUMP-THUMP!

The light blinded Kila as a mercus sphere floated into the closet ahead of Winnea and someone else. The light went out and the door slammed shut. The latch scraped back into place. Darkness.

A weight hit her, driving her to the floor. She pounded at her assailant, driving her fists into arms and back. He pressed his face to hers, kissing her cheeks, her eyelids, her forehead, her lips.

"Kila! Ah me. My beloved Kila. Are you injured? Are you well?"

With a hard shove, she created a few inches separation between her and the young man smothering her with unwanted affection. The voice was familiar, but so thick with devotion it took her a moment to remember it. "Ragin? How did you get here?"

"A woman dymensed me here." He tried to pull her close. She fought his hands way.

"Let me go."

He reluctantly obeyed. Kila scooted away from him. She

knew he loved her. But last she'd heard, he'd turned his eye toward another. The young devotee of Pol who had freed Dunne Yples from the Way of Til's imprisonment, Tia On'Liette.

"We must escape," Ragin said. She heard him shuffling about and then pounding on the door. "Kila. You can trust no one. Everyone seeks to use you."

Kila knew that. But how did Ragin?

"How long have you known Winnea?" she asked.

"Who?"

"The woman who threw you in here."

"I don't know her. She—" A weird silence overtook him and he returned to sit near to her. "The Sensuals on Garden Island found the Derslin Wheel beneath Kil's Keep. I passed through a portal there, determined to find you. I came out in Tordain. I caught wind of the Armory and knew you'd attend, so . . . But there were nosg at the Hackwatch. I asked the first shadline I saw where you were. That woman brought me here."

Such an earnest story. But much rang false in it. Kila decided it was because she was hurt by Winnea's betrayal. It was easy to be suspicious, hard to trust.

But Kila knew why Winnea had seized the opportunity to bring him here. She would use him as leverage when she wasn't close enough to force Kila's obedience through the *vaz'on*. What a demaynic woman.

"Winnea said Yioth wants me alive," Kila said.

"Who is Yioth?"

A subtle test, but he passed it. There had been no pause, no moment of evasion in his response. "Can you use the mercus?" she asked.

"I almost lit a candle once, but it slips through my control. But you can. Why don't you dymense us away from here? Take us to Starside."

She told him of the *vaz'on,* which resulted in him fumbling around at her head and futilely spinning the gems. Without the mercus he would never be able to loosen them. She tried to teach him how to feel for the tap gems. If he could access her power, he would have more than enough to blast the door from its hinges.

He couldn't find the tap gems. He truly was useless.

His hands drifted down to her face, then to her shoulders. Then his lips were seeking hers. The flat of her hand caught his cheek. "Get yer lips off me!"

Sniffling, he retreated again. "When I heard that Gian left without you, I thought perhaps . . ."

The image of Gian Delp's face came to her. His dark hair, his intense gaze. The strength and fluidity of his form. Feeling again his lips on hers. The kiss that had pulled the mercusine from her in swirls of light. The power of emotion had lifted them from the grass. Such ecstatic passion. The memory was replaced by the disgust he'd thrown at her at the Armory.

The brief time she'd loved Gian had taught her the danger of furious passion. She hadn't truly known him. Which was why her love of Henley resided more deeply in her heart. As for passion, they'd not had enough time together for that. Henley had been healing from grievous wounds. Kila had been busy training with Jil and Flau-mishtak.

Flaumishtak!

"Hey smoke-head! I know you can hear me. Come here and help me out of this *vaz'on.*"

"Smoke-head," Ragin echoed, wounded. "Why do you hurl insults at me?"

"Not you. I'm calling Flaumishtak. He can get us out of here."

"A demayne? Have you lost your wits?"

Kila called for the demayne several more times, but he did not come. The one who did was the last person she wanted to see. Winnea.

The door swung open and the mercus light floated in. Kila realized the brightness was intentional, to keep her looking away. The woman did not want to risk her unarmed attack. That was odd. She had the blade, Kila had only her hands.

The light faded a bit and Kila found the woman looking down at her was changed. The clothes were plainer and her nose and chin were more rounded, more comely. She looked to be in her third ten-year, with a tumble of blond hair. Her pink lips were twisted in a moue of consideration.

"You both reek. I've had basins brought into the cellar. You will wash and change into the clothing provided." She turned away, leaving the door open.

Kila and Ragin came out into lantern light. Two steaming half-barrels stood in the middle of the floor. Towels, cakes of soap, and a stack of folded garments stood near to each.

Winnea was going up a flight of stairs. An elderly woman stood by as a sort of guard. Kila thought she could topple the woman with a hard puff of air. But then the gnarled fingers produced a small vial, which glowed red. "I drop this and you will burn. It will not be a quick death."

Kila turned to Ragin. "Go into that closet. If you come out before I say, I will beat you into engleberry jam. Do you understand?"

He obeyed and she undressed and washed her disgusting flesh. The water in the half-barrel turned silty black.

"Wash your head," the old woman ordered.

Kila did her best, dunking her head into Ragin's clean water and then soaping the hair, working her fingers under the *vaz'on* where she could. Another two dunks rinsed the soap and grit away. And a bit of dried blood.

The clothing set out for her was not so fine as she was used to now. The trousers were for riding. The shirt, waistcoat, and jacket something a merchant man would wear. A fur-lined cloak went over her shoulders. It would be too warm here. And that meant they were going somewhere. Kila's guess: Ceronhel.

She changed places with Ragin and waited for him to knock that he was clean and dressed. When Kila came out, Winnea was waiting for her. Her sable cape and fur hat made her look like a Radiant's wife, ready to ride out for Winternight visits in the neighborhood.

Ragin was dressed for warmth as well. Winnea motioned for them to don the fur-lined boots near the stairs. Satisfied that her captives were ready for travel, the woman dismissed the elderly lady. Once she had climbed the stairs, Winnea walked around Kila, eyeing the gems of the *vaz'on*.

"In all my years here, I have never used one of these. In truth, I do not like to rely on the mercus too much. It drains the challenge from life and exposes one to the scrutiny of meddlesome Donse Masters. But today I welcome the addition of your power. I hear it is considerable, but I confess I've doubted it. Now, let's see . . ."

There were two tap gems on the *vaz'on*. Winnea latched onto the one over Kila's right temple. Since the mercus relied upon physical sensations and emotion, it required the merculyn to manifest those sensations and emotions in order to form bolts of power. Winnea did that now, wielding a dizzying array of emotion with the deftness of a juggler. For Kila, who could not control it, the experience was liquid fire.

Winnea stumbled backward, jaw slackening as she encountered the full force of Kila's power. Ragin stammered, "I—I can feel it. Like the hum of uncountable insect wings. I've never felt the mercus in someone else before."

Winnea formed light from the power, made it swirl around her like vergent wisps told of in stories. The primary emotion was awe, and it only affected Kila slightly. But Ragin fell to his knees, tears streaming from his face.

The source of the awe was Winnea herself. Whatever bolts she had intended to form were overridden by her own awed disbelief of Kila's power. The struggle in her face was clear. She fought to handle the power, which was too much for her. Kila recalled that Highest Fley had required a Sink Gem to use Dunne Yples's power, a relic that allowed a merculyn to dump excess power lest they be annihilated by it.

Winnea had no such artifact, and so she desperately shunted Kila's power into light. It was not an efficient method. Heat would have done better, but that would have burned them all alive and destroyed the mansion above them in the bargain.

The drain squeezed down, then stopped, leaving Kila and Winnea breathless. Ragin wept openly, his mind overwhelmed by the mere chance exposure to Winnea's awe-infused light.

The woman swallowed hard and smoothed her sable cape. "Oh, Yiothizandra. You've made a terrible mistake." A delighted grin transformed her into a strikingly lovely woman.

Perfect teeth, full lips. She took Kila by the shoulders and kissed her sweetly on the cheek. "Had I known the extent of your power, I would have ravished Shad Ault the day of your arrival. The Revulsion at the Hackwatch hid you from me. I did not credit the stories told of you at the Armory."

Kila longed for Cayne. At this range she could gut Winnea in less than a heartbeat. But she had her voice. "How do you know Yiothizandra?"

"She is my sister, dearie. Come here, Raginalt. I want you both to listen carefully. We are going to collect my children, whom Yioth has hostage. Raginalt will be my ransom for your good behavior, Kila. If you misbehave, he dies."

Kila bit her tongue. Not because she feared hurling curses at the woman, but because Winnea didn't need Ragin to assure Kila's obedience. The gem above her ear was the strongest will-shift imaginable. If Kila tried to run, Winnea could latch onto it and make her crawl back on her belly if she wished. But it occurred to Kila that the woman might not know that.

Not woman, she reminded herself. Dragnithan. How many more were there in this world? "What's your real name?" Kila asked.

"You may call me Lady Winnea. Now, prepare yourselves."

She didn't give Kila any time to prepare, not that it would have mattered. The mercus tore through her and Winnea formed it into bolts of dymension.

Weight returned to Kila's feet as darkness returned to her vision. She immediately sensed the chill air and the hollowness all around her. A cavern. To her right arched a great stone opening. In the gray gloom beyond were ice tipped mountain peaks.

Her eyes adjusted and noted the small fire in the rear

corner. And her mercus senses showed her a hot presence occupying part of the snow drifted floor. The shape of it told her it must be a dragon, but she could see no other details.

"Come quickly," Winnea hissed.

"What about the dragon?" Kila asked.

"I can shield us from his flame. Come. Stay close to me." Kila and Ragin had no choice but to follow as she went straight for the fire. "Children? It's mother. Come quickly."

Two faces rose into view. The children had been sleeping upon furs. A boy and an older girl. Upon seeing Winnea they cried out and raced toward her. Winnea knelt, arms wide.

A shadow dropped from the darkness above, landing behind the children. Slender arms curled around their waists and drew them in. The figure was in silhouette, but wings spread out behind it.

"Well done, sister," said the figure. The children wriggled in her arms. The boy reached toward Winnea and cried. "But the children will have to stay another day. Or until you finish your task. You were to bring me our little cousin's head."

"You never said that, Yioth. You only said to kill her. I have done that." The pull of mercus came through Kila again and Winnea brought forth the swirls of light. This time she allowed more heat into them. Ragin put his arms protectively around Kila, though he trembled more than she.

The mercus light played upon Yiothizandra, showing that she was not the hideous monster Kila had imagined. She was beautiful. Woman-formed, bare of leg and arm. Heat steamed from her flesh. Her eyes gleamed with inner fire and her hair drifted all around upon unseen currents of air.

Her belly was round. Upon seeing this outward sign of Yioth's pregnancy, the entire moment stilled for Kila. She felt the presence there. *His* presence. There was nothing mercusine about it. And yet the connection was there despite the twenty paces that separated her from Yiothizandra.

Can you hear me? she thought at the babe.

The answer came softly and without words. But it filled her mind.

Thump-thump. Thump-thump.

Like the distant menace of war drums.

Thump-thump. Thump-thump.

The heartbeat of a god.

The pull of power through the *vaz'on* jerked her attention back to the confrontation in front of her. Winnea had her hands out, violet flames shooting up from her palms. Kila did not recognize the mercus bolts.

"You threaten me?" Yioth said. "Have you forgotten the lesson Klayne learned? I cannot be harmed while I bear this child within me."

"She is flesh like us," Kila blurted. "Kill her!"

Winnea did not release her bolts. Kila sensed the strain her flow of mercus placed upon the woman. She was stretched to her limit. The light swirls continued to blur around her, hotter than before.

"Yes, listen to the girl. Throw your power at me, Eckso."

"Do it!" Kila urged. "Kil may protect her, but—"

"I cannot attack without destroying my children. I dare not try." Winnea—Eckso—released her hold on Kila's mercus and the tap went cold. The violet flames dissipated and the swirls of light faded to nothing.

Something huge stirred in the darkness behind Kila. The dragon. She turned to look for it but saw nothing. Ragin clung to her now, using her for support.

"Give us light, Eckso," Yioth said, lifting the children. Their legs kicked, but her grip was iron. "Put it very high. It has been ages since you've seen Bazron."

Eckso did not access Kila's power to send up a great white sphere. It shed light over the floor of the cavern. And there, crouched upon enormous claws, was a dragon. The mercus light did not reflect much from its scales. And only its eyes showed where its head was. "Behold, the Blackdread! Bazron, eldest of the Narlhel dragnithor."

The beast spread its great maw, exposing gleaming white fangs. Yioth lifted the children and thrust them in. Bazron closed his mouth, and muffled screams came out. "Now don't swallow them. Just keep them safe."

Eckso's fists strained at her side, but she could do nothing. What a fool, Kila thought. She'd believed Kila's power would protect them from Bazron, but hadn't anticipated Yioth lying in wait?

"Go on, sister," Yioth said softly. "Finish your task. You have a day remaining. But you will leave Kila Sigh with me. Now, who is this boy?" She stalked toward Ragin, wings folding in and vanishing. She stood before Kila and Ragin, a bit taller than both. She emanated heat. Kila's eyes dropped to the protruding belly. The connection between her and the babe remained. If Yioth felt it, she said nothing. Her attention was on Ragin, who had straightened and put his arm in front of Kila, a pathetic shield.

"I am Kila's champion," he stammered. "Her protector. I was warned all seek to use her. I am the only one who will speak to her truly. She is my heart. My deepest heart. My love."

Making an amused nod and sideways smile, Yioth

accepted these words. "I understand your purpose now. You were brought here to keep Kila Sigh under control. That was wise, Eckso. Boy, go tend the little fire over there. When Bazron releases the children, they will seek its comfort. You must look after them."

"My duty is to Kila."

"Your duty is whatever I say it is." She clutched Ragin's wrist and twisted. A horrific snap echoed across the cavern and Ragin shrieked in agony. Kila sought to comfort him, but Yioth hefted him over her head and threw him toward the fire. "Move, boy. If the fire goes out, you will be the fuel for the next one."

Ragin thumped onto the floor and let out a groan. Turning on her sister, Yioth said, "Eckso, why do you tarry? Bring me Ell's head."

Eckso stomped a foot and vanished in mercus green. Yioth laughed in delight. Now she turned to Kila. "I expected you to be older, girl. And the sketch I saw is not a fair likeness. You are lovely, in your way. I see your hair has grown out a bit. I rather like it."

Kila wanted to go to Ragin, aid him in some way. But she had no power here. No weapons aside from her hands and feet. What could that do against a dragnithan immune to all attack? Cooperation was the only way forward. Bide her time. Wait for a chance. She couldn't imagine what that would be.

The babe inside the dragnithan seemed to shout at her with its dire heartbeat. A heavy presence, the stillness of expectation, pressed against her very hard. It made concentrating on Yioth difficult.

"You will come with me for a late repast. Nosg food is not good, but it is well cooked." Her long fingers went to Kila's brow. She stroked the fringe of blond aside and tucked a few strays behind Kila's ear. Her touch was hot as embers, but soft. Almost loving, if such was possible from a dragnithan devoted to the destruction of the world.

The hand snaked around Kila's waist and pulled her close. Yioth's strength was incredible. With a whoosh, her wings manifested again. Leaping, she pulled Kila into the air. Heavy flaps of her wings carried them toward the arch and over the ledge.

Kila's vision swam and the impossible drop provoked a reflexive squeal of fright. Her arms sought any refuge, and she found herself latching onto her captor. This displeased Yioth, who easily disentangled herself from Kila. "If you scream on the way down, I will not catch you."

And then Kila was falling. Arms and legs flailing, mind smashing at the glass separating her from the mercus, heart hammering and threatening to explode with animal terror.

Kila kept her teeth clamped shut. Moans escaped her, but she would not scream. She would not.

The wind rushed past her ears, roaring now. The icy air burned and numbed her cheeks and fingers. The fear was agony. But the agony was focus.

Thump-thump! came the godling's heartbeat.

The mercus yearned there just out of reach.

The world below was a gray smear of snow in the dark, illuminated by weak starlight. It crept closer.

Thump-thump! Kil's heartbeat connected to Kila's. Her fear drained away, her own heart slowed to match time with his. Spreading her arms wide, she endured the ripping blast of the wind.

Something inside her scrabbled and clawed. It reached into her with oily fingers. The Revulsion.

It is always there, Nax had said. And here it was. Not as thickly as at the Hackwatch. Not as insistent. But it was there. In desperation, Kila reached for it. Prepared herself to receive it, as if opening her mouth to the foul runoff of Starside sewers.

Yioth's hands caught her shoulders, pulled her in and clamped around her middle. The leathery wings filled and strained and now Kila was flying, held above the glaciers by her enemy. Ahead, a black fortress thrust up from the mountainside, battlements aflame with watchfires.

Ceronhel.

Kila retreated from the Revulsion, a bitter taste making her tongue curl. It had been so close.

Thump-thump.

An odd calm held her as surely as Yiothizandra did. Her heart rammed out the slow and steady cadence of war drums. The Revulsion still reached, yearned, but the tendrils were weak and could not force themselves upon her as they had done at the Hackwatch.

Yioth swooped into a steep dive, carrying Kila home.

33

THE PROBLEM OF THE MOTHERLIGHT

Tordain shone in the predawn, a topography of pearly domes tinged orange by the rising sun. The city spread along the eastern shore of the Sorgeal Sea, which glimmered just beyond it. At the furthest reach of the horizon lay the hazy shore of the Kovi-Mest. Henley felt for Kila on the bond and confirmed that she had moved. North. Very far.

The sudden shift had awakened him from his horseback slumbers. Worry gnawed at him, for he knew what lay far to the north.

She must have used a Derslin Wheel, Huff. She's never been anywhere up there before.

Huff had no opinion on it other than to ask, *Why did she leave Nax behind?*

Kila's cat was still to the east.

He didn't know why and there was nothing to be done about it. He couldn't follow Kila. It seemed that the force of destiny wanted them parted for now. So strange. He'd been repeatedly pulled into her chaotic fellstorm of a life. And now he had to find this Motherlight relic.

He turned his eyes back to the city. It was obviously a First Race creation, for the craftsmanship to erect such huge domes was beyond the ken of humankind. He rode Sassy down the road, easy in the saddle now, if a bit sore. Yiqa kept ahead of him, back erect but pliant, like the shaft of a whipaxe. He didn't bother asking questions about the city. If she knew the answers, she wouldn't offer more than a few words. If she didn't, she'd ignore the question entirely.

A salty breeze came to him, pulling with it the dry and tea-like scent of the pale green shrubs that covered the land here. Winter did not touch this region with such icy claws as it did Starside, and he enjoyed the warmth of the air.

Huff sat in front of Henley, balancing easily as a sailor on the deck of a gently rolling ship. The cat had developed a condescending fondness for the beast, whom he had named Sassy for no reason Henley could divine. Huff assured him several times that he had not spoken to the horse. Henley wasn't convinced.

The city is elnisian, Huff. Look at the spires to the north. Maybe that's the palace of the Autarch.

Huff humored him by looking in the general direction of the spires. They thrust from the tops of two enormous domes. As far as Henley was from the city, it was hard to gauge the domes' size, but he guessed each covered an area as large as Dunne Medow Plaza. The spires shot up from the peaks of these white wonders to spear skyward, thinning to needle sharpness at the tops. Hard slanting rays of the peeping sun glinted from the pinnacles, shooting flares of gold into Henley's eyes. Huff squinted and looked away.

Tordain was surrounded by rolling hills covered with vineyards. This was the land where coveted Tordanaise wine originated. Henley's father had never secured a license to import it to Starside. That honor was held by the Keel family. Depending on the mark, a single bottle of Tordanaise red could fetch between five and five hundred gold skillets. By comparison, a raven-weight hogshead of good trezz could be had for five gold.

The city was surrounded by a wall made of the same pearly material as the domes. It reminded Henley of opalescent shells he'd seen on his sea voyages. But it was not possible that so much shell could exist in the whole world.

Yiqa reined in her horse, which Huff had named Surly, but which Yiqa did not call by any name at all. "The dohmesss are the palaccce."

Henley had feared as much. That meant the palace was enormous. Even if they could get in, he didn't see how they could search all of it.

"Do you fffeeel eet?" she asked.

She spoke of the Motherlight. She'd asked the question daily. The answer was the same now as it had been in Starside. "No."

He knew a relic of such power as the Motherlight should give off some resonances of the mercus. But that he didn't feel it now didn't mean it wasn't there. It could be protected with a mask or perhaps it was housed in a box that masked it. All speculation. He didn't even know how big it was. "You're the one who discovered the Autarch had the stone. Where did you see it?"

"The palaccce."

"Where in the palace?"

"In the Katteshhhann Thronnne."

The Katteshan Throne? "A chair? It was on a chair?"

Yiqa barked a noise that was part disgusted laugh but mostly scorn. "Nnnot a shair." She made an expansive motion with her arms. "You vill ssseee." Heeling her mount, she continued down the road.

"How are we getting in?" he called after her.

"Sssneeeking."

Did you hear that? he sent to Huff. *Her plan is to sneak into the palace.*

It's what I would do.

Henley clucked his tongue at Sassy to get her moving and settled into a good grousing. Picking pockets was well within his abilities. Breaking into palaces was not. He could take comfort in his abilities with the mercus. If things got too chaotic, he could dymense away.

He blew out his cheeks. That was all well and good if saving his own skin was all that mattered. But it didn't solve the problem of the Motherlight. The only solution to that was to succeed in this inane quest the Voluptuary had sent them on.

Sensing his antsy irritation, Huff passed a sleepy sort of feeling through the bond. *You concern yourself too much with the world. Feel the breeze and the warmth of the sun. All will be well.*

Henley sent back a feeling of love and stroked the cat's orange fur. *Ah me, Huff. What would I do without you?*

Nothing at all. You'd be dead by now, surely.

34

A LOVELY DIVE

Noy shuffled into Yiothizandra's audience room. The great hall of Ceronhel now held trestle tables, her nosg-made throne, and a crowd of men and nosg who fed upon venison and winter berries and drank the ale brought north by Tarek PiTorro's caravan. The so-called Highest of Kil, Kila Sigh, sat on the floor at Yiothizandra's feet.

She thought it rather fitting that the girl wore the *vaz'on*, which looked like a crown. All queens and kings would soon sit at her feet, assuming she allowed them the same privilege as she did Sigh. The chance to live.

Lifting her gaze from the girl, she smiled to see PiTorro's men and nosg dining together in this once barren elnisian hall. Noy came closer, bowing and scraping the whole way.

Everything that Bizt-Ma's g'galas had stolen had been delivered to the Citadel. The armies under Razk-Ka's command were forging west with Bazron's dragons melting the passes before them. Smaller forces continued to file into the Derslin Wheel, passing through the portals Klayne had opened and which the shamans maintained. They would remain in the Derslin chambers at their destinations until she commanded otherwise.

Except the ones at the Hackwatch. Eckso had used them poorly. But what did Yioth care about three or four hundred nosg? She had Kila Sigh and soon she would have also her little cousin's head. Where would she put it?

An interesting question. Perhaps upon a stake at the entrance to the hall. But that would never do. Yioth would rarely see it there. No. She'd have it mounted close by. Right next to her throne.

Noy came forward, still bowing and uttering obsequious praise.

"What is it, Noy? Can you not see I am dining?"

She had a haunch of deer to herself, laid across her lap. Overseeing her armies and the repairs to Ceronhel was taking too much time to allow for the pleasures of hunting. This deer was the bounty of one of the hunting parties she'd sent south. That meant the meat was a ten-day old before it returned here. She had flamed it to a delightful crispiness herself and now gnawed chunks from the charred haunch to sate her unending appetite.

"PiTorro speaks to me," Noy said, circling a forefinger around his ear. His beady eyes darted side to side and a lopsided grin exposed the upthrusting lower fangs that made the nosg look so stupid to Yiothizandra.

"Report."

Noy composed himself and fell into a strange reverie. She knew it was him surrendering to direct communication with the man far away in Starside. When the nosg next spoke, its voice came out as rough as ever, tongue fighting the Ennish that poured so easily from PiTorro's mind to his. But the face did change somewhat, a haughty aire coming over it. This was PiTorro speaking directly to her now, a necessity since Noy had proven to be unreliable in relaying the details of his messages.

"Your Eminence, Yiothizandra of Ceronhel, Mother of Kil, and Queen of all Realms. . ." he began. Yioth enjoyed the string of titles and used the remaining minute of introduction to swallow two more enormous bites of venison.

"I have news. Her Enlightened Maj—"

"My little cousin," she corrected.

"Ah, forgive me, great Queen. I have managed to insinuate myself quite closely to your little cousin's primary advisor and administrator, Dunne Marlow, who I have come to learn was the Hargothe's brother."

"I told you to ingratiate yourself with *her*, not with her lackeys."

"Yes. But your little cousin is away in Tearling at a shad-line ritual of some sort."

Yioth already knew this, but found that expressing constant displeasure made underlings meek and fearful. The ideal state to encourage unquestioning obedience. "Why are you not in Tearling then?"

"I? Uh, I had not thought to travel there because she may return here at any moment. She has the ability to dymense. And as I am not a shadline, I would not be admitted in any event."

All true, but she didn't like him making excuses. "Have you made any effort to find someone to dymense you there? Perhaps you could secure a shadline blade?" These were ridiculous suggestions, but they had the proper effect. PiTorro began to gibber apologies, which made Noy's face contort in amusing fashion.

Kila Sigh was staring at the nosg with a mix of horror and fascination.

But this was enough diversion for now. "Stay where you are. Now that you have a position in the Citadel, surely the Radiancies are willing to give you whatever you wish."

"Yes, Great Queen. But I do not know what you want from them."

"I want the city. Perhaps a few ambitious Radiants could take the Citadel before my little cousin returns." She would never return, but PiTorro didn't need to know that. What he needed was a sense of urgency. Even with Ell dead, conquering Starside would take a hundred thousand nosg at least, and likely several years of siege. She had no time for that.

"Ah, I see. But her Fell Guard remains. I do not think any number of Radiancy armsmen could overwhelm them here."

"Fell Guard?" This was a new term for Yiothizandra. But she had avoided Starside all these ages and knew little of its defenses.

"Their ranks are drawn from the strongest recruits to Her Enlight—I mean, your little cousin's—army. At age twelve they go to a secret camp to live and train. Those who fail, die. Those who succeed become members of the Fell Guard. They are the fiercest, most loyal armsmen in the world. Each could account for a hundred regulars in battle. Likely more."

They would all have to die. Yioth did not want to squander her forces taking the Citadel when the time came. She doubted such men would stand long against her, or Klayne, or Eckso for that matter. She ruminated on which was the best to send to clear out the Citadel. PiTorro took her silence for disapproval.

"I do hear war plans from Administrator Marlow," he blurted. The force of his words produced a dangle of spit that hung from Noy's lips.

"Speak of these plans."

"Preparations focus on supply chain. Food, medicine, arms, horses, atlen. Starside's armies do not number more than ten thousand men. Recruitment on the streets has begun, entirely voluntary at this point. That will change soon. Marlow believes general conscription is planned to begin once Ell returns."

"She intended to send her forces away from Starside?"

"Yes. Marlow has revealed they are bound for the Sablefort on the southern fringe of the Sackwood."

That made sense. Any nosg approaching from the north would necessarily pass the Sablefort, an enormous old ruin of a fortress. It showed how confident Ell was that Starside could not be taken that she dared send men to open battle west of the Honor Mountains.

"Does Marlow have any concept of how many nosg I will send to war? Ten thousand men will be but an anthill before my hordes."

"I've told him the nosg number no more than fifty thousand."

Yioth laughed in delight. "Did he believe that?"

"Marlow took much convincing that the nosg existed at all."

Ell would not have been so skeptical, and she would surely divine the truth of the nosg numbers. But she was dead—or soon would be—so this was good news. "You have barely satisfied me, PiTorro. You must do better. I want to know the Watch schedules. Buy off those men if you can. Promise them positions within Starside after my little cousin has been deposed. I would have the Moritteran Pass secured for my armies before they arrive."

"And when will that be?"

The question alerted her to the possibility that Marlow suspected PiTorro was a spy. She would never give him such information. And to remind the man that his life depended upon her continued satisfaction, she concentrated upon the mark she'd placed on his forehead. It required a moment's will to heat it. Noy's face crumpled as agony returned through the dym-bond.

The gibbering resumed and Yioth let go of the mark, allowing it to cool. "You are dismissed."

Noy's face went slack and he staggered as PiTorro relinquished the communication. "Begone, Noy. Razk-Ka! Attend me."

Her Prime wurgu pushed back from his meal and approached, skull-topped staff clicking upon the stones. For most present, he was the fearsome commander they answered to day to day. To her, he was but a servant.

He bowed low, dipping the skull to the floor. "My Queen?"

A great tear of deer haunch filled her mouth. She spoke around it. "When will the main force be ready to take Stallid?"

"A fortnight. No longer. Bazron and his dragons melt forty miles of passes daily, but their efforts require much sustenance and half a day is lost as they range for game."

Yioth understood hunger and could not fault the dragnithors for it. Placing a hand upon her belly—swollen from meat and from the godling within her—she considered her next steps. Klayne was in Tordain even now. The Motherlight would soon be his and Tordain with it. That alone would secure the southern peninsula, bringing Sorgan and Jallisea swiftly into her control.

Rask-Ka was watching her. As was the skull atop his staff, the blue eye gems glowing softly with the resting swarmlight he kept at the ready. She did not fear it. In fact, the weird light suggested a course of action that would further her aims while protecting her from Klayne's ambitions. "Bring me a shaman you can spare, one of considerable power."

"You describe Ahl-Mish-Lah of G'galas Oopax. She is a tsugu."

Tsugu were war shamans, each in charge of a nosg fighting gang called a gr'hil. "I said one you can spare."

"Ahl-Mish-Lah's warriors all died falling from a mountainside. She is greatly shamed and tends beasts now."

Female shamans were rare among the nosg. Yioth suspected her supposed shame was less about the loss of her warriors than it was the delight her male peers took in her misfortune. "Send her to me. She must bring mimak mushrooms. Tell Wurgu Zir-Fir to supply her with strong varieties, for she shall need them in my service."

"My Queen, the mimak of each wurgu are sacred secrets. We cultivate them over centuries, choosing each to show us different sparkles of the wilter-realms."

Nonsense. The mimak mushrooms served only to addle their minds, opening them to the mercusine. "What do you think will happen to Wurgu Zir-Fir if he refuses to obey my command?"

Rask-Ka's mouth worked a moment as he chewed over the

question. He knew Yioth's temper and he could well imagine many terrible tortures. And if he couldn't compel Zir-Fir's obedience, he too would be subject to her punishment. The swarmlight in his skull's eyes swelled momentarily. He bowed and backed away. Yioth turned her attention from him.

Kila Sigh watched all with keen interest. It amused Yioth to show her power in front of the girl. This next guest would likely terrify her, which would be pleasurable to witness.

"Flaumishtak, come."

Sigh twisted to look up at her, astonished.

The demayne appeared at once. Human and nosg-kin scattered, overturning platters and benches in their haste. One of the hounds growled and barked. Its master took hold of its lead and pulled it back. Yioth did not like dogs, and several had already become piles of ash for displeasing her with their noise and stink.

Yioth nodded to the creamy felnithel in Flaumishtak's arms. Seeing it always delighted her, but she would not reveal such feeling to the yoznithan. The creature crawled to Flaumishtak's shoulder and hissed and spat at the hound. The beast's master cried out, lifted the dog from the floor, and scurried out of the hall. The felnithel settled at once, though its tail tip switched to and fro in reasonable agitation.

And then it noticed Sigh. With an irritable chirp it leapt down from Flaumishtak's arms and padded near to Kila, stopping just out of arm's reach. It sat primly upon the stone, curling its tail around its feet.

Kila stared into its eyes.

Flaumishtak paid Sigh no attention whatsoever, and waited expectantly for Yioth to speak.

"My spies?" she said. "Why do you delay in recruiting more?"

"I have done nothing but recruit spies for you. I have them in Jallisea, Tordain, Tearling, Wantin, Jilin, Lockt, and Ittiti. And just now I placed a will-slave bond upon one in Slirya."

"Not Stallid?"

"Not yet. The Barrazh tribes are in uproar. The queen died recently and the heir is absent. The best subjects for will-slave may no longer have the trust of the crown."

"I must communicate with my spies. Dym-bond them to Noy."

"All of them? Surely it would be best to assign a different nosg to each spy."

"No. The more nosg I must use, the more they will discuss what my spies learn amongst each other. I cannot have that."

"But his mind will—"

"Noy will serve. If he should go mad, you will dym-bond the spies to another. Do as I command."

The yoznithan glowered at her, but made no more arguments. "Is there aught else I can do for you?" He meant it sarcastically, but Yioth ignored the tone and delighted in pretending to think of something.

"Why yes, dear Flaumishtak. Dymense me to the eyrie above this fortress. I would speak with Bazron."

"I thought he was melting the snowpack in the passes."

"Yes. But he has returned just now. Can you not feel his presence?"

Flaumishtak tilted his head and looked up. "I do not sense the dragnithor as you do. They are of a different sort than we yoznithan. Now, should a yoznithor come to this world, I will let you know." He flashed a wicked, sharp-toothed smile as the flames in his eyes flared. With a flourish of one clawed hand, he offered to help Yioth descend from the dais.

"Shall I bring this be-crowned girl?" he asked. "What is she, anyway?"

The girl shrank away from him, hands going to the *vaz'on* as if she meant to rip it from her skull. The felnithel spat at her and climbed onto Flaumishtak.

"This is Highest of Kil, Kila Sigh. Doesn't she make a lovely pet?"

"Quite."

"Bring her."

Flaumishtak's enormous hand clamped over Kila's head, *vaz'on* and all. He dymensed them to the blustery edge of the eyrie. Bazron rested deeper inside, the gray light of the cloudy day soaking into his scales.

The creamy cat jumped down and raced to greet the dragon.

Eckso's whelps were tending to his wound, which required them to first chip the hardened salve from the opening with mallet and chisel before reapplying the sticky goo. The boy, Trev, knelt on the dragon's neck, hammering away while the girl scurried about to collect the chips in a basket.

Evidence of their work was plain to see. The eyrie's great floor had been cleared of snow and filth. A fire crackled in a stone hearth in a far corner. Buckets of water stood ready for them to sluice away dung or ichor should the need occur. Industrious children. Yioth approved, though she offered them only a narrow look of dissatisfaction lest they grow lazy.

The dragon turned to regard the new arrivals, forcing the boy to drop and clasp his arms to the serpentine neck. Upon seeing the felnithel, the dragon lowered his head to the floor.

Oly nosed the great dragnithor, just a crumb compared to the beast. Yioth sensed a communication passing between the creatures, but she didn't hear it.

Poli bent over and beckoned to Oly, making cooing sounds. The cat suffered this attention and allowed its chin and rump to be scratched.

With the formal greeting to the Beloved One complete, the dragon turned to look at Flaumishtak. Bazron snorted, acrid smoke billowing from his nostrils in outspreading rings.

You think this yoznithan serves you? Bazron asked Yioth. *If you trust him, you are a fool.*

And what does that make you, dear Bazron?

Flaumishtak was not privy to this exchange, as Bazron wouldn't include him in such a mental communication voluntarily. The dragon-kin had ever been at odds with the yoz-kin.

Flaumishtak studied the children, who were now staring back in abject horror. One would think them immune to such shocks, considering where they were. Clearly their mother had never shown them her true form. To them a demayne like Flaumishtak was a hearth-horror figure out of stories. The girl hugged the felnithel to her chest.

"You may leave me, Flaumishtak. I shall fly back when I'm finished. I need to stretch my wings and feel the icy air upon my flesh."

Oly raced across the floor and climbed Flaumishtak as he started to make his usual showy flourish. He stopped. "How many dragnithor have come?"

"How many do you see? Now go dym-bond my spies to Noy."

He dymensed away, wisely leaving little mercus green behind. Yioth made her inspection of the eyrie, pointing out quibbling things the children had failed to address since her last visit. They assured her all would be done immediately once Bazron had been tended to. She took the boy again, since the felnithel had shown the girl favor, and held him over the ledge by one arm. She waited until his screams subsided before setting him on his feet. His fear was a delight to her, and it made her lordblade sword stir, hungry for violence.

Hush, Flayshui, you will soon gorge yourself upon the mortals of this world.

Bazron's voice came to her. *I assume you came here for reasons other than tormenting these children.*

Indeed. I wish you to recruit the wyvoks of this world.

Sigh had edged away from the drop, moving closer to Poli. Yioth allowed it. Perhaps if they spoke a bit, both would derive false hope from it. Breaking people was Yioth's great skill. She knew Sigh played cautious, but there was a haughty confidence in her manner still. But not for long. Soon she would be bowing and scraping like Noy.

Wyvoks? Bazron sent. His answering snort had flame in it. Dragnithor had total distain for the flying lizards native to this world. The resemblance between them was remarkable, but wyvoks were no more demayne than a chicken was a hound. But like those lesser creatures, wyvoks could be put to good use.

I will mount nosg upon the wyvoks in battle, she said. *You may assign Faxnishek or Tortyr to lead them.*

Wyvoks will eat the nosg. Bazron spared an eye to watch Kila kneel by Poli. Trev joined them. She hugged them and brushed hair from their foreheads. Both cried and clung to her.

They will not eat the nosg if you command them otherwise.

Must we have this argument? You know how that will end, do you not? She met the dragnithor's hateful gaze and held it, hand on Flayshui's hilt. The blade pleaded with her to draw and release the blood madness that drove it. But she was its master and resisted the temptation.

Bazron's lower lids rose in an odd squint, then he relented and turned his massive head away. *I shall see to it, but the wyvoks will deplete the southern ranges of meat the dragnithors need.*

Soon there will be so much meat available it will spoil under the sun. Now go. I wish nosg to be mounted and aloft within a fortnight.

"Come, Kila Sigh."

The girl disengaged from the children and said something low and soft to them. They rubbed their eyes and wiped their noses on their sleeves. But their spines had straightened a bit.

Sigh came to her obediently.

"Jump," Yioth commanded. "Do not scream."

The girl's jaw clenched. She took a moment to secure her cloak and tuck her hands inside her sleeves. Then in four strides, she hurled herself in a lovely dive, into empty space.

Yioth went to the ledge and jumped as well, manifesting her wings as she fell. She narrowed herself to better slice through the wind, quickly catching up to the girl who now had her arms and legs spread wide to better catch it.

Yioth stayed with the girl as they plummeted, waiting for the helpless scream. It didn't come.

Catching the girl, she lifted out of the dive and soared toward Ceronhel.

35

IF HE SAW YOU TRULY

Tordain was chaos. So incredibly crowded with swarms of busy people, all occupied with industrious undertakings. Wagons upon wagons of melons, leaf-wrapped beancobs, and green gourds rattled through the streets, all bound for one of seven vast markets. Handcarts loaded with turnips and fennel scraped through where they could, while children hawking twine and bead necklaces or bracelets accosted every person they saw.

Old women filed through the gates, bent over and propped up on walking sticks to bear the weight of the bundles on their backs: boughs from pines, bundles of kindling, and baskets loaded down with berries and mushrooms.

The streets were lined with stores and stalls, all filled with goods of every sort. There was no order to any of it. A potter's stand stood shoulder to shoulder with a smithy and a glass blower. Tailors kept company on the same lane as scribes and apothecaries and atlen dealers.

The pearlescent stone comprised every wall, making

Tordain glimmer in a strangely mystical way. Henley didn't like looking directly at it, finding the creamy depths dizzying.

The smell of cooking was everywhere due to the stewpots plopped indiscriminately on the streets, braced over fires fed by small children. The ladle-masters shouted at passersby, holding up gourd halves steaming and ready to exchange for two sliver plugs. A hunk of bread for five copper.

Riding horses through this madness would have got them nowhere, so Yiqa had paid to stable them outside the city. Huff went in Henley's pack, as cats were not safe here. The Way of Til had an enormous presence, with a massive cathedral near the palace and scores of towering temples in each district. Brown-robed Donse Masters patrolled the streets like the Watch, offering sharp words to stray children or to women who did not keep their ankles hidden.

"At this rate we'll get to the palace next year," Henley shouted to Yiqa. She had removed her head covering before they arrived to the city. She hadn't explained why, but Henley guessed Alnassi killers were known here and she didn't want to draw that sort of attention. As it was, she drew every eye anyway. Her hair was nearly white, and her gray eyes drew stares both for the exotic shade and their beauty.

Henley reassessed her age now that he could see her in daylight. He'd thought her at least fifty, perhaps ten years older. But now he doubted she had yet seen forty. She glared at him but said nothing.

To his surprise she turned away from the crowds, heading up a gentle slope to a quieter neighborhood with breathtaking views of the lower markets, the docks, and the sea. Here she guided them to a sleepy inn called The Wilde Moon. A wooden sign hung over the entry, a perfect circle cut in the middle. The moon, Henley supposed.

Inside the housemother took Henley's coin and showed them to a room with one big bed, basin, and whale oil lantern. Once the stout proprietor had closed the door, Huff burst from Henley's satchel and peeped through the window.

"I'm surprised we're stopping," Henley said to Yiqa. "Has removing your head covering made you lazy?" He'd meant it in jest, but the woman's cheeks flushed. She eyed the bed and then Henley. "You vill nnottt tutch mmeee inn this bett."

"Fear not, friend. I belong solely to Kila Sigh."

"I knnow mennn. You vill nnott tutch me. Now I vill vash ffilth."

And then she began to remove all her clothes. Henley's face burned and he turned away, though he caught an eyeful in a looking glass in the corner. Yiqa had no modesty when it came to her body, except for her face and hair.

Coughing from embarrassment, Henley excused himself and headed downstairs to the common room. The low ceiling and mismatched tables and chairs gave the space a homey feel. The only other guest sat near a banked fire, teacup fuming before him, as he scanned the pages of a small book. No warrior this. Likely a merchant in Tordain on some business and seeking a moment's quiet from the madding markets.

Henley found a round table under a window and eased his saddle-weary body onto a chair. He sat there a quarter of an hour before a girl came through to check on the reader. She yelped at the sight of Henley and hustled to ask if he might require any refreshment. He asked for a pint of beer.

She returned sparkly-eyed and carrying a foaming tankard. She was pretty, if a bit long in the nose and narrow of jaw.

Charm was surely her greatest asset. With the unguarded glee of a devoted gossip she bent and rested her elbows on his table. Henley was rewarded with a clear view down her bodice, and the mysterious landscape deafened him to her words at first. She tapped his hand to get his eyes back to hers.

"That man behind me," she said, neither offended by his intrusive eyes nor concerned enough to change her posture. "He's been here *fifteen* days."

"A good bit of coin for the house, Miss . . . ?"

"Aye, but who cares about that? Mistress Sqinn pays me one silver, five, regardless of how many beds and tables are full." She again whispered, "All he's done is read and drink tea. From morning until eleven bells, night. Read, read, read. Tea. Tea. Tea."

"There's much to learn. Perhaps he's a scholar, Miss . . . ?"

"Him a scholar? Ha!" She smacked her palm on the table. The man looked up from his book in annoyance, then returned to it. Casting her voice to a raspy whisper again, the girl said: "He's an Earl or Baron or Markis or somesuch. I'd marry him, but he won't even look down my dress. What'd I do with him, anyway? All that money and land, though. Mind you, I'm not greedy or nothing. I'd make for a shocking Markissa, wouldn't I?" She let out a cheerfully scandalous giggle.

Her aspect suddenly changed as she looked Henley up and down, truly seeing him for the first time. "And what are you? I smell merchant on you? Sheepskins and casks of pickled beets. No? Then it's trezz."

This guess startled him and it must have showed on his face. "Trezz. My father was—" He cut off, realizing he was telling a stranger far too much. His name was already associated with Kila's and her image was traveling around the world on strange little handbills sent out from Garden Island. "My father was a captain of a trezzer before he died. I'm a landman myself. I have a license from Annso to sell trezz here if I can find enough buyers."

"Mistress Sqinn won't be buying trezz. She says it's Kil's own brew and she's already lost an inn to fire thanks to over-trezzed patrons."

"Ah."

She continued to study him and came to some decision, for she hooked a chair with her foot and drew it next to his, whereupon she slid into it and bumped his shoulder with hers. "You married?"

"Not yet."

"Who is she? Don't tell me. Some sailor's daughter. No. I think she's poorer than that. What, you found some alley waif who wormed her way into that soft heart of yours? Ah me, where were you when I was stitching linens in Afbor Street?"

"Afbor?" he said, sucking in a breath. "You're from Star-side? What's your name?"

She made a wooshing noise and waved her hand to dismiss her past. "I hear Terriside all over your voice. Trezz, eh? Did your father captain for Keel or Mast?"

This was getting very strange very quickly. He availed himself of a long swig of beer before answering. "Mast. He wouldn't have sailed for Keel if the oceans were filled with wine and his ship made of gold."

"A funny ship that would be." She still leaned on the table, like a workman after a long day's labor. But with her seated beside him, the view down her top was too oblique to tempt him much. She turned her head so that her blondish hair curtained to hide her face from the reader by the fire. "Is Markis Limpnoodle watching us?"

"No."

She made a disgusted face. "He's been reading the *same* book for *fifteen* days. You sure you're not married? You feel married to me."

"I'm, uh, promised." Well *that* was a startling admission to make. Especially since he and Kila had come to no such understanding. It felt true, nonetheless.

"Pity. Don't you think it's strange about him?"

She said everything with a smile curling one side of her mouth. This was a girl who needed to know things. Desperately. It struck him that he rather liked her, and had he never met Kila, he might have been rather smitten by her. Likely to his eventual misery. Her nose and jaw were not unbecoming. Not the usual sort of prettiness, but a unique sort. Come to think of it, Kila was the same way. A pang of longing hit him, and he hit the beer.

Wiping foam from his lip, he said: "If he's still reading the same book, that would be strange indeed. Perhaps he is a poor reader."

The girl flipped back her hair and looked at the man. "I've seen the words. It's First Race writing or I'm Ori in Ecstasy right here in front of you."

Henley's cheeks and forehead burned at this reference. He cursed his red hair and pale skin. Another swig and he had regained some composure. The girl was quite amused to see this reaction, which meant she'd be offering more scandal soon if he didn't divert her or end the conversation outright. "First Race, you say? That's interesting. You sure he's no scholar?"

"He's a Markis or Viscount or somesuchthing. I've seen his

purse." She made a rather obscene squeezing motion with one hand, showing the fatness of said purse. "Why does he keep reading that book?" Her voice was no longer a whisper, and Henley sensed she wanted the man to overhear.

"Have you asked him, Miss . . . ?"

"What? Ask? Are you daft? If Mrs. Sqinn caught whiff of such nosiness I'd be balming my street-skinned arse with oxfat in a smithy's hayloft by eight bells, night."

Henley couldn't help himself. "Is the smithy married?"

The pause in her breathing alarmed him. For a balanced second he wasn't sure if she was set to explode with outrage or hilarity. It was the latter, and her bawdy laughter filled the room, again drawing an annoyed brow-furrow from Markis Limpnoodle.

"He is. But his wife's a cold carp most nights and he's gentle with me. I don't see him anymore since she had her babe. It isn't right when there's a babe at home."

Henley was so astonished by this revelation that he simply stared at her.

"I've done it, haven't I?" she said. "I've rattled on too much. Kil's eyes, I'm such an atlen tongued fool." She didn't look the least ashamed. Quite the contrary. "Did you know that the girl you've an understanding with isn't the woman who's sharing your bed tonight?"

"Uh . . ."

She patted his hand, then left hers on top of his. She had warm hands, small and corded along the tops from years of hard work. The nails were trim, not bitten, nor dirty in the slightest. Henley couldn't say the same of his after all these days in saddle.

The housemother's voice boomed from the kitchen:

"Terissa Irgan Viller! Get your skinny legs in here and help me with the potatoes!"

Henley chuckled as he watched the girl dash away, skirts flying. The silence she left behind sort of left a frenzied stir in the air next to him. He felt he'd been assaulted by her gossip and charm and rather worn out from the experience. He leaned back and savored the last few swallows of his beer.

Figuring he'd given Yiqa plenty of time to wash and dress, he decided to return to the room and do the same. But the man by the fire was staring at him, book closed on the table.

Henley nodded and made an apologetic face. "I swear I've never met her before. I'm sorry if she embarrassed you, sir."

"Embarrassed? Why saying this? Surely not for her calling me the Markis Limpdoodle."

It had been Limp*noodle,* but Henley didn't correct him. And curiosity about the man's book drew him into an approach, hand outreached in greeting. "I'm—uh—I'm Senny Odok—from Starside. Miss Terissa was saying your book is in Elnisian?"

"Yessi. I'm progressing this last ten-days. But it is the confusing mess to me." His accent was sharp, and Ennish was clearly not his native language. His skin was neither paler nor darker than the mix of races who called Tordain their home, but his dress was rather exotic: a long white shirt that draped to his knees, under which he wore loose trousers and sandals. A gold hoop hung from one ear, and a cropped but luxurious beard covered his lower face with such wiry density that it might require a curry comb each evening.

"I studied Elnisian as a boy," Henley said before realizing that a sea captain's son would have received no such education. He tried to cover his mistake: "I was the ward of a merchant who valued education. He allowed his House Donse Master to instruct me as long as I completed my chores timely."

The man brightened at this and beckoned Henley to join him. "Excellent! Please, I am questioning about a few passages."

And so, a half hour later, when Terissa reappeared with a fresh pot of tea, she stopped cold at the threshold of the kitchen and glared eager questions at him. He simply smiled and waved her to come over.

"My father knew the First Race tongue," she said casually, speaking to Henley and ignoring the man. Henley realized he hadn't even asked the man's name he'd been so engrossed in his translation efforts.

"Is that so?" Henley said absently, re-reading the same passage for the tenth time. It truly was thick going. "Educated, was he?"

"In ways," Terissa said. "He read a lot, when he wasn't gorging himself to the size of an ox or watching his dogs tear up the girls his men abducted from Cheapsgate alleys." She said all this with such dismissive amusement that the words slid right past Henley's understanding for a moment. But then they registered and he looked up from the book, finally seeing the girl clearly.

Terissa Viller.

"You're Dox Viller's girl?"

She grinned. "One of a hundred, I'm sure. I never met him, but I use his name. Scares off a certain type." She poured two cups of tea and departed, but not before tossing her hair and flashing the most coquettish smile Henley had ever seen.

"Beware that one, friend Senny," the man said softly. "She is hunting for the husband."

"I'd wager she'll catch a dozen before she's through."

At this the man laughed, deep and resonant. Finally he patted Henley's back and said: "I'm Harl Illis, Markis of Dol near Slirya."

"Truly?" Henley had always wanted to go to the western-most city of the known world. It was said to be full of natural beauties, mountain, lake, sea, and human. "You must miss home dearly."

"Yessi. But I will not returning for long while yet. Not until after war, should I surviving it."

He offered a grim smile in return for Henley's sudden silence. "You thinking me madman, don't you? Yessi. I seeing it in your face. But you looking back will see. War comes. Years to come, you looking back and thinking: Harl was right! Dem-Kisk. Why and when? I hoping his book to answer. But instead, this book only asking." He looked up. "Ah, Yiqa coming to us. Good."

The Alnassi woman was back in her black clothes, head covered, but face not masked. A compromise that gave her no comfort if her flushed cheeks were any gauge. But she met the man with something verging on affection, kissing his cheek and murmuring something about him looking well. This greeting complete she sat across the table and waited.

Harl smiled broadly. "I'm calling for supper and then we talk. Deciding how you two will stealing the Motherlight. Terissa!"

Henley looked from him to Yiqa and back. "Why didn't you tell me we were meeting someone?" Henley demanded of his companion.

"We are mmmeeeting sssommeonne."

"No. Do not being mad with her, young man. Yiqa, me.

We discussing much when she was last here."

Terissa chose that moment to return with more tea and a tray of day-old sweetbake. She gave Yiqa a narrow-eyed once over before bending deeply to temp Harl with her bosom. The man ignored it. Henley was not quite so successful, despite being perturbed at Yiqa for keeping this man a secret.

When she departed, Harl said: "Please, friend Senny. Let us bending our minds to task ahead. The Motherlight. Yessi?"

"Since you know Yiqa, I guess I can tell you my name is actually Henley."

"Ah. Pleasing to meet you, Henley." He flipped through the little book and turned it on the table so Henley and Yiqa could see. It was open to a page unlike the rest Henley had seen. It showed a drawing. The style of it was not consistent with the manner of the rest of the book.

The writing had been scribed by a skilled hand, letters uniform and adorned with elegant flourishes. Each section was illuminated with brilliant reds, blues, and gold leaf. But this drawing, three quarters of the way through the book, had been done by a much less skilled hand.

"I am considering this map forty years. Only coming to Tordain three years ago did I see! This map is palace of the Autarch!"

The circles on each side represented the domes. The outlines connecting the two circles showed hundreds of rooms, long galleries, vast halls, and countless courtyards, tiered gardens, and fountains.

Henley had read a few passages of the book, which seemed to refer to banking and livestock. "The text has nothing to do with the map."

"Yessi," Harl said sadly. "It is seeming so. Look here." He

thumbed through several pages of text. "Border around each page. But not around map. Not same hand. Different and strange. Why?"

"I don't know. Perhaps the scribe took up the wrong book when she decided to make a sketch."

"No. I am not thinking so. This volume very small. Meant to carrying, perhaps merchant's journal. I believe map sketching in haste. Someone take blank book, they grabbing it moment of need." He mimicked urgent hands flipping open the book to a random page and scribbling a drawing. "Years later. Yessi? Centuries later! The book coming off shelf. Nobody remembering it. Ah ha. Empty! Can use for the banking text. Scribe thinking happy things. Until . . . what's this!" He mocked shock upon seeing the sketch. "*Crosi nesti fri'Kil!* But it is only the banking and the cows and the crops. Scribe shrugging and skipping map. She finishing the book, forgetting map. Yessi?"

"If the text isn't about the map, why have you reread it so often?"

Harl smiled and spread his hands out. "I am owning bank!"

Henley studied the map again. The sketch might prove useful, assuming they could get into the palace. Unfortunately, none of the rooms were labeled.

"You vill reet thees boook, Hennnley. I vill scout palaccce." With no ceremony at all, Yiqa departed, her tea unsipped, her sweetbake untouched.

"A dangerous woman," Harl said approvingly. "Marvelous dangerous woman. Ah, but what woman not so?" He patted the table and stood. "I am leaving you to reading. I am in room opposite yours."

Henley found himself alone with tea for three and a rather inscrutable book. But not for more than three minutes before Terissa returned to collect the dishes. Instead of moving them onto her tray, she shoved the cups aside so the tray could rest on the table while giving her elbows plenty of room for propping. She eyed Henley, hair again curtaining to one side. "You didn't tell me you knew the Markis."

"I didn't know him. My companion did, it turns out."

"It turns out . . ." She mulled the phrase and popped Yiqa's sweetbake into her mouth. Around it she said, "Funny how things just 'turn out,' you know what I mean? It's another way of saying it's a coincidence. Right, Sen?"

"It's Senny, and I suppose you're right. Coincidences happen all the time. Unless you think Pol is stirring us up."

Swallowing she reached for Yiqa's tea and threw it back. "Pol is a child's tale, you ask me. You know what I think? I think we're all cooked and Kil-damned." She shouldered him again. "Your woman left. That room upstairs is getting cold. Want to go warm it up?"

Henley blew tea across the table and gawped at the girl. She covered her mouth, eyes crinkled with mirth. "You ought to see your face. I never knew someone could get that red! You glow!" Waggling her eyebrows she began to clear the table. "I know, I know. You've an understanding. Lucky girl, whoever she is. I think she's an alley waif with fine eyes and you're tied to each other as sure as two cherries. It's romantic, you ask me. But it's a pity. When you going back to Starside?"

"I don't know. When our business here is done."

"It have to do with that book?"

"The Markis thinks so."

"He *is* a Markis! I knew it. Ol' Limpnoodle's rich and I'm

poor. It's a perfect match. Kil's eyes I wish he'd look down my dress just once. I bet I'd hook him then."

Henley scooped up the book, wanting to make an exit before his cheeks burned off. "I suggest you get him to look into your eyes, Terissa. I doubt any unattached man could resist long if he saw you truly."

With that he walked away, feeling a small victory. But as he ascended the stairs he was puzzled by the sound of quiet crying in the dining hall behind him.

In the room, Huff greeted him with a soft meow and accepted a few strokes from head to tail before plumping a pillow and curling into it.

The water in the basin had been refreshed, probably by Terissa during the meeting downstairs. He undressed, washed up as best he could, then put on his road-dusty clothes and flopped onto the bed, book propped on his chest. Sleepiness came up to wash over him, but he resisted, intent on discovering if the text had any hidden meaning.

The pull of sleep made his eyes lose focus and for an instant he saw the blank space between the thick letters of the text pop forward, as if the ink was the background. Cursing, he sat up, disturbing Huff who flicked a tail tip and extended a forelimb to cover his eyes.

The entire time Henley had been in Tordain, he'd been masked. Not because merculyns were undesirables, but because of the squads of Donse Masters walking about. He hadn't wanted them to sense his ability, which by their standard would have been remarkable.

But now he risked dropping the mask.

The book hummed with the faintest hint of mercusine.

36

TO BE ALIVE FOR IT

Voluptuary Harrisan Minn, leader of the Way of Ori, strode into the Baths in the harbor city of Wantin and snapped at the Sensual seated behind the greeter desk. "The Voluptuary. Now."

There was some confusion, a bit of argumentation, then there was total compliance. Minn strode around the great dome, breathing in the moist air rising from the pools. The water had been scented with strange oils. Allowable, of course, but strange to Minn's nose. Lavender and something else. The scents of calm, of peace, of healing.

What were the scents of war? she wondered. Blood. Decay. Ash.

The Voluptuary Tritto of Wantin was a man. Minn had met him once before when he had come to Garden Island to be questioned about rising to his current station. Minn had been a mere Sensual back then. Tritto had impressed her as a placid, earnest man whose calling since youth had been healing. An ideal candidate.

In times of peace.

First she had to prove that she was the Voluptuary of Garden Island. The mark was etched on her skull, visible to any merculyn who knew how to look for it. Just the faintest trace, put there during an abbreviated ritual at Garden Tower. She'd had to request a few Spinsters to add power to the circle, since few merculyns of her Way had survived Dunne Yples's and Kila Sigh's rampages there.

Tritto was quickly satisfied and clasped his soft hands together expectantly. He had a soft face, plump and rosy. The filmy layers of the Way's robes made his figure womanly, as did his rather pink lips.

"How many merculyns of your power or greater reside here? Including novitiates."

He blinked several times before answering. It must have been a perplexing greeting coming from the leader of his Way. Followers of Ori did not have to possess any power at all, and the Way took pains not to elevate people based on their mercus alone. "Perhaps forty. You are asking because . . . ?"

"Because I need them. Moirina?" She held out a hand toward her companion. The woman produced the handbill instantly, laying the rolled tube of parchment into Minn's palm. She passed it to Tritto. "You've seen this, no doubt. Kila Sigh, Highest of Kil."

Tritto frowned and nodded. "But her followers call it the Way of Kila. We've had dozens come through here for baths in the past few ten-days. They gather outside the city."

Voluptuary Minn shared a sharp look with Moirina. "So now she's recruiting followers. And naming the Way after herself to mask its association to the Despised God is almost more alarming than being forthright about who she serves."

"Surely she does not serve Kil," Voluptuary Tritto said.

"Who would put faith and trust into the god of war and pestilence? It makes no sense."

"She had little choice in the matter. She was destined to become what she is. It is our task to oppose her, capture her, harness her, and turn her power toward peace and healing. But that will take force. I need all your merculyns to prepare. Are they trained in circling to offer their power as source-taps?"

Tritto's pink lips paled. "The Sensuals have learned the skill, for we sometimes use such power to heal folk. We have few who can receive such power, however. I can barely manage the combined mercus of more than two taps."

That was no surprise. The most powerful merculyns had gone to the Way of Til for hundreds of years. Their recruiting had become akin to conscription more recently. "Hellers in your reliquary?" she asked.

Tritto glanced at Spinster Moirina and clamped his mouth shut. Minn scoffed. "There's no point in hiding our secret caches of mercus relics, Voluptuary Tritto. The Ways will need all they have for the battle to come."

"I'll take you to the Reliquary. We have several, but the use of most is a mystery to me."

"No time for that. Gather them all. Prepare your merculyns for travel. Make sure they have garments for every climate. They must bring food. Limit personal items. I would not have anything slow them."

"Where will you take us?"

Minn was pleased he included himself in their number. The man might be soft, but he understood his duty.

"War comes. I hope we can first capture Kila Sigh. But do not plan to return home until the nosg have been defeated and Dem-Kisk is past."

His face lost all color now. "So it is true. Dem-Kisk comes. I had hoped not to be alive for it."

Minn sucked in a breath and pushed away her frustration. Tritto was a gentle man, exactly what the Way of Ori wished its Voluptuaries to be. Taking his hands she said, "Join me in prayer."

She gave it a minute of silence, allowing her mercus to rise in unformed swirls. There was no feat in prayer, merely the offering of the essence. Tritto joined his to hers.

She said softly, with as much compassion as her short patience could allow, "And yet you are alive, Voluptuary Tritto. It falls to you to see it through. Begin preparations."

The man certainly had a dozen more questions, but Minn didn't have the time to answer them. "Moirina, lead the way to Pol's Tower. I suggest you be the one to speak to the Coin."

The woman nodded sharply. This was good. Speed above all else. Forty Sensuals and initiates of middling power wouldn't be much use against Kila. But soon the Spinsters would join their number, and then they would go to Jilin to recruit more.

And then to Jallisea and Tordain and Sorgan and Trine. Until every merculyn of both Ways was dispatched to capture Kila or to contend with the nosg. She hadn't had time to sit in meditation and feel for Raginalt since leaving Garden Island. But she would have to do so soon. Hopefully Kila had remained at the Hackwatch. But if not, she would track her using Raginalt.

37

STRONG GIRL BREAK

In the time Kila had been Yiothizandra's prisoner, she had learned three things. First, to say nothing at all. Her habitual sass had earned her a swollen eye and a headache nearly as bad as the *vaz'on* itself.

But it wasn't the so-called Queen of Ceronhel who had struck her. It had been her servile nosg, Noy. Kila would have pitied the creature if she hadn't hated him so. Yioth didn't do much of anything herself as far as Kila could see. As usual, she was sitting in her crude throne, palms on her swollen belly, hearing a report of army movements from Razk-Ka.

Ol' Razk was the Prime Wurgu. Apparently this shaman was in charge of all the nosg. He carried one of those skull-topped staffs and the other nosg bowed to him. He had given Kila a long, slow look exactly once, then banished her existence from his mind.

Kila had a good view of the proceedings because Yiothizandra kept her seated at her feet. Like a pet.

The floor was cold. The entire room was cold, for the windows remained uncovered at all times. There were several hearths in the great hall, and fires burned in two of them. The men and nosg workers who dined there stayed close to the heat. Kila was allowed to shiver.

The second thing she'd learned was that the cold was survivable if she tucked her hands under her arms and breathed very deeply and then let it out in a rush. Again and again. Father had taught her and Wen the technique, but she'd never been very good at it. Over and over, in and out. Huge breaths. Eventually she could work up an inner warmth from this technique. It tended to make her lightheaded after a while. Then she'd let out her breath and hold it, enjoying a few minutes of meditative peace. But once she'd blacked out.

Razk-Ka finished talking about dragons and nosg and the hundreds of his warriors who fell over dead each day from the cold, starvation, or exhaustion. Yiothizandra did not seem to care about these casualties. The Prime Wurgu waved to another shaman who had been hanging back.

"This is Ahl-Mish-Lah. You requested a shaman. She is powerful. From G'galas Oopax. Wurgu Zir-Fir sent her with a small bag of his sacred mimak as you commanded. I had to kill his favorite wife before he would obey."

"Come forth, Ahl-Mish-Lah," Yiothizandra commanded. She had an arch tone at all times, the sort of superior mien one saw in Radiants. "I hear you lost your gr'hil."

Ahl-Mish-Lah swept into a deep bow that ended with her on her knees, forehead mashed to the stone. A whiff of stink came off her. Kila crinkled her nose and tried to take her deep breaths through the side of her mouth.

It took a bit of scrutiny to determine that Ahl-Mish-Lah was indeed female. Her face was no more delicate, no more feminine than that of the other nosg Kila had seen. Ahl clutched her staff in a clawed hand. Every digit was encumbered by a ring. Some were finely crafted gold with gems. Others appeared to be of bone, plant fiber, or stone. Several necklaces rattled on her chest, comprised of claws, teeth, beads, and—Kila held her breath—ears.

"Demonstrate your power," Yioth said.

Without hesitation, the shaman stood, murmured something growly and low, and brought a glow to the ruby eye-gems of her skull. Kila had overheard that this was called wormlight or stormlight or something. The nosg avoided Ennish when possible and she'd only been able to ask the men a few furtive questions. Whatever it was, it made the gems glow. The brightness increased until suddenly releasing as rays of red that flashed forth to sizzle the stone next to Kila.

The heat radiating from it would have been welcome had it not been so unreasonably fierce. Kila leaned away, yelping.

Yioth studied the squiggle Ahl's rays had carved into the stone. Had the target been flesh . . . Kila thrust the thought away and shrugged deeper into her cloak.

"I do not know the ways of the swarmlight," Yiothizandra said. "But it must be mercusine. You see this girl there?"

Ahl's eyes swiveled toward Kila. "Yuh."

"She is powerful with the mercus, but the crown blocks her from using it. Any other merculyn with the skill can take her power through the crown. You must learn to do this. Your power will be unmatched by any shaman. You will do my bidding and destroy my enemies."

Ahl-Mish-Lah blinked very hard and muttered to herself. The meaning of Yiothizandra's words slowly sank in. The creature prostrated herself and began babbling heaps of praise and gratitude. "I will do as you command. I will seize the girl's power. I will destroy all of the great queen's enemies!"

"Take her out of here," Yiothizandra said.

Ahl shambled to Kila and yanked her to her feet, nearly wrenching her arm out if its socket. "Come. Obey."

Several possible attacks revealed themselves to Kila, thanks to Aggy's recent training. Pain triggered her reflexes and her fist buried in Ahl's gut, knuckles tearing on claws and teeth of the necklaces. The ornaments provided armor-like protection from Kila's blow. Ahl responded with a backhand that spun Kila in a full circle. She ended on the floor, spitting blood from a split lip.

An iron claw gripped her ankle and the stone began to scrape under her body. Ears ringing, Yiothizandra's words barely made it into Kila's mind. "Do what you must to make her cooperate. But do not kill her."

"Yes, Great Queen."

The agony in Kila's head and arm made her vision swim. Nausea clogged her throat. Ceilings and walls slid past, growing dimmer and dimmer. Lanterns gave way to smoky torches. Then dampness.

A metallic clinking cut through Kila's dazed agony. A cold, iron grip squeezed her ankle. She was in a room so dark Ahl's form was a just a gray shadow hovering over her. Red flared into existence. Not from a lantern and not from Ahl's skull eyes. It was from a flash of pain as Ahl's boot impacted Kila's ribs.

Legs bunching close to her chest, arms over her head for protection, she braced for the next blow. Her right leg dragged, weighted down by whatever had her ankle. She felt for it.

An iron band. A shackle. Thick links of a rusty chain snaked away.

"Stand."

No chance to obey. Icy, fetid water smashed over her face.

"Stand."

Hands to stone, knees down, pulling hard against the chain, straightening. Tilting, balance failing. Ear exploding in fire as Ahl smashed with a fist.

Stone on cheek. Tears. Snot. Vomit. The tang of blood on her tongue.

"Stand."

Another kick to the ribs. Kila lay there, heaving.

The Revulsion oozed in, seeking, begging.

Another blow took Kila in the head, striking the crown and jarring the bolts that penetrated her skull. The pain lasted an instant, a spark from steel on stone, then vanished into blackness as Kila fell deep into Lumne's realm.

SHE AWOKE to find herself alone in total blackness. She didn't feel rested at all. Every part of her ached or throbbed. The floor was cold and filthy, and no matter how she lay, there was no comfort to be found. A bit of sleep would be . . . everything. At least she wouldn't have to experience every desperate moment. But between the convulsions of sickness and the eye-squeezing throbs of her injuries, all Kila could do was breathe.

In.

Out.

She set a goal to take ten breathes without groaning or gagging. That's all she wanted now. Ten.

Nax. . .

The cat was so far away. Henley, too.

Kila rolled onto her stomach as a new round of retching overtook her. This felt like the effects of spoiled food. There was nothing to bring up. That was part of her problem. No water. Her tongue rasped against the back of her throat and she could no longer swallow.

Panting, she again felt for the gems on the *vaz'on*. The futility of spinning them, hoping this time the bolts would loosen, was not lost on her. She'd heard from a trapper once that some animals gnawed at their own legs to free themselves of traps. It had seemed silly to her then. Not now. She'd happily tear out a bit of skull and scalp to be free of it.

A tremendous boom reverberated outside her cell. Her mercus enhanced senses soon brought the clomp of boots to her ears. Then the nasal breathing of a nosg.

Creaking. The rasp of iron against iron. A draft of air across her face.

The sickly yellow light of a tallow candle nearly blinded her. Groaning, Kila rolled away from the nosg. From the light.

The butt of Ahl's staff clicked on the stone. "Stand."

It took Kila more than a minute to obey. This time, Ahl waited for her to do it. The chain hampered her as much as her dizziness. It was not connected to the eyebolt on the wall. It was simply massive in length. The more Kila had to drag, the heavier it was. Which was quite obviously the entire idea behind it.

"Come." Ahl turned and left.

Kila had to loop several lengths of chain over her shoulders or she'd never be able to move her right leg. Even so, a tail of five paces rattled behind her as she staggered after the retreating glow of the candle.

Ahl was not patient. "Come!" she barked.

The corridor seemed to go on for a mile before coming to a winding stair. Seeing the nosg begin to go up, Kila bent double and sobbed.

"Come!" came the voice, followed by something very threatening in the nosg's lurkmire tongue.

Father's words came to Kila. "Don't give up before your body gives out." It was one of his enigmatic philosophies, earned from his years as a hunter. He usually followed the phrase with: "Don't die before you're dead."

Young Kila had thought the advice ridiculous. But now she understood. This was a choice. To live. Right now. Because if Ahl had to come back for her . . .

The first step unbalanced her and she ended up on the floor, tangled in chain. The second attempt gained her two steps, where she was forced to stop and catch her breath. And so, a step at a time, she wound her way up, rattling and cursing, and crying.

Ahl was waiting with a bucket. The moment Kila gained the final step, Ahl upended the bucket over her head, sending freezing, foul gray water sheeting over her. It found its way inside her collar, down her bare back.

Her mind slammed into the glass separating her from the mercus, and that was fortunate indeed for every living thing within a hundred miles.

"Good. Rage good," Ahl said, and walked away. "Come!"

Rage is good. Yes. Very good.

Ahl made a strange grimace, upthrusting lower teeth showing. A smile? She reached out, as if to place a comforting hand on Kila's shoulder. Kila couldn't resist ducking away.

Ahl grabbed her shoulder and pulled her forward. The chain tugged at Kila's ankle, already rubbing the skin there raw. Ahl offered a grunting sound. It was supposed to be comforting, Kila decided. But why? After all this treatment, why would—

The blow caught Kila's cheek and knocked her to the floor. "Come!"

Kila struggled to her feet, wiping reddish spittle from her lips. That last blow had jarred something in her head, unsteadying her vision. The pain was secondary, merely a new throb added to all those that had come before. An old shoulder injury—courtesy of Yiqa—awakened as she again scooped lengths of chain over her shoulders.

Stumbling after Ahl, Kila muttered a lengthy rant of curses. Some were aimed at Ahl, but most were directed at herself. Why hadn't she seen through Winnea's act? Why had she stayed at the Hackwatch knowing the mercus was unavailable to her there? Foolish, foolish!

The chamber Ahl entered was round, with a bench along the periphery. The center was clear, nothing but a scratched and scarred stone floor, stained black. Whether it was scorched or soaked with blood, Kila couldn't tell.

Ahl pointed to the center. Kila went there, trembling.

The domed ceiling was circuited with a narrow clerestory band. Grayish daylight shone through, hurting Kila's eyes, but she basked in it.

"Give me power," Ahl said, flicking a clawed finger against Kila's *vaz'on*.

"I can't give it to you. You must take it."

The wrong way to say it. Ahl thrust the butt of her staff into Kila's gut, doubling her over. Something inside her felt broken now. Watery waves of pain flushed through her bowels.

"Give me power."

"I can't! I can't control it."

Ahl thumped her staff on the floor and stalked around Kila. A swat to her back, a crack to the back of her legs sent her to her knees. Kila rested her forehead on the black smudged stone. It stank of rot.

Again the butt of the staff found her, but this time not so hard. The blunt end pressed onto her head and pushed Kila's face up. And kept pushing until she was again kneeling.

"Give power."

Since offering any reasonable response got her smacked, Kila opted to remain silent.

Ahl backed away and dug a claw into a pouch at her waist. She lifted something to her mouth. Blueish with white blotches. A mushroom it looked like, cap severely pointed, the stalk curved and fat at the base. Ahl chewed it, open mouthed, and made a wide gaping grimace of a child forced to eat something particularly nasty. She swallowed. "Give power!"

Kila said nothing, but dropped her gaze. She didn't want to see the blow coming. She didn't want to see her tormentor at all. The Revulsion met her in this retreat, eager to reach for her.

But then the air in the room failed. Kila drew in a breath, but there was nothing to it. Hand to her throat she heaved for air. There was none.

Ahl stood still and fierce, gripping her skull-topped staff. The eyes glowed bright red. Soft, diffuse rays beamed forth to surround Kila's head.

The shaman had taken her air.

Kila tried to speak, tried to beg, but there was no air in her lungs. Panic overtook her and she heaved in lungful after lungful of nothing. Vision blackening, she tried to stand, wanted to launch herself at Ahl. Rip the skull from her hands and beat her to death with it.

Instead, she fell sideways and lost all sense of life.

THE FILTHY WATER AWAKENED HER, flowed into her nostrils, sloshed through her slack lips to taint her tongue with brownish filth. Spitting and retching, Kila rolled to her stomach. The chain weighed her down, still partly over her shoulders.

"Give power!"

Sharp jabs in her ribs. Kila tried to swat the staff away, but she barely had strength to lift her hand from the greasy black floor. But there was air. Sweet, stinking air. She didn't care about the rot stench now. It was life!

"Please!" Kila croaked. "Please. I don't know how to give it to you."

A terrible itch pinched her spine. Reflex whipped Kila's arm around and she strained to reach the spot and scratch.

Two more itches bit the soles of her feet. Two more erupted deep inside her ears. Writhing and fumbling with her boots and pressing first one ear to a shoulder then the other, she desperately tried to scratch or at least put pressure on the itches. Ahl laughed, a sucking inhalation that rasped in her throat. More itches blossomed at the corners of her eyes, the backs of her knees, her groin, her armpits, her belly, her palms.

All along her scalp, down her legs. Each the worst itch of her life, each new one multiplying the torture of all the rest.

Ahl cackled and the eye gems pulsed and flashed with delighted menace. She cracked the staff onto the floor and the itches vanished. Kila lay panting and sobbing, snot smeared, and fouled by water and the smears of black grease from the floor.

Ahl's boot dug into her side and pushed until Kila rolled onto her back. The vile shaman looked down at her as she dug for another of the peculiar mushrooms. "Give power!"

Kila cried while Ahl chewed. The Revulsion pressed at her, screamed for her embrace. The mere feel of it oozing within her mind made Kila retch. And yet . . . she would only need to hold it a moment . . .

Before the thought completed, red light sizzled in the eye-gems, focusing into hair thin beams that stung Kila's head. Wisps of smoke curled up and away. It smelled like Flaumish-tak. But it wasn't him, it was Kila's own hair burning. The heat sliced over her scalp.

"The gems, you Kil licking' goat! Use the Kil-damn gems!" Kila poked at the tap gems over each over her temples. "Take power! Take power!"

The burning stopped and Ahl bent forward to study Kila's *va'zon*. "Gems have power?"

"Gems give my power to you." Kila pressed her chest and then offered the same hand in supplication. Again and again. Ahl had to learn. She had to or she was going to kill Kila by mistake. "You take power through gems."

"Hmmm."

The face came closer. So close Kila could have dug her

thumbs into those small, dark eyes and searched for whatever tiny brain lie behind them. Had she the strength.

"Can you feel my mercusine?" Kila asked.

A light cuff to the shoulder knocked Kila sideways again. Ahl dragged her back to her knees, attention only on the *vaz'on*. Kila might as well have been a stool being set upright. "Hmmmmm."

"A buzzy feeling," Kila said. "Can you feel it? Feel for the gem. It's a tap-gem. You can feel it."

"Hmmmm." The ugly head tilted one way then the other. The necklaces of teeth and claws rattled, the ears stank. The eye-gems glowed.

"Can you feel it? If you feel it you can take my power."

Anything. Kila would have done anything to show Ahl how to use her power. Anything.

"Please."

Ahl's mouth closed and her lips pooched forward. Only the tips of her upthrusting lower fangs showed. Finally she straightened. "Girl strong. But strong girl break."

The itching flared again and Kila lost sense of time. There was only the unstoppable agony. The flesh she could reach was scratched raw. Begging had no effect. Her insistence that she could not give her power fell on deaf ears.

"Take me to Yiothizandra! She'll explain! She will! She'll be angry that you tortured me."

The itching stopped a while later. No amount of prodding or kicking could get Kila to her feet. Ahl allowed her to crawl, dragging her chain behind her, down the endless spiral steps, and finally flopping into her cell. The door slammed behind her, but Kila heard nothing else.

38

THE PALE SKIN

A day. Only one day remained before Yioth would kill one of her children.

Eckso lifted her hood and scanned the battlements atop the Hackwatch's outer wall. Motion. Small dark figures on patrol. Probably some of the Iron Scholars. No danger to her. It was the shadlines she needed to avoid. Somehow.

She pulled her hood forward and trudged toward the gate. Under other circumstances, nothing would induce her to go in there. But here she was, forced by the absolute necessity of finding Ell. Yioth would enjoy killing one of her children. She would not wait a second, would likely do it early just to show that she could.

Eckso blinked away angry tears, again seeing her boy hanging over the ledge, held in Yioth's grip. The terror on his face pierced Eckso's heart. Part of her condemned the human weakness that had seeped into her over the years. Allowing herself to love these beings had opened her to these manipulations as surely as if she'd put a *vaz'on* on her own head.

The gate was closed. That was unusual.

An Iron Scholar came forward. He wore a rusty mail hauberk over his robes. A spear in both hands, tarnished and nicked tip pointed at her chest through the bars of the portcullis.

"Show your face," he rasped. He was stout but soft, like all the scholars. This was likely the first time he'd held such a weapon. It was certainly the first time he'd spoken in years. Eckso thought he was the same man who had allowed her in before.

She lifted her hood. "It's just me. Keely. I was here earlier."

"Why did you leave the fortress?" he demanded.

"I thought I could go farther tonight, but it's so dark. Please, sir," she said in the meekest voice she could muster. "Can't you spare shelter for a weary woman? I heard that the Hackwatch was open to all in need."

"Usually it is. But nosg attacked here. You saw. We're not supposed to let anybody in now."

A squeaky gasp and a hand to her breast showed him just how frightened she was. "But what shall I do? I haven't had a crumb for hours and I'm so tired."

The man's eyes dipped to take in her figure. He was still suspicious, but also interested. "Why're you traveling alone?"

"I have no one in this world since my husband died and his cousin inherited the house. The cretin expelled me without a copper plug. Ah me, the things I've had to do to survive." She flashed a dark, vulnerable look at the man. "Such terrible things. I would pay a toll, but I have no coppers." Iron Scholars weren't interested in coin, she knew. "Is there anything I might do . . . ?"

The man looked at his companion, who leered and nodded.

The spear point dropped away and the man jerked his head to the side. "I'll go first." He disappeared into his guard room and soon a sally port opened and he beckoned her in, meaty hand finding the small of her back to guide her. It seemed that few of these men were drinking the lust-deadening brew the brotherhood supplied.

The inside of the little gate office encompassed her with warmth. A lantern flickered on a shelf. The scholar secured the door and turned back to her. He'd left his spear just inside the portcullis.

Eckso threw her arms around him and found him very eager. When Loveheart pierced his chest, he shook a bit. She allowed him to look into her eyes. "Ah, how I love you," he said. Then his body slumped to the floor.

She passed out of the guard room. The other man laughed. "That was quick."

Loveheart discovered his soul. Eckso dragged him into the guard room. She guessed she had at most an hour before someone discovered the bodies. She took the lantern.

The courtyard was quiet. The remains of a huge pyre smoldered in the middle. Bits of nosg armor and bone lumped up from the ash.

The men on the battlements paid her no attention. Their job was to look outward. She dashed among the buildings, past the little shed that gave access to the dungeon cells. Hugging a wall, she found the corner where Cinnon had smashed loose a chunk when he fought with Kila Sigh.

Up the path to the garden overlook, panting more from

nervous need than exertion. The spot where she'd left Ell was bare. No surprise, but she'd needed to be sure.

Where had Ell gone? The conversation she'd overheard earlier had made it clear that Ell was missing. That meant the body had not been found here.

Unshielding the lantern, she played a beam of light onto the ground. Jagged stones and dead scrub covered the area. A stain of blood darkened one stone.

Ell had been impaled. She should have gushed blood everywhere. Except a shadline blade might drink the blood. Yes. That was why there was so little.

She couldn't have dymensed. The Revulsion prevented that. She must have crawled away. But with a sword through her? She must have freed herself of it somehow. Ell had always been stubborn.

Qinsh was supposed to drain a merculyn's power. Such a weapon should have been death for a dragnithan, who was made of the mercusine.

Quartering the area, Eckso soon found another splotch of blood. This was a bit uphill and away from overlook. A huge flat-topped stone loomed higher up. An overgrown trail led toward it.

More blood. Yes. Ell had come this way. There, a bloody smear where she'd placed her hand on a boulder. Eckso ran ahead and scrambled onto the flat-topped stone. The highest point of the entire fortress. More blood. No Ell.

Qinsh lay there, blade unstained, steel reflecting Eckso's lantern light. A cry came from downhill. More answered. A gathering of lanterns and torches congealed in the courtyard, then started toward her. They'd spotted her lantern light.

She could kill them all with the mercus. Except she didn't

have the mercus. She was no blademaster, and her rondel dagger a poor defense against so many in any case.

The answer to both problems came instantly to her. She did as Ell must have done. With a deep groan and shudder, she manifested her wings. It had been so long since she'd last done it, a rending agony tore down her back. The wings did not sprout from her back so much as explode from it. Hers were more like Ell's than Yioth's. Gray feathers, the tips trailing into demanyic smoke, ruffled in the wind.

Dropping the lantern, she leapt from the stone and glided. Ell must have done just this, gliding over the wall, waiting for the Revulsion to thin enough that the mercus became available. And as soon as it was, Eckso did as Ell most certainly had done. She dymensed.

She appeared in Ell's apartment at the top of the Citadel spire. She shed her wings instantly, relieved to be rid of them. Yioth did not suffer so when she manifested hers, but that was her nature. She had always been more strongly aligned with her dragon nature than Eckso. In this world, wings were much more painful to bring forth than in the demaynic realms.

Eckso had not been here in a long time. But it was just as she remembered. Tidy, richly appointed, and cold.

Ell was not there, but her blood was. Eckso followed the trail from the office chamber, through a curving corridor to an arched door, which stood ajar. Eckso pushed through, mercus bolts formed and ready to flame Ell on the spot.

She let them go when she found her quarry lying on the floor, surrounded by a dome of blue mercusine light. The buzz of power was overwhelming, seeming to come from everywhere at once. Ell lay on her back, hands to the wound in her chest. A seep of blood spread away from her. She was not dead, for her chest rose and fell in uneven breaths. A trickle of red drew a crimson line from the corner of her mouth, down her fair cheek, and disappearing into her black hair.

Her shadline dirk lay next to her. Good, that would be useful.

Eckso lifted her skirts as she approached, loath to get blood on her hem. A silly instinct, she realized, laughing coldly. She would soon be soaked with it. She took up Ell's dirk. Nothing happened, which was a relief. The last thing she needed was an ecstatic bonding.

In fact, the blade seemed rather shoddy. But it was sharp enough. And if Eckso had to add a little mercus to the edge to ease the cutting, so be it.

Lips clamped tight, she brought the blade to Ell's throat. No point belaboring it. She pressed down.

The blade passed right through Ell's throat and clicked onto stone. No resistance at all. And no blood. In fact, Eckso's entire hand had passed through her cousin's flesh. Because she wasn't real.

"I'm disappointed in you, Eckso," came her cousin's voice. From behind her. Spinning, Eckso hurled bolts of power at the hunched figure emerging from the shadows of the office. The green flashes made it no further than the walls of the blue mercus dome that enclosed her. They broke against the barrier, sending scintillating sparks all around Eckso that sizzled against her face and hands.

The illusion of Ell faded from the floor. Eckso slumped when she saw the circle embedded in the floor. A summoning circle.

Such a simple, elegant trap. The truth of her situation penetrated her shock and Eckso folded forward, dropping the sham blade and hugging herself against the sobs that threatened to shatter her. Poor Trev. Poor Poli.

Ell shuffled closer. Her pale face glowed from the blue light emanating from the dome that now imprisoned Eckso. Blood stains blackened her front, glistening wetly. "You killed us both. For what? Are you so weak that you let Yiothizandra bully you into suicide? Did you truly think you could kill me and remain unscathed? I have always been stronger than you, cousin."

"I thought Qinsh would make the difference. I thought —" But sobs stole her words. There was no point explaining herself to Ell. No point in anything.

"Qinsh is not what told. The blade alone did Yioth's work. Qinsh drank from my power only a moment before realizing who I was. Did you think that Jil carried her around me all this time merely because she could resist attacking me? No. Qinsh knows me. Knows my nature. Qinsh hates merculyns of a certain flavor."

"Kila Sigh?"

"Jil hated Kila, not Qinsh. Why did you do it, Eckso Ezeel?"

"Because Yioth holds my children hostage, Ellishan." It felt right that they used full names now, here upon the verge of their deaths. They had been playmates once, long ago. Friends, even. Perhaps they would vanish into the evernight together. Perhaps they would be renewed. Or perhaps the Hel Lords would feed upon their souls. Now they could pass from life together.

Ell eased herself to her knees, bracing herself with one hand. "I see your quandary now. Ah, Eckso. You flew in twilight, the sun just gone, a purple glow upon the horizon. I remember it well."

"You walked under the midday sun."

"And I would never have flown had I been allowed not to. But do not mistake my walk for infallible goodness. For I do not mistake your twilight soar as irredeemable evil."

"Amoral, Flaumishtak calls us twilight folk."

"Can an amoral being love her children?" Ell asked. "It has been my constant question these few months, watching Kila Sigh come into her power. For her mother was such. And Kila . . . she was to be Kil's mother. She was raised a thief."

Eckso wiped her eyes. "I would do anything to save my boy and my girl."

"And what of the rest of the world, which Yioth surely seeks to destroy? Do you care nothing for it?"

Eckso let weariness draw her to the floor. She sat cross-legged, shoulders slumped, facing her cousin through the wall of azure glow. "I care for it as much as anyone cares for a gameboard. It has been my occupation for ages. At first it was mere diversion from the anxiety of my imprisonment here. Now . . . I have lived scads of lives and each has revealed something new. It is like the art of arranging flowers. Beautiful, ephemeral."

"Beautiful because it is ephemeral," Ell said, nodding in agreement. "Which is why we were meant to be barred from it. And now it may be broken apart and only those who survive will remember it. Like a lovely vase of roses enjoyed for a ten-day, then discarded upon a midden."

"Ah me, my roses. Poli and Trev. I burn with love for them, cousin."

"What does Yioth demand for their lives?"

"Your head."

"Ah. I see. I see." Ell's chin dipped to her chest. Eckso thought her asleep, but she managed to look up past her regal brows. "You realize your children would never survive Kil's reign, my head in Yioth's hands or no."

"There must be some way. They must come with me when the world breaks. They must!" Catching herself, Eckso dipped her head. "Though I don't know how that could be."

"You should have sought me out at the Hackwatch. I could have helped you. Klayne will not lift a finger to aid you or your children, you know. I hope you weren't counting on him."

"I know it. He and Yioth . . . They are more alike than you and I are. And yet, she dominates him utterly. I saw him attack her. All his power is nothing. The babe shields her. Even with Kila Sigh's power, I could do nothing."

"What?"

"Kila Sigh's power is incredible. But Yioth had my babies in her arms. I dared not attack her lest they die. Ah, I see that you didn't know. Sigh wears the *vaz'on* and I used her power. Such an enormous deluge of mercus. But it is nothing against Yioth, for whom the mercus parts and does not touch."

"Where is Kila now?" Ell tried to stand, but failed. Her hands glistened with her own blood.

"Yioth has her now. But Yioth is no merculyn. She relies upon distant shouts to call the dragnithor to her. It's how she called me and Klayne. She will never be able to access the tap gems."

Ell lifted her head. Tears streamed down her cheeks. With unsteady movements, she again tried to gain her feet. "She keeps your children with her?"

"No. They bed in the eyrie above Ceronhel. They are to tend the dragons. There's another with them now. Kila's friend Raginalt. He is likely dead. Bazron was there."

"You should have sought me out. Together we could have saved them." Ell raised her hands and closed her eyes. The blue light faded and vanished. And then Ell was falling. Eckso lurched forward and caught her up before she struck ground.

Looking down, Eckso saw that her feet straddled the brass ring embedded into the floor. Ell had released her from the summoning circle. Ell had given herself into Eckso's power. Sniffing hard and blinking tears away, Eckso grasped for the mercus.

In a minute they reappeared in the cellar of her mansion in Trine. Ell still breathed. Eckso called a mercus light into existence.

Setting her cousin gently onto the floor, Eckso fetched Kila Sigh's blade from where she'd stashed it. She dimmed the light as she brought the black steel to her cousin's throat, set the edge to the pale skin.

Tears blurred her vision and she held the dagger, poised to sever Ell's head. Ell had freed her, knowing this was what Eckso must do.

"What is sacrifice to an amoral being?" Eckso said to herself, sniffing. "You are a fool, cousin, to have freed me. Did you think I would be grateful? Do the Lightshades sing your name already? It is nothing to me."

The lie was bitter upon her tongue. As was the truth. Ell's head would but delay her children's death. Lips quivering, she pulled the blade away from her cousin's neck. "Ah me."

With mercus amplification, Eckso shouted for her servants. Within five minutes old Hazel was bent over the monarch, plying her with salves and draughts while a bundle of sage smoked in a dish nearby.

"Save her, Hazel. Save her."

The old woman muttered to herself words of mooncraft. Eckso felt odd resonances upon the mercusine but could make no sense of what the healer was doing.

Eckso sent a man to fetch clothing for Ell. "Trousers. Shirt. Fur-lined boots and that grayfox cape. Gloves, too! Hurry."

Hazel set aside a small vial, now empty, and bent close to Ell's breast. With gnarled fingers she widened the tear that Qinsh had pierced through the monarch's blouse, exposing the pale smooth flesh and the puckered red wound to air.

A footman who was looking on, hissed and backed away, for the wound began to close upon itself, torn skin reaching across the gap to touch and meld with torn skin. And in this manner the wound knitted and sealed. When the process completed, an angry red scar remained and the skin around it was inflamed and swollen. Hazel bade the footmen help her turn Ell onto her face and repeated all these ministrations upon the wound in Ell's back where Qinsh had first driven in.

Clothing appeared, as did a stack of towels and a basin of steaming water. Hazel wiped away the blood, and roughly scrubbed at Ell's cheeks. The entire time, Ell remained asleep, her body limp and unresponsive to Hazel's manipulations.

"I need her awake and walking," Eckso said. "I need her ready to fight."

Hazel lifted her watery eyes. "I can do all that, but . . ."

"Do it. Ell wished to sacrifice herself. She can do so with her head on her shoulders. She is stronger than you suspect."

"Ah I know. I know her kind. Hand me that purse."

It was a satin bag, cinched closed with a golden cord. Hazel pulled from it a tin box. Inside was a shallow tray of finely chopped substance, some weed or flower or leaf. With deft motions, Hazel wetted it with spit and stirred it with her pinky. Taking up small wet clumps, she rubbed this salve into each of Ell's nostrils, then clamped her hand over Ell's mouth, forcing her to breathe through her nose.

The effect was instant.

Ell's eyes popped open and she struggled free of Hazel's grasp. She was on her feet, hunched and ready to fight. The hum of forming mercus bolts beat at Eckso's brain. "Hold, cousin!"

Awareness of her surroundings and Eckso's placating gestures broke through. "Where am I?"

"My mansion. In Trine. I knew Hazel could bring you around."

"Not for long," Hazel warned. "No matter the craft, healing comes from within the healed. Her weakness will tell sooner than later, and when it does, she will sleep."

The dark, sunken look of Ell's eyes showed how weary she was. But her shoulders were back, jaw set. Her glance fell to the dagger still in Eckso's hand. "I thought you would take my head."

"I thought you'd let me die in the circle."

Hazel collected her things as the two dragnithans faced off. Eckso barely noticed as the old woman barked at the remaining servants to leave. A strange stillness filled the cellar as the cousins weighed each other's hearts in their minds. For Eckso it was simple. Ell could help her save her children. And she was a creature of Day, for whom such a cause should require no thought at all. And yet Ell hesitated.

Eckso knew why. Even a creature of light would hesitate to aid one who had betrayed her by driving a sword into her back. But no amount of pride would restrain Eckso from doing what was needed to save her children. She lowered herself to her knees and offered her palms in surrender. "Help me, Ell. I beg you. I didn't want to harm you. You understand why I did what I did."

"I understand. You are weak. You have always been weak. Especially when your sister uses you."

Ell's words rankled. Because they were true. "And now I'm weaker still. You value honesty. You cherish truth, no? What must I do to gain your trust? Tell me."

"An oath. And not the weak words of this world, which I well know find no purchase in your heart. The shadline oath was as a drop of rain upon your brow. I require a promise-binding. And one of exceeding severity."

Tears came to Eckso's eyes. "I will say whatever words you require. And I will submit to your mercusine leash."

Ell nodded and formed bolts of heat and the scent of herbs only found in demaynic realms. To this she added the notion of honesty, love, and a strange sort of inverse pain. This last was the enforcement of the promise binding. Should Eckso attempt to act against her oath, the pain would remind her of it. And given the strength of the bolt, the reminder would be unmerciful.

Ell spoke: "Vow to me that you will never betray me or Kila Sigh again. Vow that you will turn your mind, heart, and power to the service of Day. Vow to obey me in all things. Vow to me that if I die, you will counsel Kila as best you can to serve the force of destiny and the preservation of this world through the culmination to come."

Eckso spoke the vow, and as she did so felt the bolts Ell had prepared settle upon her, constricting around her limbs, her head, and sinking into her torso. A swell of love warmed her heart, then subsided. She blinked and wondered why she had ever answered Yioth's first summons. What a fool she'd been.

Ell said, "And I vow to you, Eckso Ezeel, to pull as lightly as I can upon your oath, to cherish you as an ally, and to release you once the culmination has passed."

Eckso shivered as a white presence surrounded her. Ell placed her hands upon her head, bent and kissed her. "It is sealed. Stand."

"My children?"

"Let's fetch them. You said Bazron guarded them?"

"Aye."

"We'll need help." Ell's eyes were hollow, but fierce. She changed into the clothes the servants had brought, stomped into the fur-lined boots, and swung the grayfox cape over her shoulders. Checking her dirk, she nodded in satisfaction. "Keep Cayne with you for now. Take my hand. Come."

39

GRAY SHADOWS LOOMED

Harnzyne snorted and snuffed at Ell, and she repeated her assurances that she was quite well enough for the task ahead. Eckso had never been a good judge of dragon temperament. They all looked angry to her. For the ages she'd lived before coming to this world, she'd avoided the beasts as much as possible.

But she knew Harnzyne, who had always been Ell's frequent companion. He had been a bit jealous of Eckso even then. Now he threw amber glances at her, and snorted blue smoke.

"She has submitted to a promise binding, Harnzyne," Ell said. Eckso knew that she said this for her benefit, since Ell could speak directly to the dragon through that strange mental talk she favored. Eckso didn't like that either. Maybe Yioth was right. Maybe she had become too human.

"I've never been to Ceronhel," Eckso said. "So . . ."

"You'll have to ride with me, then. Come."

Harnzyne dipped a wing to make it easy for Ell to climb

onto his neck. Eckso went up after and took a position behind her cousin. The dragon was warm beneath her.

"Put your arms around me. Harnzyne likes to swoop."

Remembering how Klayne had dymensed while falling, Eckso clutched her cousin hard. There was no chance she could mimic such a feat.

"Your wings?" Ell prompted.

The plan required it. The pain was not as bad as the last time, but it still brought tears to Eckso's eyes. She folded her wings in close. Ell would manifest hers at the last second so Eckso could hold onto her. Harnzyne lumbered to the ledge and leapt into open air.

He did not spread his wings, much to Eckso's horror, and they plummeted down, the lights of Starside coming close very quickly. Eckso closed her eyes and bit her tongue to keep from screaming. She hated flying.

And then the beast extended his wings, which caught the wind like leathery sails.

"Ready?" Ell called. She didn't wait for an answer before forming the bolts of dymension.

A flash of blackness engulfed them, then vanished. The air bit Eckso's face with incredible ferocity. The cold was alive with greedy hunger. Ceronhel lay far below, like a child's toy fortress.

"That one!" Eckso shouted, pointing to the black archway high upon the closest mountain. The eyrie where her children were.

Ell elbowed Eckso. "Go!"

Sucking in a breath, Eckso released her hold on Ell and flung herself off the dragon. Her wings caught air and she glided toward the eyrie. Ell followed, wings sprouting and catching air. She joined Eckso and motioned for her to ascend. With hard flaps, Eckso strained higher, circling and circling.

Gliding below, Harnzyne let out a challenging bellow and shot blue flame before him. Bazron did not rise to the bait. But two other dragons emerged from the eyrie. Faxnishek and Tortyr. They screamed in outrage and strained skyward to confront the interloper of Day.

Bazron isn't here, Ell sent. Eckso shook her head, dizzied by the sudden voice inside her head.

More shrieks came from the south. Three more dragnithor winged their way to join the chase. Eckso recognized them. Grizzly-mouthed Fritor, sleek and speedy Liansher, and the enormous and ponderous Qranzi who once contended with a qiznithor and lived. He lacked a forelimb and an eye, but should he manage a deathlock upon any dragnithor, his foe's death was certain.

I knew they gathered for Yioth, Ell sent. *I did not know so many had already come.*

Harnzyne bellowed again and darted north, trailing five dragons of Night behind him.

Hurry! He will not outfly Liansher for long. If forced to turn, there are enough to cut him off.

They dove for the mouth of the eyrie and alighted in the dreary cavern. Eckso had bolts ready for Bazron. Ell was brimming over with potential power.

Bazron was not there. In the far corner a small fire threw orange shimmers against the wall. Long gray shadows loomed there, cast by the three pathetic humans sheltering by the flames.

"Trev! Poli!" Eckso called. "Come children."

They threw themselves at her, weak and thin and shivering. A wave of love caught in her throat and she folded her wings around them and kissed their filthy hair and crooned promises of safety to them.

Ell was speaking to Ragin, who seemed frantic. "I must find Kila! I must!"

"There is no time for that. I will take you away from here."

"Mother! You have wings!" Trev marveled at the gray wings and Poli touched them with tentative awe.

"I shall tell you of them later. Come. Hold tight to me."

Eckso dymensed to the Citadel. Ell's chief counselor gave a start and leapt from his chair, nearly dropping the book he'd been reading into the fireplace. "Ah, who—who—are you?"

She kissed her children. "Sit by the fire there. This man will order tea and food for you. Obey him."

His questions went silent as she dymensed back to the Ceronhel eyrie. Raginalt was shouting and stomping. "No! I came for Kila. I must be with her. She must not trust anyone else. They all seek to use her. I'm the only one she should trust. I'm the—"

Ell pressed a hand to his head and he fell into her arms. "A bit of sleep will do him good. Take him. I must aid Harnzyne. He's injured."

Eckso scooped the lad up and dymensed again to Starside.

She put him near to the fire and again took her children in her arms. They had crumbs on their chins and empty cups told of greedily consumed tea. Marlow looked on with a furrowed brow, but he said nothing.

They waited there a quarter of an hour before Ell appeared in a billow of mercus green. She stumbled. Marlow caught her up in his arms. "Harnzyne needs . . ."

Ell's eyes rolled up and her wings vanished. Marlow shouted for help. Two huge Fell Guardsmen barged in, spears ready to impale everyone in sight. Only Marlow's quick orders spared Eckso. One man dashed for help while the other stood guard over the fallen monarch.

40

WAS IT AN HONOR?

It might have been the next morning. It might have been two days later. Kila did not know for there was no light, no way to gauge time in her cell. At some point a bowl of sludge appeared. The rank slurry surrounded a hunk of burned meat. Kila devoured it all.

The searing light of a lamp came into her awareness. The staff prodded, the itches came and went, air vanished and reappeared. Kila had no defense for any of it, and she lacked the will to scratch or gasp. The suffering continued, filling her awareness totally. When it stopped, she slept.

She awoke again when the back of her *vaz'on* clanked onto the corner of a step. Again. Again. Something pulled hard at her right leg. The chain. It was slung over a nosg's shoulder as it dragged her up the spiral stairs. Clank. Clack. Clank.

She was deposited on the char-smeared floor beneath the dome. Ahl-Mish-Lah sat on the bench, forearms resting upon her thighs, staff lazily held in one hand. Kila's dragger grunted and left.

"Strong girl is weak," Ahl announced. "Weak. Weak.

Weak. I make her strong again. Come." Ahl bent for a bucket at her feet.

Kila knew what was coming, but she couldn't do more than cover her face with her arms. The splash of fetid water coursed over her, shocking her to pained alertness. She didn't wait to be asked to get up, though she felt every ounce of the iron chain as she did.

Ahl led Kila from the dome and outside. The air was still but frigid. The water in Kila's hair quickly crisped to ice. A scream came from inside the fortress. Something shattered in the great hall. Ahl chuckled ruefully. "Queen full of rage. Work hard or maybe she kill you."

"I'm hungry."

"Work for food."

They came out into a vast flat yard behind the main fortress. It was so large Kila wondered what purpose it had served. Perhaps marshaling great armies or practicing battle formations. It was surrounded on two sides by crumbling walls, the rear abutted the steep face of a towering cliff. Above that reached a white-capped mountain peak.

A band of men and nosg worked ahead. Piles of black stone lay all about. Masons chiseled away at them, then passed the stones to the gang who relayed them to a wall under repair. Ahl thrust Kila into the line between a burly man with a ragged beard, and a squat nosg with a peg in place of his lower right leg.

The man hardly looked at her. His gaze was inward, the sort a condemned man had. He took a stone, pivoted and tossed it at Kila. She dropped it onto her foot and screamed. The peg-legged nosg shoved her hard, plucked up the stone and passed it along. He cuffed her upside the head. "Work! Ratch likes to kiss."

Ahl ambled away and took a up a spot by a brazier. She ate a mushroom and leaned against a sunny patch of wall. Kila shivered and rubbed her elbows.

Another stone came at her. Kila caught it in her arms, the weight propelling her into peg-leg. A nosg nearly as wide as he was tall rushed forward and snapped a short whip. The crack drew all eyes. "Work or kisses?" he gurgled at her. His breath smelled of fish. He had leather armor over his shoulders and mismatched steel greaves on his shins. Cast offs of some ancient war, it looked like. He wore a curved sword. "Work or kisses?"

"Work!" Kila said, thrusting the stone at peg-leg. She tested the mercus automatically and was denied by the *vaz'on*. The Revulsion oozed into her awareness. Her mind fingered through the sludge, but recoiled as a hot wave of nausea bent her double. A smattering of nosg porridge flecked onto the ground. She didn't have anything else in her stomach.

The tip of the whip stung her bottom, hotter and harder than the jack hornets that used to nest under the front eaves of the Warren in Cheapsgate. "Kiss for lazy!" Ratch said.

The masons hurried their chisels and the gang tossed stones from one to another with more speed. The burly man took more care passing the stone to her, but not for her sake. Gauging by the red stripes on his arms, Ratch had favored him many kisses already.

The stones would have been too big for her even had she been rested and fed. As it was, she could barely stand under their weight. Soon her arms were scraped and burning. Each new stone made her stumble more, made her gasp harder.

Ratch stood nearby, eagerly waiting for her to drop a stone or fall.

Ahl watched keenly. Peg-leg cursed Kila in his lurkmire language. He grew angrier and angrier. When her stone dropped before reaching his hands, his slap and Ratch's kiss struck at the same time. Face and bottom stinging, she again reached for the Revulsion. Again she bent double and heaved up nothing until her abdomen ached.

Peg-leg got a kiss as he bent to pluck up the dropped stone. After that ol' Peg-Leg started shoving his peg into the back of her knee every time Burly turned to pass a stone to her.

The third time he did, she fell. The stone thwumped next to her head. Ratch lunged and kissed her shoulder. The lash lost some of its sting on her cloak, but the sheer stupidity of punishing an exhausted worker enraged her.

The Revulsion yearned for her and she felt for it again. And again she retched and convulsed. Burly yanked her to her feet. Her chain rooted her to the ground.

"Keep yer chin up, lass. Ratch'll kiss yer eyes from yer skull."

A pause in the work gave her a chance to catch her breath. A hunchbacked nosg came forward with a pail and ladle. It was cold broth and tasted of old shoe leather, but Kila drank it down greedily. When peg-leg's turn came, she thrust her heel hard into his peg. It gave a loud crack, then split, sending him down. Ratch was on him in seconds, whipping him so unmercifully that Kila reddened with shame. The downed nosg screamed and curled up into a ball, but Ratch did not relent until Ahl barked and smacked her staff onto his shoulder.

Peg-leg was sent off for repair. He threw Kila hateful look

and hissed. Burly dumped a stone in to her arms. With peg-leg gone, she had to side step and hand off to the next nosg in line. It occurred to her now that all the nosg on the work crews were debilitated in some way. Missing eyes, missing limbs, general frailty of old age. These were the only nosg Yiothizandra was willing to spare. But even with these challenges, the nosg were stronger than their human crew mates.

The men kept to themselves and it was clear they were as much prisoners here as Kila, even lacking shackles and chains.

Ahl went back to her sunny wall and resumed munching her mushrooms and watching Kila work. The stones were smaller now, whether by necessity of design or because the masons sought to reward Kila for taking out peg-leg she couldn't say. Burly refused to talk and only responded to her inquiries with meaningful glances at Ratch.

More screams came from inside the hold. They sounded like nosg. And it was clearly pain and terror in their voices. Yiothizandra was mightily upset about something.

The work continued throughout the afternoon, and Kila slowly warmed to it. Now that the stones were more manageable, she found a bit of solace in the rhythm of the relay gang and the steady beat of hammer on chisel.

The broth had restored her more than expected, and a second round a few hours later cleared her aching head of its cruft of weariness and confusion. Even the bruises on her face did not bother her. It was just pain.

The air was cold, but the work warmed her well enough that a bit of sweat began to dampen her shirt beneath her disgustingly soiled cloak.

A surprised shout pulled her from her mindless reverie. Burly stood still, stone in hand, eyes to the sky. All the men and nosg were looking the same way. Even Ahl was peering skyward.

A flight of black birds approached. They were huge, but not shaped like any crows or ravens Kila had ever seen. And the flap of their wings seemed strange, when they flapped at all. Ratch's mouth hung open, his whip held loose at his side. *"Achetli!"*

They weren't birds. "Dragons!" Kila gasped.

"No," said Burly. "Wyvoks. Far north creatures. Vile as snakes and hungry as bears."

More appeared, then more still, winging into view from behind a far mountain. Bringing up the rear was the unmistakable form of a great dragon, so black it looked like a gash torn in the sky. This creature roared and spat flame. The wyvoks answered in choruses of teeth-rattling shrieks and squawks.

The nearest flight glided toward the fortress, growing ever larger. Kila had thought them the size of sea eagles, but now saw they were several times larger than atlens, with enormous wings, and long tails tipped with curved spikes.

The work gang crouched as the wyvoks swooped low overhead. One reached with black talons and plucked a nosg mason from the top of the wall, then beat its wings to carry its prey over the valley below Ceronhel.

The dragon flamed down at it, roaring. Two more nosg were snatched up. Ratch was running with all speed toward the safety of the great hall. He didn't make it. A wyvok plucked him up. Kila saw the whip fall, then witnessed the wyvok pull the gang boss's leg from his body. Still in flight, it curled in on itself to grab the leg and chomp it down.

The dragon roared and flamed, and suddenly the other

wyvoks dropped their prey. A nosg screamed from directly above. Burly dropped his stone and pulled Kila back. The nosg impacted just feet from where she stood. The work gang broke and fled, desperate for shelter. Wyvok after wyvok glided in to land in the long open yard behind the fortress. The men and nosg had nowhere to run.

The dragon flapped down, vast claws rending furrows in the frozen turf as it landed. Kila knew this beast. The one who'd held Eckso's children in its mouth. Bazron.

Even under the light of day, the black scales reflected almost no light. Kila blinked and tried not to look directly at the beast. It was enormous, its tail alone stretching half the length of the great hall. It towered three times as high as any of the wyvoks, making them look like its brood of hatchlings. They screamed and spat and backed from the dragon, who leered at them each in turn with his baleful green eyes.

Ahl-Mish-Lah edged away from the dragon and beckoned for Kila to follow her. "Not our work." The shaman seemed very eager to leave the vicinity, and Kila found herself agreeing with her captor for the very first time. As weary as she was, she looped half of her chain over her shoulders and shuffled after Ahl.

The quickest retreat took them to the open doors of the great hall. Several others of the work gang were huddling just inside. Ahl hugged the wall, arrowing straight for an interior passage. Kila did her best to keep pace, throwing furtive glances toward the crude throne at the far end of the hall.

Yiothizandra stood before it, deep in conversation with Noy. The nosg servant swayed side to side and grumbled his responses.

Ahl had just made it to the passage when Yioth's voice boomed out. "Ahl-Mish-Lah, come to me."

The shaman froze, then turned and obeyed. Her necklaces rattled as she brushed past Kila. "Follow."

Kila did not know how long she'd been captive here. She thought it a few days at least. Apparently it had been much longer, for Yiothizandra's belly now protruded like a mother expecting child within a few ten-days.

A trestle table lay on its side, crockery shattered all over the floor. Three dead nosg lay atop the wreckage, scorched black. Whatever had infuriated Yiothizandra, she had taken it out on bystanders bent over their meals.

Ahl bowed low, dipping her staff skull until it tapped the floor. "Great queen."

Nostrils flaring, Yiothizandra looked down upon the shaman. "Demonstrate for me your mastery of Kila Sigh's power."

Ahl prostrated herself. "Forgive. Girl is strong. Break her takes long time."

"Break her? I did not command you to break her."

"She not give power, great queen!"

"Take it! Use the *vaz'on* gems, you ridiculous hog!" Yiothizandra descended and stepped over Ahl to confront Kila. "Look." She flicked a black-nailed forefinger against one of Kila's tap gems. Standing this close to the woman, Kila felt the enormous heat of her body. It felt good after being so cold.

Ahl was saying something and shaking her head. Yiothizandra answered angrily, but Kila could not understand the words. The heavy presence of Kil surrounded her.

Again her heart pulsed with his. *Thump-thump.* All her senses numbed . . . as if she was experiencing what the godling babe experienced in the womb. Without realizing what she was doing, she reached for the child. Hands pressing to Yiothizandra's belly. On contact the dragnithan's skin burned Kila's palms, but the pain was far away. A rush of sound and feeling washed over Kila, like rolling waves washing up a beach.

Thump-thump!

Her vision blackened and resolved into a starry sky. It spun slowly, then faster. Wind buffeted her back. Twisting, she discovered she was falling. Far below lay a city, streets alight with mercus lamps. Starside. The Divide made a hard edge to the sprawl. Moonside made a black void on the other side.

Kila stretched her arms out. The falling sensation was exactly the same as plummeting from the eyrie ledge. There was more exhilaration than fear in this moment. Her arms pulled back, then brushed on something soft but firm. Looking over her shoulder she discovered wings. Black wings. Raven's wings, like Ell's.

She spread them, catching the air and lifting into a smooth glide.

The wind that held her aloft failed, and strain as she might with her unskilled wings, she could not catch the air again. The city spun as she plunged, straight down. Divide to her right, Moonside directly below. The roiling black that masked Moonside reached for her, groped up to receive her with oily black fingers. Reached to embrace and be embraced. She recognized it, felt the nausea of the Revulsion roll through her gut.

Her vision blanked and returned. Something cold pressed against her back. Stone. The ceiling of the great hall soared over head. Yiothizandra looked like a giant standing over her. "You dare to touch me?" she spat. "You–" Her foot swung back in preparation for a kick, but abruptly stopped as a convulsion bent her forward. Her hands clutched her belly and she sank to one knee. Her lovely face contorted in agony. "So soon?" she gasped. "I'm not ready!"

Kila rolled away and struggled to her feet. Her vision still swam, made dizzy by the strange vision of flying. Ahl was getting to her feet, swarmlight in her red gems casting a crimson stain onto the floor. Kila's right hand felt extremely heavy. She looked down to discover her ring still on her pinky. Highest of Kil. Why hadn't it been taken from her? In fact, where had it been? She didn't remember it there when handling the stones, or at any time since coming here. It must have been there, though. It felt as heavy as the chain. It picked up on the swarmlight coming from Ahl's staff.

Yiothizandra's pain slowly passed and she too regained her feet. "Kil stirs. His time is near. And I still have no realm to gift to him." She seemed to be talking to herself. Was that fear in her voice? Kila wondered if the woman had seen any of her vision. The Elnisian words were burned into her mind. *I'il ish enizsh eyl. Lumne scor ish dragnithor! Epil ach, Kila Sigh. Epil ach!*

Kila had no idea what they meant, except for her name and the word "dragnithor." But she was certain of one thing. The vision and the words had been Kil speaking to her. Just as she was sure he reached to her heart and matched her pulse to his.

And Moonside. That roiling smoke reaching for her.

She recognized it now. It was flooded with the Revulsion. Why hadn't she felt it before?

"You will take her power, Ahl-Mish-Lah," Yiothizandra was saying. "She cannot give it to you any more than she can deny it you. The gems tap her power so you can drink from it." Yiothizandra seemed to have forgotten Kila's transgression. That, or she realized her time was running out and Kila's power was more important than wreaking vengeance upon Kila's body. "If you cannot take it, I shall find a shaman who can. Be ready to demonstrate your power at sunset. There are many hungry wyvoks here. I must feed them something." Yiothizandra strode from the hall. The wyvoks screeched in deafening chorus to greet her.

Ahl came to Kila, bent close to inspect the gem. "Why you not tell me?"

"I told you, Ahl-Mish-Lah. I told you but you didn't listen."

"Tell again."

Kila's explanation was a repetition of what Yiothizandra had just said. Ahl considered it with narrow eyes while pushing her tongue around her cheeks and pooching out her lips. "No feel mercus."

"The mushrooms give you power," Kila said, guessing at what she'd deduced so far. "What do the eye-gems do?" She balled her right hand into a fist, and pulled it into her sleeve to hide the garnet ring. The weight there was less now that Ahl's swarmlight had faded somewhat.

"Mushroom open eyes." She stamped the staff onto the floor. "See through skull. Make swarmlight."

Eating mushrooms reminded Kila of ferneater magic. She wondered if it was like that. She wished now she'd been less prejudiced against Zirhine. The woman clearly knew much about the craft. But Zirhine hadn't used any gems. There had been words though. She couldn't remember if Ahl had said anything when torturing her or not.

"Maybe if you give me a mushroom . . ."

Ahl clunked Kila's head with her staff. "No! Mimak sacred. Not for *ickli*."

Rubbing the top of her head, Kila forced herself not to reach for the shaman's throat. She didn't need another lesson to know that *ickli* meant human.

Ahl had been munching on mushrooms the whole morning. Her eyes must be wide open by now. Kila did not want the shaman to take her power. But she knew more beatings and itchings were coming, and the closer to sunset they got the worse the tortures would be. "Look at this gem with your skull eyes." She pointed to the one over her right temple.

Ahl grunted and cracked the staff against Kila's shin. "No command Ahl-Mish-Lah." But the eyes glow increased again. Kila put her hand behind her back to further shield her ring from the swarmlight. The last thing she needed was another weight on her body. The trinket hadn't done anything before. But now Kila recalled that she'd touched Yiothizandra with that hand. Kil must have done something to awaken it. The thought made Kila shiver.

Ahl's eyes squeezed shut and the eye-gem glow intensified. The skull came very near to Kila's face. She saw the empty holes where upthrusting fangs would have been seated in the jaw. She wondered who the poor nosg was who had been sacrificed to become a staff skull. Was it an honor? And the eye gems . . .

The thought vanished as a buzz took hold of her mind. Her right temple throbbed. "That's it," she said, coaxing Ahl. If the shaman succeeded, terrible things would happen. Shame heated Kila's face as she realized she *had* been broken. Tears streamed down her cheeks. It shamed her more to know these tears were from relief. The torture would stop now. Surely.

An enormous pressure built in Kila's head, forcing her to shut her own eyes and clamp her jaw tight lest she scream. Ahl was so close.

And then fire tore through Kila as her mercus found an outlet. Ahl yowled and backpedaled, falling onto her bottom. Swarmlight blasted from the eye-gems, shedding heat and a thunderous low tone, like the infinite gonging of a demaynic bell.

Wyvoks responded with shrieks outside. The work gang still huddled by the door covered their heads and wept. The flood of power increased as Ahl pulled more and more. The feeling was familiar to Kila, for Sensual Thine had once pulled power from her through the *vaz'on*. But not this much. Only the Hargothe had dared to wield this much.

Ahl again got to her feet, though she trembled like a newborn fawn. "Come." She strode from the hall, back out amongst the wyvoks.

Kila looped her chain over her shoulders and followed, staying well back. She scanned the yard, looking for Yiothizandra. The queen was not there, but Bazron was. He raised his carriage-sized head and glared at Ahl as she approached a section of the wall that had collapsed inward, and which repair crews had not yet started on. Ahl stood before it, staff thrust forward, red light glazing the rubble to a bloody black.

The air behind Kila hissed. Yiothizandra swooped down upon her dragon wings and alighted next to Kila. "What's this?"

"She has my power," Kila said. Whether the shaman knew

what to do with it was another question. "I think she's going to—"

A flash of red burst from the skull and smashed the rubble. The force pushed back on the skull, but Ahl dug in, leaning forward as if against a strong gale. The outward force of her swarmlight was infinitely greater. With an earth-shaking boom, the rubble exploded away, sending stones as large as nosg flying down into the valley, crashing into and destroying ancient pines.

Ahl released the power and all that remained was a clean gap in the wall. Several days' work completed in an instant, the wall now ready for the repair gangs to fit new stone. Some of the blown out rubble had not even landed yet and still arced far out into the gray gloom.

Yiothizandra went to Ahl, who bowed low and dipped the skull. The queen placed a loving hand on Ahl's head and spoke low words. When Ahl straightened, her small eyes gleamed with worshipful devotion.

"Come, Kila Sigh," Yiothizandra said. "Join us."

Obedience came without resistance now. It was over. Yiothizandra had won. She had made Kila a weapon, and Kila knew that it foretold the defeat of humankind. Knew now that the prophecy that she would doom her world had come to pass. All that remained was to avoid pain. That meant obedience and hoping the end would come swiftly when it came.

"The western passes are clear. Razk-Ka's armies convene, preparing to spill toward Stallid. We will join them. Ahl-Mish-Lah, you shall destroy the so-called Indomitable Wall, and all foes who defy my demands. Choose a wyvok, make it obedient to your will, for you both shall fly to battle and strike horror into the hearts of men."

Ahl's lips sucked in, and Kila knew well that the shaman did not relish the idea of riding upon one of these wild flying lizards. Had Kila still been a thief girl in Cheapsgate, the idea would have thrilled her. Now it merely sent new waves of weary defeat through her body. She had no fear of falling. Yiothizandra—and Kil—had cured her of that.

But she envisioned the view from Stallid's battlements as flight after flight of wyvoks swooped over the divisions of sieging armies, each mounted by a shaman ready to throw beams of swarmlight death from above. But one carried a girl and a shaman, and the brilliant red light burst down and hundreds of men were thrown like boulders back into the city. She imagined pinpoint rays of heat searing flesh and setting homes afire. Then a bubble of empty air surrounded entire sections of wall, depriving the soldiers their breath until they perished. Then Ahl sundered sections of wall, allowing the nosg hordes entry. It might as well have been prophecy she saw it so clearly.

Kila could not allow it. And yet, how could she stop it?

She eyed the nearest wyvok, a dragon-like beast with a long snout and flared nostrils. Its eyes were coal black, teeth black and gleaming like obsidian. The wings rustled and it stamped the earth with impatience. Its sinewy neck could support them easily, though the spines thrusting up would make for dangerous seating. No doubt the nosg would fashion some sort of harness and saddle.

The answer to Kila's problem came abruptly. The simplicity of it almost made her laugh. "That one," she said, pointing at the wyvok. "It is larger than the others, fit for the queen's prized shaman warrior."

Yiothizandra nodded. "Wise choice. Ahl-Mish-Lah,

Bazron has command of the wyvoks. They will obey. But they are not tame and must be brought to hand."

Ahl said nothing, but glared pinpoints of hatred at Kila for usurping her choice in the matter.

"I would be stronger if I had more food, more sleep, and less abuse," Kila said.

"I care nothing for your physical strength," Yiothizandra said, sneering. Wincing, she gripped her belly. "But to best serve Kil, your health is a practical concern. Ahl, see to Kila Sigh's care. I expect her bruises to heal and none more to replace them. And she is too wan, too thin. See that she gets choice cuts of venison and hearty servings of porridge." Sniffing, Yiothizandra made a disgusted face. "And see that she bathes. Her scent offends me."

Ahl could do nothing but bow and scrape and mutter assurances. Noy appeared at the entry to the great hall, waving to Yiothizandra and shuffling down the steps. "I have word! I have word from Tordain!"

Yiothizandra went to the nosg, and he immediately fell into a strange trance. Kila wished to hear what he said and could have done so easily with her heightened senses, but Ahl grasped her elbow and dragged her toward the wyvok. "I feed you. First you feed wyvok. You learn fly."

Ahl departed swiftly, skirting wide of the wyvok and keeping her head down as she passed Yiothizandra. Kila watched her go, then turned her eyes to the wyvok.

It arched its neck, a clear challenge. Kila's heart did not respond to the icy stab of fear that went through her body. She knew what it felt like to be prey. The wyvok was no doubt hungry, and she would make three or four good mouthfuls. But her heart beat slow and steady. *Thump-thump.*

Yiothizandra had taken Noy into the hall. Several nosg had come out, cowering and armored in rusty breastplate and helmets. Several dragged chains, which were clearly meant for the wyvoks. Kila snickered at the idea. They might as well try to chain Bazron.

The squeak of wagon wheels came from behind her. A nosg drove a team of shaggy, hooved beast with blinders over their eyes. The bed of the cart was full of dead deer, a few mountain goats, and various small game.

The wyvoks shrieked and started toward it, but Bazron's roar sent them back to their spots. Kila's wyvok watched the wagon with ravenous interest. "Bazron!" Kila shouted. "Hey!"

The dragon swiveled its great head toward her. It was a good twenty paces away, but she was well within range of its fiery breath. "Let me feed mine. It must be first among its flight."

The beast's eyes burned with green fire. *Wise,* he sent. *Kil favors you.*

Kila stopped the wagon driver, a nosg with one arm. Together they dragged a doe from the back of the wagon. It weighed more than Kila did, but she took the hind hooves and dragged it toward her wyvok. The others screamed and stamped and flapped their wings, but their fear of Bazron was greater than their hunger. Kila wasn't sure how long that would last, especially with such delectables so close.

Kila held a hand to her wyvok. "Wait. Wait. Wait."

With backward steps, right leg straining under the weight of the chain, she continued to command the wyvok to wait. It watched her and the deer with absolute focus. But it obeyed her. Bazron must have ordered it to do so. That was good. If Bazron granted her authority, she would take it.

"Eat!" she cried, and dropped her hand. The wyvok pounced, sank its teeth into the deer. With two sharp thrusts of its head, it folded the deer in half and swallowed it whole. The other wyvoks screamed in outrage. Kila's wyvok crowed at them and flourished its wings.

Kila found a small goat in the wagon and dragged it down. She noted that more nosg had come out to watch. None were shamans. Kila realized that each wyvok would have a nosg handler. The shamans would mount behind.

These recruits mimicked her, dragging out game and forcing their mounts to wait for permission.

Kila's wyvok downed the goat. She went closer, slowly, dragging her chain behind her. "Bend down, you big scaly crow." The head lowered. She arched a brow and pointed to the ground. The chin dipped, then the head came to rest. The top of the snout came to her shoulders. She patted it, surprised to find it warm. The coal-black eye regarded her, narrow with suspicion. The body inflated with each short breath. It was panting. Kila's heart rammed out a slow and steady thump-thump though her limbs coursed with nervous thrill.

Had she freedom to use her mercus, she could have force-bonded the creature right then. Could have made it hers. Her hand trailed over the scales of the head, over the prominent eye ridges. The scales were different from a dragon's, not as infinitely deep. Nor were they as hard. Each had a leathery quality to it, like patches of thickened skin. They would be vulnerable to arrows and blades.

Good.

She stroked the wyvok's neck and muttered softly to it, assuring it that she would not hurt it. After five minutes of this, the creature inhaled hugely and let out in a long sigh. The eyes closed and it went to sleep.

It was hers now. As long as she fed it, anyway.

She was tempted to name it. But that would make it her friend. It could not be her friend.

"Girl, come!" Ahl called from the door of the hall. Kila gave the beast one last pat then dragged her chain along to the shaman. But as she climbed the steps to the doorway a word came to her mind. A name.

Jathesh.

"Kil's eyes, Bazron!" she said, turning back. The huge dragon was not looking at her, but she knew he'd shared the wyvok's name.

"Come, girl. I try power."

"Can you cut through this iron?" Kila asked, shaking her chain. "I suppose you do not have the skill."

Ahl did not take the bait.

41

A SHUDDERING BREATH

What the nosg lacked in deftness of their craftwork, they made up for in the sheer strength of the final product. The wyvok saddles the nosg crafters had fashioned were made from deer hide stretched over wooden frames. The peculiar cordage the nosg used trailed from tie points, each strand as thick as Kila's thumb.

"I'll be Ori in Ecstasy if I'm going to tie this on Jathesh's back," Kila said to Ahl-Mish-Lah.

The shaman did not understand the statement, for she nodded in agreement. "Yes. Tie on." The shaman kept back from the wyvok, swarmlight well established in her skull. Kila eyed the flying beast, who eyed her back with restless suspicion. She had fed it a goat earlier that morning, hoping to strengthen the bond of trust they'd established the day before. She had a strong notion that trust with wyvoks extended only until the next meal.

Since she couldn't use the mercus to calm the creature, she had to rely on her voice and posture. The saddle was not heavy. The nosg were bright enough to know that mounting riders would put plenty of strain on the wings and that every additional plug of weight would reduce their range, height, and endurance.

What those crafters had not considered, however, was the act of saddling the wyvoks. "Well friend, this is going to be unpleasant for both of us." She hefted the saddle and shuffled to the wyvok, chain dragging. The creature's serpentine neck curled so it could keep an eye on Kila. She dropped the saddle next to it and backed away. Jathesh sniffed at it, shoved it around with his snout, then crunched it in his jaws and spat the pieces all over the yard. This act of destruction was repeated by scores of wyvoks, as their assigned riders continued to do whatever Kila did. A few nosg got caught in the teeth and were killed.

Bazron, bored with playing housemother to so many unruly lizards, had flown off that morning, leaving another dragon, Fritor, to oversee things. But the dusky golden beast merely watched with what Kila could have sworn was amusement as the wyvoks destroyed their saddles.

Ahl-Mish-Lah stamped her staff in the yard and went on a rant in her lurkmire language, but she didn't punish Kila this time. No surprise there. Ahl didn't want to fly, so the destruction of the saddle suited her just fine. The display of outrage was just that. A display.

She was soon to be disappointed however, for the nosg crafters had anticipated the likely destruction of their work and had simply made more saddles than needed. Many more. The wagons came out and soon Kila had another saddle placed next to Jathesh. This time she did not back away to let him destroy it. Instead she sat on it and bobbled a dead snow rabbit in her hand. This got the wyvok's attention.

Kila put the rabbit on the saddle, then lifted the saddle over Jathesh's neck. The wyvok scurried away, arching its neck around to nab the rabbit. Kila swatted its broad snout. "No. No. No. First the saddle. Then the bun-bun."

The wyvok did not like this and spread its jaws wide, clearly intending to swallow the rabbit, saddle, and Kila in one chomp.

"NO!" she shouted, a wave of gold upon her voice.

Jathesh froze. All the wyvoks froze. Ahl-Mish-Lah gaped, lower jaw a bit sideways in confusion.

Kila had done that in the past. The gold upon her voice. It was something Ell could do on purpose. But she knew it wasn't of the mercusine. Neither was it of the Revulsion. It was something else. And she'd be Kil-damned if she knew how to do it again.

She had to content herself with the fact that the wyvok was now docile enough to saddle. And so she placed the frame over the neck, between two spines. The cords looped underneath, where she tied them as tightly as she could. Two more pairs went fore and aft. These she secured around spine spikes. Jathesh endured this indignity with surly grunts.

"Knots bad," Ahl announced. "No good."

Kila did not know a single kid from Cheapsgate who had not mastered half a dozen sailor knots. Such lore just sank into one's knowledge when surrounded by so many seamen. Her knots were as strong as the cordage itself.

"Go! Fly!" Ahl ordered. "Knots bad. You die."

Kila shook her chain. "It can't fly with this."

Ahl-Mish-Lah sneered and pursed her lips. But the swarmlight built and hot rays of red shot forth to sever the chain, leaving a foot of dangle remaining. The shaman grunted in satisfaction.

Letting out a low curse on a big out breath, Kila jumped up to get her belly over the saddle, then wriggled herself to the seat. The chain jangled against Jathesh's flank. Kila found the hand hold loops at the front of the saddle. "Jathesh! Fly!"

The wyvok curved its neck to look back at her. A foul-breathed squawk washed over Kila's face. The beast stamped and flapped its wings and turned in a circle like a dog chasing its tail. Jathesh did not want anything tied to his back, and he certainly did not want Kila riding on him.

Too bad. "Hey, Fritor! Tell this lazy lizard to fly."

Fritor was lying in the sun, not unlike a lazy lizard himself. The dragon's head was so massive it could have bitten Jathesh in half. The great skull lifted and a spurt of smoke came out one nostril.

Jathesh whined and stamped. Fritor insisted.

With cries of outrage, the wyvok made a few preparatory flaps, then leapt skyward. Reflex made Kila's fists clench the hand loops and squeeze her thighs. The cordage creaked and thrummed. And much to her alarm, grew slack as the flying posture raised the beast's neck. The whole back humped and dropped with every sweep of the wings.

Kila's left boot slipped off her foot and tumbled away. It smacked onto a wyvok's head, provoking a thrashing response that drove a spiked tail into its nosg tender.

Ceronhel slipped away below as Jathesh beat higher and higher. The ice-clogged river Griln snaked away below, surrounded on all sides by snow-masked lowlands. A party of nosg driving yak wagons stopped and pointed. Had Kila carried a spear, she could have dropped it on them.

The wind cut at her face and she dared to release one hand to pull up the hood of her cloak. The fur fringe was greasy with black filth but the stench never made it to her nose as the wyvok picked up speed.

Jathesh began to circle, presumably at Fritor's orders. This disappointed Kila a bit, because she'd hoped the beast would make a flight for freedom, and that somehow she could coax it to go south. But instead the wyvok gave her a stunning view of the ancient elnisian fastness. Ceronhel's front walls thrust up, black and nearly seamless. Arrow slits gave the fortress a fierce visage. She was reminded of the hateful face of the Hackwatch. But where that had been mean, this was gracefully fierce.

Aside from the crude repairs made by man and nosg, the entire fortress was a picture of elegant beauty. Indignation arose in her that such inhabitants fouled the halls below. Beneath that outrage was another, subtler anger. The elnisians had fled. And in doing so they had shirked a great responsibility. All they left behind were shells of cities and impenetrable prophecies.

Jathesh stopped flapping and simply glided now. This steadied the waves of its spine and made staying on much easier. If the nosg added loops for her legs, she was sure she wouldn't need the hand holds at all. What she absolutely must have was warmer gear, thick gloves. And a new boot. She couldn't feel her right foot at all.

"Let's go back!" she called to the wyvok.

Of course the creature didn't understand her words, but it understood her meaning. It folded its wings back and dove. Kila let out a string of curses but couldn't suppress a flush of elation. She'd flown before, by the power of her own mercus. It was nothing like this. She'd fallen before. Twice. It was very much like this.

Her heart beat slammed faster and the infant godling that Yiothizandra carried did not pace it this time. With a hundred feet separating the wyvok from total obliteration on the yard, it spread its wings and caught the air. Kila was thrown forward at the sudden slowdown. This was followed by a sickening spiral that ended with a gentle landing.

Trembling with leftover excitement, Kila slid from the saddle. Her knees gave and she welcomed the ice crusted kiss of the ground against her cheek.

Ahl bumped her head with her staff. "Knots no good."

It took the rest of the day, arguing with Ahl and a nosg crafter named Twilk, to get the cordage lines, knots, and leg loops sorted out. At dusk a flight of twenty wyvoks took to the air, nosg handlers in saddle.

The entire day passed without so much as a back-handed smack from Ahl-Mish-Lah. And then Yiothizandra came out.

"ONLY TWENTY?" she said to the nosg shaman who had apparently been assigned as chief of the wyvok flights. Kila had seen him lingering on the far side of the yard, watching and doing nothing. This shaman turned out to be a wurgu, which Ahl explained was "big shaman."

Wurgu Larq-Si was the head of G'galas Pikork, apparently far to the east. His staff was very tall, with a wolf skull atop it. The eye-gems were onyx. Eschewing the teeth and claws common to the other shaman's Kila had seen, he adorned his chest with shells and colorful stones, the effect of which was a distinct clatter and rattle with every step.

Judging by the silvery quality of his hair, he was much older than Ahl-Mish-Lah, but there was a keen intelligence in his eyes that suggestion depths of thought Ahl would never know existed.

His Ennish was excellent, if encumbered by his thick tongue and fat fangs. "Twenty the first flight. Fritor struggles to control them as readily as Bazron. May I ask when the Blackdread will return?"

"I want the remainder mounted and aloft tonight," Yiothizandra ordered. "Bazron will return with another flight of recruits in the morning."

"The haste will cost us," Larq-Si said. "But the great queen knows best." He bowed and dipped his wolf skull.

Kila listened to this exchange with great interest. More wyvoks coming. She wondered just how many there were. By her count there were at least one hundred already. A chance bit of eavesdropping had revealed an entire second flight had been preparing in a snow field several leagues to the south. They had not met with much success. A runner had been sent with Kila's techniques and saddle modifications. A dragon named Tortyr had been assigned to oversee the unruly wyvoks there.

The thrill of the flight had long receded by this time. Kila understood just how dire this force of flying lizards was. Once mounted, the shamans would be able to rain their swarmlight destruction on armies and cities alike. How could anyone withstand it? Arrows could only fly so high. And the wyvoks' undersides were so tough that only close-range bolts would have any chance of penetrating.

The dragnithan's eyes turned toward Kila. "Semūin's

daughter . . ." she mused. "Ah, you did not suspect I knew? Kil may spare you in the end. I know not. Consider carefully the day that soon comes. He will know those of his lineage."

"Everyone knows Semūin is Til's daughter. He's the one who forbade her the love of mortal man."

"Til may have believed that. But Kil *had* played a wonderful trick on his sour older brother. Surely you know the truth of it as well as I."

Kila did know. She'd known since she'd uttered the phrase *Open for Kil's Daughter* to open Annisforl's door at the top of Kil's Keep. "The games of the gods are not my concern, Queen Yiothizandra. I did not choose any aspect of my life."

Yiothizandra was in woman form now, wings stowed away in whatever dynamic byworld they went to when unmanifested. She wore a silky robe of black, barely closed around her swollen belly. Had she been a true woman, her naked legs would have made Kila's eyes pop to be so exposed for all to see. Despite her pregnant proportions, she walked with the languorous sensuality of an expensive pleasure woman.

Gone was her initial disdain for Kila. There was an eager hunger there now as she reached for Kila's chin, lifted it on a slender finger. "Look at me, child."

Yiothizandra's eyes were human. They weren't always so, for Kila had seen how they flamed when her anger was roused. But now they were clear, amber, large and lovely. A fake gentleness came over them as she turned Kila's head this way and that to study her features. "Like a wee elf, you are," she pronounced. "I once lived in Slirya, where the street performers often mount skits of vergent tales. The fey ones are always played by children. Thin, sharp featured, pretty. Like you." She was standing very close now.

The thump of Kil's heart rose in Kila's awareness. She felt the influence of it over her own heart. She restrained her hands, which sought to again touch the belly. Yiothizandra tilted her head as if listening. The fake gentleness in her eyes vanished, replaced by suspicion. "He feels you, doesn't he?"

The finger under her chin slid under her jaw, a sharp thumb clamped on the other side. A moment of pressure, a curl of lip. Kila knew the woman could crush her throat, or break her neck in a second. She looked tempted. Maybe it would be for the best if she did.

Thump-thump!

The moment slowed and the pressure built. Peace spread through Kila's chest. Yes. Let me die. Better that than for you to use my power against my kind.

Yiothizandra released the pressure, curved her hand around the back of Kila's neck and pulled her nearer. She bent closer, until her eyes filled Kila's vision. "You could be my greatest ally," she whispered. Her breath was hot and sweet. Then she pressed her lips to Kila's, so hot they burned. Pulling back, Yiothizandra drew in a shuddering breath. "I could make you . . ."

Kila did not ask the question Yiothizandra wanted her to ask. Didn't utter the burning "Make me what?" that wanted to pour from her still flaming lips. The dragnithor's desire was plain now. The kiss was meant to manipulate, to drain Kila's will. To fill her so full of want that she would do anything asked of her.

"You could," Kila said. "I'm in chains. I wear the *vaz'on*. I can do nothing but what you command. Did Larq-Si tell you I was the first to fly?"

Thump-thump!

It was clear by the Yiothizandra's expression that the wurgu had told her nothing of the sort. The big shaman bowed to his queen but said nothing. Kila's attempt to change the subject did not succeed for Yioth again took hold of her chin, this time roughly. "Had you no power, I would kill you. But all must serve in the battle to come." Releasing Kila, she again turned to Larq-Si. "All wyvoks fly tonight."

"Yes, Great Queen. It is well. The handlers need practice."

"I care nothing for practice. The shamans shall ride as well. They will not return here, but fly west to an encampment already prepared with goats and sheep and bedding. The following morning you will continue on to join Razk-Ka's forces marshalling in the foothills above the desert."

Larq-Si didn't blanch so much as draw in his cheeks. But the effect was the same. The wurgu feared flying as much as Ahl did.

"Surely your mimak will give courage to the weak-hearted among your forces," Kila taunted.

The onyx eye-gems radiated a weird black flare, but Larq-Si did not release his power against Kila. Instead he bowed to his queen and retreated, barking orders for the riders to mount up.

Thump-thump. Kila's hearing became hollow and distant as the godling again reached for her. She kept her hands to her sides. Yiothizandra dropped her own hands to her belly and winced. So little time had passed, yet the babe would come soon.

Dem-Kisk was coming.

42

THIS VILE PLACE

allo PiTorro unfolded the sketch and placed it before Wykie. Of all the men at the Hackwatch, Wykie had struck Fallo as the most amiable. That might have been due to the inordinate quantities of beer the man imbibed each morning. But dealing with a swaying man who slurred a lot was better than the sour-faced ones who said nothing at all. That was because Wykie wasn't an Iron Scholar here. He was visiting from Wantin. Apparently he'd been visiting for thirteen years.

"A farlinbright showed you writing on this?" Wykie said. "I didn't know any of those existed outside of a few libraries that won't admit me anymore. Did you know that the atlensmackers at the imperial archives in Stallid have the authority to remove digits?" He waggled the three remaining fingers on his left hand. "I was just borrowing a manuscript."

Fallo tapped the sketch. "This peak is a mountain at the east end of Cigil-Tine. A waterfall spouts from here," Fallo pointed to a spot not drawn in. "The stars and moon—"

"Ah yes. This tells the time. But why all this blank area

here?" Wykie thumbed the paper below the sketch of a mountain peak bracketed by the constellation of the Goblet and the horned moon.

"Vergent ink," Zirhine said. The sketch was hers, a fate's-piece she had shown to Fallo and the Cloak upon their first meeting. "That's where the farlinbright showed writing."

"This was not drawn by a vergent," Wykie said. "They never ink paper. Only flesh."

"We didn't say it was," Cloak Einlin barked. "Can you tell us when this alignment will occur again?"

"Of course! It is a simple thing. I just need to refer to a few texts." He gulped down half a tankard and wiped his lips on his sleeve. He gave a quiet belch, then eyed the sketch again. "Cigil-Tine, you say? I can't give you an exact day unless I know where the city is located."

Fallo had anticipated this. He unrolled the map Kila had brought with her to the Hackwatch. Cigil-Tine was not labeled, but Zirhine had copied a map of vergent passes she'd found embroidered under a rug in Illizshian's bedroom. That allowed them to place Cigil-Tine at the location of a labeled but unidentified Derslin Wheel on Kila's map. "It's here," she said, stabbing the spot, far to the west of Tearling.

"Truly? We always thought Cigil-Tine nearer to Misen-Tine. But perhaps that city is also further west than believed."

It was not. Fallo knew exactly where Misen-Tine was, having had been there once. Even now that adventure gave him shivers.

"What does the hidden inscription say?" Wykie held the sketch close to a whale oil lantern, turning it this way and that.

"Mati il waun Kil. Entir il umak," Zirhine said. "Birthplace of Kil. Tomb—"

"Of man, yes yes. I know my First Race back to front, dear."

Zirhine's eyes crinkled dangerously.

Fallo cleared his throat and urged Wykie to be swift in his research. "I need to be at Cigil-Tine at the appointed time. I feel it absolutely." Simple truth, though it vexed him to admit it. Not knowing *why* he must be there added to his irritability. Or maybe that was the nosg in him. He trusted his shadline instincts now, but they seemed to be in service of a higher interest than his own. He wasn't made for all this hero work.

The scholar retrieved several dusty tomes from nearby shelves and referred to charts and tables of figures, humming to himself and scribbling notes onto a scrap of paper.

"Will you go with me, then?" Fallo asked the Cloak.

"Uncertain. Since Kila Sigh has dymensed north, I do not feel the pull."

"She didn't dymense there. She was taken there."

Cloak Einlin apparently didn't think that distinction mattered. Only the pull of his shadline instincts did. They pulled him or they didn't. "I've been counseling with the Dirth. They have asked me to join the Knights."

"What?" Zirhine and Fallo said together. Another scholar shot them an angry glare from where he was hunched over a tiny book of verse.

"I have accepted and spoken the oaths."

"You're still in your black," Fallo noted.

"I shall remain so. The Dirth will disperse to follow the call. Already a dozen of good reputation have left to petition the courts of Slirya, Wantin, Jallisea, Sorgan, and other realms for soldiers and supplies to be sent to the Sablefort. All must be on a war footing now. The vergent passes will make their travel much swifter."

"And who will command this army?" Fallo asked.

The Cloak blinked several times. "Shad Maz Nool is Prime now. I suspect she will counsel with whomever the Autarch of Tordain chooses. They have the largest force in the east. Another will counsel King Gian Delp in Stallid, where the western line will form."

"*King?* That lad who slandered Kila in the Armory?"

"The same. Do not judge him too harshly. He spoke as a newly sworn shadline. I did not hear falseness in his testimony."

"Kila sure did. I thought she was going to shatter her own teeth the way she ground them."

Zirhine touched Fallo lightly. "One can speak honestly and miss the truth. You of all people know that can be done."

That was true enough. He looked down at Kila's map. "Will these realms answer the call?"

"They must or they will perish. The nosg will outnumber us. And they'll bring more than nosg to the battle. That giant you helped slay in the courtyard surely has brothers and sisters. Who knows what else lurks in the north."

"They have a Derslin Wheel at Ceronhel," Zirhine said. "I suspect Yiothizandra will send similar raiders elsewhere. The realms must be warned."

"The shadlines disperse with sketches of this map. The vergent passes and Derslin Wheels are noted. That is all that can be done."

Wykie continued to hum while he jotted more numbers and figures on his paper.

"What of Nax?" Zirhine asked.

Fallo motioned at the map. "Lop says she's going north."

"There are vergent passes that could have shortened her journey. I fear she has little chance of success. Nosg or foxes or wolves or worse will claim her if the cold and starvation do not."

Fallo feared the same. He'd urged Lop to convince Nax to return to the Hackwatch. The small gray could have come with him and Quinn to Cigil-Tine. But Lop only replied with assurances that Nax was doing what she must. Kila needed her.

Wykie slammed shut a tome, sending a billowing cloud of dust over the table and making everyone sneeze and rub their eyes. After swallowing the rest of his ale, he took up his scrap of paper and beckoned them to follow him to the Stardome.

The bodies had been cleared away, though the mosaic floor was still stained with blood. Critt Sanglo had been cremated along with the other dead shadlines. His bier was gone and only his weapon Shatter remained to tell of him. "No one dares to touch it," Zirhine said as Fallo gave it a sideways look. "It rejects people in rather dramatic fashion."

Scholar Wykie went to a cabinet on the periphery and opened the doors. Inside was an array of levers, which Wykie began to move while repeatedly referring to his notes.

Overhead the starfield began to move more swiftly, until it finally blurred with a swirling motion. Fallo had to look down lest he become sick from the dizziness it provoked. Finally the motion ceased and the stars were frozen.

"There," Wykie said, pointing. "The Goblet and the moon."

"When will this alignment occur in Cigil-Tine?" Fallo asked.

"Two ten-days."

Twenty days. Not much time to travel so far. "Too bad the vergent pass we took out of there goes only one way. I'll have to travel up the coast to the tomb." And that meant contending with the vergent wards that had made it so difficult for him to pass through the last time.

Lop, wake up. We'll be leaving soon.

The response he got was a shudder and the sense of burrowing under warm covers. Which Lop was likely doing. Quinn had returned to her cot after the battle. Zirhine had insisted she sleep and eat and do nothing else. Lop felt it her duty to keep Quinn warm. Or so she said.

Shad Lykea burst in, sword in hand. "The traitors have escaped. Another scholar is dead near their cells."

The shadlines moved swiftly, emerging from the library to find the compound aswarm with shadlines and scholars, all armed. Fallo had been to the cells before when Kila had vanished. His hackles rose as he descended to the oppressive prison block. Shad Grickel and a shadline he didn't know bearing a war hammer stood over the body of a scholar. The dead man was unrecognizable, for his face had been stove in.

"Cinnon's work," Cloak Einlin said. "The scholar must have brought his club to him. And Mack'Ti his blade."

Shad Grickel clicked his tongue. "I doubted Shad Ault's decision to hold the Amory in this vile place. But he insisted. He despised merculyns too much. I regret not standing more firmly against it." His face was red, and he gripped his short sword in a meaty fist. His great axe was still on his back. "And here are all the shadline gathered and none heard a hint of it? How can that be?"

"We didn't feel the wrongness in Winnea, Cinnon, or Mack'Ti either," Fallo said, eyeing the splatter of blood on the floor. Since the battle with the nosg, such carnage didn't bother him at all. Zirhine said it was because of his daggers. Since pulling life from the nosg, his eyes had changed again, no longer as silvery as when he'd killed the elnisian warden in Cigil-Tine. Now they had a dark amber cast. And the sight of the scholar's demolished skull made his stomach rumble with hunger.

He looked away. "They wouldn't go to Tearling. The citizenry is too orderly and law abiding to shelter them from us."

Cloak Einlin tilted his head as if listening to something. Nodding, he said, "They took the Hackwatch Road to the Wantin Pass. They'll be easy to track. A dusting of snow has fallen these past few hours, I'll gather supplies. Fallo?"

"The vergent pass to Cigil-Tine is that way. Zirhine, I'm going to ask Quinn to stay behind. That means she will surely be coming with me. Do you have any, uh, potions to revive her a bit for the road?" Zirhine had sustained a nasty slice to her left arm in the battle. The limb was bandaged and tied close to her body. Fallo said, "I could, er, you know . . . help get out whatever toad teeth or worm eyes you need, if you'd point them out in your sack."

A momentary anger surged in her eyes, followed by an unwilling blurt of laughter. "You truly are a study in offensive politefulness. I wonder if you ever think of what you say beforehand."

"My mother wondered the same. I never understood the

question. I don't mean to give offense, but then how does one discuss ferneater tricks without giving offense?"

The Cloak nudged him. "You could start by rubbing 'ferneater' from your tongue. The mooncraft is sacred, and you'd do well to speak less and listen more."

"I know. I know. Listen and obey."

Zirhine did not need his help, and within a quarter of an hour, Quinn was scurrying about stuffing all her things into a pack. Zirhine had warned that the strength would eventually fail and Quinn would sleep. She made enough doses to keep Quinn awake for a ten-day, though with a severe warning not to let the girl do so.

"You're not coming?" Fallo asked her, crestfallen to lose the only shadline who'd laughed at any of his jokes.

"With this injury I'd be a hindrance. But I also hear a call I must answer. Ulagatin still seeks the dragons of Day. He has heard only Harnzyne."

"How many are there?"

"Ulagatin says six in total. Haptenar. Harnzyne. Quill'sh. Povnavni, and Noxianthenes. He worries they still sleep while Night feeds for war. I shall help find them and wake them." Fixing him with a warm look, she took hold of his shoulders. "You have been blessed, Fallo PiTorro. You see that do you not?"

"Quinn is more beautiful than I deserve. Can't say truer than that."

"That is not what I mean and you know it. Your blades. Your instincts. They have come to you just in time. For ages scholars have worried over the prophecy of Dem-Kisk. They did not trust the force of destiny to bring everything that is needed to this culmination. You, Fallo, are as important as

Kila Sigh. Perhaps not as powerful. Perhaps not at the center. But never doubt that you are drawn forward for a purpose." She kissed him softly on the cheek. "I have something for you." She fished a small blue jar from her pack.

Fallo popped the lid. "Weeds! You probably shouldn't have, Zirhine. I don't have a gift worth giving at the moment. Unless you want more of Lop's fur."

"I have plenty, thank you. This jar holds dried and cut maknek leaf. Chew a small pinch and let your spit build. Spread it on a wound to ease pain and advance healing. Use very little, for all healing draws from the healed. And this is fillishader leaf. Same technique, but for light. You remember me using it in the tomb north of here."

He did remember. "Did you say a magic word along with it?"

"An incantation, yes. The maknek needs none. The fillishader needs 'rahsh.' Can you remember that?"

"I can. Thank you, Zirhine. For this and . . ." His throat tightened and he could say nothing more. His eyes were burning from an unaccustomed feeling of gratitude and loss.

She kissed his other cheek. "I'll see you again, Fallo. I'm eager to hear of your adventures."

43

I WILL EXPLORE

"The power is immense," Henley said to Yiqa and Markis Harl Illis. They stood just inside the gates of the Katteshan Palace. That didn't mean much, since the gates stood open all the time. The so-called Palace was a city unto itself, with streets and innumerable structures housing bureaucrats, visitors, nobles, servants, and a very large number of armsmen.

And Donse Masters. They were everywhere. But to Henley's surprise—and delight—he had not passed a single one with an ounce of mercus potential. Unless they were all going about quelled or masked, these men were just men. That didn't ease any of Henley's distaste for their order. He doubted he'd ever look upon a man in brown robes with anything but resentment.

"Yessi. Autarch is known as merculyn. Everyone is knowing that, young Henley."

"Her sister didn't mention her being the most powerful merculyn who ever existed next to Kila Sigh. It has to be the Motherlight." Something was strange about the thrum of mercus potential coming from somewhere far off. It was too steady, too regularly formed.

"Veee musst go to thrronne," Yiqa said.

"What? Just walk in? Haven't you noticed the guards? They look like they've recently had a hard dressing down and are ready to stab anyone and everyone in sight."

Harl turned his bearded face toward a passing patrol. "Yessi. Sensing very tense. What is book saying?"

Henley held the elnisian book tucked under his elbow. It too hummed with mercus, but so faintly he couldn't really feel it here. It was a residual of mercus. So far he had not even sniffed out a hint of what bolts of senses or emotion might have been used on it. "Nothing. I think the map is of the palace proper, not this area. How are we going to get in?"

Neither of his companions had an answer. Yiqa could have gotten in alone, most certainly. Henley might have done if he'd dared to use his power here. Even with the mute Donse Masters roaming around, he knew there were some merculyns somewhere here. He wasn't masked at the moment, which was risky enough. But he needed his senses alert.

It's hot in here, Huff complained. The orange cat was once again riding in Henley's satchel. He'd tried to convince Huff to remain at The Wilde Moon, but Huff thought Terissa would come to nose around their rooms. Henley couldn't help but agree, though he doubted she would harm the cat. And now that he was here, he realized that Huff might be able to help. "We need to find an entry Huff can use."

"Commme." Yiqa strode off, taking the perimeter street along the outer palace wall. This area was home to the Autarch's personal tradecrafters, from tailors to cobblers to smithies to bakers. The stores were freshly painted, windows full of fine examples of their wares, and shop girls standing at the ready to greet their single customer.

"Are no citizens allowed in to patronize these shops?" he asked again.

"Ah, no," Harl said. "Each serving only the Autarch."

"And they open and show samples hoping she wanders in?"

"Ah, no. She would not coming so far from home. She is sending her Masters of Wardrobe and such to procure what is needed. The shops are taking wares out for sale in the city. The Autarch keeping half the profit, of course. Yessi?"

"Yessi." Henley had known of Tordain's extraordinary wealth, but seeing it so brazenly flaunted made him a little ill. Terissa had told him that the Autarch never wore a garment twice and that she changed at least five times a day.

They turned onto a boulevard lined with more shops and residences, all made of the same pearlescent stone as the rest of the city. A corner tavern offered a moment's normalcy to the tour. Apparently people within the palace city were allowed to at least dine here.

They had to stop as a large patrol marched past, heading deeper into the palace city. They surrounded a group of raggedly dressed prisoners in chains. They had lank hair and smudged faces. Several were bruised and bandaged. The leader wore a white robe made from bed linens. A familiar symbol was crudely drawn on his back. A crown with spear tines. The symbol of the Way of Kil.

"Comme!" Yiqa hissed.

But Henley didn't move. He watched the prisoners being herded into the square ahead where a fountain bubbled and finely dressed folk milled about. He followed the patrol, ignoring Yiqa's irritated commands.

The captain of the patrol squad shoved the leader onto a platform and roughly tied him to a post. His robe was slashed open. No sentence was read before the whipping began. The man cried out with each stripe across his back. "When will Kila Sigh come?"

The other prisoners responded to each call with: "When we're ready."

Yiqa grabbed him and ushered him away from the scene. He'd known of the Way of Kila in Starside. To find it here was astonishing. And disturbing.

He felt Kila on their bond, far to the north. She had dymensed there and stayed. Hopefully in Lockt and not Ceronhel. Huff said Nax was venturing north, slowly. Which meant they weren't together.

"Here," Yiqa said, stopping in a dead-end ally. "Up."

"Huff can't climb a wall like this. Never mind. Watch for patrols."

The alley was dim. A downspout offered good handholds, though it had been a while since Henley had climbed to roof in this manner. His old thieving skills had never been quite as sharp as Kila's or Fallo's. He handed the book to Harl for safe-keeping.

The roof was flat, which offered good protection from eyes below. He was more worried about the series of inner towers that offered clear views of his position should any armsmen happen to look down.

Once on the roof, the view was rather magnificent. The nearest dome arced up to blot half the sky. Its spire shot to an impossible height. It made him dizzy to look at it. He saw the path Yiqa had meant for Huff.

I need you to go in a hole and look.

Huff immediately squirmed free of the satchel. Henley pointed out the hole in question. Huff said nothing as he ghosted along the ledges, leaping across alleys and finally approached the last gap.

Henley's vision swam suddenly as Huff sent the catsight. Directly below him was a ten span drop to a wide boulevard that opened into a square in front of the dome. There was no way Huff could jump to the dome. This gap had been invisible from the first rooftop. But it didn't make any sense. Why would Yiqa have sent him up here knowing that?

Look around.

Huff swung his head wildly around, making Henley stumble and fall onto his bottom. Nausea claimed him instantly. *Stop! You did that on purpose.*

I only did what you told me. Would you care to be more specific?

Henley had a number of very specific things he wanted to tell the cat, but refrained. There would be time for that discussion later. Hopefully.

Huff made a more deliberate and slow inspection the second time. And Henley finally spotted the course Yiqa must have intended. *You need to go to the other side of this roof and jump to that tree. From there you can go tree to tree to the low wall above the cart vendor. That will take you to the opposite side of the plaza where another tree will get you to the stables, and from there it's an easy climb up that stone wall to where you can jump to the dome ledge.*

Huff sent the feeling of a tail tug to Henley, which was a very peculiar sensation that made his tailbone ache.

You'll be in the open on that plaza wall, so go fast. But let go of the catsight first.

Normal vision returned and Henley got to his feet, though his knees remained a bit shaky. He moved to better watch Huff's progress. Despite a couple inelegant landings between trees, the route went smoothly enough. *See? Easy.*

Huff groused and sent the feeling of being dunked in cold water. Henley kept further comment to himself. Stupid cat couldn't take encouragement.

Once Huff had gone through a hole in the dome, Henley slid down the spout and rejoined his extremely impatient Alnassi guide. He shrugged. "It takes longer for a cat. Let's get somewhere I can sit down without drawing attention. The catsight makes it hard to stay upright sometimes."

Huff, don't go too far in and wait to send the catsight until I say I'm ready.

Yes.

Harl knew of just the place. He led them to a lovely eatery overlooking the plaza. Being a Markis, he had the demeanor of a lord and the air of command. A serving man guided them to a shaded table and provided them with water, wine, and fruit. Yiqa sat bolt upright, looking about as comfortable as if she'd been seated on a cactus.

"How did you get in last time?" Henley asked her.

"I ssneeekt."

Harl laughed and raised his wine glass in a toast to Yiqa's skills. Yiqa drank nothing.

Show me, he sent to Huff.

His vision filled with greenery and bright colors. A breathtaking garden lay below, filling the floor of the domed space. Paths carved through the garden, stopping here and there at little gazebos, or arched bridges. The smells were verdant and lush. Birds called throughout the dome, and occasional flits showed the swoop of swallows as they dove for a meal of insects. Huff restrained himself from following these flights, which Henley greatly appreciated.

What's that in the middle? he sent.

Huff slewed his gaze toward the great column occupying the middle of the dome. It was the base of the spire, surely. Huff's vision did not provide much detail. Henley relayed what he was seeing to Yiqa.

"Thetsss eet. I sssaw Motheerlight therrre. Ketteshannn Thronnnne."

"The whole dome is the throne?"

Harl snickered and shook his head. "Yessi. Autarch always must having biggest. True throne on spire."

Do you see a way down? Henley sent. *We need to get inside.*

You will not sneak through holes. Perhaps only Yiqa should come. Old man must stay out. Huff did not mean to slight Henley. The cat was protective when he knew Henley was about to march straight into danger.

"Markis Illis, Huff does not think you will be able to sneak in."

"The cat is wise, indeed. I'm not sneaking. Perhaps getting permission." He pressed a hand to his chest. "I am Markis of Slirya. Dignitary!"

Huff dropped the catsight. *I will explore.*

The afternoon might have been enjoyable. It was winter in Starside, but here it was warm enough in the sun to enjoy an outdoor lunch. Perhaps when all was done he could convince

Kila to move here. They could get married and find a home up on the hill near The Wilde Moon. The cats would like it, with lots of sunny places to snooze in.

"Commme," Yiqa said, ruining his pleasant reverie. "Sneek vitt meee."

They did not make it five paces into the square before Henley yanked Yiqa to a stop. "Over there. That Spinster. That's Coin Inlina."

Yiqa nudged him to keep walking. "Talk."

Many others moved through the plaza singly or in pairs. They spoke in cheerful voices, apparently content with their lives and their fine clothes. The Coin wasn't alone. A Sensual walked next to her, young and serious. Henley calculated the travel times by ship and thought it unlikely for the Coin to have made it here so swiftly. Dymensing? Possible. She had been there when Kila had dymensed. And the Coin was powerful, more so now that she possessed Highest Fley's mercus relics.

"Talk," Yiqa insisted, edging them along behind the Coin and Sensual.

"She's the Coin from Garden Island. She's like the Highest of Highests. She was there when the Voluptuary tried to promise-bind Kila. I was surprised that she was part of it. I had thought her an honest sort."

"You do nnnott trrussst herrrr?"

"I don't trust anyone, Yiqa. I don't know why she's here, but now that she is, I'm certain she can feel the Motherlight. She won't be content to let the Autarch keep it."

They hung back by the low wall Huff had traversed and watched the Coin and Sensual pass through a thickly guarded gate and disappear into the dome. Harl Illis was not far behind the women, walking with the haughty confidence that came with one of his breeding. He did not gain entry nearly so easily. A runner was sent into the dome, probably to seek a superior's judgment about the Markis.

"Commme."

There are snakes in here, Huff sent.

Stay away from them.

Too late. The sensation of a full belly came through the bond. *Are you coming in?*

Yes. I hope.

Yiqa led him away from the dome, winding through streets and alleys, through residential lanes and once over a high stone fence. "Do you know where you're going?" he called.

Yiqa shushed him and made him crouch behind a stand of water barrels, set under a series of downspouts. The building was an inn. Palatial in size and decoration, Mizzy Mabbel's Accommadatory Home served visiting dignitaries who did not rank highly enough to be granted rooms within the Autarch's residential apartment blocks.

In short, that meant it was host to government functionaries, merchants, and the untitled wealthy. A sign posted by the door said rooms were available, and a fixed price menu at one gold spire.

"A gold spire!" Henley said, outraged at the price. The Tordanaise equivalent of a gold Raven, which was more commonly called a gold skillet in Starside. For that price, a man could eat for a week at the Yin Inn in Terriside.

Yiqa elbowed his gut and bade him follow her around the back where cellar doors stood open near the kitchen yard. Work men carried down casks and crates of wine.

Yiqa produced a gold skillet from a hidden pocket and slipped it to a lad in cap and breeches. He led them down into the cool cellar. It was not the dank block walled space Henley expected. It was a warren of storage rooms and offices that eventually gave into a huge two-level chamber where men and women drank and screamed as they egged on fighters in a pit below.

They skirted the balcony overlooking the fray and plunged into a darker corridor lined with curtained-off alcoves. From the laughs and moans coming through, they'd passed into the pleasure house section of the operation. Humming to himself to block out the sounds, he followed Yiqa's shadowy form through a series of doors and corridors, then down a winding stair to a sublevel. This area was quiet and empty, with only a few storage rooms full of broken furniture, moldering old rugs, and bits and pieces of forgotten kitchen ware.

The boy tore a flashtaper and lit a lantern. This he handed to Yiqa, tipped his cap, and retreated the way they'd come.

"What is this place?"

"A cellarrrr." The door ahead was unlocked. Its iron hinges squealed. Beyond it, a short course of wide steps led to water. A low stone platform held the crumbling remains of a wooden dock. Black water moved slowly by beneath an arched ceiling supported upon thick stone columns. It was clearly elnisian work.

It smelled like what it was. A sewer. The effluvium of the entire inn, and likely every building of the palace complex emptied into this waterway, carrying away the waste of stock pots and chamber pots alike.

A boat was tied at the bow with a thin, slimy cord. Yiqa hopped in so lightly the boat hardly stirred. Henley Mast, born to a seafaring family, nearly overturned the little craft and got a boot soaked with filthy water in the effort. Yiqa hissed at him as she handed over the lantern. She took up the oar and paddled them away from the little dock.

"How do you know where you're going?"

She didn't answer and he had to content himself with holding the lantern and praying to Pol that they did not happen to pass beneath a dump hole when a chamber maid emptied a pot into a needs closet. Such splashes were not infrequent.

The boat bumped softly into some obstruction in the water. Henley bent over the bow. A pale face peered back at him. Two hands floated out to the sides. A deep gash across the throat told the story. Yiqa pushed the body away with her oar while Henley heaved up his lunch over the side.

Other things bobbed in the thick stew. Barrels, potatoes, cork soled shoes used by night-shift servants to keep quiet and not disturb their masters. He saw several dead animals, including an entire hog. Aboard that disgusting and bloated porcine raft rode fifteen black rats, feasting their way to an eventual sinking.

He spotted the lights of three similar boats. Yiqa veered away, and the other crafts did too. Henley pieced together a theory about the sewers and the boats, figuring the waterway provided movement around the palace complex without prying eyes noticing. Likely many a moonlight affair was facilitated by this grisly passage. But also the usual palace murders and disposals.

Nobody down here wanted to be seen down here.

Henley was starting to nod off when the boat again bumped something. This time hard enough to jerk him forward. Another little stone dock. He looped the bow line over a post and climbed out. The platform here was more elaborate than the one they'd departed from. The stairs had polished marble hand rails with thick newel posts, topped by fanciful sculptures of fruits and flowers.

A portcullis barred entry and it was guarded within by a liveried armsman. He glared at Yiqa, irritated that she'd brought him all this way to be denied entry by guards anyone might have anticipated. This was the inner sanctum they were trying to enter, after all.

But Yiqa didn't climb the steps. Instead she went along a narrow walkway hugging a slime covered wall. This came to a dead end surrounded by black water. Yiqa looked up. Straight up. The lantern showed a square hole above them. Without a word or a glance, she jumped, fingers catching on some hidden hand hold. She slipped upward and disappeared. A minute later a rope ladder unrolled, the last rung smacking Henley's forehead.

"Ow!"

You don't even want to know where I am, he sent to Huff.

You are correct. Hurry up.

He blew out the lantern, set it on the walkway and climbed up. Yiqa scolded him for leaving the lantern, but she retrieved it. "Firrre," she said, nudging him in the total blackness that encompassed them.

"I don't have a flashtaper with me."

"Firrre."

"If I use the mercus, someone will feel it."

"Firrre." This time he got a pinch on his arm for emphasis.

He needed to see the wick in order to focus heat on the right point, so he brought a tiny spark of mercus light into existence. It felt good to use his power and the temptation to brighten it brought an ache to his heart. He hadn't realized how much he'd missed it.

The lantern lit easily and he let the mercus go. They were in another cellar storage area, this one entirely empty. And without any doors. Yiqa led the way to a block wall. From a pocket she removed a length of slender cord, which she fastened around her waist. The loose end tied to the carry ring on the lantern, which she had Henley hold.

What he feared was what she did. She climbed, finding ready hand holds on the blocks of the wall. Soon the lantern lifted from his hands to dangle from her waist. Cursing under his breath, Henley shifted his satchel out of the way and began to climb.

44

LIVING WELL BUT SMALL

"You want me to kill your sister?" Klayne said, arms folded across his chest, looking down at Yioth where she lay upon her bed. A great weariness had overtaken her after the wyvoks had departed. Noy had brought her deer, which she'd eaten with ravenous devotion. But food didn't seem to restore her.

"I do not make a habit of repeating myself," she said. "Eckso has betrayed us."

"I thought her children were ransom against such a thing. Did she not love them as much as she let on?"

Yioth stewed on the failure of the dragons to keep two children and an eighteen-year-old boy in the eyrie. Fritor said there had been two dragnithans and a dragnithor. Eckso had gotten their little cousin to assist, obviously.

"Do you know where she is?" Klayne asked. If Yioth wasn't so exhausted she would have burned the amusement off his face.

"My spy in Starside says she is at the Citadel, along with her children. I want all three. And Ell."

"Perhaps your spy is better placed than I am to do such work. Ell will not be so easy to kill. And Eckso . . ." He sighed and moved to the open window. The very window from which Yioth had thrust him not so long ago. He turned back to her. "I have news of my own that may alter your priorities."

"Yes. I want to hear why you have not yet secured the Motherlight from that little prat Saralina ri Clann." Kil stirred within her, kicking her innards viciously.

"The Motherlight is protected most cleverly."

"Not by her. You told me yourself she's incompetent with the mercus."

"I believe the protection is elnisian in origin, and the Autarch has access to the stone by means I have not yet discovered."

"Dig through her thoughts and discover it."

He shot her an irritated glance. "I did so within minutes of first meeting the woman. But there is nothing there to find. She does not use the mercus to gain access. At least, not directly. It is most puzzling. And I can *feel* the damned thing. It's concealed within her throne."

"Then blast the throne apart. I'm surprised by your wool-headedness, Klayne. This should be the work of an hour for one of your skills."

He put his hands in his trouser pockets and shrugged. "I had thought the same thing. But I have thus far failed to crack the throne. I believe the Motherlight lends it strength. But think on this: if the relic remains bound to the Autarch, then it will be little threat to your forces when they come to claim Tordain. She is ridiculously unskilled with all that power."

Yioth closed her eyes, feigning even more weariness than she truly felt. It allowed her to mask her surprise. Klayne truly did not understand what the Motherlight was. Most surprising.

Perhaps it shouldn't have been. He'd spent the ages on this world scheming and wenching and lounging, rather than seeking freedom. Unlike Yiothizandra, who had hidden in the shadows, living well but small, seeking a way out. She had read every First Race tract and tome she could lay her hands on.

The Motherlight was not a secret among the scholars of this world, though most considered it a myth, as fanciful as the so-called Dragon Tooth blades. But the elnisians had possessed the Motherlight. At one point, it had been held in Orrin-Tine, and had been the source of the empire's great power.

And now, right at the moment of culmination, it had appeared again. Yioth did not believe in coincidences any more than those fool shadlines did. No. She must have it. Even if it could not be used, it must be removed from the hands of those who would stand against her son.

"Would you like me to go after Eckso and Ell or continue seeking the Motherlight?" he asked. "I cannot do both at once. Confronting two dragnithans is not the same as abducting two children. It will be dangerous."

Kil kicked again, sending a jolt of pain through her gut. She stroked her bloated belly, hoping to soothe the babe. The way he writhed she half feared he intended to be born through the skin of her abdomen.

"The Motherlight. And quickly. And once you have it, Eckso and Ell will be simple kills. Your life depends upon our conquest. Why don't you simply kill that fool Saralina? Put yourself upon the throne. I don't care. Take control of it, then swear fealty to me and Kil."

Klayne opened his mouth to say something but thought better of it. Instead he approached her, hands now loose at his sides. Yioth had always found his human form attractive far beyond his true essence as a demayne. But now his face irked her. "Why are you lingering? You have work to do."

"Merely looking at you, dear. And remembering."

"Stop your blathering and go." Kil had settled and she felt a wave of sleepiness come over her. As a dragnithan she rarely needed sleep, and sometimes went months without considering it. But now she knew that sleep was coming whether she willed it or no. And that was well.

"Do you move against my city soon?" Klayne asked softly.

Stallid was not his city. It was Kil's. Or soon would be. "Soon, yes."

"You do not intend to wait for me to secure the Motherlight?"

"I have no need of your assistance in this matter."

He nodded absently as he absorbed this information. He seemed to come to a decision then, demeanor changing to a mocking servility. He swept a bow and dymensed.

Yioth called for Noy to bring her broth to settle her stomach, but was asleep by the time he came. The nosg watched her sleep, licking his lips with nervous consideration. But then he cowered, as if frightened by his own thoughts, and fled the room.

45

SHAMEFUL STIRRING

A stiff breeze came in over the seawall, ruffling Voluptuary Harrisan Minn's hair. Spin Moirina turned to face it, eyes closed for a moment's indulgence.

"Since our visit to Lockt I appreciate the balmy south much more," the Spinster said.

Minn had no time or concern for comforts at the moment. They'd visited five cities, recruited over three hundred merculyns. But she wasn't done. As tempting as it had been while in Lockt to march north to find Raginalt, she knew such an attempt would cost her half her forces to weather alone.

Why or how Raginalt had gone there, she could only speculate, but the most logical answer was the simplest. He'd found Kila Sigh and she had decided to throw in with whomever was mustering the nosg hordes in the north. A few rumors had spread throughout Lockt, of a demayne of some sort having deposed the Hargothe.

She thought it was Kila they spoke of. "Come, Moirina. This will be our last visit, I think."

The city of Sorgan was perched at the very southern tip of the Lower Peninsula, once called Sorgania. But that old nation had been sundered apart, leaving a powerful city-state ruling a tiny portion of the old realm.

That made the city no less impressive, standing high upon the out-thrusting bedrock, its towers imperiously posed above the crashing sea far below. The lower city lay down hundreds of steps and hugged the lee side of the rock. This was where most citizens lived, where the docks thrust out on long elnisian-built quays, and where the Baths of Ori had necessarily been founded. Sorgan was a city of Pol, and only Pol enjoyed a temple near the fortress above.

The Voluptuary cared nothing about it. She merely wanted merculyns. "The Baths first."

"Sensible as always," Spin Moirina said. "Shall we?"

THAT EVENING the merculyns of both Ways crowded through the cellars of an abandoned and ruined Cathedral of Til. Minn doubted the Donse Masters had ever known of the Derslin Wheel's presence, concealed as it was by not only the usual illusory wall, but a considerable amount of collapsed tunnel. But she and Moirina had cleared it easily, thanks to a heller she had appropriated from the Baths' reliquary in Jilin. She wore the artifact now around her neck, a band of gold that closed very tightly around her throat. It gave her triple her usual power, almost more than she could handle.

With Moirina's guidance she had learned to push stone

away, infusing anger into the bolts. Such use of the mercus was strictly prohibited by the Synod. But what of it? The Synod was broken. This was the time for expediency.

The Spinsters, Sensuals, devotees, and initiates were awed by the black cavern of the Derslin Wheel. It took a fair amount of shouting to get them in line and marching forward. "Trust me," Minn said. "It will be a walk of fifteen minutes."

Moirina leaned close. "Have you decided upon a destination?"

"Yes. Kila Sigh must bring her armies out eventually. Once to the Wheel I will check on Raginalt's location. I expect he will come with her south to take Lockt. We have to cede that city, unfortunately. I think perhaps we'll take the merculyn company to the Sablefort, but we shall see."

Spin Moirina gave a slight start, eyes widening. "I hadn't thought of it until now, but what you just described, this merculyn company, there is an elnisian name for such a force. *Kilenishza.*"

Minn grunted. As if she would ever use a word with Kil in it. Of course the First Race had called merculyn armies Kil's Swords. "They also had squads of *orishanza*. Healers. I much prefer that word."

Moirina dipped her head in deference, though her eyes blazed as she fingered her medallion. The woman had been born to be a warrior. Likely why Coin Inlina had recommended her as Voluptuary Minn's companion. But Minn had no intention of making her force of merculyns an offensive weapon. One could not heal the world with destruction.

"Let us call our force the Orishanza, unless you think the Spinsters will be offended. We must train them in healing and feats of defense."

"No, Voluptuary. I do not think that. However, consider allowing me to form a detachment of perhaps twenty to practice lethal bolts should the battle grow desperate."

Minn soured at the thought. It went against her most basic beliefs, but she couldn't help but see the pragmatic value of the suggestion. They would be facing nosg, after all. But even such vile creatures were infused with sacred Life, and so were children of the gods. Ori would not distinguish a nosg's soul from Minn's. And yet . . .

"I'll allow it. But do not forget compassion, Moirina. Remember that our enemies—even Kila Sigh—are babes in the eyes of Ori."

Moirina said nothing more and fell back to begin recruiting merculyns for her squadron of violence.

At the Wheel, Minn allowed Moirina to open the portal to the Sablefort while she sat in meditation upon the mercusine. She had marked Raginalt rather subtly, better to hide the mark from Kila. It required long concentration to feel out where he was.

Expecting him to be far to the north in Ceronhel, she was caught surprised to discover him much closer. Her sense of distance was not exact, but she was quite certain he was now in Starside.

"Moirina! Hold! The lad is in Starside. Kila Sigh must have returned home."

But the woman had already begun opening the column portal to the Sablefort. The fiery tear in the air spread wide, provoking gasps and shouts of awe from merculyns who should have known better.

Minn got to her feet and shouted for the file poised to enter to hold back. There were more cries and a shameful stirring at the front of the ranks. How could people of the Ways be so undisciplined?

Storming forward, Voluptuary bawled at those who stood in her way. Now there were screams of pain. And something else. The clank of metal. Suddenly tap circles were forming.

"NOSG!" someone screamed.

Minn moved laterally to see past the throng. Merculyns turned to flee, bunching against those behind them. Gr'hil after gr'hil of nosg poured through the portal, backed by nosg shamans carrying evil-eyed skull staves.

46

OUTMATCHED

"It has been three days," Coin Inlina said to the Autarch of Tordain. "I do not think Klayne Itopolo fully understands the urgency of the matter. You would do well to appoint someone else as Grand Marshal of your armies, auntie."

The Autarch sat upon her throne overlooking the dome gardens, satin-slippered feet dangling. She was bent forward to peer past her knees.

"Oh tish-tosh, niece. These things take time. Believe me, Klayne knows how important it is to take his time, let things build slowly. But once he's in action, nothing will stop him until you are completely satisfied. Be patient, relax, and let him do what he does best."

Inlina wasn't sure they were still talking about armies or not. From the flush of rose in the Autarch's cheeks, she thought she knew the answer. Had the woman not been tapping power from her hidden relic, Coin Inlina would have bent her over a knee and spanked her bottom as pink as her cheeks.

She needed a way to show the young woman the threat of the nosg. But before she could do that, she needed to deal with Klayne.

"I'm surprised that Klayne is allowing you to speak with us," she said. Sens Roon was already drawing upon the Coin's mercus, ready to throw up a mental probe should the Autarch strike.

"What do you mean? I can speak with whomever I wish."

"Can you? Where is Klayne? Does he leave you often? Where does he go?"

The red drained from the Autarch's face. So there it was, the jealousy Inlina had known was boiling inside the woman's love-drenched heart. Saralina had always been a clingy child, never satisfied unless one's attention was entirely devoted to her.

"I suppose a man of his charm must have many close friends. Many young women who need his counsel."

"Shut up!"

The Coin braced herself for a squeezing fist of air, or a flash of heat, but her aunt did not attack. One slipper began to waggle side to side though. Good. That nervous energy was a clear sign that Inlina had found a tender spot.

"Do you know what a Derslin Wheel is?" the Coin asked.

"Of course I do. I studied at the Garden for years. The most boring years of my life."

"You have one here. Did you know that?"

"Of course I know!"

"Ah. Then you know how magnificent it is. How beautiful it is. Klayne knew of it too. Did you notice that? When I mentioned it, he became momentarily worried. I wonder why. It's very private there."

"Is it?"

"I thought you'd been there."

"I—I don't recall now. Perhaps I'm thinking of a different Derslin Wheel. They all are so similar."

The young woman didn't know just how right she was about that. Coin Inlina offered her a smile, as warm as she could muster given the nail-pointed ache in her belly. "You would love it. And I know how to open portals there. You could visit Starside or the Garden Island or perhaps even Wantin. Just as quick as stepping across the threshold to your bedroom. Why, we could get a mochin cake and milk from a genuine Starside inn. I recall you loved mochin cake at the Garden. Believe me, the Starside sweetbake is even better."

As expected, Klayne arrived just in time to interrupt and destroy the Coin's progress. She had not truly expected the Autarch to take her up on the excursion, but if she had . . . alas. At least Klayne had come, which is what she'd wanted. It was time to remove him from play.

"Coin Inlina. What a pleasure to see you. I was just speaking with my generals." He offered a flat, apologetic smile. "They are in agreement with me about the Sablefort. Leaving Tordain and traversing innumerable miles of winter terrain does not strike us as wise. The generals do not think more than five hundred nosg could band together without starting a war within their ranks." He pressed a hand to his chest to show just how much he regretted this. "*I* believe you. But these generals have never seen nosgs. They believe them defeated an age ago by Sephie of On'lin Keep."

The Coin moved casually to the railing overlooking the dome garden. Swallows dove and swooped below. A burbling stream cut across the view. A small animal nosed from beneath the underbrush to sip daintily at the water. She spoke very softly, letting her shoulders sag in defeat. "I am sorry to hear that."

Being the sort of man he was, Klayne wanted to appear to be magnanimous in front of the Autarch. He came to stand beside her, strong hands upon the railing. The dome made odd currents in the air, and his long shirt rippled in the light breeze. He was a repulsively pretty man. He too spoke softly. "You are outmatched here, Coin. I have been patient, but it's time for you to go. There will be no marshaling of armies to march north."

"I see that now," she pretended to admit, removing her medallion from her necklace and worrying it in her fingers. "Sensual Roon, release my source tap." The woman obeyed and the Coin let the mercus go. Klayne would feel it.

The medallion fumbled in her aged fingers. Ah, what a silly old bat she appeared to be. The invaluable disc clinked on the rail and tumbled away toward the shrubbery below.

Klayne bent to watch it. The Coin stepped backward, summoned her will and released the unique power of her crane-shaped bracelet.

A fellstorm wind blew past her, picked the man up from his feet and sent him plummeting after her fallen medallion. Moving her attention to the heller ring on her finger, she reached for her medallion and caught it before it struck soil. It returned along its path and slapped into the palm of her hand.

"Coin Inlina!" Roon yelled.

Inlina felt the heat building behind her as the Autarch lashed out with wild rage. Roon snatched her back, pulling her into the little passage inside the throne. Fire engulfed the railing where she'd stood, blackening the stone.

"I can't block that," Roon said. "And her mind is boiling. I can't—"

Slippered feet came into view from above, then the whole woman made an ungraceful landing as she jumped from her throne to the balcony. She raced to the rail and peered over. "Klayne!"

Inlina took four steps forward, took her aunt by the waist, and hefted her over the rail. A thin cry followed her down, ending in a concussion and upward wash of searing heat. Then nothing.

"Open this damnable throne, Roon. Hurry!"

"Yes, but—I feel a merculyn down there still. Maybe more than one."

"Never mind that. Get that stone."

47

WHAT FOUL TREACHERY

The donkey proved its worth on the third day in the Wantin Pass. Prior to that Fallo had eyed it with a mix of jealousy and irritation. For one, both Quinn and Lop loved it. Quinn was always sneaking it bits of apple, and Lop rode atop the animal's burden of sacks like a queen on a palanquin.

But the animal was not fast, and Fallo felt a hard pull to catch up to Cinnon and Mack'Ti before they got to Wantin. Worse, Cloak Einlin—he had ordered Fallo not to call him Shad Einlin—decided that Fallo's impatience with the pace meant the pace *should* be slow.

Shadline logic. "Discomfort is the way," the black-cloaked man had said.

The Wantin Pass was high in the Kovi-Mest range, bordered by snow-shrouded pine. It was a breathtaking land of solitude and silence. Only the occasional snow hawk or fox told of the living things that inhabited the forest.

Great peaks towered overhead, jagged and imposing, and encased in white. The two had been pushing hard, trusting in

Fallo's instincts and Einlin's keen eye to trace the path of the fugitive shadlines.

Game trails left the main road frequently, and it was one of these that caught the Cloak's interest. Leaving the road, they had wound uphill and down to hidden ravines where frozen over creeks rested and waited with infinite patience for spring.

Boot prints stood out here and there, such that even Fallo could see them. Night enclosed them early, forcing them to stop. Cloak did not allow a fire, and so they huddled together under the branches of a pine and endured the keen wind that found out every little gap in their collars and sleeves.

Fallo enjoyed holding onto Quinn, feeling her warmth, her slim strength as she slept. A bit of frostbite was a cheap cost for such rich pleasure, he was thinking, when a voice cut across the air.

"Kil's eyes, Mack. Run!"

Beyond that came a disturbance of branches and hoots of nosg pursuit.

The Cloak awakened instantly. Quinn took a bit more coaxing. The moon was bright in a cloudless sky, casting long shadows over the silvered snow.

Quinn drew Black and slipped deeper into the shadows. Fallo knew she was there, but he couldn't see her.

The fugitives slid to a stop before the two shadlines in their path. Fallo chose Telt and Skeye. Cloak held Tosuin ready, flames licking up the blade in anticipation.

"Hold," the Cloak said.

"You'll have ta kill us," Cinnon said, unlimbering his club. Mack'Ti looked back, sword already clutched in his hands. Even in the moonlight his eyes were bright with fear.

"Pray let us go, gentlemen," he said. "Join us. For your own sakes. Nosg come, and in great number."

Fallo heard the hoots and grunts clearly now. His skin thrilled and he twirled Telt in anticipation of the battle to come. Zirhine was right. He truly had become part nosg. The notion of battle excited him so much, he had to restrain himself from running toward the onrushing creatures.

"You cannot outrun them," Cloak Einlin said. "Ready yourselves."

They spread out and waited. It did not take long. The first two gr'hils raced in, moonlight flashing on iron blades scraped raw on honing stones. The swarmlight eyes of shaman skulls followed, already full to bursting with accumulated power. The first shaman released his bolt, shooting forth a ray of yellow that struck Mack'Ti's chest. He flew back, writhing and screaming.

The second shaman loosed her feat, a rapid pulse of violet beams, like flickbow quarrels. Fallo's body moved with impossible coordination as he ceded control to his shadline battle instincts. Telt met one violet pulse, deflected it back to strike a huge nosg girnt leading the charge. It bore a hole through his forehead and he dropped, tripping five of those running behind him.

The Cloak closed with the gr'hil, Tosuin carving fiery death as it blazed with its own righteous fury. The orange light pushed long shadows of dying nosg in all directions.

Three more gr'hils came behind, slowing at the sight of battle. These did not rush in, but spread out to encircle the shadlines.

Cinnon swore and rushed toward the nearest, club blurring as he flourished it. The first nosg to meet that crude hunk of wood soared high into the air and disappeared into the pines. The skinny man flailed in a circle, turning skulls to mist, ripping off limbs, and launching several more nosg into the forest.

Fallo could spare it no further notice as he ducked and weaved, thrusting with each dagger, careful not to double-stab any foe. Hammers tousled his hair, spears pierced his sleeves and pant legs, an ax tickled the nape of his neck. Death reached and receded five times, ten times, as he spun and jabbed, and trusted his instincts to guide him.

A gr'hil of ten died before him, some continuing to convulse from Skeye's shocks, some bleeding out as Telt severed arteries in their necks or probed through eyeballs and into brains.

The shaman's staff split in half from Fallo's kick. The swarmlight released in an outward globe of heat, searing the shaman and threatening to crisp Fallo's skin. Only a last second dive into deep snow spared him.

He popped up, sucking in a huge breath, realizing he had barely breathed during the entire assault. His muscles screamed with his efforts. The blades reveled. Shinane, still unblooded in this battle, cried for action, demanded a part in the slaughter. Fallo switched Skeye for Shinane and met the next gr'hil as it swept in.

A sword licked his shoulder, drawing blood. A mace connected with Telt, sending a numbing jolt through Fallo's arm and spilling the blade into the snow.

The shaman's skull eyes flashed a brilliant red. There was no escape, no pull of instinct one way or another. Fallo flew back, landing in deep snow on his back.

A dark figure loomed over him, dagger in hand. Then it reached for him. A small, strong hand. Quinn!

He thrust past her with Shinane, taking out the eye of a nosg about to decapitate her. It fell atop her, and she atop him. The sounds of battle muffled until they struggled free. Quinn's lips were moving. A hearty curse. Her eyes caught the moonlight, full of glee. And then she was gone, fading into shadow.

Fallo pulled Skeye as he assessed the battle.

Two more gr'hils were in flames from Tosuin's rage. Another surrounded Mack'Ti, who jabbed and sliced like a swordmaster. But he was slow, heavy of limb. A great gash spilled blood from his thigh. His offhand arm was slack at his side. His chest smoked from the initial swarmlight strike.

Fallo ran toward the battle, daggers up.

The girnt of the group rose up from the snow, lacking an arm. It clutched a battle axe and its small eyes were glazed over with madness of the fight. With a sharp stroke, it clove the blade into Mack'Ti's skull. The man pitched forward and vanished among a mob of nosg eager to get in a blow.

Fallo arrowed toward the shaman, thrust in both daggers before he could think not to. His body went hot and cold. His daggers came free, now clutched in what appeared to be shaman's claws. The skull staff intensified. Fallo backed away, arm over his face as the skull exploded. The gr'hil burst into pink flame and the nosg capered in a horrific dance of agony before they fell, steaming in the snow.

The final gr'hil paused ten paces from the shadlines. The shaman was screaming at his warriors. The girnt of the gr'hil was shouting back and pointing his spear at all the fallen nosg. The shaman's swarmlight grew as a threat to the balking girnt.

But then the shaman collapsed, revealing a dark figure

behind. Quinn. She caught the skull staff, tossed it at the girnt and shadowed away. The swarmlight released and the nosg fountained into the air. Those that survived enough to stand, were quickly struck down as the Cloak and Quinn swept amongst them.

Fallo trembled and coughed as his body struggled to recover from the exertions of battle. Then the Cloak was charging him, blazing blade raised high.

Quinn tried to shout, but her voice was silenced.

"Cloak Einlin, stop!" Fallo raised his claws, saw his blades and dropped them. "It's me!"

"What foul treachery is this?"

"It's the blades," Quinn said, breathless. Black was now sheathed and she was rushing forward in a panic. "Which ones do this, Fallo?"

"Skeye and Shinane." He explained the effect of a double-stab with those weapons. The Cloak lowered his blade, but did not put it away.

"Let me pick them up and show you."

Quinn put herself between the Cloak and Fallo. "He just needs to stab himself."

"Just?" Fallo said. "I'll have you know it stings like a firehornet."

"Just do it."

He retrieved the blades and pressed the tips to his shin. After swearing and cursing for a minute he was able to return the blades to their scabbards. "See? I'm me." A few minutes later he had retrieved Telt from the snow.

The Cloak still did not sheathe Tosuin. "Cinnon is gone."

They returned to their camp and found the donkey standing over a nosg, its face crushed in. "Aww! Tolky's a hero!" Quinn cooed. Lop was resting comfortably atop the beast, eyes squinting at the humans in irritation for the racket of battle.

What happened? he asked Lop.

The nosg was about to cleave me in half. Tolky put his foot in its face. I told you, this is a good donkey.

"I'm going after Cinnon," the Cloak said. "Quinn, see to Fallo's wounds. Follow when you can." The man did not wait for an answer before dashing into the darkness.

Fallo wanted to object, but Quinn's arms sneaked around his neck and suddenly her lips were on his.

"What's gotten into you? Not that I mind, but . . ."

"It's my shadline instincts," she teased in a sultry tone he'd never heard before. Her body pressed closer to his, very warm amidst the chill of the mountain winter.

It got much colder for them both soon after, but neither noticed.

48

WISE LITTLE FELNITHEL

The sound of voices faded away. Only the rush of Henley's pulse disturbed the silence that followed. Yiqa never made any noise. If she had been nervous just now it hadn't been enough to increase her breathing. He knew this because he was hugging her like a lover.

She was proportioned much like Kila, but there was no softness to her. No yield to her muscles. And despite the intimacy of the moment, there was nothing sensual in it. Just two people occupying a space barely large enough for one.

They squeezed from the shadowy alcove and into the dim passage. The soldiers who had passed hadn't noticed them due to Yiqa's black clothes, which had masked most of Henley's body.

She had her head covered again, the scarf across her chin and mouth. Though she did not possess the mercus, an odd energy flowed from her. Intensity, as if the focus of her mind shed rays of pressure into the world. He'd known many dangerous people in his life. Yiqa was easily the most lethal-minded of them all. Sure, Kila could ash her without a thought. But when it came to pure animal flesh against animal flesh, Yiqa would always be the victor.

Two people just fell into the garden, Huff sent.

Fell? Fell from where?

A burst of catsight—made blurry as Huff recalled the vision—showed him tiny figures leaping over a high railing. The first dissolved into a haze of green just as it reached the treetops. The second crashed through, sending up a flight of frightening birds.

Yiqa caught his elbow as he swayed. "I'm all right. Huff was just showing me something."

"Theees waayyy."

They moved quickly now, a welcome change from the tense creeping and sneaking of the past hour. He'd lost track of how many stairs they'd climbed only to retrace their steps to avoid meeting a servant or guard. Yiqa seemed to know this under-realm of the palace quite well. But if Voluptuary Sinlop had sent her to find the Motherlight, she had no doubt lived in these passages for several ten-days at a stretch in order to finally get close enough to see it.

Now she moved with silky speed, forcing Henley to run. His satchel banged against his back, and his boots scuffed on the floor. All at once the corridor opened up and they emerged into the vast garden dome. Henley stumbled as his head swiveled all around. The sheer vastness of the space gave him vertigo. Yiqa pulled him off the path and into a dense thicket of berry vines. The thorns caught his clothes, but Yiqa picked her way through easily.

He could feel Huff off in the distance. *We're in the dome. Where are you?*

Rather than explain, Huff showed him a view of the great

central column. Working his way to a clearing, Henley studied the column. It was so massive, so incomprehensibly heavy looking, his mind could not accept that it had been crafted by mortal hands. All the credit due the First Race for their architecture could not answer the enormity of the effort required to build this. He pictured the spire rising from the dome. He'd seen it from the outside, but he'd not understood its scale until now.

More incredible, there was a duplicate spire and dome on the west end of the palace city.

"That blocky thing on the balcony there," he said to Yiqa, pointing. "Huff is straight out from it. Two people jumped over the railing."

The thrum of the Motherlight pressed on him. It had been present in his mind for a while now, but something had changed. It was louder. More insistent.

Do you want to see the woman?

What woman?

The one who jumped. She's dead.

That was no surprise. The first one had lived, he knew. That haze of green. He knew mercus green when he saw it. Why had the second jumped? Was it a merculyn, perhaps joining a dare to see who could dymense out of a fall? It seemed utterly stupid.

I don't want to see it.

The fall didn't kill her, Huff sent. The comment had the weight of an afterthought, a curiosity.

Not to Henley. *How do you know?*

Do you want me to show you?

No. We'll come there.

The garden offered plenty of cover, and there was nobody

around to see them anyway. After darting into the open to cross a quaint stone bridge, they had plunged through brambles and hedges to finally reach Huff. The cat sat on a stone, licking his paws. Beneath him lay the woman, flat on her back. Her limbs were not mangled, her body not flattened or exploded or damaged in any way one might expect from an impact from such a long fall.

She was dead from fire. Her skin was blackened to a cracked crispness, cheeks drawn taught so that her lips pulled back to show a black tongue and teeth. Not a scrap of clothing remained on her body, and the greenery around her was seared away in a radius of three paces in all directions. It looked like she had combusted from within. But if that were so, why hadn't her body blown apart too?

"It's like a sudden, uncontrolled release of a mercus feat," he said.

Yiqa waited for him to explain.

"Two people fell. One dymensed. She did not. I think she was holding a feat when she fell." He looked up, saw charred limbs above. "I think she panicked and lost her grip on it. Maybe the blast cushioned her landing even as it crisped her."

It took you a long time to get here, Huff sent.

Henley scratched the cat's head and offered a shoulder. Huff hopped aboard. *You should be grateful you didn't have to come the way we did.*

You often tell me how I should be grateful. And yet I never am.

Yiqa pointed up to the blocky structure on the balcony. "Thronnne. Mootheerlight therrre."

"How did you get up there?"

"I sneekt." She held up her hands, waggling her fingers. "Tennn daayyss, eet took mmmeee."

"Ten days! We don't have ten days."

"Go up."

"I'm not Kila. I don't know how to fly."

She made a disgusted wooshing noise and flicked the strap of his satchel. "Wherre ees booook?"

"The book? Oh, the book!"

He dug Harl Illis's book from the satchel and flipped open to the map of the palace. He'd been so preoccupied with sneaking he'd forgotten all about it.

"This is the dome we're in," he said, tapping the circle on the right. "The central spire has a stairwell in it. The opening is on the other side. There's not much detail—What? What's this?" New lines were coming into view as ink seemed to seep in from below the page.

An inscription drew in across the top: Orrin-Tine.

"Kil's arse! This is Orrin-Tine." He wished Fallo was there to shake loose the old song about the fabled city. The seat of elnisian power for thousands of years, during the Age of Harmony. Orrin-Tine was lost before the long decline. Well before Illizshian was born. Before Misen-Tine was built. Henley had not studied that much about the First Race, but there was song about Orrin-Tine. "I think it went, 'blah blah something truesight. She sat upon the throne. Scepter, sword, and swarmlight. From Mother true day shone.'"

An enormous boom resounded from above, flakes of stone broke from the column and rafts of dust rained slowly down.

"That was a mercus feat." He smacked his lips together, tasting the bitter anger someone had overloaded the feat with.

The pressure of the Motherlight increased. If it didn't let up soon, he was going to have a rip-roaring headache.

"If this is Orrin-Tine, the Motherlight wasn't found and brought here. It was always here. The Autarch must have discovered it. Probably right where it's always been. What did it look like?"

Yiqa held her hands out, indicating an object the size of an atlen egg. "Inn thronnne. Eet blinnnd meee."

They needed to get up there now. Another merculyn was there. Maybe the one who had dymensed while falling. It struck him then who the dead woman was. "You must have seen the Autarch. Is this her?"

Yiqa bent over the burned corpse, turning her head this way and that. She toed the woman's right hand, which flaked away to a pile of ash. She plucked something up from the black debris. A ring. "Herr ssseeall."

He bent over the book, scanning the map for a way up to the balcony. It showed a passage into the column. "More stairs. Come." It felt good to order Yiqa for once. Clutching the book, he ran for the path and sprinted straight to the column. Getting his bearings, he skirted along the stone edifice, dragging his fingers. "It should be right about . . . here."

There was solid stone where the map showed an opening.

Remembering the illusory wall masking entry to a Derslin Wheel he strode boldly at the wall. And smacked his nose hard. "Kil's snicken in a biscuit! Damned fire hell and throbbin' suck dung goat bender!" Blood poured down his face. Yiqa grabbed his nose and pinched it shut.

"Ssstop makeeng sssoooo mmmuch sssssound."

He found a kerchief in his satchel and stuffed the corners up his nostrils.

Why did you do that? Huff sent.

I thought the wall was an illusion. The book shows an opening here. Holding the kerchief to his nose, he looked at the map again. The new lines on the sketch were clear enough. He again checked his bearings. "It should be here."

Yiqa searched the stone, pressing her hands to it and sliding them all over. Nothing.

There must be something else to do, he decided. A secret phrase or a mercus trick. It was hard to concentrate with the throbbing in this nose and the constant push of the Motherlight. "I must be quiet for a moment."

Ignoring Yiqa's grunt of skepticism, he closed his eyes and sank into the mercusine. The Motherlight filled his awareness. Not a haze of potential, but a blaze of power. A sun-like presence far above him. Three other merculyns were within the dome. Two near the Motherlight, another a bit farther away. They weren't moving.

He bent his focus toward the book. Its mercus had been subtle even in the quiet of the Wilde Moon. He switched his senses to touch, bringing more attention to his hand. The book vibrated ever so softly. He formed a bolt of mercus touch, simply adding to the book's vibration. He realized that it might be the simplest of all the mercus senses to create. And that would make sense if the book was a tool to show the secret passages of the palace. A person with the slightest ability could use it.

He opened his eyes. The map was unchanged except for one detail. A tiny blue dot had appeared. It marked the spot where he stood.

Pulling the kerchief from his nose, he absently stuffed it in a pocket, then reached to touch the wall. His hand passed through. He stepped forward. "Hold my shoulder, Yiqa. Do not let go."

They moved together, more slowly this time, and passed into the still solid-looking stone. Inside was a narrow foyer and the bottom of a staircase. Though they had no lantern, everything was awash in green light that came from nowhere. The walls glimmered with it, the edges of the stairs too. "Keep holding onto me," he said. "We are in solid rock. If you let go, you'll be . . . I don't know, but it will surely kill you."

The stairs went up a short distance before ending at a landing. There were no more stairs. Odd. The map now showed the blue dot on the opposite side of the column. He moved forward, and stepped into open air. Yiqa came out behind him and sighed softly. She let go of his shoulder.

A railing curved away before him. He peered over. They had ascended to the balcony. "That was only ten steps," he said.

"Theese vaaay," Yiqa said and started to follow the balcony to the right.

Henley released the mercus and stuffed the book back into his satchel. Huff hopped from his shoulder to the railing.

Be careful! Henley sent.

The cat walked along the railing with surefooted nonchalance.

Henley glared at Huff and got a dismissive meow in return. Grumbling he rushed to catch up with Yiqa. It didn't take long, for she was standing still, facing a man in a long shirt and sandals. His hair and beard were oiled. He wore gold chains around his neck and wrists, and large gold hoops hung from his ears.

The man had his arms crossed and was smiling at Yiqa. She had one foot back, weight on her toes. Nobody would suspect that meant they were seconds from death. But this man was charged with the mercus. A very strong merculyn.

He smiled at the sight of Huff and tilted his head in a respectful bow. "Well met, noble felnithel. And who are your companions? I see an Alnassi lay-esh and a young merculyn of considerable power. Is that blood on your face?"

Henley wiped at his lip. He could feel two other merculyns on the opposite side of the column. They were wielding a lot of power, a constant barrage of feats. It felt like hammering.

"I've heard of the return of felnithel to this world. It seems that several friends of Kila Sigh are bonded to them. You must be Fallo or Henley."

"Henley Mast. Who are you?"

"Klayne Itopolo, of Stallid. I was chief counselor to the Autarch." He laughed and shook his head. "Had I known she was so easily killed, I would have pitched her over the railing a ten-day ago. I suppose you are here for the Motherlight as well? The Coin and her lovely assistant are banging their heads against the throne right now. They'll never get to it." He unfolded his arms. Yiqa crouched and lifted her hands.

"Easy, my lovely Alnassi. I do not seek a battle with you or young Henley."

Huff stepped lightly along the rail and stopped near the man. His nose waggled and the tip of his tail flicked. *This one is dangerous,* Huff sent. *He is like Flaumishtak, but different.*

"You are a demayne," Henley said. "But you don't look like one."

Klayne gave Huff a wounded look. "You betrayed me. Yes, Henley. I am a demayne. A dragnithan like your monarch in Starside. But I am quite comfortable as a man. I haven't manifested wings in a thousand years. Believe me, it's quite painful if you don't keep up with it."

"And you are allied with Yiothizandra in Ceronhel."

"Allied? No. Bound? Yes. She will bring forth Kil very soon. I was never as committed to the evernight as Yioth, but now that she has reminded me of how stuffy it is in this world, I do grow eager to escape it. And in truth, it is that or die. I'm still young, so . . . But who sent you? Surely Kila Sigh didn't know the Motherlight had been found."

"The Voluptuary in Starside." Henley formed the subtlest mercus bolt he could, a strand thinner than the finest hair. Surely the racket of the other merculyns and the Motherlight would conceal it from this man. "The Autarch's sister."

"Sister? I didn't know she had any sisters. But then, I did not know her well. Although, I did know her intimately." He laughed, pleased with his joke. "You don't have to die, young man. And neither does this fearsome Alnassi. Kil will sit upon a large throne, and there will be much room at his feet, especially for ones of your power. All you lack is skill. And that I can teach you."

Henley reached for Yiqa. "You can't beat him, no matter how fast you are." He sent his little hair of mercus floating ahead of him, also reaching. If Klayne saw it, he would surely answer with something terrible.

But Henley did not think Klayne as powerful as the Hargothe. And he'd learned much since the blind seer had died. "I didn't come here to die," Henley said. And he didn't intend to. Klayne interpreted the phrase to mean that Henley was backing down. The man smiled broadly. He was truly charming, even likeable.

"I won't ask you for much," Klayne said. "Merely allow me to perform a little promise-binding on you to assure your loyalty to me. It won't hurt a bit, as long as you behave. Come forward."

The thread of mercus Henley controlled wavered right at the man's ear. Henley stepped forward, arms loose, chin down. Yiqa hadn't moved. She fairly trembled with potential violence. But she was trusting him so far. How long she would continue to do so was questionable. The Voluptuary had given them a mission. Yiqa would succeed or die.

"Kneel, lad."

Henley knelt, and simultaneously thrust in with his mental probe. And passed into a mercusine fellstorm. It was more disorienting than the catsight. A human mind was always shrouded in clouds of thought and emotion, but this dragnithan's was roiling with thunderheads and sheeting rain. Kila had said Ell was made of mercusine, that all demayne were. He'd never imagined it would be like this.

Klayne coughed in surprise. "What? What is that?"

Huff, distract him.

The cat mewled and jumped from the railing and onto Klayne's shoulder. "Hey now, Beloved One. I thought you a bit stand-offish before."

"Yiqa, go around to the others. Quickly."

"No no," Klayne said. "She must submit to the promise-binding first."

Henley pushed into the fellstorm of Klayne's mind,

pressing harder and harder. The man scratched at his ear and squinted. He didn't know what was happening, but he knew *something* was happening. "Are you trying to speak to me?" he asked Huff. The cat nuzzled his ear.

Henley's thread broke free of the clouds. The topography of the demaynic mind swept beneath Henley now. He had to close his eyes. "Please don't make me hurt Kila," he said, hoping the tightness in his voice came across as submission.

He had to switch away from the visual representation of Klayne's mind, for it offered no deeper pathways. The man was pulling together bolts of certainty, adoration, commitment, and truth. Attached to those was despair and agony. Henley gave himself over to the emotional plane, feeling through Klayne's mind, following the bolts the man was forming for promise-binding to their source.

If he could just reach that point, Henley thought it could place a force-tap on him.

"Repeat this oath," Klayne said. "I, Henley Mast, swear to obey my master, tell nothing but truth, and wield my power only in his service."

"I, Henley Mast, swear to obey my master . . ." It was there, right there. A hot flow of white brilliance, throbbing with confidence and self regard. The dragnithan felt no fear at all, had no doubt, no hesitation. Hovering this close to such overwhelming self regard, Henley felt it course through him. "I swear to tell nothing but truth and wield my power only in his service."

Klayne's bolts formed and he brought his hands to Henley's head.

Henley lunged with his power, bringing all he could muster to bear. His feat drew upon Klayne's own confidence, split the man's own pulse of mercusine, diverting it to Henley.

The shock of this interruption shot pure doubt through Klayne, disrupting his feat and dispersing the bolts out in a flash of light. The backlash pushed him onto his heels. Huff jumped free, alighting again on the railing.

"You—You dare probe into my mind!" Klayne raged.

Henley stood, smiling. Tapping half of Klayne's power was rather ingenious, he thought. So much easier than quelling him entirely. Klayne formed bolts of fire, but Henley felt it happening and easily negated the heat that burst from Klayne's hands.

"Yiqa. Go see to the others. It must be Coin Inlina and that Sensual we saw in the plaza. Be careful, they are joined in power."

Klayne backed a step. His haughty confidence was shattered now. "How did you do this, boy? It simply cannot be done."

"I'll give you a choice now, dragnithan," Henley said. "Submit to a promise-binding, or see if you can dymense while falling again. It might be a bit more difficult with only half your power. And I'll probably negate your bolts on the way down."

Spheres of blue shot from Klayne's hands. Henley sapped their sting, and felt the remainder pass as a slight breeze. He tilted his head and waggled a finger. "I'm disappointed in you." Henley's mind probe thickened and he pressed a hard willshift into the chaotic mind.

Klayne stiffened as he struggled against Henley's commands. But his own power was joined to Henley's, a force too great to resist with will alone. He turned and shuffled to the railing. Henley forced the man's hands to grip the smooth surface. Huff sat primly and watched with keen interest as Klayne lifted a leg and put a foot on the railing.

"Go on up," Henley said smoothly.

Klayne pushed up and over until he was straddling the railing. Henley gave him freedom to speak.

"I'll speak the vow. I'll speak it! It won't matter in the end. Kil will devour us both."

A great throb of mercus shuddered through the dome. A small voice cried out then went still. Yiqa must have found the Coin and the Sensual. Far below, a chorus of shouts arose. Squads of armsmen, drawn by the racket, were swarming in.

"Swear to me. I, Klayne Itopolo, swear to obey Henley Mast, speak only the truth, and use my power only in service of his will."

Klayne repeated the oath as Henley placed his hands on the demayne's head. He knew the bolts well, having just seen Klayne form them. They settled over the man's mind, making him shiver. With the promise-binding in place, Henley released the willshift. "Come with me."

Huff jumped to Henley's shoulder. He did not look back to see if Klayne followed. He did not need to.

He found Yiqa standing over Coin Inlina who lay next to a ridiculously massive throne. Yiqa held a bracelet, necklace, and something else cupped in her palm. The Sensual was lying face down. "Did you kill her?" Henley asked.

"Nnnooo." She handed him the jewelry. Mercus artifacts, confiscated from the Coin. "They verre downnn wheennnn I founnnd themmm."

Henley offered the Coin a hand up. She accepted,

grimacing and gripping her belly as she straightened. She didn't attempt any mercus on him.

"What happened?" he asked.

The Coin rubbed her wrist, which was red and raw. "Sensual Roon and I were attempting to shatter the throne. Since you are here, you obviously know—What's he doing here? Kill him!"

"Klayne has been promise-bound to me," Henley said absently, looking at the mercus relics. "He can do nothing to you now."

Klayne bowed to the old woman, making a flourish with one hand. "Madam Coin, I regret to inform you that I will no longer be able to lead the forces of man against the nosg."

"You never were."

"It is my duty to tell you, Henley, that the Coin tried to kill me. Blasted me over the railing and did the same to Autarch."

"I did what was needed. The nosg come. We must prepare. You and she stood in the way of the greater good."

"And here we all are. Tordain's finest armsmen will soon join us. Will you kill them all too? The very forces you sought to recruit will be set against you."

The woman had always been pale. There was a gauntness to her eyes and cheeks now. A sickly pallor on her throat.

"Where is the Motherlight?" Henley asked Yiqa.

"Een therre. I sssaw Autarch oppennn doorr."

"There is no door," the Coin said.

The distant clatter of men in armor was louder now. Klayne smiled. "They've reached the throne balcony. Will you kill them, Henley?"

Henley pushed into the little passage in the base of the

throne. The Sensual lay face down. A few chips had fallen away here and there, and the white stone was tarnished black in spots, all evidence of Sensual Roon's attempts to break in. Henley could feel the Motherlight's pulse in his bones.

"Yiqa, did the Autarch have a map in her hand when she opened the door?"

"A sscrolll."

Henley understood. He retrieved Harl Illis's book and opened to the map. A thread of mercus brought the blue dot to the surface, showing him right where he was. And a little opening in front of him. More of an alcove than a passage. He stepped through.

The Motherlight rested on a golden stand. It was as Yiqa had described it, the size of an atlen egg. It glowed with severe white light that pulsed in the unmistakable rhythm of a heartbeat.

Huff slipped from his shoulder and nosed at the stone. *Warm. Alive.*

Henley reached for it, let his fingers brush the hard surface. It was faceted, like a gem. A living gem.

The glow brightened as he lifted it and backed out of the alcove.

Klayne watched with open envy. The Coin with relief. Yiqa's dark eyes hardly reflected any of the relic's light. Sensual Roon groaned and sat up, wiping at a trace of blood seeping from her nose.

Behind them, a squad of armsmen, swords bared, stood frozen in shock.

"You haven't claimed it, you fool," Klayne said. "I swear what I do, I do in your service." Then he laughed with glee and reached for it himself. Yiqa blurred, striking Klayne's knee with her foot. The Coin reached, but bent double as her abdomen convulsed.

Henley lashed out with a willshift to stop the man. Klayne's pinky brushed the stone, and it erupted in light. Huff screamed. Sensual Roon echoed him. Henley felt himself fly backward, into the throne passage. The stone slipped away from him, pulled hard by Klayne's mercusine.

Henley's tap on Klayne's power ceased and his mind probe was forcibly ejected. Ears ringing, he scrambled to his feet, losing his grip on the Coin's mercus jewelry. The world was flooded with mercus, blasting away all his sensitivity. He felt Huff running past him, away from the light. Henley followed.

"Come back, boy!" Klayne's voice thundered in the dome, coming from all directions.

Stumbling and covering his eyes with his hands, Henley chased after Huff. Behind him the throne shattered. Shards of stone flew past his head.

Jump! Huff sent. A second later Henley felt Huff fall. He followed, leaping the railing. Mercus bolts formed almost of their own volition, seeking Huff, grasping him, pulling him back into his arms. The instant the soft fur touched him, he dymensed.

He came out of dymension amidst berry brambles in the garden, falling and rolling, thorns stabbing and scraping. Huff wriggled free and burrowed deeper into the garden shrubbery.

Overhead, the Motherlight shone like a white sun.

"I feel you, Henley Mast." Klayne's voice came as a whisper.

Bolts came from Henley's right. A reflexive negation pulled the heat from the fire Klayne sent at him, but an oven-like blast washed over him. The Motherlight was now there, ten paces away and coming closer. Klayne held it aloft like a lantern. "You cannot elude me forever. Submit or die."

Henley dymensed to the spot at the base of the column where the secret stair was. He fumbled for the book. Sent mercus into it and dove into the stone. The column quivered as immense spheres of power impacted behind him.

Klayne's voice was muffled now, passing through the stone that encased Henley. "I will bring the spire down, boy. I am next to a god now. You should have claimed her."

Henley scrambled up the stairs. He doubted Yiqa still lived, but he could feel the Coin and the Sensual's mercus. He came out of the secret stair and sprinted back to the shattered throne. He found the merculyn women there. Yiqa was gone, probably thrown over the railing by the blast.

The Coin was flat on her back but still breathing. Henley bent to rouse her.

The Sensual crawled toward him. She was reaching for something in the debris, a gleam of silver. The bracelet. Henley snatched it up. Saw the necklace and ring. These he donned swiftly, hoping one was a heller.

The ring was.

"Hold, son," barked an armsman. He was covered with dust, and blood ran from a wound in on his head. He held his sword out. "Where's the Autarch?"

"Dead. Her counselor Klayne killed her." Not true, but close enough.

"I did no such thing." Klayne's head rose above the railing, then his body, held aloft on mercus power. He floated over the railing and alighted behind the armsman. With a clutch of one hand he gripped the man's head and sundered it from his body with flame. Henley hurled blue spheres at Klayne, leavening them with rage.

Klayne waved them away. The force of the man's power stunned Henley. It was a match for Kila's at the height of her rage. "Sensual, I need your power," Henley barked. He didn't wait for her to offer it, lancing in and force-tapping her. She gasped in violated horror. Her power was half his, but joined to his and amplified by the ring, it mattered. Henley threw up a curved wall of blue light.

As hoped, Klayne thought the feat was an attack and brought forth negations. Henley used the precious seconds he'd bought to grab the Sensual's wrist, and lunged to lay over the Coin's body. He dymensed back to the garden.

Incoming bolts warned him, and he dymensed back to the balcony, still gripping the Sensual, still lying on the Coin.

Beams of red heat seared through the floor of the balcony, and the section Henley was on pitched forward to spill him and the women toward a long drop. He dymensed to the garden and rolled off the Coin. He released the Sensual's wrist and dymensed again to keep Klayne from blasting the women.

He masked his mercus and scurried through the garden, keeping low and off the paths. A squad of armsmen tromped past.

He unmasked and amplified his own voice. "You can't prevail, Klayne." He dymensed to the entry of the garden, and instantly masked. No time to think. He ran and dove behind a stone figure of Ori.

Klayne appeared at the entrance, billows of mercus green rolling away from overpowered bolts. The Motherlight was straining with power, as if it couldn't release even a fraction of what it wished to.

"I have already prevailed," Klayne said. "Yioth didn't know what she was giving me when she sent me for the stone."

The man stalked forward, eyes scanning. Henley held very still.

"I do not wish to harm the felnithel. I urge you to release its bond before you die."

It didn't work that way. Huff had chosen him, not the other way around. But that explained why the man hadn't killed Henley from the start. It was only out of regard for the cat.

Huff, why do bad demayne love you felnithel?

Oly says it is because we are magnificent.

I'm not asking Oly. I'm asking you.

I don't know. They are . . . kindred.

Klayne respects you. And I think he fears you.

"I can hear your heartbeat," Klayne said. He stopped on the path and turned slowly.

Henley dropped his mask and sent power to the crane bracelet, hoping it would do something useful. A terrific gust blasted the greenery flat and pushed Klayne backward, tripping him. Henley reached with mercus touch for the stone and pulled it free of the man's hand.

It flew toward him, but instantly stopped to hover over the path. Klayne was pulling with his own power. And he was winning, for the Motherlight was giving him enormous rivers of mercus.

A figure stumbled into view and threw herself at the gem. The Sensual. Her fingers grazed it and the mercus abruptly cut from Kayne's control and went into hers. She pulled the Motherlight to her breast, eyes glowing with victory and total greed.

Mouth gaping, she tilted her head back in ecstasy as she drank in the enormous flows. She mirrored the statue of Ori next to Henley, the ecstatic freedom of total surrender. But then her face twisted in agony and her body jerked forward.

In a desperate attempt to release the power, she threw the stone from her. It struck the path and released all that she had not been able to bear. Henley dymensed to the balcony. The dome rumbled and white light blotted everything for a few heartbeats. Chunks of the dome ceiling fell in a tumbling rain of house-sized slabs, crashing into the garden, streams, and pathways.

Henley dymensed back to Ori, appearing in a blackened circle of ash. The ground glowed under his boots. A great crater lay in the center. The Motherlight was there, deep down. He ran for it. Across from him, Klayne did the same.

Henley launched spheres and another blast of crane wind at the man. Klayne negated them, sending the power flying away to strike against the dome. More great chunks shook loose and crashed down. Armsmen screamed in the hollow distance. Henley jumped into the crater, feeling for the Motherlight. Klayne came down after him. The hole was deep and black.

Water engulfed Henley, thick and foul. It rushed up his nose, seeped through his clamped lips. The sewer!

Flailing and disoriented, Henley didn't know which way was up. He opened his eyes. A piercing light came from the depths. He reached and grasped with mercus touch, pulling the Motherlight back toward him.

Arms wrapped around his neck. A blade drove against his side. Again. Again.

Henley gulped in a mouthful of fetid water. His mercus

bolts pulling the Motherlight began to fade as Klayne pummeled him with mind probes. Henley released the Motherlight and dymensed, taking Klayne with him.

This time he came out of dymension on a lush rug in front of a blazing fireplace. Several feet shuffled back.

"Til's tears!" Marlow cried out. "Why do you people keep doing this to me?"

A noble woman Henley did not know hissed. "What's he doing here?"

"Help me quell him, Marlow!" Henley said, choking on a mouthful of sewer water. He simultaneously drove hard mental spikes at Klayne's mind and punched the man in the gut. Henley's waterlogged satchel weighed him down, so he didn't bother to stand.

Klayne writhed and sent forth his own feats, but the strange woman negated them and another man stepped in to press a hard probe into the man's mind.

It was Highest Quiv, whose face was pale, but determined. Marlow joined in next, still pressing his chest as though his heart might burst out of it. Klayne gritted his teeth and fought, but with so many pressing against his mind, Henley was able to reestablish his partial force-tap. This done, a simple willshift froze Klayne to the floor.

"You smell awful, Klayne!" the woman said. "Who is this boy?"

Henley looked to Marlow. "I'm going to release the force-tap. You have to keep him quelled. He's a dragnithan."

"I know him well," the woman said, pinching her nose. "Ugh."

Marlow and Quiv nodded their readiness. Henley released

the force tap and the three merculyns slammed the quell on Klayne.

"I'll be back directly." Henley dymensed once again.

This time he did not jump into the crater. The Motherlight came up on mercus touch and landed in his palms. He did not hesitate to claim her, and the inrushing power nearly destroyed him. Gritting his teeth he sought a way to shed the excess that flowed at him. There were plenty of holes in the roof of the dome now. He shot heat and light straight up and into the sky.

The Motherlight shone so brightly Henley couldn't see anything but white light. Huff crept from under a wide-leafed plant and toed through the ash. *This is like the ash barrens.*

An entire Fifth of Garden Island had been muddy ash when Henley had traversed it. Only rocks and burned stumps had stood up from the plain of destruction. And that reminded Henley of what he'd found out there in the ash. "Oh Huff my boy, you wise little felnithel."

He set the Motherlight onto the ash and dug into his soggy satchel. He pulled forth a red disc—a dragon scale—which was really seven of them nested like dinner plates. He laid one face down and moved the Motherlight atop it. Another went over the gem. He'd hoped only to block the light, but the relic attracted the scales, such that they clicked and stuck. Curious, he took another scale and placed it on edge. It snapped onto the end of the Motherlight and seamed together with the other two. Snap. Snap. Snap. The rest of the scales fit together to completely enshroud the Motherlight. With each one in place, the flow of power eased, as if the stone slipped into a light sleep.

Once the last was attached, the light was extinguished and

the flow to Henley reduced by half. He could now hold it or use it as he willed. He put the Motherlight, which now had a distinctly egg-like appearance to it, into his satchel.

Armsmen were still patrolling the garden, but now more cautiously. They looked up to the dome, fearful it would collapse on top of them. Henley returned to where he'd left the Coin. She was conscious but in obvious agony, clutching her stomach and squeezing her eyes closed. Yiqa stood over her, black garb singed, torn, and filthy.

"Is she injured?" he asked, kneeling next to her.

Yiqa ignored the question. "You haff Mootheerlight? Vee must go too Ssstarsssite."

He threaded a bit of mercus into the Coin. He was no healer, but he saw where the pain was concentrated. Merely by probing it, he felt the pain for himself. He didn't know how to ease her suffering, so he simply motioned for Yiqa to grab hold of him and dymensed with her and the Coin back to the Citadel.

49

TO PERISH SLOW

The man was shabbily dressed in shirt and short pants, mud up his bare calves. A mouth full of brown teeth grinned at Fallo. Quinn had nearly stabbed him once already, so Fallo had to walk between them.

"Cloak don't pay for hard work," the man said, hand up in the universal gesture. Fallo weighted the man's palm with a silver skillet and nudged him forward. "Another when we reach the cache."

Wantin was a low-built city, surrounded by a thick wall, and filled with mud. The citizenry kept to plank walkways, like piers, that coursed through the streets. These were not always in good repair, with many gaps, rotten boards, and more than a few dead ends.

Their guide, Fathben, jumped the gaps and expected his shadline guests to do the same. Tolky had been stabled outside the city for a stunning three gold skillets a night. Fallo had never been parsimonious, but he expected old Tolky to come out in ribbons and slippers.

There were no wagons, atlens, horses, or any sort of carts

in view. Everything was carried, and all by women. The men, according to Fathben, had more important tasks to see to. By Fallo's observation this included drinking in taverns, walking along in peaceful contemplation, and guiding visitors. The women bore large pots on their heads, bundles of firewood on their backs, children on their hips, and heavier burdens strapped to shoulder poles, which they carried in pairs.

The city was flat and stinky, the stale ocean smell pervading everything. Fallo had gotten one quick glimpse of the Iopsean Sea, far out beyond a mudflat, where children and women bent to collect clams.

Further inland a section of city had been built upon a stone foundation. A square tower was the seat of power, such as it was. The temples of three Ways surrounded it. Access to that portion of the city was thickly guarded, probably to keep the filthy-footed commoners out.

The shadline cache was in the basement of an inn, built hard against this inner wall. The ground around it was soggy, but bore up under their feet without sucking off their boots.

The proprietor greeted Fallo warmly. Quinn a bit less so. "Please cover your head," he said to her. "I run a respectable establishment." He was wiry, pants splotched with mud, shirt-sleeves bunched up around his elbows.

Fathben leered at her and bobbled his silver coin. Fallo paid him off and he went to the bar to spend it. Quinn did not cover her head.

"Cloak Einlin is here?" Fallo asked.

The man guided them to a storeroom where a great floor hatch stood open. Wooden stairs led down. The Cloak was there, seated at a polished wooden table, mug of beer before him and a pipe in his teeth. A fire burned cheerfully in the hearth and another barman leaned against the board. He wore a leather apron.

"Doesn't the damp seep in, Shad Einlin?" Fallo asked, dropping his weight into the chair opposite the Cloak's. The barman choked on his own sip of beer and coughed until this face turned red.

"You didn't know, sir?" Fallo called cheerfully. "Ol' black-cloak is a Knight now. Does that come with special privileges by any chance?"

Einlin's nostrils dilated a bit, but he otherwise did not show irritation at Fallo's obnoxious greeting. Fallo was not best pleased with the man, who had never returned to their battle-side camp. He'd left no word at the small villages and farms along the way. He'd also never mentioned where in Wantin the shadline cache was.

Quinn joined them, opened her satchel, and let Lop out. The lazy beast had chosen her pack because, in her words, "*It's much softer and smells nice.*"

The cat stalked across the table, first nosing Einlin's mug, then jumping the two-pace span to the bar, where she proceeded to meow.

The barman watched the cat with slightly horrified fascination. "You'd best find a bit of meat for her or she'll never shut up," said Fallo.

Einlin drank off the rest of his beer. "I've been waiting two days," he said.

"Tell it to Tolky. We came as swiftly as we could. Where's Cinnon?"

"Gone. That club he bears drives him on. He doesn't sleep if he can get enough food. He stole plenty along the way."

Quinn nudged Fallo. "That's why nobody wanted to talk to us. They'd been robbed."

"Did he come here?"

"Seul?" the Cloak called. "Come tell about Cinnon."

The barman set out a dish of cream for Lop and came to take the fourth chair at the table. His hands were thick and callused. He wore a dagger at his hip.

"Cinnon was here," he said. "Ate enough for five, took a new pack, loaded down with food and supplies for a long journey. Didn't say where he was going. You know I don't ask. Listen and obey."

"You're a shadline?" Quinn asked. "Why weren't you at the Armory?"

"I'm not a shadline. I'm a crafter."

Fallo remembered Crafter Exalin at the Hackwatch, who had set up a smithy and repair shop in the stables there.

"The caches are in most cities," Seul said. "Easy to find if you want to. I don't understand how Cinnon could be a fugitive."

The Cloak didn't explain. Fallo almost started to, then thought better of it. Perhaps it was his instinct guiding him. Perhaps it was mere tiredness. "Might we get a mug of that?" he asked.

Seul jumped up and muttered apologies. He returned with beer and said he'd send up for eggs, bacon, and bread. "An atlen leg is on roast, too."

"You stayed," Fallo said to Einlin. "Cinnon's going to get away. Ah, but you are listening and obeying. You need me."

"I do not need you. Others come, I think. Shadlines who left the Hackwatch after us. They will come here. In the meantime, eat, rest, resupply. Seul will provide all that you need."

His eyes narrowed and turned to Quinn. "I will train with you. The inn will provide you rooms. Or perhaps you need only one. Yes. I see that clearly." His eyes softened and a wolfish grin spread his lips. But he leaned forward and patted Quinn's hand. "You could do much better."

Quinn arched an eyebrow. "So could Zirhine."

Fallo spat beer across the table. "What?"

"Didn't you know about them?" Quinn asked coyly.

"No! That cannot be. I spent night and day with them and never saw more pass between them than cooperative courtesies."

Einlin merely eyed Quinn for a few long moments. "You are correct, Lady Peline. Zirhine could do much better. Let that be my counsel to you. Loving a man married to his blades is to be heart-cut daily. I wouldn't wish it on anyone. Do reconsider this dalliance with Fallo. He is perhaps the greatest shadline I've known. And that will mean nothing but hardship for him and those who love him." Einlin stood and nodded a parting. "We shall train in an hour."

"I'm not sure if I want to stab him or shake his hand," Fallo said. "He has a way of insulting that leaves one feeling rather proud."

Quinn kissed him. "After we eat, let's go find that room the Cloak mentioned."

The rest of the day passed quietly, especially after Quinn left to train with Cloak Einlin. A piping hot bath did wonders for them both, and Lop remained in the cellar with Seul who extended shadline privileges in the form of choice slices of atlen roast.

Her overstuffed sleepiness crept through the bond and Fallo enjoyed languorous hours unconscious in the warm bed.

But it was Lop who told him of the shadline visitors. *Loud men have come.*

There were two of them in the cellar bar. Shad Grickel and Gian Delp. Fallo did not like the younger man, who had spoken against Kila at the Armory. He was too good looking, for one thing. For another, he kissed Quinn's hand and asked after her mother and began discussing with great fluency the Radiant families of Starside. While she answered his inquiries civilly, Fallo saw how sharply edged her looks were. She did not like Gian for how he'd abandoned Kila on Garden Island.

"Shad Einlin," Grickel bawled happily, slapping the newly minted Knight on the shoulder. His huge axe leaned against the table. "You slipped away from the Hackwatch so quickly, the Dirth had to convene without you."

"I'm sure you handled it fine. I had to obey the call."

"Did you catch Cinnon?"

"Yes. He's in the cell."

"What?" Fallo cried. "You said he was gone."

"He was. He came back an hour ago, famished, and covered in mud. It seems he tried to take a shortcut across the mudflats and got bogged down."

"Let's bring him out," Shad Grickel said. "Did you get that club away from him?"

"I didn't dare. I'm sure he'll die if he doesn't have it on him.'"

He was going to die anyway, Fallo realized, as soon as he saw the man's face. Cinnon had always been rail thin, but now he was skeletal, with cheekbones and collarbones protruding. His lips were pulled back, exposing pale gums and loose teeth. Sunken eyes held a look of continual surprise.

Seul put a bowl of porridge in front of him, but he refused

it. "I wanna die," he said. "I deserve nothin' better. Would ya be so kind as ta do it quick fer me?"

"Where is Kila Sigh?" Einlin asked.

"Dunno. Winnea took her. Said somebody called Yioth wanted her alive. Mack and me, we did what she said."

"Why?"

"She said Klayne wanted us to. He's a slick one. Dunno. I s'pose he made me an' Mack'Ti his men with all the coin an' women an' luckshree he gave us."

"Klayne?" Gian said. "Klayne Itopolo of Stallid?"

"Yup. Women love him. Course, he's rich, so why wouldn't they? Kil's eyes, I wish I'da never saw him. Don't like merculyns."

"I know Klayne," Gian said. "A minor nobleman of the Bazhro tribe. He was a supporter to my mother for many years. He is as this man describes him. Charming and unsavory. I never heard that he was a merculyn."

"We must find him," Einlin said.

"I am returning to Stallid," Gian said. "I intend to organize an army in preparation for the war to come."

"You told Kila you weren't a shadline," Quinn said, cutting in suddenly.

"I wasn't." Gian patted the hilt of his sword. "My mother was, thanks to the generosity of this sword. Revenir."

Fallo coughed. "That's Revenir?" Zirhine had told him of the famous blade during their travels.

Quinn was not so impressed. "If you spoke the oath, how could you then speak to ill against Kila at the Armory?"

"I spoke the truth as I knew it. This man says Winnea took Kila away, but consider this. Perhaps she and Winnea worked together. Perhaps Kila brought the nosg to—"

"I nearly brained Kila tryin' ta get her ta go," Cinnon said. "She weren't workin' with Winnea. In fact, she threw her dagger at the blasted woman. If it weren't for that screw crown she was wearin', we'da all been dead."

Quinn grabbed his shirt and lifted him from his chair. "What's this about a screw crown? Describe it."

Cinnon's huge throat apple bobbed. "Gold, with gems all 'round the band. I saw Winnea screw sharp bolts inta Sigh's skull."

"Shadline Ault's *vaz'on*," Shad Grickel said. "Winnea bore Loveheart, did she not? Ault's body was drained of blood. Pierced through the heart. It must have been her who took it from his room. I had thought it one of the Iron Scholars."

"Nax said Kila was far to the north," Fallo said. "Winnea must have taken her to Yiothizandra. With the *vaz'on* on her head, she's helpless."

"Likely dead by now," Shad Grickel said.

"No. Nax would feel that. And no matter how far away Nax is, Lop would feel the agony of Kila's death through Nax."

"And where is Sigh's cat now?"

Lop, where is Nax?

Lop looked up with squinty torpor. *That way.* She aimed her nose north and west. *Farther than the last time.*

"North," Fallo said to Grickel. "Trying to get to Kila."

"We must question Klayne Itopolo," Einlin said softly. "But if he's a merculyn aligned with Yiothizandra, he will be dangerous. I wish we had Jil with us."

"Killed her, too," Cinnon said sadly. "Winnea wanted that blade. She stabbed Ell LiMinluit with it."

Shad Grickel sat heavily and put his face in his hands. "Ell went missing during the nosg invasion. We found Jil's sword in the overlook garden. A bit of blood. Ell wasn't there."

"It is time to move," Einlin said. "I feel drawn to Stallid to question Klayne Itopolo. With your leave of course, Gian Delp."

"You are welcome anytime, Shad Einlin. All shadlines are welcome in Stallid. Fallo? Quinn?"

"I must return to Cigil-Tine," Fallo said.

"Cigil-Tine? Nobody knows where that is."

"I do. Cloak Einlin and Zirhine were there with me. A rather long tale."

Shad Grickel's face went red. "And you did not share this at the Armory?"

"There was clear evidence of corruption there," Einlin said. "We did not know who to trust, for the Hackwatch is a sinister place that clouds the force of destiny."

"I don't feel that here," Fallo said. "Not with these men. Cloak?"

Einlin nodded, giving Fallo permission to share the story. It ended with Fallo presenting Zirhine's fate's-piece sketch and the message revealed by the farlinbright. "And I have thirteen days to get there," he concluded.

"Come to Stallid first," Gian said. "My archivists have something you'll need. The key."

"The key to what?"

"The gate to the Tomb of Man."

Gian didn't know more than that. The key had been in the family for generations. It had been taken to innumerable tombs, but had opened no gates. "I wish to leave today. Within the hour. It is a long ride to Stallid."

"Fallo, bring out Kila's map," Einlin said.

The men marveled at the map and pored over details about the world they had never suspected, including the location of Cigil-Tine. "These are vergent passes," Fallo said, pointing to various symbols Zirhine had added to the map. "These others are Derslin Wheels, according to Kila. They are like the passes, as I understand it, but require merculyns to open portals."

Cloak Einlin dragged a finger north of Wantin, following the Sable River north and east to the northern edge of the Kovi-Mest range. "This vergent pass will take us here." His finger traversed north and west to a spot in the Rachtooth foothills east of Stallid.

Grickel's mouth worked a moment as he chewed his tongue. "I—I don't like going through a vergent pass."

"It's easy," Fallo said. "Cloak Einlin and I have been through several now and our souls are intact. I think. Mine is, anyway. Not sure if Einlin has one."

Grickel's beard bristled and he barked a laugh. "Til blame me, it will not be said that I'm a coward. Shadline Delp?"

"I do not fear vergents, which are revered throughout Losstra. But if such a pass exists in the Rachtooths, it is a wonder we have not discovered it."

"They go in one direction only," Fallo said. "The exits are never visible. You'll see."

"An' what of me?" Cinnon said. "Will ya leave me to perish slow?"

"No. You shall come with us," Einlin said. "You will arrange to meet with Klayne Itopolo so that he comes freely to a place of our choosing. Now eat!"

"Ya canna make me!"

Cinnon was wrong. The shadlines left the inn an hour later, Cinnon laden down with bags of food, from which he constantly withdrew large hunks of ham, beef, and chicken. Lop shadowed him mercilessly.

Outside of Wantin, they followed the Sable River, Cinnon riding Tolky to spare his energy. When Tolky lagged, the Cloak took his lead from Quinn's hand and pressed his forehead to the beast's muzzle. He spoke in low tones to the animal and fed it an apple from Cinnon's pack.

Tolky perked up and stepped much more lively from that moment on.

What did he say to the donkey? Fallo asked Lop.

How would I know?

You could ask the donkey.

Do you think I talk to donkeys?

Yes.

Well . . . Tolky doesn't talk. But I can tell he likes the Cloak. I don't like him though.

Why not?

He makes me hunt. Will he make Tolky hunt?

Tolky eats grass. He just needs to bend forward and nibble.

Lop sent a wave of disgust through the bond. Despite her poor regard for the Cloak, Lop did not hold it against Tolky. And since Cinnon was riding on the beast with his bags of goodies, Lop spent even more time aboard. Cinnon didn't relish sharing out his food, but Lop had a way of finagling large tidbits through sheer annoyance.

50

RED-CAPS

Jathesh flared his wings and reached his hind feet for the snow-covered clearing. With the added weight of girl and shaman, the landing came abruptly. Kila was thrown forward and Ahl-Mish-Lah's weight slammed into her back. A huge plume of snow rose all around them, caking Kila's cloak and hat in white.

She slipped from the saddle, legs frozen from cold and the long stretch of immobility. Ahl jumped down behind her, looking like a snow spirit she was so frosted over from the flight. Her staff's skull eyes glowed dully through a crust of ice. With a soft word they brightened sending forth red radiance that warmed her and Kila.

More wyvoks began to land, inelegantly and without regard to the safety of their passengers. A few nosg handlers were tossed free, face first into deep snow.

Several hundred paces ahead blazed the enormous signal fire that had guided them to this field. A train of wagons waited there, laden with deer, goat, and sheep. It took the remainder of the evening to distribute the game to the ravenous wyvoks, first requiring shamans to melt pathways through the snow to allow the wagons passage. The last thing they wanted was for the wyvoks to ransack the wagons. There was a natural pecking order among the beasts, but younger ones were always testing their elders, inevitably leading to pitched battles of writhing wyvoks, who indiscriminately crushed nosg under their bodies or impaled them with incidental lashes of their spiked tails.

Fritor and Tortyr landed at the fringes of the field to oversee the unruly feeding, then they leapt skyward to find perches upon the windswept crags. Dragons didn't seem to notice the chill, though it caused great tendrils of vapor to rise from their bodies.

The nosg horde stretched westward from the wyvok field. Kila and Ahl had overflown it prior to landing. Miles and miles of campfires, crude hide tents, and jacks trenches. Kila had been surprised by the rather orderly arrangement of the camps. But despite the crudeness of nosg craftsmanship, and the general lack of education among the lower castes, they had a remarkably efficient organization. Ahl had told Kila of some of it, though not out of any interest in educating her. Her admonishment had been for Kila to not embarrass her in front of the other shamans.

There had been twelve g'galasi, or tribes, until recently. Ahl-Mish-Lah was a shaman in G'galas Oopax. She had been a tsugu, or shaman of a gr'hil of warriors. But her gr'hil had fallen off a mountainside during an avalanche. This was incredibly shameful, but now Ahl-Mish-Lah was more powerful than any of the wurgus because she had Kila's power.

One of those wurgus now stood before Ahl, a familiar figure with a wolf skull staff and silvery hair. Wurgu Larq-Si wore a huge cloak that looked like sea-hound fur, but thicker. The hide from the beast's head remained attached and flopped atop his head. Snowflakes melted before reaching him, and Kila could feel the heat emanating from this wolf skull. She didn't know what he was saying but Ahl bristled.

More shamans came in, all covered with frost from the flight. They had not been allowed to use mimak for their own warmth, having been instructed to save their supplies for the coming battle. Ahl had sneaked some anyway in order to then draw upon Kila's power.

Apparently, Ahl had explained this because Larq-Si grunted and changed the subject, which had to do with the camp arrangements. Soon tents sprang up and Kila and Ahl were cramped under a thick hide supported by bones of a beast she did not recognize. She was glad to be out of the wind. Another hide served as a floor.

She woke the next morning, sweating and clutching her throat. Her head throbbed. She found Ahl-Mish-Lah sitting cross legged, swarmlight bright in her eye-gems.

"Strong girl get Roon-Jek visit." It was a question, Kila thought.

"Dream!" Ahl insisted. "Roon-Jek give bad dream." The shaman laugh-snorted then jabbed Kila with her staff. "Up. We fly."

Jathesh took to the air an hour before sunrise. The flight was as long as the previous day's. She saw Larq-Si aboard one of the wyvoks, squeezing the nosg handler so tightly she almost pitied the thing. Almost. Her head still hurt from her dream. She thought Roon-Jek was a nosg god.

Kila was astonished to find another enormous nosg army encamped a day's flight west. The wyvok field had been better prepared for them this time. Kila and Ahl ate in silence, slept instantly, and were aloft the following morning as the sun turned the impenetrable clouds a steel gray. The wyvoks flew beneath the clouds when they could, but often soared through them, relying on pulsing squawks and the answering echoes to keep them from smashing into mountainsides.

They landed at midday at the final wyvok field. Yet another massive army was encamped there. After the wyvoks were fed and settled, Ahl wanted to parade Kila before the tsugus there because the gr'hils of G'galas Oopax formed a good portion of its force. Ahl encompassed herself and Kila with a large bubble of heat, thanks to Kila's power, then draped several of her own tooth and claw necklaces over Kila's neck. Ahl surprised Kila further by opening a sack full of clacking bones and beads and fixing more strings of them around Kila's arms and waist. She was being decorated for show.

As they set out among the gr'hil tents, Kila felt a rise of energy in her breast, and a bit of bounce in her step. She felt . . . almost good. She hadn't been beaten or suffocated in several days. The camp food was better and fresher than what she'd become accustomed to. Face heating with shame, she berated herself for the cheap price of her happiness. Ahl had dressed her like a doll. Had it taken so little to burnish Kila's pride? Seeing herself in this getup, walking among a race set on killing every human they encountered, she thought of her father.

"Why making water eyes?" Ahl growled. "Strong girl weak?"

"Strong girl shamed. Prisoner. Slave."

"Yes. Shamed. Very shamed." Ahl laughed then and made

her skull eyes flare. Itches sprouted in the middle of Kila's back, unreachable and unscratchable anyway due to her layers of clothes and cloak. Kila bore it as best she could, wriggling futilely to rub the fabric of her shirt against the itches. It did no good except to make Ahl laugh. "Dance shame girl!"

The shaman relented as they approached a tsugu shouting at his warriors. Kila had learned that each gr'hil of nosg had one lead warrior called a girnt. These were always the biggest and meanest. They deferred to the tsugu in all things, of course, but they were often left in charge of the gr'hil when the tsugu had to attend to other things.

In this case the girnt was dead, head cloven open and brains spilling over the snow. The remaining warriors stood with their heads down, shamefaced as the tsugu berated them. One held an axe that dripped blood onto his shoulder.

The tsugu was pointing at the dead girnt. Kila didn't understand what he said, but his meaning was clear. He was demanding to know who had killed the girnt. Nobody was saying anything. Kila wondered if the tsugu was that stupid.

"If other warriors blame him, bloody axe dies," Ahl explained. "If no blame, he is girnt now. Gr'hil hate dead girnt. Like new one. See?"

Kila saw. The tsugu was testing the gr'hil to see if they'd point a claw at the murderer. If not, he would take the girnt's place. A rough tradition, but it made a sort of sense to Kila. Things worked a bit like that in Cheapsgate.

They continued to wind through the camp. Ahl enjoyed the long stares she and Kila received. Occasionally, Ahl would throw beams of heat around, melting snow and scoring trenches into the ground. The other shamans were impressed by this, and though Kila didn't understand their language, she saw their hideous envy quite clearly.

Ahl appeared to be looking for someone in particular. And soon she found her. A fellow shaman she apparently hated. They exchanged insults, then Ahl brought her to the ground with itches and suffocation bubbles. Ahl laughed and stamped her staff into the ground. When the shaman's gr'hil came to defend their tsugu, Ahl tortured them all with itches. Other gr'hils laughed and hooted as the nosg scratched bloody gashes into their own flesh.

Ahl ended the encounter by immolating the tsugu and commanding her gr'hil to move their camp to Ahl's tent. "My gr'hil now," Ahl said, pilfering all the dead shaman's mimak. A few of these she ate immediately, others she crooned over and tucked away in her pouches. Kila saw the more prized ones were red-caps, the common ones bluish.

Kila didn't know what Ahl needed with a gr'hil. They couldn't ride on Jathesh with her. But she knew better than to say anything. And words nearly failed her anyway when she saw what lay beyond the nosg camp.

"What are those?"

Another camp was spread out upon a rocky field rising toward a distant glacier. More campfires, but no tents. The creatures there sat upon boulders. They looked a bit like nosg, but they were huge. At least ten feet tall, with great spears, clubs, and axes with heads made of sharpened bone. Their flat-faced heads thrust forward as they hunched before their fires, huge hides draped over their shoulders for warmth. No evidence of gr'hil organization here. They sat singly or in pairs, doing nothing much but looking into the flames.

"Esgin," Ahl said. "Stupid. Strong."

"How many are there?"

Ahl shrugged, necklaces clattering. "Come. Queen will come soon."

The gr'hil that Ahl had commandeered had moved their camp to surround Ahl's tent. A hearty fire already burned there, and one nosg had a black pot on the boil. It would be more of the odd porridge the creatures lived on. Kila's stomach growled at the smell of it. The nosg warriors did not look at Kila at all. The new girnt had not cleaned his axe or the blood spatter from his face. Kila understood this to be a sort of badge, which he wished all nosg to see.

Ahl allowed Kila to return to the tent. She lay there, huddled in her thick cloak and necklaces. She took off her gloves and rubbed her palms together, disgusted by the filth under her fingernails. There had been a time not long ago when she'd never have noticed it. But Quinn had cleaned her up, kindling a pride of appearance in her. She was glad the nosg didn't bring looking glasses to war. She feared she might look too much like a nosg now, arrayed as she was in their clothes and jewelry.

The tent flaps were cinched open and light from the fire glanced off the garnet of her ring. She considered it again, and wondered why Ahl hadn't taken it. The only conclusion Kila could reach was that Ahl didn't trust it. Perhaps she thought it might be cursed. The shamans guarded their staffs jealously.

Seeing it, noting how its beauty and elegance contrasted so with her current state of dress, Kila decided it was time to try something that would likely make her very sick. She didn't fear the risk, though this was much bigger than running the roofway in Starside and making big leaps over alleyways.

Much bigger than climbing to the top of the bell tower over the Baths of Ori, as she and Nax had once done.

Ell had once told her that she was a thief for a reason. It was time to put that to the test. She continued to rub her hands together, seeking to heat her fingers and loosen the muscles. For what she was going to attempt, gloves just wouldn't do. But neither would frozen fingers.

Ahl came in after yelling at her new gr'hil for a while. She thumped down and warmed the tent with her skull and Kila's power. Kila spoke.

"I know the mimak lets you see through the skull's eyes."

Ahl grunted but said nothing.

"Do you have enough mimak for the battle?"

Ahl shifted and twisted her head until her neck popped, but she didn't answer.

"If you ate all your mimak, would Wurgu Larq-Si give you more?"

"Queen demands mimak, I get mimak." Ahl was irritated by these questions. She always was when Kila dared to talk about the sacred mushrooms.

"But I see you eating it all the time. I think Larq-Si doesn't give you good mimak." She had watched other shamans closely. They did not eat so much as Ahl did, but their power endured much longer. At first Kila had thought it due to the amount of power Ahl wielded. But even when Ahl did minor things with her staff, she had to eat a mushroom. "Why don't you take mimak from other shamans?"

"Queen not like me killing too many."

"She told Razk-Ka that you should have the best mimak. You have Kila Sigh, you must have the best mimak. Who keeps it from you?"

This struck a gong within the shaman. She again shifted uncomfortably, but now steamed inwardly. "Wurgu Larq-Si takes best, gives worst. He know I too powerful."

"Why don't you tell Yiothizandra?"

The swarmlight flared and a terrible itch sprouted in Kila's groin. She gritted her teeth and writhed around the tent for a minute. Ahl released the itch, but didn't laugh at all. Kila had spoiled her mood. "*Queen* Yioffissantra," Ahl corrected Kila. "I bother queen. I am shamed."

"But you can't kill Larq-Si. She would be angry about that too. She is hard to please. But what if you steal Larq-Si's mimak?"

"Wurgu Larq-Si sees me. Knows I steal it. Tells queen. Maybe she laugh. Maybe she breathe fire at me."

Ahl's cowardice was nothing new to Kila. In fact, she counted on it for her ploy to work.

"Ahl-Mish-Lah, you know I am a thief? I steal many gold coins. I steal gems. I steal right from men's pockets." Kila swayed side to side and pretended to snatch a purse. When she opened her palm, she showed a tooth she'd pulled from one of her own necklaces.

Ahl gasped and looked at her own chest, as if Kila had stolen it from her.

"Tonight I sneak to Larq-Si's tent. I take mimak. Bring it back to you. Red caps!"

Ahl's face crumpled as she considered this plan. Her lips pooched together and she hummed to herself. Her cowardice was too strong. Kila could just see a no forming in the shaman's mind. Hastily she said, "Think about juicy red-caps in your hand. Eating red-caps. They belong to you. Larq-Si steals your red-caps. Queen will be happy you took them. She will say. 'Ahl-Mish-Lah, you did well to take your red-caps. Larq-Si is too greedy.' And Ahl-Mish-Lah! What if Queen Yiothizandra thinks Ahl is better wurgu than Larq-Si? Wurgu Ahl-Mish-Lah!" Kila flopped back and sighed. "But maybe Ahl too scared to be wurgu. Cannot be wurgu without bags and bags of red-caps."

Most of Kila's speech had been stolen from Terriside corner vendors, eager to sell people fishbroth medicines. They always made their marks imagine already having the bottle of their worthless brew. Already having the cure it offered. Then they would finish with another trick, which Kila employed now. "Perhaps there is not enough red-caps to go around to all the shamans. Maybe Larq-Si knows the shamans go to battle with few mimak. They eat too many to make themselves warm. What will happen to the shamans who fail in battle? Queen Yiothizandra will make them *very* warm."

Ahl sucked in air. "Not enough mimak? Hmmmm. Strong girl sees greedy truth, I think. Hmmm. Strong girl can steal?"

"It's my specialty. I go tonight. Bring back red-caps so Ahl-Mish-Lah has power in battle."

The nosg settled down to sleep soon after sunset. No watches were posted because none were needed. No men came to these barren and inhospitable places. The fires were banked low when Kila crept out of the tent and into moonlit night.

Ahl had told her to look for Larq-Si's tent in the center of the encampment. The position of honor. Nosg snored in their tents or under piled hides. Kila had asked for a knife but Ahl had forbidden it in case Kila was captured. Ahl wanted to be able to blame Kila if she got caught.

Kila's first mark was a nosg warrior in her own gr'hil. The new girnt himself, who slept face down with his claws over his head. His axe was close by his side, and an unsheathed dagger beside it. She could have slit his throat easily.

She considered going back into the tent to stab Ahl, but the shaman was not asleep. In fact, she was eagerly anticipating a bag full of red-caps.

Kila did not bother to creep through the camp. The moon was too bright and the nosg had extraordinarily good sight in dim light. Their hearing was sharp too. Their sense of smell was only slightly better than their taste, which was why they could eat slightly rotten meat as happily as the shamans could eat uncooked mushrooms.

A few nosg stirred as she moved through the camp circles. A few opened their eyes and watched her go. Word had spread about her, especially after Ahl had marched her through the encampment. Any who saw her would assume she was supposed to be there. And after Ahl's murder of a rival shaman, no warrior wanted anything to do with her slave girl.

Larq-Si's tent was huge, and in it were three nosg. Moonlight played on the wurgu's silvery hair as Kila squeezed through the flaps. She waited for her eyes to adjust, but there simply wasn't enough light. She thrust the flap wider, which helped a little. It also let in cold air. Larq-Si stirred and pulled his furs more snugly around himself. The other two rolled hard against him for warmth.

Kila didn't think he'd wear his mimak pouches while he slept. The tent was large enough for her to remain standing. She hugged the wall, feeling the way with her feet and hands. Her toe bumped something soft. She bent to feel it, hoping it was a bag of mimak, but it was a fourth nosg.

She froze and waited for it to settle before stepping over it and continuing her search. She found the remains of supper next, the cold porridge sticking to her fingers. Still probing, she found a stack of books, and a metal pot full of liquid that stank so badly she heaved and gagged, covering her mouth with her arm to keep quiet. It was a chamber pot. Finally she found some packs made of deer hide. They were cinched with leather thongs, which she cut using the girnt's knife.

It was the fourth one that rewarded her. The mimak mushrooms were somewhat soft, but the odor was unmistakable. She continued searching bags until she was sure she'd found the only two with mushrooms.

She retreated with her loot, secured the tent flap and returned to Ahl-Mish-Lah's tent. But not before stuffing several red-caps into her sleeves. She considered keeping the knife, but she didn't dare hide it in her cloaks. The girnt would surely complain and Ahl would know Kila had been sneaking around.

When Kila presented the bags of mimak, Ahl immediately ate a red-cap. It seemed to relax her greatly, for she lay back, mouth open and gazed at nothing until finally falling to sleep.

Kila pulled a red-cap from her sleeve and bit off a hunk. It was cold and dry and tasted like old socks. She ground it to a paste with her teeth and forced herself to swallow. This was what she'd undertaken the whole caper to achieve. A desperate hope.

She raised her hand to her face and concentrated on her garnet ring, willing the swarmlight to come to it.

Nothing happened.

At first.

51

THOSE WINGED VILLAINS

"Are you sure about this?" Gian Delp asked. "Stallid just lost their queen. I'm not keen on them losing the heir before he's even officially crowned. Ha ha."

The handsome young man was trying to make light of the situation. Fallo recognized the attempt at humor for what it was. But as was common for most people, Gian had ruined it by laughing at the end. That's not how humor worked. If you were going to use a joke to alleviate an extremely uncomfortable moment, you had to keep your voice dead even.

Fallo leaned forward to peer down into the well. The vergent passes he'd been through before had been archways one could easily step through. This was a pit, a black chasm surrounded by low wall of vergent-carved stone. It was much like a well, absent the water. "Should I throw Lop in?" he asked.

Quinn gasped in horror. Grickel swore and said, "By Til and his mighty right fist, you'll do no such thing to her." Grickel had developed a fierce fondness for the cat during the journey to this vergent pass.

Cinnon glared at Fallo and reached vaguely for the club strapped onto his back. He too had fallen under Lop's fuzzy spell. And apparently, he too had a broken sense of humor. To make this more sharply clear, the usually humorless Cloak spread his lips in a grin. Not that he held any ill will toward Lop, but he thought every living creature should be subjected to daily discomforts. He probably thought being tossed into a black pit would do Lop some good.

Why don't you jump in? Lop asked.

I knew you could understand what I say aloud, Fallo sent.

Were those noises you were making words? I just thought you were whining with fear.

Another rule Fallo had about humor was never to explain a joke when it didn't work. "Lop says I should jump in."

"Hear, hear," Grickel said. "Should I assist?" the stocky man barked, laughing.

Quinn and Cinnon laughed. Fallo palmed his forehead. "I'm sure I can manage." He threw a leg over the wall, then the other. Nobody stopped him. Not even Quinn. "Perhaps a rope . . . ?"

They all seemed disappointed, but Grickel secured a rope to a thick pine and gave Fallo the end. He dropped the coil into darkness and heard it slap against the side of the well. "I don't see how Tolky is going to manage this."

Fallo climbed down, slowly, probing with his feet and trying to ignore the growing fear that something might reach up to grab his ankles. He hadn't gone more than three feet below the rim when the wall pulled him toward it. Not with hands, but with a strange invisible attraction.

Releasing the rope, he stood up. The well had become a tunnel from this new perspective. He stepped to the opening and peered over the edge. His companions now appeared to be standing on a vertical plane covered with grass and trees. It dropped away forever.

Upon seeing him standing there, Lop nosed over the wall and walked into the tunnel.

Strange, Lop announced. Then she continued on into the blackness.

They lost two hours trying to figure out how to get Tolky into the tunnel. Then Lop reappeared and meowed at the donkey. Tolky moved to the lip of the well, put one foot over and leaned forward. Cinnon and Quinn, already in the well, called to him and pulled on his lead. Lop meowed again. All at once Tolky hopped over and landed on all four hooves. The Cloak came last.

What did you say to Tolky? Fallo sent.

I don't talk to donkeys.

Cinnon mounted up, skinny legs hanging so that his feet nearly scraped the floor. Lop jumped up and found a perch among the pannier bags.

Shad Grickel tore a flashtaper and lit a pine tar torch he'd fashioned. The tunnel walls were smooth block stone. The air was cool and smelled fresh, as if a breeze blew in from a garden. The passage widened at one point where a little stone fountain burbled from the wall to collect in a basin carved to look like woven rose brambles. They refilled their skins and jugs, and let Tolky suck down his fill.

The water was cold, fresh, almost sweet, and all agreed they felt revived by it. They continued on. The tunnel appeared to go on forever. "What's the point of a vergent pass if it's as long as the overland journey?" Fallo asked.

"My torch sputters its last," Grickel said.

As the flame died they stepped into daylight.

Looking back, there was nothing but a mountainside and tall spruce laden with snow. Before them was a game trail, dotted with rabbit tracks. A slate gray sky pressed low over the tips of the tall pines. Severe peaks crowded around them in this hidden ravine.

"Ah, now that is bracing air!" Grickel boomed, tossing the extinguished torch into the snow. The air was sharp with cold. Fallo retrieved the fur-lined cloak he'd taken from the shadline cache, thankful that Seul had insisted he take warm things. The others were soon similarly bundled against the northern chill. Tolky snorted and stamped, nostrils sending forth billows of steam.

"Let's proceed," Gian said. "I hope to get my bearings once I can see the peaks more clearly."

The game trail wound deeper into the ravine, which widened into a steep canyon. They followed the course of a frozen stream west for an hour before the scent of smoke reached them.

"Campfires," the Cloak said.

Meat! Lop sent, black nose testing the air. *Someone is cooking delicious goats.*

"Lop says they're cooking goat."

They proceeded with more caution and the Cloak slipped ahead to scout the way. He returned swiftly making shushing motions and guiding them away from the frozen stream bed. Tolky grumbled and the Cloak glared at the beast.

Tell the donkey to be quiet, Fallo sent to Lop.

I don't talk to donkeys.

But Tolky made no more noises, and Fallo thought the beast stepped more lightly too. The Cloak led them upslope again, stopping them just short of an overlook. He motioned them to stay low. Fallo crept up next to the swordsman and peeked over. "Kil's throbbin' handle, that's an army."

"A nosg army," the Cloak whispered.

Shad Grickel and Quinn bracketed him, each peeping over and offering their own curse. "How many?" Quinn asked. "At least ten thousand, don't you think?"

Gian slipped further up and lay flat on the rock. He lay very still for a while then inched backward. "The encampment continues around the lower limb of that eastern mountain. This valley is known to me. There is a hunting house just west of here. Likely destroyed by now. But that way lies the only sure pass out of the mountains at this time of year."

The Cloak eyed the sky. "Another few hours until dark. We saw no nosg tracks coming down. They aren't bothering to patrol. We should be safe to wait until middle dark. Then we'll have to chance it and slip past. Does anyone hear otherwise?"

No one did. If Fallo calmed himself and listened to his instincts at all, they simply pulled him southeast toward Cigil-Tine. But they had nothing to say about the nosg army.

The respite would have been very welcome if not for the horde of nosg just around the bend. The little fellowship had no fire, so only cold food for supper. Shad Grickel rescued them with a few slugs off his flask. "Lockt spirits, friends," he said. "Aged in oak barrels a twenty-year. You'll not likely sip smoother than that."

They discussed the nosg army, but only briefly. Gian declared the obvious reason for why the horde was there. "They intend to take Stallid."

"They'll need more than numbers to breech those walls," Shad Grickel said. "I've been there and I know siege craft. I see no engines in that camp."

"They might craft what they need in the foothills," the Cloak said. "But I agree. Stallid will not be an easy prize to claim."

"The Indomitable Wall," Quinn said, nodding and gazing off as if she could see it. "I've read about it. Longed to see it. Wasn't Sephie the Archer born in Stallid?"

"She was," Gian said. "On'lin Keep is the central fortress. The Indomitable Wall was built after she drove the nosg back to the mountains. Her bow was at the Armory. Did you not see it?"

"I was asleep most of my time there."

"Ah. Forgive me. I had forgotten your illness."

"Who wields it now?" Fallo asked. He'd never considered that the legendary bow could still exist, but of course it could. A shadline weapon would endure for thousands of years.

"Balik Tol. He was a commoner—a sheepherder—which is a usual choice for Dark Smiter. The arrows become empowered with shadline effects through use. A curious effect, really." He proceeded to tell how any common arrow would increase in power if loosed from Dark Smiter often enough. Balik practiced daily to build up a supply of such arrows. Some flew longer, some faster, others burst into flames when they struck, still others could pierce into stone and were strong enough to support ropes. "The stone piercers require the most patience, for he must loose them at stone with just the slightest pull on the string, many times, lest he blunt or split the arrows before they have accumulated enough power to withstand hard impacts. You will likely see Balik at work soon. If he can return in time."

"If the force of destiny wills it, and he listens and obeys, we shall see him," the Cloak said with finality.

Night seeped in from above and quickly crept down the mountainsides, but the clouds cleared. A bright moon lit their way across the snowy slopes. The Cloak let Gian guide, stopping him frequently to first consider the path with the most tree cover.

They paralleled the great nosg army for an hour, astonished by the extent of it. The leading edge grew ragged, with fewer tents and campfires, and then it was behind them. They passed the burned out ruins of the hunting house, which to Fallo looked like the foundations of an enormous mansion equal to a Radiant's greathouse.

"We will leave tracks," the Cloak said. "If the army moves in the morning, they will know of our passing. I fear we will have little rest until we are safely behind the Indomitable Wall."

They moved from the mountains into the foothills. Stallid was still more than two days' trek away. Another nosg encampment lay before them, this one smaller. The Cloak guided them wide of the fires and tents. A weird animal squawk sounded in the stillness.

Shad Grickel spun, hand reaching over his shoulder for his axe. "Til hold me!" he muttered. "I'd know that sound as sure as my own mother's crooning. We must move faster, shadlines. The nosg have wyvoks."

They spotted a flight of the beasts a few minutes later, inky shapes roosting on a snowy slope. "How did they tame those winged villains?" the stout shadline knight said. "I've never known them to rest on low hills like this either. No wall can bar them entry."

"Their hides will feel our ballista bolts should they wing too low," Gian said.

The Cloak glared them both to silence and Fallo added his own stares. A shadline should know better than to blather on when surrounded by enemies. Tolky was keeping quiet, for he instinctively knew that he was food for wyvoks.

Skirting still wider of their path, they left the nosg behind. The land flattened and the snow vanished, giving way to hardpan supporting little plant life save for wiry scrub that sprouted in dense clusters.

Soon their warm cloaks were shed and packed. And the long trudge continued, always too slowly. Fallo's instincts screamed for him to run now, but they couldn't leave Tolky behind without leaving Quinn, and probably Lop.

Cinnon kept looking over his shoulder. "I don't unnerstand why nosgs are attackin' Stallid."

"It's the culmination, you idiot," Grickel muttered. "Are you a shadline at all? Did you ever feel the call? Or are you just a faithless mercenary?"

Cinnon had no answer for this except to repeat that he hadn't asked for any of this. Didn't want the club. Didn't want to be tricked by Winnea into killing Jil. Didn't even want the coin and women Klayne had given him. Not much anyway.

Quinn walked beside Fallo, saying nothing. There was no fear in her, he noted. In fact, her eyes caught the moonlight and reflected back excitement. She no longer favored the stump of her right wrist, letting it swing easily as she walked rather than holding it close or hiding it. Seul had fitted it with a steel cup, held in place by clever straps. "You can stove in a man's nose with that," Seul had said. "Harder than a fist, and no broken knuckles for your efforts."

Fallo felt a rush of fondness for her. No matter how lousy the times, and how burdensome his responsibilities as a shad-line, he couldn't regret them. For Quinn was part of it. And for her love, he would face any danger. Anywhere.

GRASP THE CHANCE

The raven soars above the Haelshok Range, far higher than any bird ever flew. Below, the moonlit mountains curve away, revealing the spherical shape of the world.

Tiny pricks of light shine up from the vast stretches of snow-covered wilderness. The raven folds its wings as it spears through the wind.

Dive, Kila Sigh. Dive!

KILA BOLTED UPRIGHT, sucking in a wheezing gasp of air. Her mouth was dry, tongue thick with the aftertaste of the red-cap she'd eaten.

Ahl-Mish-Lah lay next to her, snoring softly. The interior of the tent was ablaze in crimson light. It came from Kila's ring. The redness chimed as she raised her hand to look at the ring. The gold letters scribed around the jewel became strangely magnified before her eyes. The letters detached from the ring and floated before her. *Ot Kil, Tuin Pri*—God Kil, His First.

The gem appeared to have grown enormous too, weighing her hand down like a boulder. She forced it up, felt it with her other hand. It was its usual size, the script still smooth under her finger. And yet, it appeared huge before her, filling the tent.

The gem's facets gave off different qualities of red, pink, rose, and crimson. Deep inside the gem was a black inclusion, a flaw. But upon closer scrutiny it had a peculiar shape. Wings. Tail. Beak. A raven.

The chime of the light went on, each ring resonating forever, each new ring adding to the sound, until her bones vibrated with a ceaseless gong tone. It thrummed at the base of her spine, accumulated there, then rose in tingling urgency to groin, belly, chest, throat. Her skull vibrated as the sound warmed her forehead then released in a great fiery rush from the top of her head.

Surely the tent had been seared away. Even the sky could not absorb such light. Though Kila's eyes were squeezed tightly shut, the inscription and the gem filled her vision.

The thrumming light oozed past her, full of bubbles and faces and flowers and words that tasted sweet and salty and dense and crisp. The *vaz'on* constricted, the skull bolts crushing inward. Kila opened her eyes and looked down, discovered she was a thousand feet tall. The mountains were stones. Oceans surrounded her, puddles she could displace with a stomp of one foot.

The secret words her father had hidden behind a thief's mirror sprang to mind. *Open for Kil's Daughter.* They formed on her tongue like castles, tasted of smoke, and crunched under her teeth. A vine grew upon the words, winding up and blossoming with black roses, thorns dripping with blood and tears, stalk curling around a high tower. Words that were love, a citadel, a carriage, a sip of wine, a broken broom handle, sang like drifts of sand.

With a texture like rough spun wool, the words erupted in her mind, all golden and full of teeth: *"Words cannot contain, nor the mind apprehend, the unconscious will of time. The force of destiny has meter, but, alas, no rhyme."*

Pennie's words. Roya Reth's words.

In answer came a snatch of verse, plucked from a memory. A play she'd read in a Radiant's greathouse.

> "Oh, darling dagger, cut this mortal gown a
>> life-spilling seam,
> Join me to my love, in Lumne's wakeless
>> dream!"

The thrumming light coursed through her body, relentlessly, until her head pulled back, her jaw dropped, lips curled in an unwilling snarl of agonized ecstasy. The ring throbbed, weighing a thousand pounds. A million. So heavy. The ring became the world upon her finger.

The gem. The light. The sound. The insane rattle of unrelated words.

"Hush."

The voice was deep, soft, but insistent. "Hush, child."

Kila found herself on her back, panting, sweat pouring from her brow.

The tent was awash with red light. She raised her hand,

looked at the ring. The light faded. The sweat froze upon her forehead and she shivered.

An hour later—or perhaps an age had passed, Kila had no sense of it—Ahl-Mish-Lah jabbed her staff into Kila's side. "Up. The queen calls."

BY THE TIME Kila had attended to her needs and splashed water on her face, her mind felt as clear as the cloudless sky. Her chest was light, her shoulders at ease. She went to Ahl's side and waited.

Yiothizandra wore a sable cloak that gaped up the front to where it was loosely belted under the bare and protruding belly. Her wings were gone. She wore a sword on her hip but no armor. She addressed the shamans, who had gathered in a half circle.

Kila glanced at her ring. Its garnet was dull, nearly black.

"The armies move forward tonight. They will race to Stallid, to the so-called Indomitable Wall. The first gr'hil to touch the stone shall be honored above the rest and become my personal guard."

The tsugu shamans cheered and thumped their staves on the ground.

But Wurgu Larq-Si's head hung low. Finally he prostrated himself. "Great Queen. My mimak has been stolen. My bedmates were killed in the night."

Kila had not killed anyone. Larq-Si had probably killed them himself in a wild rage. Yiothizandra stood over him. "If you cannot summon the swarmlight, then you have no use to me. Will anyone give him mimak?" she asked of the assembled shamans.

None volunteered.

"I believe G'galas Pikork lacks a wurgu now. Pity." With a single fluid movement, she drew her blade and drove it into the Larq-Si's neck. And then something utterly strange happened. The blade blurred. Kila realized it was thrusting up and down of its own accord, a frenzy of stabbing. Soon the nosg shaman's head had been severed and the sword continued to plunge until Yiothizandra gritted her teeth and yanked the blade back. With obvious effort she returned it to its scabbard. "Who took his mimak? Step forward so that you might be recognized. Do not fear, I cherish those who grasp the chance. Larq-Si was weak to have been so easily robbed."

Several shaman stepped forward, but when they could show no red-caps, they were dismissed. Finally Ahl-Mish-Lah stepped forward to show her bag, stuffed nearly to bursting with red-caps.

Yioth touched her head gently. "Well done. And wise. Much will be asked of you Ahl-Mish-Lah. It would have gone poorly for you had you failed me in the battle to come." The dragnithan motioned to her servile helper, Noy, and he placed a small bag in her hand. She withdrew a fine golden necklace, heavy with a purple-gemmed pendant. This she placed over Ahl's head, where it rested against her chest on a bed of claws and teeth. "Wurgu Ahl-Mish-Lah, of G'galas Wyvok. Pikork exists no longer."

Ahl beamed and licked her lips. Her devotion to Yioth increased tenfold in that moment. Kila was content, still so clear of mind that none of her past tortures haunted her.

Whatever the red-cap had done to her in the night, at least it had given her this momentary peace.

Nax? she sent, knowing the cat could not hear her. *I think I will die soon. I would go easy except that I would never wish to hurt you.* The cat was somewhere far to the south and east.

When Yioth departed, Kila returned to the tent. Ahl did not come for her, but probably set out to flaunt her new trinket and begin making the shamans of Pikork dip the skull to her. For a long time, Kila didn't have any thoughts at all as she sat in the chill stillness of the tent. When Ahl did finally return, the light outside had dimmed. Night was falling.

Was it possible she'd sat there for so long? When she emerged, the nosgs were gone except for the wyvok handlers and shamans. Jathesh was restive and eager to fly. He leapt into the air the moment Ahl-Mish-Lah had settled into saddle behind Kila.

The new wurgu was generous with her heat, enclosing Kila within the bubble of warmth. Jathesh was now the leader of all the wyvok flights, so hundreds of flyers fell into disorganized formations behind them. Below, the nosg army marched swiftly forward.

53

THEY INSULT US

The final watchtower lay far behind, barely a bump on the horizon now. Fallo forced himself to keep his eyes forward, to not look for the signal fire that would flare atop it as soon as the men there saw the approaching army. They knew the exact range at which such a force could be seen. On a clear day like this the flare atop that tower would mean the nosg were just thirty miles behind them.

"It's burnin'," Cinnon said an hour later, looking back from the bed of the wagon. "It's burnin'."

There was no more speed to be added, pulled along now as they were by a team of three atlens in harness. Gian had commandeered it after spending ten minutes convincing the last tower captain that he was indeed the uncrowned king of Stallid.

"Another few hours," Gian said, looking back. "I know this road well."

They were on a well-maintained cart road, used to supply the series of watchtowers between Stallid and the Rachtooth

Mountains. They had replenished their water, taken some food, and fed Tolky at the last tower. A stop of barely half an hour. The donkey was keeping up admirably, despite the pace of the draft birds. Had they not pulled a heavy wagon, the donkey would have been left far behind.

"Will your watch guards retreat?" Quinn asked, looking back now that Cinnon had announced the signal fire.

"No," Gian said. "Their duty is not complete. They must signal when the nosg arrive there."

Fallo heard the iron in his voice. The watchtower guards would never retreat. The tower would fall quickly, and they would die.

"What's that ahead?" Cinnon asked.

A gray smudge rose upon the horizon. The land was absolutely flat, desert scrub and lizards the only things to break up the monotony. It had a bleak beauty to it, Fallo supposed. But it was difficult to appreciate when an enormous nosg army was following.

"The Indomitable Wall," the Cloak said.

"Then we are nearly there," Fallo said.

"No." Gian laughed. "You do not appreciate the size of the wall."

It was as the heir said. Fallo did not appreciate it, for he had never seen it before. He had thought the Divide in Starside an enormous structure, built as it was in elnisian perfection. But as they approached, hour by hour, the scale of Stallid's wall began to kindle in him a deep awe.

Fallo had no training in fortification architecture, but it was obvious that the builders had considered a nosg attack to be like an ocean of bodies washing against a mountainside. It stood one hundred feet high and stretched north to south for half a mile before turning to encompass the city.

"The corners are fortresses in their own right," Gian said, pointing out the great blocky protrusions. "Three wedges thrust forward between them, offering choke points where arrow, ballistae, stone, and oil may be concentrated. My father is the Anjel General of the army. He used to have me watch the mock sieges."

Despite the flat land surrounding the city, the final mile was anything but level ground. A series of wide trenches carved around the city, so that any force would first have to bridge them to get to the wall.

They crossed bridge after bridge, Gian explaining the great swinging arms at each end that would swing down to dislodge keystones, thereby collapsing the bridges. The watchtower road joined to the Slirya-Wantin, a wide stone-paved road built by elnisians. Traffic was heavy here with merchants and desert folk who had seen the watchtower signal.

They joined more wagons, driven by men who cursed the slower foot traffic. Small horses bore men in the long white shirts and loose trousers common in the desert. The air was brisk and clear.

A huge plaza opened before the gate, where each wagon was stopped, inspected for contraband, then sent on to a dozen teams of customs inspectors, who rifled through every bag and box, scratching numbers of slates which were then relayed to a scribe and teller. Coins were exchanged.

Gian drove them to the leftmost team, spoke a few words. They were soon surrounded by a guard of fifteen men on horse, who escorted them past the customs teams and through another series of gates.

The Indomitable Wall was not a single structure, but a series of three walls, each twenty feet thick. The gates were not aligned, but required a parallel journey of two hundred paces before turning in past more guards, and then repeating the parallel journey between walls two and three to the final gate. Any enemy breeching the first gate, would be subject to arrows, stones, and oil from above for a long time before even reaching the second gate.

They came through the final gate and into an enormous open plaza. Men in bright yellow shirts stood upon platforms, waving wagons one way, horses another, and folk on foot still another.

"Through long tradition we have prepared for this day," Gian said. "By the time the nosg get here, this plaza will hold an orderly encampment for those who live outside the city."

"And those who can't make it in time?" Quinn asked.

Gian didn't answer except to shake his head.

It was the largest city Fallo had ever been to. Larger than Starside by half again in population. The streets formed an even grid, very unlike the typical elnisian style which valued beauty more than function. Stallid had an elnisian core, where the fabled On'lin Keep lay. But the city—including the Indomitable Wall—was the work of men. It lacked the elegance of the First Race builders, but Fallo noted many elnisian motifs and techniques on display, including fluted columns and decorative cornices. The streets were wide, paved, and nearly as well maintained as those in Tearling. The people were alert, but calm. And no surprise. They clearly trusted the Indomitable Wall.

From the great plaza Fallo saw the battlements of the surrounding wall enclosing the city. There were no hills in

Stallid, and no buildings were allowed to be more than three stories high. But watchtowers were set at regular intervals among the shops and homes so that the streets could be observed at all times.

"Should the nosg breech the walls, they will not easily swarm through the city," Gian said. "Every block will come at a great cost. The people of Stallid will shed the last drop of their tribes' blood to preserve their homes."

In addition to the enormous numbers of liveried guard patrols and army columns moving about the city were cohorts of well-organized militia. The men and women in the ranks were not as strong, nor were their steps as evenly paced, but they all wore blue shirts and corresponding arm bands. They carried spears.

They stopped at a watchtower, where Gian bade them step down from the wagon. Tolky was led onward toward the stables. Quinn gave stern instructions that the beast be unloaded, rubbed down, and watered.

Lop drew an enormous amount of attention from the guards, most who gaped and pointed. Some made a symbol with their hands, tucking the middle two fingers and thumb, while extending forefinger and pinky. Fallo couldn't tell if it was a superstitious ward or a sign of sacred respect.

"Lop is a cat," Fallo said to the closest man. "She won't hurt you."

"Sheia's heart! I would think not," the man said, again making the sign. "I once saw a cat when I was a lad. I've had good luck ever since. Sheia rarely graces the eyes of men in her true form."

They thought Lop was a goddess. That was the last thing the arrogant cat needed. But hearing of another cat's existence intrigued him. "You saw a cat in this city? What color?"

"Gray, as I recall. White flag on the tip of the tale, face blazed with white. Like a horse. Bigger than that one, though not as, uh, rotund."

Are there other cats in the city? Fallo asked Lop.

I am aware of three.

Can you talk to them?

I don't talk to cats.

Fallo sighed. He'd had this discussion with Lop dozens of times. *You know what I mean.* The cats didn't talk to each other in words, but simply knew each other's thoughts.

They are not awake. They will not welcome my thoughts.

Aren't you curious about them? Don't you want to meet them?

No.

A squad of riders on fast horses tore away from the tower for a long ride to notify Slirya of the attack. The guard said solemnly: "Blessed Wayol, give them strength, speed, and endurance for the journey."

"Who's Wayol?" Fallo quietly asked Quinn as she emerged from the stables. "One of those Losstran gods?"

"Probably. They have hundreds of them."

Gian conferred with the captain of the watchtower a minute more before joining his traveling companions. "I must return to the keep. Shadlines, you are welcome there or anywhere your instincts lead you. Fallo, the archives are adjacent to the keep. Ask for Stannin Dio and give him this token. He will provide you the key we discussed." Gian handed Fallo a small silver coin, burnished to mirror brightness. A Stallid Favor, which he'd heard of but had never seen before. Only a Losstran royal could give such a token.

"I will take Cinnon to find Klayne Itopolo," the Cloak said. Shad Grickel nodded and said he'd join him.

"It is well," Gian said. "I will likely be at the wall before sunset, should you need to speak with me. You will of course find the captains ready to aid you, should you require such." The young man straightened. "Here I am king, though my vows as a shadline are no weaker than before. But my city is my trust."

"The shadline order has never commanded kings against their interests," Shad Grickel said. "We won't start now. Listen and obey."

"Listen and obey," Gian said. And then he was gone, already immersed in conversation about the siege to come.

Fallo bade the Cloak and Grickel goodbye. They planned to reunite upon the wall at sunset if it was the will of destiny.

Lop was not interested in traveling further and found a cozy spot for napping in the stable loft overlooking Tolky's stall. The truth, Fallo thought, was that Lop smelled a hearty stew simmering and intended to exact a tribute from soldiers hoping she would grant them luck.

It took half an hour to get to On'lin Keep and locate the archives. Gian's token smoothed every interaction, allowed them to skip queues, and finally resulted in a middle-aged man running through library shelves to greet them. Stannin Dio was very short, slight, with curly brown locks sprouting from a receding hairline. He wore black and a great silver pendant on a leather thong about his neck. It was shaped like an open book.

He inspected Gian's token, then returned it. "How may I be of service?"

"I need the key to the Tomb of Man."

This resulted in a widening of eyes and a few stammered objections. Fallo merely flipped the silver token and caught it. Stannin looked to Quinn, as if she might offer some explanation of why Gian had given such a hideous man his token. Quinn merely arched an eyebrow. "It's rather urgent, sir."

They key was kept in a small room beneath the archives. "These shelves hold all the books that reference the key, where it has been tried, and what the result was. I can save you an enormous amount of time by saying that invariably the key has not yet unlocked anything."

He continued on with several discursive monologues about what tombs had gates in Losstra, Slirya, and Wantin and how none had accepted the key. Fallo interrupted him with a pat on the shoulder. "My good man, perhaps you show us the key."

It was held in a wooden box, sitting on a shelf. Stannin took it down, placed it on a reading table in the center of the room. He lifted the shade on a mercus lamp to allow more light.

The box lid came off and there was the key. A black iron key. "It looks like it belongs on a jailors keyring," Fallo said, plucking the artifact up. The barrel was as thick as his thumb, and four bits thrust out from it. "It doesn't look like much to me. How do you know it's for the Tomb of Man?"

"The inscription," Stannin said. "Just there on the barrel. It's elnisian script."

Holding the key close to the mercus light, Fallo angled it until he could see the engraving on the side. *Entir il umak.* "Well, there it is." He realized then that he'd hoped Gian had been mistaken, or that a legend had coincidentally sprung up about some random key found in a tavern basement. He snorted, realizing that the force of destiny would use just that sort of happenstance to guide the key into his hands.

Stannin leaned forward, brows up. He expected some explanation, it seemed, for why this royal artifact was being removed from his collection. "The Tomb of Man is in Cigil-Tine," Fallo said. An hour later, Kila's map spread on the table, and Stannin Dio's numerous notations and additions sketched in, Fallo leaned back and drained the last of the tea the archivist had brought in.

"The vergent passes have never been mapped with this degree of precision," Stannin said, tracing a quick copy of the map for his own records. "And you say they go only one way?"

"The ones I've been through. I believe I'll have to use this one here, travel back down the Kovi-Mest and then come through to Cigil-Tine by way of the one I used before. I'm not sure it will save much time, actually."

Stannin tugged at his lower lip. "That is an ill-conceived route, sir. You'd have to cross a five hundred miles of desert to reach the pass at this coast. Then another hundred on the Kovi-Mest. And you have how many days remaining?"

"Twelve, now."

"Can't be done. No. You'd be better off trekking south to the Boil. If you survived that, and the descent into the Shaddle Rift, you'd be able to make it to the Shanala Range and find a pass through to where you claim Cigil-Tine is."

"Why is crossing mountains preferable to crossing the Destig Desert?" Quinn asked. "And I don't see how that can be done in a hundred days, much less twelve."

Fallo waggled his nose and sighed. "That's *if* we had twelve days. The city is besieged. I don't see how we'd get out anyway." A cold sweat prickled the back of his neck. He had to be to Cigil-Tine on the appointed day. The pull was so strong he had nearly decided to risk going out among the nosg and seeing if he could break through to the west. "There must be an underground escape passage from the city. The sort of thing royals use in a siege or to escape a coup."

Stannin shrugged. "If there is, I'm not privy to its existence. But it would not be in character for a Losstran monarch to flee a siege. Not even Gian Delp would do such a thing."

Not even? That was curious. "Do you not approve of the new king?" Fallo asked. He caught Quinn's eye. She was suddenly very attentive.

"It isn't for me to approve or disapprove. You must excuse my haphazard phraseology. Surely young King Delp will stand upon the wall and fight behind his men." There was just the slightest emphasis on "behind." Fallo had seen no evidence of cowardice in the young man, and he had been determined to return to the city to lead its defense.

When Fallo said nothing more, Stannin went on. "It is natural for a young king to be timid, I suppose, and seek the counsel of elders." Now Fallo understood. Stannin was talking about the shadline Armory Gian had attended.

"You do not approve of the shadlines?" Fallo asked.

The man eyed their daggers before answering. "By all accounts, the shadline are a noble order."

It was clear that Fallo would never get a direct answer from the man. And that was fine, for he was done with him. "Thank you for your assistance. I will return the key if I can."

By the time they emerged from the archives, the streets were quiet. Those with homes were locked inside, those without were in camps tending cookfires, and awaiting news of the siege.

Gian's silver token allowed them easy passage through checkpoint after checkpoint. Heavy wagons were set at angles in the major cross streets ready to be rolled forward as barricades. Fallo discovered dozens more of these, all manned by squads of militia.

The gate plaza was arranged in orderly rows of tents. Folk watched him and Quinn pass. A soldier directed them to the base of a corner stair that lead to the gate battlements. From there they walked upon the inner wall, across a bridge to the middle, and from there over another to the outer wall where the token was again required.

They found Gian with his advisors and the shadlines. Cinnon stood aside from them, leaning his skinny body against the wall and gazing across the dusky desert. His club was on his back, his hands shoving bread in his face.

"What happened with Klayne Itopolo?" Fallo asked.

"Wasn't home. His servants say he's been gone a while. Somewheres east, they think."

The nosg army was in view, a stormcloud of dust spread wide behind them as they marched toward Stallid.

Gian was arguing with a man in breastplate and blue cloak. A sash of rank crossed his breast. A very fine sword hung on his hip.

"Yes, Anjel General," Gian said irritably. Fallo recalled that this man was the head of the army, and also Gian's father. That explained the argument. He moved to the Cloak and Grickel, standing well out of the fray. The Cloak eyed Quinn, who held her dagger.

He pointed to it, eyebrow questioning. She gaped at it in surprise and returned it to its scabbard. "The sight of nosg . . . Black still catches me by surprise sometimes. I know we saw the encampments, but I never imagined so many nosg existed in the whole world."

"And this is but a portion," Shad Grickel said. "Outriders just returned. There are miles and miles more of them coming."

The closest ranks were still a few miles off, the rest masked behind the dust cloud. A soldier stood upon a circular platform nearby, peering through a brass tube. "Swords, axes, spears. The usual weapons. More archers than expected. Gr'hils of twenty to thirty. Shamans with skull staves. I see swarmlight in the eyes. Bridge builders! Oh. It will go quickly. They bear timbers upon long wagons. I count . . . twenty within my watch area."

Fallo held Quinn as they watched the rising dust cloud and the tiny figures of swarming nosg.

"Trenches bridged," the observation man announced. "The front ranks come faster. They have begun to trot."

"Surely they do not mean to assault the wall upon arrival," the Anjel General said. "It would be pure folly."

"They have sped up," the soldier said, clearly not wanting to contradict the general, but also committed to declaring the facts as he saw them.

More men with the brass tubes were posted at intervals of a hundred yards. They called out their observations to the captains nearby.

The wall was thinly manned to Fallo's eye. But that appeared to be about to change. File after file of armored soldier was pouring into the space between the middle and outer walls.

Fallo stood at the tip of one of the wedge formations that thrust from the wall. The wedge had appeared to be very sharp from the ground. Now that Fallo was upon it, it seemed as broad as a boulevard. The tip of the wedge projected several dozen paces from the plane of the wall. A bunker was built into the floor where men waited below.

When Quinn asked why no soldiers were taking position atop the wall, Shad Grickel offered his guess. "The Indomitable Wall has never been besieged before. It was designed to counter the same attack as Stallid endured during the last nosg war. The walls were much lower then. The nosg bore down with siege engines and towers. Many men were killed by flying boulders, and splashes of flaming tar. These bunkers will allow protection from some of those attacks while keeping men close to hand to defend the wall and drop death on any nosg who approach with ladders or towers."

"Nosg gr'hils running! They attack!" the observation man called.

It didn't require a glass for Fallo to see that dozens of gr'hils had broken away from the main body. The shamans charged behind their squads, shouting and shooting forth colored rays from their staves. These served like lashes of a whip to drive their warriors to great speed.

All down the wall, similar ragged attacks were underway. There were no signs of any engines of war among the nosg yet. A captain barked to the men in the bunker and they stormed out to array along the wall. Every other one carried a bow; the remainder held stones. The ranks were backed by soldiers ready with quivers of arrows and gangs of boys ready to relay more stones to the droppers.

The sergeant of the closest files was shouting at his soldiers to remain steady. "These nosg are no threat to us. But they insult us. We will gladly kill them for it."

"I say let them mill about down there," Shad Grickel grumbled. "These gr'hils were obviously sent to test our response. When the others see the arrows and stones, they'll know better how to prepare for the next assault."

Fallo agreed with the stout shadline. It seemed foolish to waste the arrows on nosg that had no chance of breaking through.

As the nosg neared the wall, a flash of blue shot forth from one of the skull staves and struck another shaman in the head, dropping her instantly. Her staff struck ground and exploded, sending bodies flying forward to smack against the wall.

"They kill their own!" cried the observation man.

The girnt of the forward-most gr'hil, reached the wall first. He smashed straight into it, bounced back into his comrades and fell onto his back. He didn't move. The gr'hil cheered, hoisted their fallen comrade up and began jogging back to the nosg lines.

"Flyer coming!" the observation man shouted. "It does not appear to be a wyvok. But rather a . . . a woman."

The winged creature glided to earth very far away. The other gr'hils stopped their charge and ambled back to the line.

"What was the point of that?" Fallo asked.

"It looked like a foot race," Quinn said. "Perhaps they were to be rewarded if they reached the wall first."

"But why?"

"Winged woman greeting the gr'hils. She is giving the shaman a favor. A necklace I think. Hard to make out."

"I told you," Quinn said, nudging Fallo. "A footrace."

"It is well the men held their arrows and stones," Shad Grickel said. "Young Gian won that argument, at least."

The soldiers retreated to their bunkers. The observation

man called out all that he noticed about the gr'hils demeanor, number, and distance. This last measure was well established by the placement of the trenches and by stone markers placed on the ground. The ballistae mounted upon the walls could strike with deadly accuracy anything within that range. The nosg seemed to know this, and kept well back of it.

The dust cloud continued to build as the trailing horde moved to surround the city. Soon the air was full of grit that stung the eye and caked the back of Fallo's throat. The observation man dunked a rag in a water bucket and swiped it across his eyes and cleaned the end of his brass looking tube.

"Do those nosg look larger?" Quinn asked, pointing to a band off to the left.

They did indeed. Fallo called to the observation man, who slewed his brass tube to take in nosg in question. "Damn me!" the man shouted.

"What is it?" the Anjel General demanded irritably.

"Nosg. Huge ones. At least twice the height of the regulars."

Shad Grickel was there in an instant, demanding the brass tube. He placed it to his eye, jaw muscles bulging. "It is as I feared. We fought such a beast at the Hackwatch. These have crude weapons, but they will tell in close combat." He returned the tube to the observation man and went to consult with Gian and the Anjel General.

The ranks of the huge nosg continued to grow over the next quarter hour. As invincible as the wall was, it felt just a bit smaller knowing such beasts were out there.

"Wyvoks approaching!" the observation man shouted, voice cracking.

Indeed they were. Black shapes high up, where the dusty

cloud was thinnest. The wyvoks began to grow larger against a dust-red sky quickly fading to black as the sun set behind the city.

"They will not attack until dark," the Cloak said. "We will not be able to see them, but they will see us."

"Riders upon the wyvoks!" the observation man said, voice cracking. "Riders upon the wyvoks. I see . . . two nosg upon each."

Shad Grickel cursed. "Gian! Gian Delp! A word!" he shouted, voice booming like a sailor's. It carried to where the young monarch was conferring with his father and a passel of other military men. Gian motioned Grickel forward. Fallo followed.

"The wyvoks are mounted," Grickel said. "I assure you, such has never been done before."

The Anjel General spat. "Chekk preserve us. Those nosg could drop stones upon us here."

"That is the least of what I fear," Grickel said. "Surely you see it. They will mount shamans. The wall will be no barrier to them at all, and they will unleash their swarmlight upon the city."

"I should not be here," Fallo said, body thrilling with the certainty of it.

Grickel frowned. "Do not be ashamed of fear, lad. We all feel it."

"It is not fear of nosg," Fallo said. "I need to be in Cigil-Tine in twelve days. I do not see how I will make it, even without this siege. The need to go there is throbbing in this ugly skull of mine." Which was true. What he didn't say was that the prospect of battle thrummed in his blood. That he wished the nosg would attack so that he could lose himself in the fever of combat. That was the doing of his nosg blood.

"Rider!" the observation man shouted.

A man on horse came out of the south, riding hard. He had flanked the nosg horde and was riding along the wall. Several gr'hils saw him and started to race toward him.

"It is Balik Tol!" the observation man shouted, following it with a whoop. "Gr'hils giving chase!"

A cheer went up, but the Anjel General shouted them down. "Archers!"

Files of longbowmen returned to the battlements. With strict uniformity they nocked arrows, pulled, and loosed at the direction of their sergeants and corporals. The first flight arced out and down, smattering into the disorganized rush of nosg pursuing the horseman.

With thirty inches of wood behind them, the bodkin points drove into armor, flesh, and turf alike. The gr'hils wavered and Balik raced beneath the wall to the cheers of his countrymen above.

"Order the postern gate open for him!" Gian shouted to the nearest captain.

Fifty paces down the wall, men worked a ballista, which they cranked to draw tight a thick launch cord. Another man dropped a pan full of iron balls into a cupped tray. The captain sited the machine and cried, "Loose!" With a snap the ballista flung the balls away so fast Fallo could not follow their flight.

Nosg charging forward were suddenly knocked backward as balls impacted their bodies. The ballista men cheered and began to reset their machine.

The archers loosed flight after flight, murdering the pursuing gr'hils with vicious efficiency. Balik Tol drew his bow, loosing arrows without seeming to aim, horse galloping at full speed. The long bow made it impossible for him to draw fully, but the arrows soared. None missed that Fallo saw.

Nosg returned with volleys, but their arrows fell well short of the speeding horseman.

"Bring Balik up," Gian said. Two runners dashed away to greet the shadline archer in the courtyard.

Quinn's eyes were all asparkle. Nosg blood or no, Fallo did not crave a fight as much as Quinn did. And now she was as antsy as a child on Winternight at the prospect of meeting Balik Tol. "I read all about Sephie when Kila and I were at Ori's Home. And now I'm about to see Dark Smiter. I wish I hadn't been asleep through the whole Armory. Did you know Critt carried Shatter? And Gian carries Revenir. And Shad Grickel is holding Halish-Hel right now. All may be blooded soon. Ah, the glory of it!" She went on, but was muted when she drew her blade.

Balik Tol was smiling when he gained the top of the wall. He swept a courtly bow to Gian, then nodded respectfully to Shad Grickel. "I need to report a band of nosg threatening the city," he said to all assembled. He smiled broadly, weather-beaten face flushed from his ride.

Gian smiled at the man's joke and grasped his shoulders. "How did you get past them? And how did you get from the Hackwatch so quickly?"

"Didn't you know? I left the very day yon raven-haired lass came. Apologies to you, Shad Grickel. But I had to listen and obey. Smiter here was humming with urgency. And so I rode off. Got delayed in the Boil."

Several men cursed in astonishment and murmured about

traversing the Boil alone, much less at the speed Balik must have gone.

The bowman ignored them. "I hope I didn't miss anything important at the Armory."

Gian's face grew grave. "You missed much indeed. We can discuss it another time. You must eat and refresh yourself. Find an almen below to grant you sleep." Balik Tol bowed again and descended into the nearest bunker. Cheers of welcome followed him.

"Is it truly the best time for him to sleep?" Quinn said. "If Grickel is right about shaman on wyvoks, then every archer will be needed."

"Ah, I see your error," Gian said. "An almen's prayers will rest him as if he's had three nights of good sleep."

Fallo understood, somewhat. The almen were like Donse Masters, though they prayed to the multitudes of gods the Losstrans worshipped. "I haven't seen an almen since arriving. What do they wear?"

"Whatever they wish," Gian said. "You cannot identify one by her dress, but by her presence."

"Will they fight against the shamans?"

"No. Almen do not fight. They ask favors of the gods, to protect, heal, and strengthen. If they ask for harm against an enemy, they become sheelek and risk going mad. But almen have their ways to aid in the battle. They will pray to strengthen our arrows, bows, swords, and armor. They pray to strengthen the Indomitable Wall. They will pray to make our skin tougher, our muscles stronger. In that way, the enemy will feel their might."

The sun had set, the last glow fading to the west.

"Camp preparations," the observation man said. "A mile out. The closer ranks are building fires."

Thousands of campfires came alive, spreading along the width of the wall. Runners came to report similar lines surrounding the city. The siege of Stallid had begun.

54

IN THE SERVICE OF DAY

Her Enlightened Majesty's counsel chamber was crowded, the mood somber. A cheerful little fire burned in the hearth, and so that's where Henley kept his attention for as long as he could. It reminded him of long pleasant hours, steeping in his studies, near to a similar fire in his father's study. A lifetime ago.

The monarch sat upon a blue chair, wearing tan trousers and a blue blouse. The dragnithan, Eckso, sat to her left, looking like a Radiant in a flowing cream gown. Marlow sat to the monarch's right. Henley was sure there was more silver in his hair and beard than there had been just a ten-day ago. Across from him was Highest Quiv, lean, attentive, and seemingly calm.

The quelled dragnithan, Klayne, was next. His sewer sogged garments had been replaced with simple layman's clothes, but he still managed to look dashing. He was quelled by the combined effort of three merculyns: Quiv, Marlow, and Eckso. Ell held him in a willshift.

Coin Inlina sat bolt upright next to Marlow. Ell had

performed a healing on her but said the disease was beyond her abilities. She had eased the woman's suffering such that she could down a bit of food without grimacing.

Henley sat opposite the monarch, feeling a bit silly in the fine garb the servants had given him. Huff rested on his lap, shedding orange hairs onto the black of Henley's pants. Before them was tea, sweetbake, several books, and a large map.

The attention of everyone else there was upon the dragon-scaled object in the center of the table. The Motherlight.

"It was there in the palace all along," Henley said, pulling his gaze from the fire. "I think it was dormant, else every merculyn in the city could have felt it. She must have discovered a mercus map somewhere in the palace which led her to it."

"These secret passages you discovered . . ." Quiv began. "The map in that book showed them to you?"

"And allowed me to move through them. It was very odd. I think had I released the mercus, I would be encased in stone right now."

"It sounds like phasic mercusine," the scholarly Donse Master said. "The Markis of Dol had this book?"

Henley repeated Harl Illis's story and hoped the man had left the palace before it was locked down. With the events in the dome and the dead body of the Autarch in the garden, there would be city-wide repercussions. He hoped the intrigues didn't reach The Wilde Moon and poor Terissa Viller.

"Are we truly going to ignore," began the Coin, "that three demayne sit at the table with us?"

"Four, if you count the felnithel," the monarch said. "Though they truly are more than demayne."

"It is so," Eckso said. Even Klayne, who was willshifted

into immobility, closed his eyes in a sort of nod of agreement. "But there are demayne of Day and then there are demayne of Night." As if that meant anything at all. But Her Enlightened seemed to agree.

"And which are you?" the Coin asked.

"I flew at twilight," Eckso said, "as seemed reasonable. Nothing is all good or all bad, and most of life's delights lie somewhere in between. I have no love for my sister, I assure you. Nor for Klayne."

"Nor for Day or this world or humankind," said the Coin.

"I do love some humans. Two of them at any rate."

Henley was containing his anger fairly well, he thought. After hearing what Eckso had done to Kila, he was ready to blast her from existence. But Her Enlightened had stopped him, saying she was promise-bound to her now. He decided to bring his concerns up again. "I promise-bound Klayne, and he was able to disregard it easily."

"You have to phrase it just so," the monarch said. "And the bolts for a demayne are different. But promise-binding a dragnithan whose first flight was under the stars . . . almost impossible to make it last, even for one of your abilities. The demayne of Night do not value promises. It goes against their very nature. But enough of this. Coin Inlina, what led you from Garden Island to Tordain?"

"I intended to recruit my aunt's armies to stand against the coming nosg invasion. From there I intended to do the same in Jallisea, Sorgan, Wantin, and Trine, and Trist, and Slirya, and in every realm with a militia, until all were united and prepared. And such is still my intention."

Henley thought the woman was about to say something else, but she clamped her mouth shut. What was she withholding? "There was a Sensual with you at the palace. Who was she?"

"Sensual Roon was attached to my service by Voluptuary Minn, to assist me in realms where the Way of Ori holds more sway."

It sounded reasonable enough, but Henley thought something was hidden in her words. Not a false note—but another hesitation. There was more to it than she was saying. But the woman continued. "I had not intended to come to Starside until the last, knowing that Your Enlightened Majesty would most certainly send troops to the cause."

"We would and we have, isn't that right Marlow?"

"Indeed. Five thousand men have already left, supplied by a train of wagons, tradesmen, and camp attendants. They are likely half-way to the Sablefort now."

The Coin brightened. "That is excellent. I had thought the Sablefort the best base for such a force, though it is likely in disrepair after all these years."

"Since when is the Way of Pol a military religion?" Eckso asked. "Who granted you the power to demand these realms subject themselves to your will?"

"No one grants such power," Coin Inlina said. "One takes it. You surely know I'm dying. I am no tyrant planning to conquer the world. That may be Yiothizandra and Kila Sigh's way, but not mine." She ladened Yiothizandra's name with great skepticism, as if the dragnithan didn't truly exist. Or wasn't the true force behind the nosg gathering now that the Hargothe was dead.

"Kila is no tyrant," Henley said.

"She is a prisoner," the monarch said after a long silence.

"Eckso fitted her with a *vaz'on* and now she serves Yiothizandra."

"If she still lives," Marlow grumbled sadly. The man had an uncle's fondness for Kila, which endeared him to Henley.

"She lives," Henley said. "Huff would feel Nax's suffering should the bond be broken by her death." He didn't add that Huff had sensed a vague feeling of pain from Nax, but he wasn't sure if it was from Kila or simply the trials of Nax's trek. "Nax has been journeying north, apparently to Ceronhel, but just recently she turned westward."

"Westward?" Ell asked. "Why didn't you tell me immediately?"

"I was in Tordain fighting with Klayne."

"Did she turn west because Kila had moved west or simply to skirt an obstacle on her northerly route?"

"I don't know. She covers very little distance each day. The move west was so subtle Huff didn't notice it at first."

Ell stood and surveyed the map. "Put a marker on Ceronhel," she commanded Quiv, who sat closest to Yiothizandra's northern holdfast. He put a red disc on the map. "Dearest felnithel Huff," she said addressing the orange cat. "Would you please look in the direction in which you feel your sister Nax?"

Huff chirped and hopped onto the table then swiveled his head left and right until coming to a stop. Ell went to the wall and put a finger on it. "Here or left or right?"

To help the cat, Henley tapped his right forefoot. *Is Nax directly past the monarch's finger or on this side of it?*

The other side.

"To the left."

Her Enlightened slid her finger along the wall to the left.

Huff meowed and the woman stopped. "Here?" she asked.

Back a little, Huff sent to Henley.

Henley motioned the monarch to make an adjustment. She moved in small increments, pausing until Huff chirped.

Highest Quiv came forward with a quill and inkpot. Ell bade him mark the spot beneath her finger. He rushed back to the map. "The Citadel faces east. That window over there overlooks the city, and that one looks west toward the eyrie. The mark is . . ." He began to mutter numbers, then sent a man to fetch a knotted rope used to measure for construction.

With this he measured from the window to the mark and noted down some figures. "This isn't as precise as I would wish, but . . ."

He took a straight edge and placed it upon the map, one end on Starside. It pointed west and slightly north. "It appears Nax is heading to Losstra," Henley said. "Why would Yiothizandra take Kila there?"

"Stallid," Eckso said, eyeing Klayne. "Did Yiothizandra say she was moving against Stallid?"

Klayne blinked. Henley felt the monarch release some of the willshift, allowing the man to use his mouth. "Might I have a sip of tea first. My throat is—" He yelped and coughed. "Yiothizandra intends to take Stallid first. Now may I have a sip?"

He was allowed freedom to drink his tea.

Quiv put a marker on Stallid. "Even with tens of thousands of nosg, Stallid will withstand it. I've seen the Indomitable Wall."

"A siege is not about taking a city quickly," Coin Inlina said. "It is to deny the city resupply. To starve the citizenry."

"But time is not with her," Eckso said. "She will birth Kil

soon. She must have a realm ready before he comes of age. She expects to give him the entire world."

"And what age is that?" Marlow asked. "Ten? Twenty? I would say she has plenty of time to starve out Stallid."

"Kil will grow much faster than any human," the monarch said. "I agree with Eckso. Yiothizandra will not be content to wait out a prolonged siege. Patience has never been her strength. She knew of the Indomitable Wall as well as any of us. She would not attempt Stallid if she didn't believe it would fall. And do not forget, she has a dozen dragons to fight for her. Raginalt counted seven during his time at the eyrie above Ceronhel."

"Raginalt Keel?" Henley asked, incredulous. "I thought he was on Garden Island."

"No longer. Eckso took him to Ceronhel as leverage over Kila. We rescued him when we recovered her children. But the fool boy left Starside last night to search for Kila." Her Enlightened dismissed the boy from her thoughts with a wave of her hand. "The shadlines have dispersed, many go to courts where they have influence, to raise the armies of men, much as you sought to do, Coin Inlina."

"Shadlines serve their own ends," Inlina said. "They claim to serve Pol's will, but they merely seek to strengthen the power of their own cult."

"We have never claimed to serve Pol's will," Ell said. "We serve only the force of destiny. You are ill, Coin, but you can still aid us. I know you have coin-talkers in your service. Such communication will be essential in the days to come. We need to know what transpires in the far-flung realms. And they need to know what we've learned of Yiothizandra's plans. Do you think you can help us with that?"

"I can." She twisted her crane bracelet, which Henley had returned to her with her other relics.

"What about Kila?" Henley asked. "We have to rescue her."

Marlow nodded in agreement, but nobody else did. The Coin smirked. She'd made it very clear that she thought Kila an ally of Yiothizandra's, no matter what Eckso said about her wearing a *vaz'on*. "We have to *capture* her," she said.

Highest Quiv tapped the marker he'd placed on Stallid. "Kila must attend to herself. We cannot charge into the midst of a nosg army looking for her. The Way of Til is already spread thin searching for Dunne Yples. We caught scent of him in Traye, briefly. I cannot even be sure it was him, though the description sounds right. The odd thing is that he was seen among a band of Kila's followers."

"The Way of Kila," the Coin spat. "I hear they are organized even here, Your Enlightened Majesty. Why do you tolerate it?"

The monarch fixed the Coin with a steely glare. "I have tolerated much that I dislike in service of Day. The Way of Kila is misguided, not evil. Many of those who attach themselves to her are the lowest and most unfortunate, who would necessarily turn to crime or be victims of crime without the protection of the Way. If you have strength enough, venture to the Blasted Quarter and see for yourself what they have already built in this city."

"They are harmless enough," Marlow said. "Let us discuss the war. I do not yet hear a unified strategy in our discussion. Who will command the forces the shadlines recruit? Where shall they be stationed? They cannot all be posted at the Sable-fort. And shouldn't a sizeable army be sent to break the siege at

Stallid? And what of Tordain? It will erupt in civil war since the Autarch had no heir. Will we allow the greatest army in the world to fight against itself? And what of Kila Sigh? If she wears a *vaz'on*, then what merculyn does Yiothizandra have to wield her power now that Eckso and Klayne are here? Her power alone would be a threat to Stallid. And what about Kil? What is to be done when he is born? Won't it be too late for us all then?"

Klayne, still free to lift his teacup, grinned. "It was too late for you all when Yioth bedded the Hargothe the first time. All your efforts are like the futile thrashings of a drowning man in the middle of the ocean."

55

MY TRUE AND HONORED FRIEND

Yiothizandra came to Ahl-Mish-Lah at midnight. Her arrival was expected and all the wyvok shamans were there, ready to hear their queen's orders.

Yioth cupped her belly as she spoke. "Go aloft, set fire to every rooftop, destroy all the watchtowers, burn every human to ash. If your mimak runs low, the wyvoks should be given free rein. Ahl-Mish-Lah, you already know what I want of you." The new wurgu of G'galas Wyvok bowed low.

After a hearty cheer of *"Aggalamas alamas!"* the nosg dispersed. Kila followed Ahl to the wyvok fields, heart thumping hard but steady. Her pulse was locked to that of Yiothizandra's child now, no matter how far away she was. She wished that her experiment with the mimak had not failed, for now she had to fall back to her original plan. Ahl must not be allowed to breech the walls using Kila's power.

Longing for Nax, longing for Henley, Kila forced down an ache in her throat as she fed a haunch of goat to Jathesh. The beast wanted more, but Kila didn't want him laden down with food just now. He would be performing some rather severe stunts soon. Kila checked the saddle straps once more to make sure they were as she wanted them.

Ahl was more comfortable with the wyvok now, and eagerly clambered onto the saddle behind Kila. She'd had a special cupped stirrup added to hold the butt of her staff. Already the red gems glowed with menace.

Jathesh took to the air, letting out eager squawks. He took direction from Kila easily now, banking into a left wing circle as the remainder of the flight formed behind him. Ahl communicated her wishes to Kila through smacks on Kila's shoulders. A hard punch at the top of her spine signaled to head to the city. Kila readied herself for the action that would certainly result in her own death. A solemn sadness came over her.

I love you so much, Naxie. I wish I could have held you one last time. I wish you could hear me and tell Henley that I love him too.

Her tears froze on her cheeks as Jathesh beat for more height. The nosg fires sparkled below, and the great black wall of Stallid grew larger, jagged and imposing even seen from above.

Kila knew what it was to fall from a great height. She didn't fear it.

Thump-thump.

She had seen to the straps on the saddle herself. Had made sure the fore and aft ties were loose, the series of belly straps just snug enough to keep them on as Jathesh climbed.

The bracing straps that kept her legs tight to Jathesh's flanks were a bit looser than usual. Ahl hadn't noticed, for she wore thick fur boots that made up for most of the slack.

Kila couldn't gauge their height, but it overtopped the wall before them. The wyvoks behind did not shriek. As night hunters, they knew not to warn their prey. They would be invisible against the cloud-covered night sky.

Fallo leaned against the wall, rubbing his arms and stamping his feet against the cold. "I thought deserts were hot," he said.

Nobody answered his complaint. The observation guard had just announced midnight. The bunkered cohorts had been relieved by new archers an hour past. But Gian and the rest had stayed on the wall, waiting.

"Maybe they plan to starve us out," Fallo mused.

Quinn leaned against him, stealing warmth. "I don't think so. I feel . . . I think I can hear something. Not with my ears, but like how you say the force of destiny calls to you. I feel battle. It's as if the nosg are charging right now, like the beat of war drums in my chest. But all there is silence. It's maddening." She'd drawn Black half a dozen times in the past hour, only to drive it back into the scabbard and sigh.

"Aye," Shad Grickel said softly. "I feel it too."

"As do I," said Cloak Einlin.

"Aloft!" gasped the observation guard. He had his brass tubed trained up. "I see sparks of light. Red. Blue. Green. Here and there."

"Swarmlight!" Grickel said. "Shamans mounted on wyvoks, damn me."

With his words came the first strike. Rays of red beamed from the sky and swept across the wall. Men leapt away, cloaks smoldering. The beam continued across the inner two walls and then into the encamped refugees in the plaza. Tents burst into flames, screams rose, people ran, arms wheeling and blazing.

More beams burst down, igniting more tents. The sky was filled with colorful rays of swarmlight death. A watchtower in the city came alight as green pulses hammered the crenellations, throwing chunks free to fall onto the people below.

In these flashes Fallo could see vague winged shapes swooping low.

"Move!" Shad Grickel cried, pushing Fallo and Quinn along the wall like a bull set loose at a market. The stone exploded where they'd been standing as a red blast erupted from above. The entire width of the wall blew out over the flaming tents, crushing man and wagon.

"Such power!" the Anjel General shouted. "No nosg ever possessed so much!"

A furrow ten feet deep had been carved in the wall and now separated Fallo, Quinn, and Grickel from the Cloak and Gian. The observation guard and his platform were simply gone.

Bells began to clang. Archers rushed up, but they dared not loose their arrows over the city lest any that missed fell upon their comrades and citizens. Wyvoks began to shriek, and their mounted shamans threw down blast after blast of swarmlight.

KILA SAW the wall burst apart ahead of her, annihilating a lone guard on a platform as small figures dove away. She hadn't expected Ahl to strike there, since she'd been charged with destroying the gates. The shaman was pounding on Kila's left shoulder, indicating she should guide Jathesh in a circle. Apparently, Ahl had been eager to get an early blow in. Perhaps testing how much of Kila's power she needed to bring to bear.

Kila bumped her fist on Jathesh's neck once, twice, and then a third time. This signaled the steepest turn the wyvok could manage and stay aloft. Kila threw her weight into the turn rather than leaning against it.

The saddle slid. Ahl screamed in startlement. The straps caught. Kila yanked her right leg free of the strap and twisted, reaching for Ahl, snagging a fistful of the shaman's tooth necklaces. The points dug into her palms.

She threw herself sideways, hoping to dislodge the strap and slip the saddle under Jathesh's belly so that both riders would fall.

Her body froze and a great pressure struck over her right ear.

"No! No!"

Ahl knew. Somehow Ahl knew about the *vaz'on* willshift gem.

Total willshift claimed her. Jathesh came out of his bank, the saddle askew, but not so much that Ahl couldn't shift off it and onto the wyvok's spine. With nosg strength she hugged Kila to her chest. Using the butt of her staff, Ahl signaled Jathesh to land.

Kila screamed inside, infuriated to have her plan—her sacrifice—made useless. Jathesh winged down and alighted. Ahl was off the beast in an instant, and then Kila's limbs were moving of their own accord until she was kneeling. Slowly her hands raised to her throat and began to squeeze.

Ahl smashed the staff into her ribs, but the willshift kept her there unable to curl into the pain, unable to scream, unable to do anything except experience the agony fully and choke on her own cries.

Ahl struck again and again, cursing with rage. Jathesh screamed and flapped. Ahl sent a warning burst of red heat into the creature's side and it bounded away, squealing.

The staff cracked into Kila's ribs and something inside her broke. Still she held there, forehead grinding into the dirt, tears dripping, pain and her own hands choking her throat.

Her heart did not beat faster. Kil would not allow it. Anger —righteous outrage—hatred! It rose within her, like her gorge rising to spew out her guts. The same nausea, the same convulsions, except that Ahl's willshift forbade the muscles to spasm as they needed to.

But Kila's stomach was not trying to rid itself of her last meal of nosg porridge. It was her very soul trying to expel her rage.

Sludgy fingers grasped for her, deep inside of her. The Revulsion was thin here, but it gathered around her nonetheless.

Ahl allowed Kila to release her throat. She grabbed Kila by the collar, then flung her over Jathesh's back. The beast again leapt into flight. Kila gagged, raised her head. The willshift had released. Fires twinkled below. The nosg camp. Ahl tapped Kila's power and fiery blasts of swarmlight erupted from her skull eyes.

Ahl steered the wyvok with taps from her staff. Kila felt the beast swoop low, heard it scream, felt the insane blast of power flow from her into Ahl's staff and then outward. Rending iron squealed and clanged, men and nosg cried out.

Thunderous rumbles pummeled the air. Kila choked and spat as fine grit filled the air, covered her face and tongue.

The broken bit of her, the ribs and whatever organs they protected, felt like shards of pottery lodged in her flank.

She again tried to climb off of Jathesh. Forget about taking Ahl with her. She would at least deprive Ahl and Yiothizandra of her power. She had become what she swore she would never be.

Willshift weighed on her, so hard and unrelenting she might as well have been a newborn babe crushed under a carriage wheel.

FALLO AND QUINN stumbled toward the palace. They didn't need to show Gian's silver token. There was no organization left to the scattered clumps of soldiers and citizens. The world was on fire. Orange and red hatred illuminated every street, and the wyvok shamans continued to seek out anything that could burn, be toppled, or blown apart.

An arrow smacked into the street next to him, tip sparking on the stone. Archers had begun loosing over the city now, realizing that everyone would die if the wyvoks continued to fly. Four more fell in quick succession. "They must be aiming at something," he said.

In answer a shriek tore the air behind them. Instinct drove him to the ground, pulling Quinn with. Wind pushed him flat as a shadow passed overhead and crashed into the wall of the inner fortress of On'lin Keep. The wyvok peeled back from where it impacted, shedding the bodies of its riders. It fell backward into a burning stables, sending up heavy black smoke.

They picked themselves up and stumbled on. A man trotted past, clothes blackened with char. He held a bow. Balik Tol nodded and said, "Sorry about that one. Nearly got away. You folks well?"

"Well enough, shadline," Quinn said, eyes gleaming. "Listen and obey."

"Listen and obey." Balik tipped his head and dashed onward, nocking and loosing without pause. Everywhere his arrows flew, screams answered.

The pull on his instincts had split. The strongest pull was south toward Cigil-Tine, but another, more immediate pull was toward the keep. There wasn't much choice, since the keep was the last bastion of protection available. He doubted it would stand long, but at least they could get a mug of beer there. Trezz would be even better.

A shadow lumbered across their path. An animal, it brayed in terror.

"Tolky!" Quinn cried, grabbing the lead and pressing her forehead to its muzzle. Now leading the beast, they continued toward the keep. "Where's Shad Grickel?" Quinn asked, looking back.

"He joined a barricade team."

Stragglers were limping toward the keep's gate, which was open for all. A man in vest and billowing pants handed them cups of water as they entered. "Are you injured?"

"No."

"I cannot ask for blessings for anyone who is not injured. Go on."

He was an almen. Kindly, it seemed. Fallo felt a pull now,

downward. He recognized the feeling, for he'd felt the same in Cigil-Tine. The shadline instinct. "Cellars? Dungeon?"

"Such won't protect you long," the man said, "but through the baily, right along the gallery to the kitchens. Someone there can guide you."

"Why the dungeon?" Quinn asked.

Fallo shrugged. "It's what I feel."

She elbowed him. "You never let me use that excuse."

KILA WAS aware that a rock was poking her spine. She opened her eyes and instantly regretted it. The sun was lightening the eastern sky and sending daggers of agony directly into her brain.

Ahl-Mish-Lah sat nearby, eating something. Wyvoks were resting in the distance. Kila rolled over and instantly decided it was enough exertion for the day. Cheek pressed to the dry ground, she watched the shaman chew. For some reason the way Ahl's jaws worked and the intent look in her small eyes reminded Kila of Parlo Odok's strong man, Jocko. Ahl was much smarter than Jocko, but you wouldn't know it by looking at her. The resemblance made Kila chuckle, which made her innards grind against the broken pottery pain still lodged in her side.

Kila forced herself onto her hands and knees, and then to a seated position. Huge towers of black smoke rose from behind the Indomitable Wall. An enormous hole drew her eye, boring through each of three successive walls. Wide enough for fifty nosg to march abreast. Her power had done that, though she could hardly remember it.

The nosg were swarming through the gap now. Kila's mercus-heightened hearing picked up distant cries of terror and agony as they rampaged.

"They will kill them all, won't they?" she said.

Ahl grunted and bit off another bite of what now looked like ham. Apparently some food stores had already been looted from the city.

After swallowing her mouthful, Ahl hefted herself up and went to shout at her shamans and wyvok handlers. Kila simply breathed. She wished she had a flask of trezz. Usually she didn't drink the stuff, but it might ease the pain. Wen had used it during those lean days when they ran out of his medicine.

This thought brought up Finta Sahng's face. How long had it been since Kila had seen her last? Old Finta would have something to ease the pain. She always did. Enough of it would ease it permanently.

Frowning, Kila forced herself to stand. Finta would never allow Kila to kill herself. Never. She'd have some bit of wisdom and a big smile. Maybe a draught of something to ease the pain, but not to alleviate it entirely. Finta didn't believe the body could heal without some pain.

"In that case I ought to be the fittest I've ever been," Kila said, wishing Fallo was there to appreciate the joke.

Her hand searched for Cayne. Not there of course. Winnea had taken it. Her ring was there, heavy, useless. Highest of Kil. She tasted blood on her lips and spat a red glob into the dirt. Something was definitely broken inside of her.

She tugged at the ring, determined to fling it into the scrub.

It wouldn't come off. Her knuckles were too swollen.

The garnet caught the early sunlight, dazzling her for a moment.

For no reason a snatch of *Ana and Forli* rose to her mind.

> Oh, darling dagger, cut this mortal gown a life-
>   spilling seam,
> Join me to my love, in Lumne's wakeless
>   dream!

For no reason? No reason. No—

The mimak dream.

Hands shaking, she searched in her sleeve. Two red-caps came out. "Looks like medicine to me," she mumbled, laughing and noting the tinge of madness in it. She didn't relish having more of the strange hallucinations, but the real world before her wasn't offering much solace.

She shoved the mushrooms in, ground them to a nasty paste, and swallowed. She returned to her seat, feeling more than a bit nauseated. It wouldn't do to sick up the medicine.

That wouldn't do at all.

FALLO AND QUINN found Cloak Einlin in the kitchens, swallowing the entirety of a flagon of ale in one long backward tilt of his head. He gasped and handed the empty flagon to the man next to him.

His cloak was torn, the tail end singed ragged. Blood smeared his face, and open wounds wept on his arms.

"Please, sir," said a young woman in servant's livery. "Allow me to ask for healing. It won't take but a moment."

"Do not waste it on me, almen. I know others are more grievously wounded."

"Nonsense!" barked Gian Delp. He too was filthy with blood and grime. His eyes were sunken and part of his luscious black hair had been burned away, leaving a bubbling wound across his scalp.

The Cloak submitted to the woman's care. She took his face in her hands and bade him look into her eyes. She spoke very softly, calling upon the god of blood, if Fallo heard her right. Next she spoke to the god of flesh, saying, "And her of this flesh, be sealed, and her of all flesh, aid in the sealing. Make whole what is severed, return to wholeness that which has been rent. God of this man's strength, give strength to this man. God of all strength, give strength to this man. Fill him with vitality so that which needs rest is rested."

The wounds stopped bleeding then knitted closed, leaving only the drying blood behind. The Cloak straightened, lips parting, and a gasp of utter relief escaped him. The young woman pulled his face to hers. She kissed his cheeks, then bade him sit and accept another flagon of ale. When she was done, she ruffled his hair as if he was a boy and moved on to Gian.

"Well met, shadlines," the Cloak said to Quinn and Fallo. "I sense you are called. Go. Listen and obey."

Fallo gripped the man's forearm, wanting now to thank him for all he'd made him endure. The training, the travels, the hardship. He'd become a man, true and independent, thanks to the Cloak's endless patience. The Cloak cut him off before he could embarrass himself. "Where is Lop?"

"This is the kitchen. She's got to be here somewhere." The cat had made it to On'lin Keep earlier in the assault, he knew.

Lop, where are you?

The cat hopped onto the Cloak's lap, seemingly out of nowhere. The man gave a start, then relaxed. A wolfish grin spread his lips.

"How is it that this animal grows so fat so quickly?" But then the man's eyes gleamed with moisture and he stroked Lop from ears to tail. "Be well felnithel. Take care of Fallo and Quinn." Lifting his eyes to Fallo's, he swallowed before continuing. "My true and honored friend, noble shadline, bearer of the Dragon Tooth Blades. Hope fades like the dying day, but a spark remains as long as true hearts serve the cause of good. Go my friends. Listen and obey."

"Listen and obey," Fallo said, Quinn echoing him. Her voice hitched and she turned away. Fallo could do nothing but follow her, choking upon the ache in his throat.

Come, Lop, the force of destiny calls.

56

A QUICK STOP

"I cannot go with you, Henley," Marlow said. "You understand."

"I do. Just show me how this thing works."

They stood among a circle of columns at the Derslin Wheel beneath a jewelry shop in upper Terriside. Marlow pointed. "This symbol here is for Stallid. I think it represents On'lin Keep, but as the elnisians thought of it." He went on to explain how a column portal was opened and demonstrated the bolts. It was simple enough.

Henley had his satchel over one shoulder, weighed down with spare clothes, food, and the Motherlight still encased in dragon scales. Huff sat at his feet, taking care of some last minute grooming.

Marlow gave him a very roughly sketched map, showing what symbols went to what places. "Which one is Trist?"

The monarch's counselor blinked. "This one here. Why Trist?"

"Just a quick stop. Thank you, Marlow." He found the needed column and formed the bolts. The portal burned open before him, revealing a Derslin Wheel on the other side. Huff hopped through and Henley followed.

Dozens of campfires lay before him in the Derslin cavern. Out of the darkness came a nightmare of brutish faces and glowing eyes. Nosg, it would seem.

He drew upon the Motherlight and destroyed them all with fire.

Fifteen minutes later he found a simple wooden door. The passage beyond dead-ended in a stone wall. Henley walked through it and came out in a wine cellar. Servants cried in alarm as he and Huff climbed a staircase which opened into a butler's pantry. They strode out the kitchen door into the garden, ignoring the alarm being raised about the strange intruder.

Well, Huff?

That way. Huff looked east.

How far?

Not far. Nax says she is hungry.

You can talk to her?

I just told you she was hungry. Let's go find her.

57

THE SAME AS IN FLESH

Ahl forced Kila back onto Jathesh using willshift. "What other gems do? I will know soon."

Kila didn't care. The mimak had eased some of her pain. It also gave a shimmery outline to everything in the world. Ahl's was red. Jathesh's was yellow. The effect was not as dramatic as the first time. In fact, it was rather pleasant. The world appeared to be alive in ways she had never suspected. The shimmer was a sheen of mercusine, surrounding and infusing everything.

Jathesh winged upward, the flight again forming behind him. Ahl said that humans were fighting nosgs and that the great queen wanted them all burned. It was taking too long to clear out the city. "Maybe I bring G'galas Wyvok here. I make this home for my drikks. Mountains too cold."

Kila drank in the eerie world as seen through the mimak, delighting in the shimmery glow surrounding the wyvoks. Another beast flew higher up. A dragon. Bazron, his scales eating light, but also sending forth sparkles of blackness. A remarkable effect that made Kila uneasy. She looked away and found Fritor and Tortyr.

They dove and sent forth flames, but it appeared to be for sport rather than from any sort of strategy. Still another figure swooped over the city. That was Yiothizandra, soaring upon her dragon-like wings as she inspected the work of the night before.

She sparkled too, and her aura changed from red to green to black. Kila felt even more uneasy looking at her. The thump of Kil's heart came louder to her when she was looking.

Kila pushed her hand from her sleeve to peep at her ring. The gem was aglow with swarmlight. Smiling, Kila reached for it, as she had so often reached for her own mercus power.

It retreated, slipping away like so much water.

That wasn't the *vaz'on's* doing. No. It was the nature of the power. It could not be wielded the same way she was used to.

The eyes. The skulls' eyes. The shamans' power had never been about the skulls. That was a nosg tribal tradition. The eye-gems were the secret. They collected the swarmlight. The eyes projected the power. Kila turned her hand palm up, so that the ring faced down at the saddle leather. Closing her eyes, she felt for the swarmlight.

Yes. There it was. Warm, ready. If the gem was her eye, what would she see? The leather, the grain of the leather, the stretch of it over the wooden saddle form. And what if she saw that leather begin to smoke, to sear away in a tiny line as she swiped her vision across it?

A flame sprouted on the saddle. Kila released the swarmlight and patted it out. Ahl didn't notice, for she was watching Yiothizandra.

Kila considered her choices. She could sever the straps

with the swarmlight. But Ahl would notice before she got all of them. The willshift would return and then she'd never be able to direct the ring where she needed to.

Patience. She needed patience.

Yioth directed shamans to destroy barricades, demolish watchtowers, burn fleeing soldiers. She made Ahl begin to smash a new hole in the wall, this one on the west side. Kila endured the searing flow of her own power as Ahl pulled it through the *vaz'on* and shot it from her skull. With practice Ahl had learned how to focus the power to do even more damage. Boulders blown from the wall flew into the desert, smashing into nosg ranks on the western perimeter. Ahl did not stop, for Yiothizandra demanded immediate action.

Only when a gap in all three walls allowed the western ranks to flow in, was Ahl allowed to land and rest. It didn't take long for the shaman to doze. Kila stood, knees weak, side aching, but mimak still making the world scintillate. First she snatched the skull staff away from the shaman, then she took her bag of mimak. It was nearly empty.

Ahl stirred, then shot up. There was no demand for Kila to drop the staff. Ahl charged, fangs bared.

Kila saw through the skull's eye gems, saw Ahl-Mish-Lah gasping for breath, saw her clutch at her throat. And so it was. The air around the shaman's head retreated, leaving her gawping and drawing useless breaths. The small eyes widened as she collapsed onto her knees. Kila drove the butt of the staff into the nosg's gut, folding her over.

Kila released the feat, allowing Ahl to suck in air. Through the skull's eyes, Kila wished to see pinpricks of irritation on Ahl's skin, like thousands of insect bites. And so it was. Ahl scratched desperately, now writhing upon the ground as unabating itches assailed her.

Kila laughed and slammed the staff into the shaman's torso.

Inside her mind, greedy fingers wove into the void where her mercusine should have been. *Yes*, it seemed to say. *Yes. Now me. Use me too!*

Kila let the itching go and heated Ahl's flesh with rays of red. Not too much, slowly at first. *Make her cook! Make her sear!*

She shook her head. Those weren't her thoughts. That was the sludge. The nauseating sludge. But it didn't sicken her so much now. Her rage, her thirst for vengeance, her desire to witness Ahl's suffering was stronger. The Revulsion surged, drawn by Kila's hatred.

"Enough!" Kila shouted at herself. "I can't—I can't—I won't be that."

The wurgu of G'galas Wyvok flailed and shrieked. Kila went closer and closer, until she was standing over the tortured shaman. With all her might, she swung the skull into Ahl's face, releasing swarmlight fire and obliterating her hated captor's entire head in a red mist.

The Revulsion slithered out of her as she brought her vision into her own eyes and not so much through the skull's eyes.

That was close, Naxie. It almost had me. She felt the bond inside her, no weaker than it had ever been. But she wished she could talk to the little gray. Wished she could draw strength from her as she had done so many times before. But perhaps it was well that Nax was far away. Safe from this war.

Other nosg had noticed Ahl's death. They were crying out

and pointing. Shamans were peering at her but keeping their distance.

Kila stretched and steeled herself. There was more fighting to come. She had been willing to die. She still was.

"Jathesh, come."

Once aloft, she guided the wyvok with gentle nudges and taps. She seared through other wyvoks' wings, sending them tumbling into the city. She'd felled a dozen before the others realized what was happening.

Shamans sent rays at Jathesh, but Kila understood the mercus. She saw negating bubbles around her and her mount. And so they sprang into existence. Their red and green and violet attacks sizzled out. She returned them with fire. There was no reason to aim for riders. The wyvok's wings made them utterly vulnerable.

Yiothizandra had returned to camp earlier. She was no concern at the moment. The dragons were enraged and Bazron ordered Jathesh to dump his rider. The terrified wyvok struggled to obey, flapping low over the burning plaza, twisting and banking. The inner wall loomed ahead as Jathesh struggled to climb past it.

Kila couldn't access the wyvok's mind as she could with her own mercus power, but she held on long enough to leap from his back and land atop the great wall.

She tumbled, lost the staff, then skidded on her belly until her feet dangled over the side. Her palms were flaming with abrasions. A roar warned her of an incoming dragon. She scrambled for the staff.

Behind her, Jathesh winged away, shrieking in fear. Kila leapt up, staff eyes flashing. She stood alone atop the wall, wind blowing her fur cloak behind her, ring and eye-gemmed skull sending beams of death at Bazron. His infinitely black scales absorbed the power, suffering no apparent damage. But he roared and circled away.

She turned more beams to the sky.

Wyvoks fell.

Deeper in the city, a soldier atop the one remaining watchtower watched her through his brass tube, marveling at the tiny figure surrounded by a dome of red light that flashed white when other bolts of power struck it.

"One of their own fights against them!" he cried. Was that a jeweled crown upon the figure's head? It was.

The figure raised its staff to throw pulses of red skyward. And all over the city, wyvoks folded and fell. Dragons screamed and flamed their rage. A great black one swooped low over the wall, engulfing the lone figure in green fire.

But when it passed, the tiny figure still stood. "That's no nosg!" he shouted. "That's no shaman, though it wields a shaman's staff. It's—it's . . ." He lowered his tube and gaped. "It's a girl . . . wearing a crown."

Tortyr plucked the watchman up in great claws, ripped him in twain, and threw the bloody pieces into a flaming barricade.

On the wall, Kila whirled with the staff, seeing through its eyes. The world was red, glazed over with swarmlight fury. She had survived Bazron's first pass, but she did not think she could negate that much heat again. Not without more mimak.

She raced along the wall, seeking a way down. There, a stairway. Down, skittering on her heels, maintaining balance with pure thievish instinct. Bodies smoldered down here. Kila crouched close to the wall, skull eyes down to hide the swarmlight from above.

The remaining wyvoks had retreated now, flying in vulture circles very high over the city. Larger forms joined their spiral. She now counted seven dragons. She pulled the last two redcaps from the bag. There would be more in the city if she could find any of the fallen shamans.

At ground level, Stallid was a fellstorm of fire and destruction. Huge boulders were strewn across a vast inner plaza. The remains of a tent camp were now a smoking black ruin. She hugged the wall, not daring to go out into the open. Nosg poured through the wall openings, grunting and screaming. They moved among the burning tents, jabbing at bodies. A nearby group found a survivor and fell upon him with vicious glee.

At the other side of the plaza were the stumps of two watchtowers that had been blown over, throwing more stone across the plaza. Beyond that, black smoke and billows of dust rose in thick columns to the heavens.

The nosg didn't notice her, for they were pushing deeper into the city. She brought the skull up, turned the eyes to face her. If she could just see the *vaz'on* through those eyes . . . she turned the gem over her left temple. It spun freely and did not loosen the bolt.

She tried again, focusing the swarmlight upon it, willing it to catch.

But it didn't work that way. The *vaz'on* was not a swarmlight relic. Perhaps it could work if she were not wearing it. She didn't know.

She remembered her father's saying when she was frustrated with her early failures at picking pockets. "You have the hands and feet you have. No sense wishing for others."

The staff and the swarmlight would do. She would wield

them until the mimak wore off. And then she would fight with her hands, and when her strength failed, she would die defiantly.

She found a door into a guard barracks for men posted at the wall. Inside everything was in disarray, tables toppled, chairs bunched together, shelves emptied as from a great shaking of the ground. But she found what she sought. Water. She dipped a cup in the barrel and drank it down. Again. Another cup over her face.

Every object shined in her vision. The red glaze had faded as she had brought her focus to her own eyes. The swarmlight still pulsed in the skull eyes and her ring. Three nosg burst in. She raised the staff. They skidded, faces going slack in confusion. Behind them crowded more of their gr'hil. The largest, the girnt, urged the others to attack. Kila waited for the shaman to appear behind the girnt. It was thin, dressed in a crudely stitched robe of hide, chest festooned with necklaces. The gem-eyes of its tiny fox skull staff glowed a brilliant yellow. Kila burned the shaman's head off. The fox skull fell, exploded, sending nosg flying toward her. She slammed a protective thickness into the air around her and dove aside.

"That's a ridiculous weakness," Kila muttered as she eyed the skull staff in her own hands. She had no sense that it was so pressured with swarmlight that it would blow apart.

Smiling grimly, she left the barracks and went into the plaza. She did not slink or sneak, but simply strode out. The shamans were easy to see, for their skull staves were like banners in the smoky chaos of the plaza.

They did not have the skill to defend and attack at the same time, and they were bent on destruction. A purple flare erupted to her right. She sent rays of red sunfire toward it. The shaman never had a chance to scream, but his skull blew apart, sending nosg bodies fountaining away.

A red flash ahead. She pulsed it with her swarmlight. Heat was easy to manifest through the skull eyes. It seemed to be the most common feat the shamans performed.

She began to run, destroying warrior and shaman alike with quick pulses of swarmlight. Her feats were clearly more powerful than theirs. She did not think it was due to the red-cap mimak, but from the experience she had with the mercus. She was able to manifest more power with the same effort. And quicker.

An enormous esgin nosg loomed over her, swinging a tree trunk maul straight down. Swarmlight blew the weapon from his hands and it sailed away. She wheeled and blasted the giant with fire, leaving it dancing and howling in red flame.

Grinning, she made her staff twirl, swinging the eyes to look at this shaman, that girnt, this warrior. Each died. A girnt lunged from thick black smoke and she cracked his head with her skull staff, misting his head into nothing.

Two more esgin lumbered from the smoke, roaring and circling to come at her from two sides. They died of suffocation.

A horrific roar shattered the air behind her, she dove, made a bubble of negation around her, but still felt the singeing heat of dragonfire pass over her. It left the stone around her black, the iron of a cookpot melted slag. Where there had been nosg and human bodies, there was not even ash remaining.

Rolling, she threw red fire at the retreating dragon. It was Bazron again. The swarmlight had no effect. And of course it wouldn't. No amount of heat would damage a beast that could spew flame from its mouth.

Clambering to her feet, she raced along the burnt-out trail the dragon's flame had seared through the plaza. More nosg were filing in from outside. She turned and blasted them, sparing shots of cold up toward the circling dragons. They were too far away to kill, but one bolt connected and the creature swerved away and descended outside the walls.

Shamans threw new powers at her. Tried to suffocate her. Tried to heat her bones. Tried to blow her down with gusts of wind. But she could feel the swarmlight coming, knew its nature before it reached her. She answered these with momentary negations, like parrying blows from a blade.

A blade. She spotted a nosg sword nearby. She lifted it upon swarmlight and shot it skyward, arrowing it with greater and greater speed to intercept Fritor. She did not bother to watch the effect, for she had to contend with thousands of nosg esgin now spreading through the plaza. Even as quick as she was with the staff, she could not keep them all at bay.

Slowly she backed away. Something shrieked high up.

The nosg stopped, lifting their gazes. Hairs prickling, Kila darted left and dove. An immense impact behind her made the ground shudder, breaking loose more stone from the ruins of the surrounding buildings.

Fritor lay in a crumpled heap, half buried in the smashed pavement of the plaza. The hilt of a nosg sword thrust out from one dimmed eye. From far away arose a howl. Of rage. Of pain.

Kila hurled swarmlight at the nosg, defended attacks, blew entire gr'hils apart. Her heart never wavered from its slow purposeful pace, but her breath sped up. Sweat coursed down her face. The swarmlight scintillations surrounding everything began to dim. Her attacks weakened.

The mimak was burning off. She drifted right, to the broken form of a downed wyvok. The shaman was pinned beneath. She rifled through its pockets, found its mimak pouch. Empty.

The nosg converged, shamans hiding behind girnts and esgin.

Desperate, Kila sought to press all the swarmlight she could into a final feat. The gem eyes glowed so brightly the world became a piercing red fire. Grunting, Kila hurled the staff. It flipped end over end, striking the plaza between her and the nosg.

It released a silent flare of light that shot away from her in a visible liquid wave, smashing nosg and shamans into the ground. A rumble returned and the ground shook so violently she lost her footing and fell. More chunks tumbled from the wall and behind her a bell fell from a far tower and resounded with doom gongs as it bounced.

Something rose into the air from beyond the Indomitable Wall. Kila knew Yiothizandra instantly. The dragnithan queen soared over the wall, then glided down to land in front of her ranks of nosg.

Kila threw ice at the woman using her garnet ring, knowing that no attack would have effect while Kil was within her. The swarmlight dissipated before it reached her. Yiothizandra held her sword in her hand as she stalked forward, wings folding in and vanishing.

She wore a cloak of fur and nothing else. The garment was open from neck to belt, belly protruding. Each stride exposed long, slender legs. Her eyes were fire, mouth pressed into a sneer.

"Enough, Kila Sigh," she said softly, but her voice carried

easily through the hush that pressed over the plaza. "Do you truly think you can defeat every nosg? The hundreds you've killed are nothing to me. The wyvoks you downed are easily replaced. Look around you. Stallid has fallen. It cannot stand against my forces, my dragons." Her eyes flitted to Fritor, then back to Kila. "For Fritor's death, you shall pay in agony."

Kila's ring weighed heavily on her hand, but the gem was dark. She backed away, saw a broken soldier. She freed his dagger from his hand and held it up, ready to fight her last fight. Yiothizandra continued toward her, swiftly, purposefully.

The dragnithan's bare feet struck the ground in time with her babe's heartbeats, which Kila felt in her own chest. Here at the end of her life, Kila felt fear drain away. Yiothizandra promised pain, but what else had Kila endured since her capture?

Kila dropped the dagger and lowered herself to her knees. She brought her hands to her heart. *Thump-thump.* The babe's heart and hers were locked together. Yiothizandra's stride was perfectly in time to the cadence.

Roya Reth had spoken through the child Pennie: *"The force of destiny has meter, but, alas, no rhyme."*

No reason to remember that now. Except for the meter of the heartbeat, the rhythm. The unstoppable stride of Yiothizandra, mother of Kil, like the lulling meter of verse.

Join me to my love, in Lumne's wakeless dream . . .

The force of destiny has meter.

Thump-thump.

"Open for Kil's daughter," Kila whispered. It was the phrase that had opened Annisforl's room in Kil's Keep. The message her father had concealed in gold script on a mirror's silvering. The message only she could see because her mercus vision showed her metal.

Yiothizandra raised her sword, her teeth gritted as she summoned her dragnithan strength. The sword would drive into Kila many times. She foresaw the blur as the blade ate and ate and ate, greedy and insatiable for blood, for more than blood. It wanted life itself, the formless fire that gave movement to matter. It would imbibe upon her soul, entrap it where it could torture her without end.

The absolute stillness of the moment came over Kila. She recalled a Winternight long ago, out on the roofway with Wen, as snow drifted down in huge flakes, lit from below by mercus light. How peaceful. How magical had been the stillness of Starside that night.

That stillness encompassed her now, punctuated by the slow and steady beat of her heart. Yiothizandra's blade arced down, point first, blazing toward Kila's chest.

"Kil, protect your daughter," Kila whispered.

The blade's name came to Kila's mind—*Flayshui!*—as tip pierced flesh and impacted her breastbone. Light blasted upward, throwing Kila back and Yiothizandra in the opposite direction.

The sword whirled straight up, a silvery blur, then tumbled down, striking stone and humming with vibrations as it stuck, half buried in rock. Kila saw dragons and wyvoks flying overhead, as if through a lacy veil of black.

Tortyr wheeled and flamed as another dragon swooped toward it. The new beast shimmered like a pearl and released its own white flame as it locked with Tortyr. More screams rose.

A shadow swept over Kila, and a heavy buffet of air kicked

dust up all around. Someone called her name, but it came to her muffled and distant.

And then a familiar face hovered over her. The lips moved but Kila couldn't hear the words, they came to her slow and low. The woman's name failed to come to Kila's mind. She was Fallo's friend. Fallo and the Cloak's friend. She had saved Quinn.

A weathered finger reached toward Kila, the tip smudged black. It lifted her lids and swiped painfully across her eyes. Then a searingly cold line drew over her forehead.

"Kila!"

Coughing and spitting dust, Kila struggled to sit up. The name came to her then. "Zirhine?" The woman had one arm bound close to her body. A dragon stood tall behind her, wings wide, acting as a shield.

Zirhine pulled Kila to her feet. Yiothizandra's sword still sang with vibrations nearby. Kila reached for it, but Zirhine knocked her hand aside. "Not that blade. Never that blade. We must go now, the nosg are coming."

Sound rushed back to Kila. The roar of the nosg army. Blasts of swarmlight impacted the dragon towering over her. Its body jerked with each impact, but it maintained its protective stance.

Kila knew the dragon. "Harnzyne? Is Ell here?"

Zirhine answered. "I don't know. I just arrived with the dragons of Day. But they are too few and cannot defeat so many of Night. We must go."

Zirhine dragged Kila toward Harnzyne.

Escape. Yes. She could live. But no. That did not matter.

"I'm not finished," she said, wrenching her hand free of Zirhine's.

"Kila, you can do nothing with the *vaz'on* blocking you. Come with me. We'll find a merculyn to remove it."

But Yiothizandra was here. Now. Kila could end it.

She moved away from Zirhine. Yiothizandra lay on the stone, curled around her belly. She moaned.

Kila stood over her, struck by the woman's fierce beauty. Zirhine tugged at Kila, but it took no effort at all to yank free again. "Zirhine, do you know anything of midwifery?"

"I—I do. But surely you don't mean to . . . but I see that it must be."

Zirhine knelt by Yiothizandra and hesitantly placed a hand on the woman's belly. The dragnithan winced and flailed at Zirhine, knocking her back five paces. When she saw Kila her eyes flared with fire. "No! I fed you to Flayshui!"

Before Kila could answer, the face contorted and scales appeared across her flesh. The mouth parted showing fangs and glowing rage deep in her throat. Kila knew dragonfire was coming. Harnzyne too, for he lurched to sweep his wing between Kila and the flame.

The dragon's veins showed briefly as it was lit by Yiothizandra's fire. Yelping, the dragon pulled its wing away, smoking. Yioth was on her knees, one hand under her belly. The other reached for Kila. With blurring speed, Yioth lunged, grasping Kila's throat. Again the fire built within her. It blasted from the twisted mouth and blew over Kila's face like a hot summer wind.

But nothing more.

"I am Kil's daughter," Kila said.

The nosg were closing in, forming a circle around their queen, Kila, and the dragon. Hundreds of skull eyes glowed brightly, full of swarmlight and ready to destroy her. Harnzyne spat a sweep of fire, forcing them back.

Yioth squeezed Kila's throat, her own face pulled back into an animal snarl. A convulsion doubled her over, and Kila slipped free.

Inside of her strange calm, Kila felt a feat building. It was powered by her rage, and hate, and frustration, and the total sum of all her suffering. Her heart beat out slow and steady, but a coldness settled into her gut. A numbness.

The oily blackness of the Revulsion reached for her. Not from desperation this time, but from a sense of supreme arrogance. What were these puny nosg to her? They didn't merit her consideration at all, not even as enemies. They were nothing. Less than insects.

Yes!

The voice was inside her. Not Nax's. Not the same at all. Not Bazron's or Harnzyne's.

The Revulsion flowed into her and she welcomed it. She formed bolts of black flame and gusts of wind and all the tricks she'd learned from Ahl. She vanished the air from the entire plaza, finding herself now above it, flying upon the upthrusting power of black mercus.

"SUBMIT!" she said, casting her voice full of black tones. These words struck not with authority, but with terror. The nosg prostrated themselves at once. Settling back to the ground she toed Yiothizandra who was grimacing in agony. With a curl of a finger, Kila roused Zirhine. "ATTEND!"

The woman crawled over the shattered and fire-blackened stone to Yiothizandra. Tears streamed down her face as she crooned comforting words to the dragnithan.

Harnzyne bellowed and took to the air. Kila spared him a

moment's glance. She had never before seen so coldly, so clearly. The world revealed itself in its true nature for the first time. All these bodies before her were no different from the stones they lay upon. She looked at one gibbering girnt and saw into it, felt with Revulsion-heightened senses the subtle bonds that held its flesh together. Curious, she released those bonds.

The girnt became smoke and blew away.

"IT IS AS I SEE IT," she said, turning her eye to the Indomitable Wall. The bonds there were the same as in flesh. She released them, and the wall became less than dust, less substantial than vapor. The entire east-facing stretch simply ceased to exist and flitted from view.

Turning her eyes down, she saw Yiothizandra as a pulsating form of mercusine, run through with thick veins of black corruption. Inside her was the bright-form, the essential, the child.

"The babe is too large," Zirhine said. "It needs to be cut out."

"So be it. Yiothizandra is nothing, as you are nothing, as this world is nothing but a vergent's dream."

Yiothizandra bent forward and shrieked, flame dribbling from her lips, tears sizzling on her cheeks.

Kila knelt and placed her hand on the dragnithan's belly.

"Kila!" Zirhine shouted. "Kila Sigh! Come back!"

58

LISTEN AND OBEY

The Derslin Wheel glowed ahead as Fallo and Quinn pressed through the darkness. "It takes the time it takes," Quinn said, leading Tolky who was determined not to go any faster than an amble. "Running will make no difference."

Fallo had never been in a Derslin cavern before. And he didn't much like it. But urgency was pulling him on. The columns were visible now, lit by a sourceless light. A blueish flare appeared among them.

"That's a portal opening," Quinn said.

Lop rode atop the donkey. *Huff is here! Nax is here!*

A familiar and welcome friend emerged from the portal. Henley held a sphere of blue power in one hand, raised and ready to throw.

"It's us, you idiot," Fallo called. "Don't jolt our bones apart."

"Fallo?"

The reunion was fierce. Fallo embraced his fiery-haired friend. Quinn hugged them both. The cats meowed and nosed each other and sent joy through their bonds. But it was short-lived.

"Huff says Kila is in trouble," Henley said.

"So nothing has changed," Fallo said. "Where is she?"

"Out there."

"What? We just came from there. Stallid has fallen to a nosg army. They've got wyvoks!"

Henley clearly didn't know what a wyvok was, but he didn't seem the least concerned when Fallo described nosg shaman and swarmlight skull eyes. He patted his satchel. "I can handle that. I have to get to Kila. Come on."

Fallo didn't move. "I can't. Shadline call. I have to go to Cigil-Tine."

"How were you going to open a portal?"

"I didn't know. But my instincts pulled me here." Fallo unrolled Kila's map and pointed at the symbol that would take him and Quinn to Cigil-Tine. The three of them split up and circuited the columns until Quinn found it. "Are you sure?" Henley asked.

"Listen and obey," Fallo said, and without a hint of irony.

Henley opened the portal and Fallo and Quinn plunged through, leading a donkey with a cat on its back.

59

THE AWED SILENCE

Kila, what are you doing? Nax sent.

Kila blinked. Blinked again. Black oil oozed across her vision. Her hand burned on Yiothizandra's belly. The pulse of the babe within hammered against her palm, even as it rammed in her chest

Her chest hurt so badly. She pressed her free hand there, found blood.

"You're wounded," Zirhine said.

Nax?

I'm coming. You . . . smell. The Revulsion has you.

The Revulsion did have her. Because she welcomed it. It didn't make her sick now. It made her powerful. She closed her eyes, feeling a deep communion with the babe yet to be born.

Kila, Henley's coming.

Henley, can you hear me?

Yes. There was strain in the bond. His voice was so distant in her mind. *What's happening?*

Kil is coming.

Kila sought to break the bonds of Yiothizandra's abdomen. But the Revulsion could not penetrate the dragnithan flesh. Was Kil protecting Yioth's flesh even as he was threatening to destroy her? Kila's head was pounding now. The smear Zirhine had drawn on her forehead burned with a deeper cold.

Men's voices rose behind her. "Stay back." That was Cloak Einlin's voice.

She felt Nax and Henley's presence, but it was still muted.

Yiothizandra screamed, back arching, fingers digging into stone and crumbling it in her fists.

"The babe grows so quickly," Zirhine gasped. "I can feel it."

Dragons began to alight in the plaza. Bazron, Tortyr, and others Kila did not know.

Bazron, go, Kila ordered. *Take the others with you.*

We will witness Kil's birth.

Pressure clamped in Kila's chest. Her heart thumped faster now. "The babe must be born."

"I feel the strain," Zirhine said. Her hand was atop Kila's, pulsing upwards with Kil's every heartbeat. "We must cut him free."

"Do it!" Yiothizandra commanded through gritted teeth. Her scales and fangs had gone. She was again a lovely woman. "Cut him out."

Zirhine pulled a dagger. "Move your hand aside, Kila."

It took all her strength to withdraw, for her palm felt melded with Yiothizandra's flesh. Zirhine pressed the tip of the blade to the taught skin. Pressed harder. She lifted and stabbed. The blade skittered off Yiothizandra's skin as if on stone.

Yiothizandra screamed. Kila fell back. Heart racing, aching, as Kil's heartbeat drove hers faster and faster. She couldn't catch her breath.

Zirhine drew Reft from her back, the curved shadline blade gleaming. It was too large for the task, but she sliced it across Yiothizandra's abdomen. A squealing scrape pierced the air, and sparks shot out. The dragnithan's skin was unmarked.

Kila felt the Revulsion swarming deeper into her. Her heart slammed.

I'm going to die, Nax.

Don't do that. I'm coming.

An enormous pressure was building inside of Yiothizandra. Kila felt it like waves of heat, like a flute's highest warbling pitch, or like a rumble of thunder of a storm about to break.

She foresaw the city utterly flattened, the land all around seared to blackened waste. A towering cloud would rise and rise and a wave of wind would flow ever outward, crushing man and tree and nosg alike. "This is it. He will destroy the world before he's grown."

Kila reached for Cayne, but it was not sheathed on her thigh.

"Cayne!" she screamed, even as Yiothizandra convulsed again. "Cayne!"

A cool voice answered. "Here. Take it!"

A hand took her shoulder, pulled her around. Ell bent over her, eyes fierce. "Take it." Winnea stood behind her, face slack with shock and fear. Ell held out a bundle. Gasping, Kila ripped the cloth away to reveal Cayne, sheathed in black, fresh doe-hide leather on the hilt.

She tore the blade free. It resonated with the moment, vibrating with eagerness. "Zirhine, show me."

Zirhine dabbed black smudge from a small pot and smeared a line across Yiothizandra's belly.

"Do it!" Yiothizandra screamed.

Cayne bit into the flesh, parted it as if it were paper. Zirhine directed the cut. "Go no deeper than that. Yes. That's it." Yiothizandra screamed, long and shrill.

Kila's heart raced faster than it had ever done. The keening whistle of pressure filled the air. The rolling thunder of imminent destruction built to a roar until all she could hear was the boulder crash of doom.

Cayne jolted of its own accord, freeing itself and throwing Kila backward. She struck her head on the pavement, vision flashing white. Voices called her name. A warm softness pressed against her face, a purring warmth so familiar and so heartbreakingly welcome. The sludge of Revulsion drained from her, skittering and oozing into hiding.

"Nax."

I am here. I shall keep the Revulsion away.

A squalling cry cut through the awed silence. Bazron roared. The other dragons of Night answered. Gouts of flame shot skyward in respectful tribute.

Gasps and low curses brought Kila's head up. Yiothizandra wept, hands over her face. Zirhine passed a small bundle to Ell, who cradled it gently. Zirhine raised a questioning brow to Kila. A bloody cloak lay over Yiothizandra's wound.

"Will she die?"

It was Eckso who answered. "Not likely. Kil will surely protect her a while longer."

Yioth dropped her hands, sat up, grimacing. She threw hateful looks around, locked on Ell. "Give me my child, cousin."

"*Your* child? I think not."

"Give him to me. Now."

Instead, Ell handed the swaddled babe to Kila. She still felt the heartbeat, locked to hers. She had never held an infant before, had never particularly wanted to. As she took the bundle, the swaddling made of a stained and torn soldier's shirt fell away. Kila quickly covered the nakedness. But not before she saw. Not before Ell saw.

Had Eckso? Had Yiothizandra? No. She could tell by their faces. Only three of them knew.

Conceal it for now, Ell said into her mind. *I know not what it signifies.*

"Give him to me!" Yiothizandra screamed again. She strained up, struggled to her knees. The cloak fell away and Kila saw that her wound had already seared closed. But she was weak.

And her words reassured Kila that she had not seen. Ell's hands went to Kila's crown, deftly loosening the gems. The pull of the bolts ground in her skull, tore at her scalp. As soon as they were free, she took hold of the mercusine, reveled in its pure wonder. On instinct alone, she sent a mind probe into the babe, wondered at the magnificent topology of innocent godhood.

Yiothizandra lunged.

Kila caught her in a thickening of air, freezing her in space as surely as a willshift. The impulse to squeeze the life from her came on hard, but an opposing force made her relent. This came from the babe, who could not form words, but who knew Yiothizandra as a mother, not to be harmed.

Kila looked around for the faces she knew. Henley was there. The Cloak was there. Huff had come to sit in her lap with Nax. "We need to lock her up somewhere. Some place strong enough she cannot escape."

Another person she knew stumbled forward, his head wrapped in a filthy bandage. It was Gian. He looked at her with distrust. "There are deep cells beneath On'lin Keep. Help us move her into one and she will never see the day again."

Kila did not have the strength remaining to keep Yiothizandra frozen in this way. So she formed another mind probe and sent it into the dragnithan. She sought nothing more than to make the creature sleep, but she could not manage it. "Ell?"

"I see what you wish to do. I do not have strength enough alone, but perhaps Henley is a better choice. His skill with the mind is superior to mine."

Henley hiked his satchel off his shoulder and pulled from it an egg. Kila felt the mercus humming from within it. And then he threaded forth the most delicate and insubstantial mind probe. It entered Yiothizandra's mind and even though she was frozen in midair, the fire in her eyes suddenly banked low. "You can release her."

Kila did and the dragnithan flopped face down. Gian ordered men forward to drag her away.

Henley came to Kila, hugged her and the child.

This is Kil? he sent.

It is.

"The nosg are retreating," a soldier called. Kila looked to the sky, saw wyvoks winging north. With angered roars, the dragons flew off. They would do nothing to harm the child, and cared nothing for conquering Stallid.

"Stallid stands," Gian said. "You have my thanks, Kila Sigh. But if this babe is Kil . . ."

"I saw what Cayne did," Eckso said, voice trembling. "Perhaps if you . . ."

Her words cut off as Kila vanished the air around the woman's head.

"Do not," Ell said. "She is merely afraid."

Kila let the feat go and Eckso choked and gasped as air returned.

To use Cayne on the babe . . . so obvious, so wrong. Kila felt nothing of evil from the child. But there was power there, unlimited, raw, unthinking. It did not seek anything except sustenance, warmth, and love.

"We must convene immediately. In private," Ell said. "I think we should return to the Citadel."

"I must come, I think," the Cloak said.

Zirhine stood, brushed off her trousers and repacked her satchel. "I must go with Harnzyne. Several dragons need my aid. It would be better for them to go to the eyrie above Starside, but it is a long flight."

Ell spoke low to Henley, who nodded. "Easily, Your Enlightened Majesty."

And so it was that Henley rode upon Harnzyne with Zirhine, and high above Stallid, dymensed to Starside. He returned and repeated this until all the dragons of Day were in the Starside eyrie.

Kila took the humans, all holding to each other and her.

And after they had washed and fed they convened in Her Enlightened's counsel chamber atop the Citadel spire. The fire burned more brightly than Kila had ever seen it and Ell had closed the windows to keep the winter wind out. Kila held the babe, perplexed and full of wonder, and still feeling the beat of her heart matching that of the child's.

When all were assembled, including the Coin, Marlow, Quiv and the shadlines, Ell said simply. "I feel this group can be trusted. In fact, must be trusted. Kila?"

Kila stood and held the babe aloft, snug in fresh soft swaddling. The babe was like any human infant, pink, ugly, weak. But the eyes were open and keen, as if fully able to see all who stared back.

"Til's tears!" Marlow said.

"Have you considered the obvious?" Coin Inlina asked. "Has any attempt been made to destroy the child?"

Kila stayed her hand. But she let her feelings be known upon her face. Nax hissed at the woman, in case Kila's feelings weren't clear enough.

"He will be the doom of us," Coin Inlina said sourly. "He will be the doom of the world."

"Not necessarily," Kila said.

"And how do you know? You're but a child yourself. He is the god of war and hatred and darkness. He will bring the evernight, mark me."

"He will do no such thing."

The Coin was too tough and stubborn to be put off by an angry glare.

"Kila, show her," Ell said. "Show them all."

Solemnly, Kila dropped the swaddling and again held the babe up for all to see. Marlow cursed again. Quiv gaped. The Coin's bright eyes widened and her mouth opened, but she said nothing. The Cloak's lips spread in a wolfish grin, and Henley, who already knew the truth bit his lip with uncertainty. Eckso squawked in most unladylike manner. Ell merely looked.

Once they'd all gotten a clear look, Kila wrapped the child

back in the swaddling clothes. "As you can see, friends, Kil is a girl."

The End of *Fortress of Shadow*
Book Seven of Starside Saga.

AUTHOR'S NOTE

So about that little twist at the ending . . . I've known about it since I started writing book 3. Whenever I got stuck or had to backtrack in the writing process, I always got a good cackle of glee when I thought about the Birth of Kil.

It amazes me to think how small Starside Saga started. Just a spunky thief girl discovering some cats. And now her story has grown to epic proportions. I had an absolute blast writing *Fortress of Shadow* (except when I had to delete tens of thousands of words because I went down a dead end.)

I'm writing this note during a break while working on book eight. I believe it will be the final book in the series, and I expect it to be just as epic as this one.

Do you want to know the second book 8 comes out? Sign up for my newsletter at ericedstrom.com/newsletter.

If you're enjoying this series, please tell a friend. And I'm sure you've heard that writers rely on reviews to help spread the word. Your honest review is always appreciated.

I'm so grateful for your support.

I'm heading back to my writing desk to discover what new mess of trouble Kila's gotten into.

—Eric Kent Edstrom (Spring Prairie, Wisconsin)